PRAISE FOR

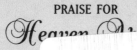

"You'll laugh. You'll _____ na, Blake, and Erin in H_____ ve lost and found . . . _____ od takes readers on a so_____ k- ing journey deep into _____ at love can conquer everything . . . even death. Jarrod knows how to create wonderfully believable characters who touch your heart, and plotlines that surprise and delight. Definitely a winner!"
—Barbara Bretton

"*Heaven Above* is at turns charming and steamy. Sara Jarrod knows just how to tug on our heartstrings."
—Tina Wainscott

"*Heaven Above* is a tale as irresistible as its central character, Glenna Tanner. From the first word, Sara Jarrod gently seduces the reader with a love story that is both haunting and hypnotic."
—Peggy Webb,
author of *From a Distance*

"Sara Jarrod gives ghostly romance a special twist in this appealing first novel. A heartwarming story that will have you wishing for some heavenly help of your own. *Heaven Above* will charm you."
—Justine Dare Davis,
author of *Heart of the Hawk*

MORE ROMANCE AWAITS IN THE HAUNTING HEARTS NOVELS . . .

Stardust of Yesterday
Spring Enchantment
A Ghost of a Chance

*Turn to the back of this book for a
special sneak preview of*

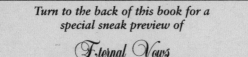
Eternal Vows

the next Haunting Hearts romance!

HEAVEN ABOVE

SARA JARROD

JOVE BOOKS, NEW YORK

If you purchased this book without a cover, you should be aware that
this book is stolen property. It was reported as "unsold and destroyed"
to the publisher, and neither the author nor the publisher has received
any payment for this "stripped book."

HEAVEN ABOVE

A Jove Book / published by arrangement with
the author

PRINTING HISTORY
Jove edition / October 1996

All rights reserved.
Copyright © 1996 by Sara Brockunier and Ann Josephson.
Excerpt from *Eternal Vows* copyright © 1996 by Alice Alfonsi.
This book may not be reproduced in whole
or in part, by mimeograph or any other means,
without permission. For information address:
The Berkley Publishing Group, 200 Madison Avenue,
New York, New York 10016.

The Putnam Berkley World Wide Web site address is
http://www.berkley.com/berkley

ISBN: 0-515-11954-7

A JOVE BOOK®
Jove Books are published by The Berkley Publishing Group,
200 Madison Avenue, New York, New York 10016.
JOVE and the "J" design are trademarks
belonging to Jove Publications, Inc.

PRINTED IN THE UNITED STATES OF AMERICA

10 9 8 7 6 5 4 3 2 1

For my daughter, Tara Danielle; my mother, Carmen; and my sister, Mary Ellen, and her husband, Michael: for always believing in me and giving me the time to pursue my dreams.

To EO for encouraging and supporting me.

Sara

To my husband, Eric, and all our children—Jim and his wife, Sedef, John, Maggie, Dawn, Carla, Paula, and Jerald—for their faith that Mom could make her dreams come true.

Ann

ACKNOWLEDGMENTS

We would like to thank all of those folks we know who have constantly encouraged, believed, and supported our dreams. To Jeanie LeGendre and Christy Ruth, a very special thank you for reading and rereading our "baby" and for offering wonderful suggestions. And to our friends in Tampa Area Romance Authors, Romance Writers of America, and GEnie Romex, a tremendous thank you for all your support and encouragement.

Chapter 1

"Blake! Our baby just moved. It was just the tiniest little flutter, but I felt him."

Glenna Tanner wanted to jump up and scream out her elation, but she settled for calmly announcing the news to her husband, who had paused from doing laps at the shallow end of the pool to ask how she was feeling. She watched his expression soften as he pushed himself up and out of the pool and headed for her shaded resting place in the gazebo.

God, how I love this man, she thought, enjoying watching the sun reflect off crystalline rivulets of water as they caressed the planes of Blake's long, muscular body. He was sexier now at thirty-seven than he'd been as a college boy, with muscles finely honed and defined with maturity. Glenna stretched sensually, wishing the difficulties of this high-risk pregnancy hadn't dictated that they abstain from the joys of sex.

"This time everything is going to be just perfect," she told him when he knelt beside her lounge chair. "Here, give me your hand. See if you can feel him, too."

"I'll get you all wet, honey." But he let her place his wet, cool palm on her still-flat stomach and indulgently tried to feel motion that even to Glenna had been so fleeting it had barely registered in her conscious mind. "Do you feel all right?" Blake asked, concern evident in his warm, loving gaze.

"Never better. There! He moved again. Did you feel him?"

"I don't know. Maybe. Isn't it a little soon?"

"We're nearly halfway there. Blake, I just know that this time we're going to have our baby. I've already carried this baby a month longer than I ever have before." Glenna sensed Blake's reserve; his fear of hoping too much that after so many years, and two heartbreaking miscarriages, they were finally going to have a child.

"Sweetheart," he said softly, "I'm hoping as much as you are that everything will turn out right. I just don't want anything to happen to you."

Glenna knew the warnings they had received from Greg Halpern, her obstetrician and Blake's longtime friend, were never far from Blake's mind. She realized her long-standing endometriosis and history of *placenta previa* made the chance of this pregnancy being a success remote. Still, she refused to let worries infringe on her joy. She and Blake were finally going to have the baby she had wanted for every day of the fourteen years they had been married.

This time she had known she was pregnant practically from the moment of conception. She was following Greg's instructions to the letter, hardly ever finding herself bored by the long hours of bed rest. And now she was nearly four and a half months along—and she had felt her baby move!

"Would you like to have lunch out here?" Blake asked, unfolding his big body from its crouched position and slinging a beach towel around his shoulders.

Glenna smiled. "It would be nice, unless you think it's too hot." The latticework of the gazebo shaded them nicely from a sultry July sun, and a fan turned lazily from the ceiling, cooling the air and shooing away the occasional moth and butterfly. "I feel lazy today," she added.

"Me, too. I'll ask Mary to bring out the food."

Glenna thought Blake looked more at ease when he lifted

her from the padded turquoise chaise lounge and set her onto one of the chairs that ringed a small, glass-topped table. Ordinarily she would balk at being treated as if she were made of glass—but not now, while the little life inside her was so tenuous.

"Your son or daughter and I thank you," she quipped, tilting her head to rest it against Blake's hard, flat belly.

"You're both welcome," Blake replied as he leaned down and brushed a gentle kiss across her lips.

They spent the afternoon outside. Even as restricted as her activities were because of the baby, Glenna liked just sitting, relaxing with Blake and enjoying his company this beautiful summer day. She sighed, regretting that the day was almost over, as she watched a bright orange Texas sun begin to disappear in the western sky.

Suddenly chilled despite the heat, Glenna shivered. "I'm cold," she told Blake, who sprang up from the lounge chair where he had been snoozing and hurried to her side.

"Let's go inside," he suggested, concern evident in his solemn gaze.

"All right." With more effort than the simple action should have required, she sat up and slid her legs to the floor. "I think you'd better carry me," she told him quietly, not wanting to alarm him by admitting just how weak and dizzy she felt.

His strong arms enveloped her, and she felt safe, until she glanced down at the chaise where she had been resting and saw the dark, red pool of blood.

"I'm bleeding," she said, unable to keep fear and hopelessness from showing in her weakening voice. "You'd better get me to the hospital."

Blake stopped pacing the length of a sterile-looking waiting room and sank down onto an overstuffed sofa.

What in hell is taking them so long?

He propped his elbows on his knees, bringing his head down to rest on his hands. With every noisy tick of that clock on the wall, his panic escalated. He shivered. They kept this room about as cold as a refrigerator, but he knew the chill in his body owed more to fear than to the hospital's air-conditioning system.

Had it been just hours ago that he and Glenna had laughed in the gazebo by the pool? Had it been today that she had held his hand to her abdomen and challenged him to feel their baby's faint, fluttering movement? Right now, Blake thought dismally, those warm, happy moments seemed light-years away. For the hundredth time, he glanced at the thin, gold Rolex Glenna had given him last Christmas. Then he clenched his fists with helpless fury.

Three hours. It's been three hours. She may be dying in there, and there's not a goddamn thing I can do to help her.

Blake got up and strode to the windows, staring out into bleak darkness punctuated with bright lights of downtown Dallas that winked in the distance. The cheerful kaleidoscope of color somehow seemed obscene.

"Blake?"

He spun around at the sound of Greg Halpern's voice. Greg looked as bad as Blake felt, and Blake's hope for a happy ending died before it had a chance to materialize.

Wearily Greg tugged off the paper surgical cap that covered his hair and stuffed it into a pocket of blood-spattered green scrubs. He looked as if he'd been through a war, Blake thought as he tried to find his voice to speak.

Greg apparently noticed Blake's loss of words. "I couldn't save the baby. It was a little girl. I'm sorry." He met Blake's gaze with sad, dark eyes.

"Glenna?" The question came out in a husky croak.

"She's in recovery."

"And . . ."

"And she's all right. We got the bleeding stopped—at least for now."

Blake finally took in a breath of air. "What happened? Not an hour before the bleeding started, Glenna was the happiest I've ever seen her. This morning she felt the baby moving for the first time. Greg, I'm afraid this is going to push her over the edge.''

Greg sank into a chair and rubbed a hand across his stubbled chin. ''You want a technical explanation?''

Blake nodded.

''The placenta separated. Remember I showed you on the ultrasound last week how low the placenta was attached? Quite simply, the growing baby put enough pressure on it to make it come loose. When this happened, Glenna started to hemorrhage.''

''You mean this is the same thing that happened the last time Glenna miscarried?''

''Yes, except that this time she was farther along. That made the situation worse.'' Greg rubbed the bridge of his nose, as if to ease the strain of bright lights on his eyes.

''Did you have to . . .'' Blake's words trailed off. He couldn't voice what he half hoped, half feared.

''I should have, but I didn't. Glenna refused permission for a hysterectomy unless it was the only way to save her life. I'll take you to see her now. Blake, tonight is not the time, but very soon we three are going to have to have a serious talk,'' Greg said as they walked together to the recovery room.

Stiffly, Glenna made her way to the breakfast room to ''visit'' with Greg and Blake. She had been home three days now, and it felt good to get out of the bedroom for a change.

Glenna had worked hard to shelve the deep sadness she felt when Blake had told her they had lost their little girl. Still, they had each other. And she had made up her mind that they *would* have their baby, next time.

''You said we needed to talk,'' she told Greg after joining Blake on the sofa. ''I'm ready.''

Glenna watched Greg look pointedly at Blake. Then she

felt Blake's hand enfold hers in a reassuring way, and her determined optimism began to erode.

"It would be tantamount to suicide for you to risk another pregnancy. For the sake of your present and future health, Glenna, you should have a hysterectomy as soon as I can schedule it."

Shocked, Glenna jerked her hand from Blake's and stared out the window at the spot she had planned for her children's playhouse. "I thought your specialty was helping couples who have problem pregnancies, Greg, not taking away their chances of ever having a baby," she snapped, knowing she was being rude as well as unfair, but unable at the moment to do more than lash out at the bearer of bad tidings.

"Glenna. Honey, let's listen to Greg." That was Blake, ever the conciliator, Glenna thought with a good deal of malice.

Still, she murmured, "Sorry," to Greg and sat back down to hear him out.

Greg sighed. "I know how much you want a child. And if I thought you could survive it, Glenna, I would be the first to suggest another try. It's my business to deliver healthy babies no one else thought had a snowball's chance in hell. I don't think you'll listen to me if I try to soft pedal the facts, and you're both my friends as well as Glenna being my patient, so here it is, straight-out.

"You have one of the worst cases of endometriosis I've ever tried to treat. I've operated three times, trying to correct it, but it just keeps coming back. On top of that, you have had three miscarriages despite our taking every precaution we could devise. Two of those pregnancies ended because of the placenta breaking away from the lining of the uterus and causing hemorrhage—and *placenta previa* is a condition that tends to recur. You're thirty-seven years old. Any of those factors alone would be sufficient for most obstetricians to caution you against trying again to have a baby.'' Greg paused, taking a sip from his drink before continuing.

"Before this last miscarriage, I had hoped you could carry the baby long enough to deliver a preemie that might have a chance for survival. Glenna, I'm sorry, but I don't believe you have a chance now of having a viable child. It is my opinion that the pregnancy itself could easily kill you. And, if you don't have the hysterectomy, your health is going to keep deteriorating until you won't be able to enjoy living.''

Glenna felt herself shivering in spite of the sunny warmth of the glass-walled breakfast room. Blake's arm encircled her shoulders, and he pulled her against him for comfort, but the chill in her soul would not subside.

"You mentioned something at the hospital about options?'' Blake said quietly to Greg. Suddenly Glenna felt a ray of hope.

Greg stretched out his legs in front of the glass-topped cocktail table. "Both of you want a baby. I see no reason why you wouldn't be able to adopt one or more.''

"No!'' Glenna sat up straighter and raked Greg with a furious gaze. "I want *our* baby.''

"Glenna, that's not possible, honey,'' Blake said, stroking her shoulder as he spoke. "I want *you*, alive and well, as I believe I've said a thousand times. I'm willing to adopt—or simply to stay as we are, just the two of us.''

"What about in vitro fertilization?'' Glenna asked, suddenly recalling Greg's highly publicized successes with helping make "test-tube'' babies.

Greg smiled slightly. "That's not an option for you. In vitro's for ladies who can't get pregnant in the usual way, not ones who can't carry a baby to term. If you don't want to adopt, exactly, you could hire a surrogate mother,'' he added. "That was the other option I had in mind.''

A surrogate. "Then the baby would be Blake's,'' Glenna said excitedly. "How do we do it?''

"Hey, wait just a minute here,'' Blake interjected. "I

don't like that idea one damn bit. Forget it.''

"No! I won't just forget it. Greg, tell us how it's done.''
In her mind, Glenna was already picturing a plump, dark-haired newborn nestling snugly in her arms.

Greg shot a helpless look toward Blake. "The procedure itself is simple. You hire a healthy woman, I determine when she's ovulating; and when the time is right, I do an artificial insemination in the office, using fresh semen Blake has collected and delivered to me. Then we cross our fingers, and if we're lucky, nine months later you bring your baby home.''

Glenna could almost feel Blake's mind formulating a scathing retort. "Why don't you explain the part that's everything but simple, Greg?'' he finally asked, before entering into a recital of the myriad legal woes that could arise from entering into an agreement with a surrogate mother.

I'm finally going to have Blake's baby.

Glenna pushed her husband's arguments firmly from her mind. Not even his closing statement, a flat-out, adamant refusal to consider letting a stranger carry and bear his child for pay, diminished her resolve.

For several days Blake made himself scarce, staying long hours at his office to avoid the inevitable showdown with Glenna. Not a word had crossed her lips since Greg had left, but Blake knew his wife, and he knew the subject of surrogate motherhood was far from closed.

Tonight he was home, closeted inside his study with work he hadn't touched. Why in hell had Greg presented the idea to Glenna in the first place? But he knew why. His wife had captivated Greg years ago, just as she enchanted everyone she met. His friend hadn't had a choice but to present Glenna with every possible way by which she might gain the one thing—a baby—fate seemed determined to deny her.

Blake understood. Every day, he marveled at the aura of

hope and optimism that radiated around Glenna, even in situations where most people would be indulging in bitter anger or sullen self-pity. Hell, when he had broken the news about this last miscarriage, she had swallowed her own tears and comforted *him*. He had expected her to scream and rail at the unfairness of it all, as he had done when he received the news from Greg. Instead, she had managed a sad smile and promised that next time things would work out—that fresh new sunshine would come and chase the storm clouds away.

Everyone loved Glenna, from the boy who delivered their morning paper to the woman-hating grouch who ran a vegetable stand where she shopped. How could they help loving her? She had wound *Blake* around her tiny finger since they shared a table in kindergarten.

Now, thirty-two years later, that love just kept growing stronger, Blake realized as bittersweet memories assailed him. He had given her his heart. But her gift to him was so much grander. Each day Glenna gave him a piece of her own unique ability to view the world with gentle humor and an enduring, childlike wonder that never seemed to tarnish as they aged.

Suddenly guilt washed over him. Glenna gave him such joy in living. Could he dismiss out of hand the possibility of fulfilling her lifelong dream of having their baby to love? Forcefully repressing an overwhelming need to reject surrogacy without considering his wife's wishes, Blake left his solitary refuge and went to find her.

Glenna looked like a mischievous angel, he decided as he watched her slide over on the bed to give him room. Her chestnut curls framed a small, heart-shaped face still pale from her ordeal of losing their baby. Blake loved the way her golden-brown eyes sparkled brightly with gentle humor.

''Are you through hiding?'' she asked, the corners of her mouth curving upward into a smile.

''Yes. I'm sorry, honey.''

"Then you're ready to admit I'm right to want our baby to be truly *yours* even if it can't really be mine, too?"

"I'm ready to discuss the options."

"There are only two. I want your baby. If you don't want us to use a surrogate mother, I'll get pregnant again, immediately." Glenna's face took on that intractable expression Blake knew meant compromise was out.

Eventually he would give in. He knew it. He knew *she* knew it, too. Trapped in a situation he believed would cause them more grief than joy, he lost his taste for trying to change Glenna's mind. "You damn well are not going to risk your life again. Didn't you even halfway listen to what Greg said?"

"I will if I have to."

"Hell, honey, I may as well give in now. I'll get Greg busy looking for a likely broodmare of the human persuasion, if you're positive this is what you really want." *And I'll set myself to drafting an ironclad contract that just may protect us from the grasping claws of our surrogate,* he added silently.

"It's really what I want."

"Then we'll do it. But you're going to schedule that surgery so you can be well enough to enjoy this baby of mine that you're so obsessed with having." Blake leaned over and took Glenna gently into his arms when she voiced no protest at his condition for capitulation.

"You want me to *what*?"

"Find us a surrogate mother. Hell, Greg, you're an obstetrician. You must know thousands of women who are physically capable of having a healthy baby."

Greg laughed out loud. "Now why does that make me feel like a high-priced pimp? You don't want a surrogate from among my patients. They're all high-risk. More important, they all desperately want their babies or they wouldn't bother with seeking me out in the first place."

"Damn it, you're the one who put this notion in Glenna's

pretty, stubborn head. The least you can do, besides eventually earning a hefty fee for the delivery, is help us find a woman willing to do the job.'' Blake handed over two sheets from a yellow legal pad.

Scrawled over on both sides of the pages were the qualifications Blake must have spent hours agonizing over, Greg realized as he glanced over his friend's requirements. ''You don't want much, do you?'' he asked, amused.

''I want nine months of this woman's time. That's all. Damn it to hell, I don't want any part of this whole farce. But Glenna does, and what Glenna wants, she's going to get. Can you think of anything I missed?''

Greg glanced over the list again. ''You want someone who isn't in a relationship and who is willing to accept celibacy for the duration of the arrangement.''

''Why should I care? I have no intention of ever laying eyes on the woman.''

''One word. Disease.''

Blake nodded. ''Anything else?''

''Ideally you want a widow or divorcée who already has one or two children. The main reason is psychological— she will already have had babies she won't be giving up. Also, she won't be an unknown factor physically. Someone who has had a normal, uneventful pregnancy is statistically likely to have another one.''

''Find us a surrogate. I don't like anything about this, and I'll be damned if I'll advertise and interview a bunch of women the way I would if I needed a new secretary. I'll do it for Glenna, and I'll draw up a contract after terms are decided. I'll pay the woman whatever in reason she may demand. But that's as far as it's going to go.'' Blake got up and paced across his oak-paneled office. ''Would you like a drink?'' he asked as he opened the bar and pulled out a bottle of fine, old Scotch.

''Can't. I've still got a couple of patients to see. Anyhow, I'm on call tonight. Blake, you do realize you're going to have to . . .''

"Yeah, I know. More or less on demand, whenever this unknown woman is ripe to conceive? I don't like the idea of doing it that way, but when the time comes I'll give it my best shot."

On the way back to his own office, Greg mentally chose and discarded possible accomplices for the thankless job of finding his good friends Blake and Glenna Tanner the perfect surrogate.

Chapter 2

"Mrs. Corwin was the last one for today," Sandy Daniels said with an exaggerated sigh of relief as she warmed Greg's coffee from the thermal pot she kept on his desk.

Greg looked up from the Rolodex file he had been searching through and smiled at his pert, young, practice manager. In six short months, Sandy had turned his office into a well-oiled machine instead of the barely controlled madhouse it had been before she came—and she had made it feel almost like home. No, he felt more comfortable here than in the sterile apartment he had called home since shedding his second wife two years earlier.

"Thanks, boss. Any messages?"

"Just this folder Barbara Ann dropped off. She said Dr. Williams told her you had asked for it. And, oh, your daughter called, but she said you didn't need to call her back because she was headed down to Saks with her mom and aunt to catch a sale."

Greg groaned. The last time Shana had hit a sale, it had cost him three OB fees. "Am I going to be able to afford her spree this time?" he asked Sandy comically.

"I don't know. You know, Greg, you could put Shana on a budget. No girl her age needs her own purse full of credit cards."

Right. Greg had no more luck dictating thrift to his

twelve-year-old daughter than he had experienced with her mother Kay—or Rhea, his more recent former wife. While being brutally honest with himself, he admitted that without Sandy's careful management of his practice, he could not have modified his own easy-come, easy-go spending habits enough to keep out of bankruptcy court.

"I know. I've gotten myself into a hell of a mess, letting women wrap me around their fingers. Speaking of messes, do you have any ideas about where we can come up with a surrogate mother?"

Sandy stepped behind his desk and opened a hidden file drawer. "Once in a while we get inquiries from women who think they'd like to be surrogates. I made a file for them and put it in here," she said as she turned and handed him the neatly labeled manila folder. Their fingers brushed together, and he felt a sudden need to prolong the physical contact.

"Who needs a surrogate mother?" Sandy asked casually, her own slight blush making Greg wonder if she, too, felt the sensual pull that was developing between them in spite of the strictly professional relationship they maintained.

"Glenna Tanner."

Sandy shook her head sadly. "I felt so bad for her when she lost her baby last month. I've never seen anyone want a child as much as she does. You're personal friends, aren't you?"

"Her husband and I roomed together in college. The three of us go back a long way. Now I've been given the impossible task of finding a Glenna clone to bear my good friends' baby. Here, look. It's not enough that Blake Tanner asks me to find a woman; he's insisting that the woman be a cross between saint and martyr—and that she has to be practically a dead ringer for his wife." Greg tossed aside the folder his colleague had provided, and leafed through the one Sandy had produced. He didn't see any prospective surrogates that he felt warranted further attention.

Sandy sat down across from him and flipped through the

two folders again. Greg tried to keep his mind off the silky thigh that tantalized him when she calmly crossed her legs. He couldn't believe it! Here they were, with Sandy trying to help him long after she could have packed it in and gone home; and he was getting hard, fantasizing about how it would feel to touch her soft, inviting body.

"What about my sister?" she asked suddenly.

Greg forced his mind off the desire he certainly couldn't satisfy. "The one with the little crippled boy?" he asked, trying to recall the woman. He had seen her once, a couple of months ago, when Sandy had brought her to the office for a routine annual exam, but he couldn't quite picture her in his mind.

"Timmy," Sandy confirmed, nodding. "He needs another operation that Medicaid won't pay for and Erin can't afford. Actually, being a surrogate mother would be great—Erin could earn good money and still stay home to take care of Timmy."

"Did you make up a chart when Erin came in for her checkup?" he asked, needing to refresh his memory. Sandy looked as if he'd insulted her, and without dignifying his question with a reply, got up and fetched Erin Winters's records.

"Here," she said, handing him the chart. Again they touched in a fleeting way that shouldn't have made Greg start to burn again.

It took a good deal of effort to focus on Erin's medical record. Greg forced himself, though, and after he had reviewed the chart, he thought he might have found Glenna's surrogate. "Do you think she'd do it?" he asked Sandy expectantly.

"I don't know. I'll sound her out if you'd like, and see how she feels about it. Oh, no! Didn't you say Mr. Tanner wanted a surrogate who was almost a clone of his wife?"

"That was only one of many requirements," he replied, tossing Sandy the sheets of paper Blake had given him. "You don't find surrogate mothers under every barrel, especially if, like Blake, you don't want to advertise for them. I believe Blake will have to take basically what he can get if he wants me to procure the woman for them.''

"Greg, Erin doesn't look at all like Glenna Tanner."

Suddenly Greg pictured Erin—tall, slender, with dark hair and blue eyes. "No. Actually, her coloring is almost like Blake's. Health-wise, your sister would be a perfect choice. If she wants to do it, I'm sure I can sell her to Blake and Glenna."

"We won't know if we don't ask. I'll call her now," Sandy said, pushing the button to activate Greg's speakerphone and dialing Erin's number. Greg listened as the phone rang once—then again.

"Hello?"

"Hi, Erin, it's Sandy. Greg and I are here at the office, trying to find a special person for—well, for a special kind of job." Greg smiled. He liked the words Sandy had come up with to describe surrogate motherhood.

Erin sounded interested but skeptical when she replied, "What kind of job? You know I could certainly use the money, but I can't leave Timmy now. It will be a long time before he'll be well enough to go back to school and day care."

"That's the beautiful part of this job. You wouldn't have to leave Timmy at all—well, certainly not for more than a few days at most. And the pay would be fantastic, maybe even enough for you to put down that deposit the hospital wants before they'll let Timmy's doctor schedule his next surgery."

Greg felt like an eavesdropper, sitting listening to the sisters' conversation without Erin realizing he was in the room. While Erin was silent on the other end, he leaned toward the fancy machine he had a hard time believing would pick up his voice without his holding its handset to his ear, and announced his presence.

"Erin, I'm Greg Halpern. I'd really like to speak to you about doing a very special favor for two dear friends of mine. Could you come here tomorrow so we can discuss it further?''

He watched Sandy's smooth, supple movements as she reached over to flip on the computer he had never really learned how to use. She pushed some keys, and magically his schedule for tomorrow, August twenty-first, popped onto the screen.

''Greg will be free at four o'clock,'' she told Erin before turning off the machine and leaning back in her chair.

''Sandy, I don't know.''

''Come on. You owe it to yourself, and Timmy, to at least consider what Greg is offering.''

''All right. I'll have to see if Mrs. Johnson next door can watch Timmy for a couple of hours. If she can, I'll be there.''

''If you can't get a sitter, call and I'll come watch my favorite nephew myself,'' Sandy offered. ''You sound tired, sis. I'm about to con my boss into feeding me, since he's kept me here two hours after my usual dinnertime. See you tomorrow. Bye.''

''Good night.'' Greg thought Erin sounded singularly confused, and he didn't know if he was looking forward to explaining the magnitude of the favor he was going to ask her to do for Glenna and Blake.

He did know that the idea of sharing a meal and some personal, nonprofessional conversation with Sandy was damn appealing. For the first time since he and Rhea had split up, Greg actually welcomed the need he felt to have a woman in his personal life.

''I accept your not so subtle hint to feed you,'' he told her with a grin. ''Go get your purse, and we can have a pizza or something,'' he said. Sandy's surprised but pleased expression fed his growing attraction to her.

Glenna put down the phone. She pinched herself to make certain she wasn't dreaming. Then she practically ran to the workout room by the pool and draped herself in a dramatic pose across the machine Blake was about to use.

"We're going to have a baby!" she announced.

Blake looked as if someone had announced impending disaster, not birth. "No, we aren't. I won't let you. Honey, if Greg says it's too damn dangerous for you, I believe him."

Glenna stood up and wrapped her arms around him, laughing as she tilted her head back to meet his angry gaze. "We're going to have our baby," she repeated, lifting a hand to cover his lips and prevent his further protest. "Greg has found us a surrogate mother."

She felt Blake's muscles tense beneath her hands. It worried her a bit, forcing him to do this when he was so dead set against it. Still, she told herself, he needed a child almost as much as she did—even if he was ready to deny that need to save her grief and guilt for not being able to bear it.

When the baby came home, she knew he would forget all his misgivings; meanwhile, she would have to work hard to combat his distaste for the way they were going to have to get that baby.

For a long time, she waited while he simply held her. "When?" he finally asked.

"When did he find the surrogate? Or when are we supposed to go to Greg's office to give him the sample?" she asked, teasing him.

"Both, I guess."

"The woman agreed just now to do it. Greg said he first talked to her and examined her about a month ago, and that she just made up her mind. Blake, I'm so excited. Greg wants to do the procedure tomorrow. He wants us to come to his office at ten o'clock to get him the sperm sample. You don't have to be in court, do you?"

"No. I don't. I'll go. But you're not going with me. Getting Greg his 'sample' will be a damn unpleasant medical procedure as far as I'm concerned. It won't have anything to do with making love, and I don't want you there."

Glenna shuddered. It was going to be harder than she thought to change Blake's attitude on this. "I wanted to meet this woman and thank her for what she's doing for us," she said in a pleading tone.

"Well, I don't. I've already given Greg a contract for her to sign—all he has to do is fill in the woman's name and the amount of money she wants for doing this job. I have no intention of ever laying eyes on her."

Tears threatened to spill from Glenna's eyes. She knew Blake had seen them when his voice softened and he brushed one gently from her cheek as it fell. "You can meet this woman later, love, after my part is done and she's pregnant. I'm sorry, but I can't help the way I feel."

"You're pregnant."

The examining table in Dr. Halpern's office felt cold and hard. And his pronouncement rang in Erin's ears. She was pregnant, but she was not going to keep the baby.

Without a whole lot of success, she tried to convince herself that carrying this child for James Blake Tanner IV and his infertile wife was just another job—a job that paid so well that she would be able to let the neurosurgeon schedule her own son's surgery.

Across the hall, Blake tried to concentrate on doing what his father had always cautioned him against when he was a boy. He tried not to think about the woman across the hall who would be getting his gift of life for the second time in as many months, with even less personal involvement than he was having, coaxing it from his body.

"Blake?"

Quickly he ceased his activity. What the hell was Greg doing, walking in on him? "Ever think of knocking, Doc?" he asked shortly.

"You can zip up, my friend. It took the first time."

Conflicting feelings surged through Blake's mind. The emotions bore no resemblance to the elation he'd felt the first time Glenna had told him she would bear their child. But then, he thought, they didn't match the terror that had accompanied her third and final announcement, either.

"Have you told Glenna?" he asked, feeling strange that he might have learned about this pregnancy before his wife.

"I thought you might want to." Greg motioned toward the phone on the counter. "You'll be parents on June twenty-fifth, give or take a few days. Very few, since I know to the minute when this pregnancy began," he added as if handling an arrangement like this were an everyday affair.

Blake stood up and zipped his pants. "You're sure?" he asked, knowing how it would hurt Glenna to get her hopes up for nothing.

"Positive. I think Ms. Winters would like to get her check as soon as possible."

"I imagine she would." Blake had mixed feelings about the woman who would carry his child. Sure, he was grateful that this woman had consented to give his wife what she most wanted in the world. Yet he couldn't help wondering what kind of a woman could carry a child for nine months and then give it up for money.

Shrugging, Blake fished in his wallet for a check and scribbled it out for fifty thousand dollars—the amount Ms. Winters had demanded for this very special favor. "She signed the papers, didn't she?" he asked Greg as he handed over the wrinkled check.

"Yes. They're in my office."

"Look, I want you to know how much I appreciate your arranging this. I couldn't risk Glenna's trying another pregnancy."

"I know. We'll schedule her hysterectomy for next week."

"Yeah. I hope knowing we're going to have a baby in another eight months will make her feel better about the surgery." As he went home to tell Glenna the first insemination had taken, Blake tried to persuade himself that this

arrangement was going to work out right despite his misgivings.

For the past few months, Glenna had frequented Greg's
well-appointed office almost as often as he had visited her
at home to check her short months ago, when they were
trying so desperately to bring her last pregnancy to term.
She had no room in her heart for recriminations over what
might have been, not now that Blake's child was growing
strong and healthy inside Erin's body. Not since she felt
stronger and better than she had in years.

As she thumbed through the dog-eared pages of a *Parents'* magazine, Glenna mentally planned the celebration
she would have with Blake tonight—after Greg pronounced
her good as new.

"Mrs. Tanner, Dr. Halpern is ready to see you now," a
nurse announced, and Glenna followed her into the examining room she knew was right next door to Greg's office.

"You're doing just fine. Better than new and ready to
resume any activities you might be missing," Greg told her
after carefully examining her incision. "Ms. Winters is
here, too. Would you like to meet her?" he asked casually.

"Oh, yes! She's all right, isn't she?"

Greg smiled. "She and that baby of yours are both so
healthy, I feel like I'm not earning my fee. Come on into
my office when you're dressed. Erin is waiting for you."

*Life is great! I'm well again, and I'm finally going to
meet the woman who is helping to make Blake's and my
lives complete.*

Glenna dressed quickly and ran a brush through chin-
length, wavy hair that a chilly wind outside had tossed into
disarray. Gathering up her purse, she hurried into Greg's
office. The sight of Erin took her breath away.

"I'm so glad to finally meet you," she said breathlessly.
"I've wanted to thank you, and to let you know how much
it means to me that you are making it possible for me to
have my husband's child."

Erin smiled, perhaps a bit self-consciously. "You've helped me, too," she replied softly. "Me and my little boy."

It was inevitable that their first conversation would be awkward, Glenna told herself. Still, after a few minutes' hesitant communication, she felt comfortable—the sort of contentment one experienced usually in the company of old, close friends. And she got the impression that Erin felt that way, too.

"Let's go to lunch," she suggested, not wanting to usurp Greg's office for a lengthy visit—yet needing more time with this new and special friend.

"I'd like that. But I have to be home before three o'clock. My neighbor is watching my little boy, but she has an appointment with her dentist at four."

Glenna noticed how Erin's pretty face softened when she was talking about her son, and she wondered what had compelled Erin to carry a child that would never be hers, as they walked to her car. Erin was quiet while they drove the ten short blocks to one of her favorite restaurants, but it was an easy silence, she decided.

"What made you decide to help us?" she asked after a waitress had taken their order.

Erin's gaze was sober, yet open. "Timmy. My son. I'm doing this so Timmy will have the chance to run and play again. He needed this operation he had last month *then* if it was to do the most good. And I had to give the hospital a big deposit before they would let his doctor admit him for the surgery."

"What?" Didn't state and federal programs make medical care available to all, without considering their ability to pay? "You mean some hospital here in Dallas would refuse to take someone—a helpless child, for heaven's sake—unless the parents pay the bill in advance?"

"Not usually. The surgeries Timmy needs now are semi-experimental, which means that Medicaid won't pay for them. His neurosurgeon is donating his services, but the hospital can't. Anyhow, the money you and your husband gave me made it possible for my son to have the first of several operations that we hope will let him walk again.''

Greg had told Glenna that Erin lost her husband several years ago. First, her husband . . . then this horrible tragedy that had crippled her little boy. Glenna's heart filled with sympathy for this young woman who must have suffered terribly.

''Has he had the surgery?'' Glenna asked.

''Yes. Now he has months of physical therapy to go through before the next operation. But his doctor believes the nerve transplants are working, so we're both hopeful about the ultimate result.''

Glenna changed the subject after offering herself and Blake to help financially—or personally if they could, with Timmy's future care. ''You know, I can't wait until *our* baby is here,'' she said with a smile. ''I couldn't be more thrilled that Greg found you. In case you've wondered, the baby is going to look a lot like you—Blake is tall and good-looking, with blue eyes and hair just a little darker than yours.''

Erin's expression sobered. ''I've tried very hard not to think of your baby at all. That way it won't hurt so much when I walk away from the hospital as if it never was inside me,'' she said, and Glenna knew the shopping trip she had been about to suggest they take to pick out baby clothes would be a cruel mistake.

Too soon, for Glenna liked Erin and enjoyed her company, their time together was over. They parted at Greg's office building, and Glenna headed home, promising to keep in touch by phone for the duration of Erin's pregnancy.

After a frustrating day in court, Blake strode into his bedroom a little after five, shedding coat, vest, and tie as he went. He was damn tired! Then he saw Glenna, stretched out on that chaise lounge she'd bought because it reminded her of a scene in an old French movie. She was vamping him, lying there wearing nothing but a see-through nightie and an enticing smile, designed to make a dead man come alive.

Desire slammed through his body. There was no more fatigue, just a primal mating urge that compelled him to scoop her into his arms and dump her into bed. He could tell from the way she clung to him that she was as ready as he to end celibacy forced on them first by her pregnancy and miscarriage, then his fear of her slipping in a suicidal last-ditch chance for her own baby, and finally the surgery and recovery period.

When they came together, it was fast and hard and carnal. Much later, he showed her with hands and mouth and body how much he loved and needed her. Afterward, as they lay in the dark and talked about the baby they would finally have next June, he started to let go of the misgivings that had haunted him. He had his wife back, to love without fear now. That made up for a lot of hours' worry about that surrogate mother and everything that could but probably wouldn't go wrong.

"Neiman's is having a sale on baby things tomorrow," Glenna said sleepily. "I'm going to the downtown store first thing in the morning. Could I talk you into lunch after I'm done?"

Blake wished she could. "Sorry, honey, I can't do it tomorrow. I'll be in court all day. Can I have a rain check?"

"You bet!"

Tenderly Blake pulled Glenna close to him and stroked her silken skin. He smiled at his own capitulation to her gentle obstinance. This had been the hardest sell ever, for her. He had resisted with all his will, but she had finally brought him around.

He knew he would backslide into cynicism every now and then; but Glenna had woven her spell. He honestly looked forward to the day they would bring their baby home—and that fact alone amazed him. More at ease than he had been for months, Blake lay back and went to sleep.

Freed for a little while from listening carefully to the proceedings, Blake leaned back in his chair at the plaintiff's table. It felt good once in a while to let a junior associate present yet another dry technical piece of evidence to add to an already impressive stack of exhibits. This case, involving software piracy, was incredibly complex; but it was not the type of dramatic legal maneuvering from which TV courtroom dramas were made. Sometimes, like now, Blake wondered why he had chosen corporate law over one of the more exciting fields—criminal defense, for instance.

Criminal defense? Did my idle thoughts conjure up that cop?

Blake took a closer look. It *was* a uniformed Dallas policeman, standing at the side door of the courtroom, whispering quietly to the bailiff. He tried to recall the last time he had seen a cop in the staid, safe courtrooms where civil cases were tried.

The police officer left as abruptly as he had appeared. With an urgent look on his face, the bailiff approached the bench and exchanged a few words with Judge Anderson.

What the hell is going on?

"I will accept the file you are presenting, counselor. Mark it as Exhibit twenty-six. This case is recessed until next Monday at ten o'clock," Judge Anderson announced. "I will see chief counsel for the plaintiff in my chambers now."

Confused, Blake swept the loose papers off the table into his briefcase and headed to Judge Anderson's chambers.

The judge wasn't there. But the policeman who had spoken with the bailiff a few minutes earlier was. "What's going on?" Blake asked bluntly.

"Mr. Tanner, I'm Frank Hernandez, Dallas Police Department. There's been a shooting. Your wife has been hurt. I'm to take you to Parkland Hospital now."

Blake felt as if Hernandez had delivered him a hard left hook. ''How bad?'' he croaked as they ran through the hallway of the courthouse and down the stairs to a waiting squad car.

Hernandez's partner hit the siren. As they sped along the downtown streets, Hernandez gave Blake what scanty details he had. Blake heard nothing except that the policeman had no idea how badly Glenna was hurt.

The harried emergency room nurse wasn't able to tell him much more, except that they had taken her directly to surgery. This wasn't the posh, private hospital where Glenna had been when she'd miscarried and later when she had surgery; it was a teeming mass of humanity running in all directions, trying to take care of the unwashed multitude of unfortunates who passed through its doors. It took Blake fifteen frantic minutes to find an overcrowded surgery waiting room.

I've got to know what's going on!

Blake's mind reached out for answers. *Greg will be able to find out,* he thought, damning the necessity of finding a medical professional to wade through this ''I don't know'' bureaucracy. Quickly he strode to a bank of pay phones and called his friend. Then he waited by the elevators, feeling more frightened than he remembered ever having been before.

He didn't keep track of how long he stood there, searching faces as people came out of each packed elevator. Finally, though, Greg stepped off one and strode to Blake's side.

''How is she?''

''Hell, I don't know any more now than I did when I called you. For God's sake, Greg, go find out something. They won't talk to me.''

Greg rested one hand on Blake's shoulder as if to restrain him from some rash action. ''I'll go in and ask some questions. You just sit down and try to relax,'' he ordered gruffly.

Why was it, Blake wondered, that time went so quickly when you were having fun and so damn miserably slow when each moment seemed like another eternity in hell? It seemed like hours, but a look at his watch confirmed that Greg had been gone less than ten minutes when he reappeared outside the ominous-looking swinging doors marked STAFF ONLY.

"Well?" Blake could barely get that one word out, after searching Greg's face. Glenna was right, he thought; their friend's expressions were easy to read. Now he saw as well as felt Greg's sense of helplessness and sadness.

Greg herded Blake into a secluded corner, away from others who were awaiting word from surgery. "It's bad, Blake. A head wound."

Blake felt then heard the wrenching sob that came from deep down in his chest before Greg went on.

"Parkland has the best trauma team around. They're doing all they can, so you've got every reason to hope."

"It's that bad?" Blake sat down on a tattered chair and stared senselessly at the shadow Greg's lean body cast across the room. He turned to his friend when Greg sank down beside him and put a consoling arm around his shoulder.

"If you believe in praying, now's the time to start," Greg said, his own voice breaking with emotion as he tried to give help and comfort.

For a long time they sat there, saying nothing. Silently Blake invoked the power of God, and every saint he had ever heard of, to spare his wife. Without asking, he knew his friend was adding his own entreaties for Glenna's life and health.

Finally they had to speak or go insane. Greg began, recalling sweet and funny memories of good times the three of them—and Greg's girlfriend of the moment—had enjoyed when they were undergraduates at the University of Texas. The stories eased the tension, and soon Blake joined in with memories of his own.

Blake looked up as a doctor crossed the waiting room. The man looked awful, his white lab coat standing out in contrast with florid skin and faded OR scrubs. But it wasn't his appearance that struck Blake so strongly; it was the look of utter, unmitigated defeat Blake saw in the doctor's eyes.

When Blake realized the man was headed straight for him, his chest suddenly felt too tight. For long seconds, he couldn't breathe. Reflexively he reached for Greg's steadying hand.

Chapter 3

*G*lenna Tanner is dead!

Erin set down the phone. Like a zombie, she sank onto the worn sofa in her living room and cried. Reflexively she clutched her distended abdomen.

Erin had worried about the arrangement at first, until she'd seen Glenna recover quickly from the surgery she'd had. But now, without warning, some deranged maniac out for revenge for being fired from Neiman's had gunned down Glenna while she shopped for baby clothes.

A sob wrenched itself from Erin's throat. Glenna would never hold this child or rock it to sleep in the antique rocker she'd described to Erin the day they had met for lunch.

"What will become of you?" she asked aloud, but the only response in the silent room was the baby's strong, healthy movement within her belly.

Erin had never met Glenna's husband whose seed had made this child. Still, her heart went out to him. *For once,* she thought sadly, *Blake Tanner has lost something his money can't replace.*

She's gone.

Blake stared at the bleak, ivory closet wall that just this morning had been hidden behind brightly colored dresses Glenna liked to wear. Why had he told Mary to get rid of them today? Then, with self-derision, he berated himself for having thought for a moment that the colors could have cheered him. Nothing would do that, not after watching the workers lower Glenna's coffin into the icy ground.

Like a robot, he shrugged out of the jacket of his dark gray suit and hung it up. Sliding the mourning band off the sleeve, he felt tears well up in his eyes again. His fist closed fiercely around the scrap of black material as he walked back into the bedroom that he and Glenna had shared for fourteen years.

Three days ago, they had laughed and loved in this room, and he had teased her gently about the baby they hoped to have in four more months. Then she had gone shopping for a layette and gotten in the way of a bullet intended by a deranged ex-employee for the manager who'd fired him.

Why in hell did I ever agree to her crazy need to have a child?

If he hadn't, Glenna wouldn't have been in the infant department. *She would still be here,* he told himself as he sat on the bed and wondered how in hell he was going to survive without her.

"Oh, God," he said aloud, for suddenly he remembered the baby was still very much alive, inside the body of Erin Winters, the surrogate mother Greg had found. He stripped off his dark tie and opened the collar of his shirt before getting out of the room. He would never be able to sleep there again.

Blake didn't want that baby now. His heart bleak, he picked up the phone and called Greg.

"What are you going to do?"

Erin met her sister Sandy's concerned gaze. "I can't have an abortion," she said with conviction.

"I told Greg that. Oh, Erin, I'm sorry I talked you into doing this for the Tanners."

"You couldn't have known it was going to turn out like this. No one could. It seemed like the only way I could manage for Timmy to have his surgery. And he's doing so much better now. The therapist thinks he'll be walking with crutches in another month or two.'' She didn't want Sandy blaming herself for getting her into this predicament.

Erin tried to smile. It was hard, knowing she was likely to be totally responsible for this new life growing inside her as well as for her seven-year-old who was slowly and painfully learning to function again.

"You could always give the baby up, for adoption to someone else,'' Sandy suggested gently.

"Wouldn't Mr. Tanner have to agree to it? After all, it is going to be his baby as much as mine. More, in fact,'' she murmured, thinking of the money he'd paid for her to carry his child.

Sandy didn't answer right away. "Yes. He would. But Greg said he was adamant about wanting you to have an abortion.''

"Even if I wanted to, it would be too late. And I couldn't. I've felt the baby moving. It's alive, and I can't kill it—not for anyone, even its natural father. I have to talk to Mr. Tanner, Sandy.''

"Okay. I'll tell Greg and have him relay your message.'' Sandy looked at her sister with undisguised sympathy. "Erin, Greg says Mr. Tanner won't leave you holding the bag, no matter what,'' she said with what seemed to be very determined optimism. "Give Timmy a hug for me. I've got to get back to work.''

Erin watched her sister go down the stairs before going to Timmy's room to check on him. Lovingly she straightened the blankets around her little boy's weakened legs before bending and kissing his pale cheek. How could James Blake Tanner IV not want his child, she wondered, knowing that Timmy was the one bright light that kept darkness out from her life after Bill's sudden death three years ago.

She walked tiredly into the living room and opened up the sofa bed where she slept. For a long time she lay there in the dark, feeling the movement in her womb.

Since Glenna died two weeks earlier, Erin was finding it harder each day to think of this child other than as her own. Glenna had become a friend since they made the surrogate arrangement. While Erin had easily been able to think of the baby inside her as Glenna's, she had trouble picturing it as belonging now only to Glenna's husband.

For the first time, Erin made herself consider the man whose sperm had been placed in her body in a sterile doctor's office, who had willingly paid her price to bear his child for Glenna—but who had coldly demanded after Glenna's death that her baby—no, not Glenna's anymore, but hers—be callously destroyed. Resentment warred with compassion as Erin considered first Blake Tanner's rejection of his child, then the grief she could so easily understand.

"I told you, Greg, I don't want anything to do with this baby," Blake repeated. "This was Glenna's idea to begin with. And she's gone."

"It will be your son or daughter," Greg reminded him. "The surrogate mother flatly refuses to abort it. Look, Blake, I know you're grieving. But think of Mrs. Winters. She's been carrying that baby for five and a half months now. She's felt it move inside her. Frankly I wouldn't think much of her if she were willing to have an abortion at this stage. If you weren't a lifelong friend and the circumstances weren't the way they are, I wouldn't do it even if she were willing."

"What is she going to do?"

"Have the baby. I think she might be willing to offer it for adoption to another family. But whether she can do that is up to you. You're the father and you would have to agree to its being adopted."

Blake swore softly and succinctly as he leaned back in the leather swivel chair behind his desk and rubbed a hand across his eyes. He appreciated his friend's coming here, to his office, instead of making him come to his medical suite where this whole mess had started.

"You know, I don't feel a helluva lot like anybody's father. Especially not a baby whose mother I've never laid eyes on, much less anything else. Right now, I just feel empty. All I want to do is make it from one day to the next."

"Maybe this baby would give you reason to live," Greg suggested quietly.

"Without Glenna? Hell, having a baby was her obsession, not mine. Even before you told us she needed that hysterectomy, I'd resigned myself to not having any children. I didn't particularly want them if Glenna couldn't be their mother."

Greg leaned forward and rested his elbows on the corner of Blake's desk. "And you thought the surrogate arrangement was dangerous from the beginning." He paused. "Don't deny it. You told me how you felt about a woman offering to give up her child for money—that you worried that she would keep making more and more demands to keep quiet about the arrangement. How could you not have second thoughts? I did, and I'm not a contract attorney."

"That's not what bothered me most. The whole thing was damn unnatural. From writing up ironclad agreements, to sitting on the edge of a cold stainless steel examining stool and collecting the sperm, to handing over fifty thousand dollars the day you confirmed that the procedure took—all of it smacked of anything but making a baby with a woman I care for."

"I offered to let you collect the semen at home."

"And I told you no. I did it, damn it, but I wasn't about to dirty my marriage bed by using my wife to help me get it up to fill that little jar."

"Would you have rather done it naturally?"

"With Glenna? Yes." Blake felt a muscle twitch in his jaw. "With someone else? Hell, no. Look, Greg, you can tell this Mrs. Winters I'll up the ante by whatever reasonable figure she asks for, and I'll sign the papers agreeing that the baby can be adopted when it's born.''

"You're going to have to tell her yourself, my friend. She's not talking to me since I relayed your desire for her to have an abortion.''

Blake's fist came down without his conscious direction and slammed into the desk. "I have no desire to meet a woman who would sell her body for fifty grand. Besides, she has to talk to you. You're her obstetrician.''

"And you're the father of that baby she's carrying. You owe it to her to meet her and tell her what's on your mind.'' Greg drilled Blake with a stormy gaze. "I think you also owe it to yourself to find out just why she agreed to this arrangement.''

"What the hell do you mean by that?'' Blake asked, meeting his friend's gaze without flinching.

"That maybe you've misjudged the lady. And that you need to see that baby growing inside her and realize it's as much a part of you as it is of her. Look, I've got to go. I'm going to be seeing patients until seven o'clock as it is.'' Greg took a folded paper from an inside pocket of his navy blazer and pressed it into Blake's hand. Then he walked out without another word.

Chapter 4

Glenna

"No, Blake. My poor, heartbroken darling, you can't mean you want to abandon our baby!"

Glenna heard Blake talking with Greg as if she had been standing at his side. She strained to visualize the man she had loved for longer than she could remember. His image was hazy now, but not so faint that she couldn't feel the agony evident in his tear-clouded eyes and uncharacteristically slumped shoulders.

What have you done? What have you done to Blake? To our baby? To Erin Winters? And to me?

Glenna's spirit raged at the twisted wretch who had ended her life with a single, barely audible blast. For a moment she hated that faceless piece of humanity enough that, if she had the power to, she would take pleasure in turning his obscene little gun on him and blowing him straight to hell.

Then guilt washed over her.

That stranger pulled the trigger that took me away from him. But it was my obsession that has brought this awful grief to Blake, leaving him so horribly alone yet responsible for the life of the unborn child in Erin's body.

He doesn't want his baby now.

My poor, sweet baby.

And Erin. What is she thinking, carrying a baby whose father wants it destroyed?

My God!

Glenna could see Blake clearly now. She could practically feel his despair as he stared, unseeing, at the paper Greg had left with him.

I've got to make this right.

Can I come back? Just long enough to help them cope?

Yes. She felt a highly charged energy deep within her being, transporting her from the limbo of nonentity to Blake's office in a high-rise Dallas office building.

Blake. Her love. Her friend. How well she knew him— her strong, earthbound anchor whose calm and analytical way of viewing life had always been a perfect foil for her own whimsical and often impractical nature.

They went back forever. Glenna's spirit lightened as she remembered the quiet, often solemn little boy who had vowed his undying love for her in first grade, teased her when they were ten, and asked her to be his wife the Christmas after they had graduated from college. He'd always been serious—but she had unearthed a sense of fun in him while he had talked her out of the most impractical of her impulsive ideas.

They had been soul mates. She, raised by loving grandparents to enjoy life's every moment, and Blake, imbued with a mighty sense of responsibility and duty by a workaholic father and socialite mother, had been the odd couple whose lives had mingled smoothly into one.

She would love him for all eternity. But now she wanted . . . needed . . . to talk to him, to convince him of how precious his son or daughter would be. She wanted to hold and comfort him, and tell him time would heal his grief. More than anything, Glenna wanted Blake not to hurt anymore.

She wanted him to see her, recognize her presence so she could tell him how sorry she was to have left him all alone and unprepared to go on without her. But she stopped short of making her presence known to him. She knew Blake like her own alter ego; he would never accept her returning this way.

If he would even allow himself to admit he saw me, he'd run, not walk, to commit himself into the nearest psycho ward.

No, I can't show myself to him. She willed her spirit to drift away.

"But I can work on Erin Winters," Glenna said aloud, heartened at the thought that she might find an ally in the kind, caring woman she and Blake had hired to carry their baby.

"Yes." Glenna remembered the pain she had read in Erin's soft, dark blue eyes when they had talked about the baby. Instinctively she felt that Erin couldn't help but love the child she had said she tried hard not to think about, that day they met for lunch.

"Erin can be a real mother, not just a surrogate, to this child of mine. If she will, she can heal Blake, too."

No longer aimlessly floating in limbo, Glenna's spirit gathered and strengthened for the long, hard task ahead.

Chapter 5

For a long time, Blake stared at the paper Greg had given him. All it contained was a name, phone number, and address. The name was Erin Winters's. The address he couldn't place; but the zip code indicated an area not too far from downtown Dallas, where what few houses remained were pretty shabby and run-down. He'd have thought his $50,000 would have bought this woman a better place to live than that.

Was she on drugs? In trouble with the law? Questions came to mind, but Blake logically put them to rest. Greg was a friend as well as a damn fine doctor. He would never have set Glenna up with a surrogate whose lifestyle would threaten the health of the child that would belong to Glenna—or him.

Finally Blake tucked the paper in his pocket and forced himself to get up and head home. Before he realized what he was doing, he was pulling his silver Mercedes sedan to the curb in front of a run-down apartment building in a neighborhood that had seen better days.

''Yes?'' Erin's back hurt, her feet were swollen, and she barely had the energy to answer the door. *The strain has really been getting to me these last two weeks,* she thought tiredly, forcing her eyes to focus on the stranger at her door. She didn't think the tall, good-looking man standing in her doorway, wearing a suit that probably cost more than she spent on groceries in a year, was just another door-to-door salesman.

"I'm Blake Tanner."

For a moment, she stared into eyes bleak with sorrow. "Come in," she murmured, remembering her manners.

She led him through the living room, where Timmy was napping in front of their old TV set, into the kitchen. "Won't you sit down?" She indicated one of two battered chairs beside an old wood dining table.

"What did you do with the money we gave you?" Blake asked without even so much as a cursory greeting. Erin watched his gaze shift from shabby appliances to the tired-looking curtain that shielded his eyes from a view of the alley out back.

"I paid for my son's last surgery—at least for most of it," Erin said quietly, hoping Timmy wouldn't awaken to hear the bitter conversation she was sure would follow.

"Surgery?"

She thought his flat, deep voice sounded a little more alive. "Timmy was hurt three years ago, in the accident that killed his father," she supplied in response to Blake's terse question.

"Where is the boy?"

"In there. Didn't you see him?" she replied, gesturing toward the living room they had passed through. "He was watching TV when he fell asleep. I brought you in here so we wouldn't disturb him."

"I wasn't looking." Blake got up suddenly and stood in the doorway between the rooms, as if he needed to verify for himself the existence of her little boy. "How old is he?" he asked, turning back to Erin and settling back down at the table.

"Seven."

For a long time, neither of them spoke. Erin had wanted, needed, to see her unborn baby's father, but now that he was here, she didn't know what to say. She had been pre-

pared to hate the man who had proposed that she get rid
of his child; now, having seen the depth of his grief, she
felt a need to console him.

Not comfortable enough to take the chair across from
Blake, Erin stood at the counter, watching his gaze shift
until it settled on her rounded belly.

"Would you like some coffee?" she asked, nervous at
the way he was looking at her.

"No, thank you. You have no idea how happy you made
Glenna when you agreed to have our baby," he murmured
suddenly, his deep voice crackling with emotion.

"But not you?"

"No. I'd have been content to adopt. You're carrying the
result of my wife's obsession that our child must come from
my body if not from hers."

Erin could see why Glenna had so desperately wanted
her husband's child. Even in his grief, Blake Tanner was
devastatingly attractive; she imagined that in happier circumstances he could easily break women's hearts.

She'd been surprised to note that he was well over six
feet tall, since Glenna had been so petite. And she couldn't
help noticing that beneath the conservative suit he wore, he
had broad, muscular shoulders and a lean, well-conditioned
torso. His sable hair, darker than her own, was a bit too
long, long enough to tempt a woman to reach out and brush
back an unruly curl from his tanned forehead. Erin sensed
that his dark blue eyes, dulled now with grief, would sparkle if he curled those shapely, sensual lips into a real smile.

"This baby is yours," Erin finally murmured, unable to
keep from imagining that the baby's coloring would mirror
his—and hers, if its genes reflected their own dominant
traits. "What are you going to do about it?"

Blake didn't answer right away. Instead he looked as if
he were trying to lift the weight of the world from his broad
shoulders. "Would you want to raise it?" he asked, tun-
neling his fingers through his hair.

The baby chose that moment to move inside Erin. "Me?" She said stupidly.

"You're its biological mother. Its only mother now." The words came from him harshly, as though it pained him to admit that he had put this life inside her.

Erin pictured this baby in her arms. Then she thought of Timmy—of the series of surgeries still scheduled for him, of the years still to come before he would be whole and she could take a real job to care for herself and him.

"It's all I can do to see to Timmy's needs," she blurted out, and she wondered if Blake thought she lived in this shabby place because she wanted to. "I couldn't."

"Do you want it to go to strangers?" She felt his gaze pierce through the thin cotton maternity blouse she wore, as if he were looking at the baby that rested within her distended belly.

No. It was going to be hard enough to give it to Glenna and you when it was born. "What choice do I have?" she asked aloud.

Blake's expression softened. It seemed to Erin that he was seeing something or someone beyond her range of vision. She watched him stand and move to the window, staring out as if entranced.

"Mommy . . . I need to go to the bathroom."

Blake turned and followed as Erin hurried into the living room. When she bent to pick Timmy up, Blake reached out and nudged her away, slipping his strong arms around the little boy and lifting him with ease.

"Who are you?" Timmy asked.

"I'm Blake Tanner. Where's the bathroom?" he asked gruffly as he strode through the only other door in the room.

Later, when Timmy was in bed for the night, Blake sat down in the living room and regarded Erin seriously. "He can't walk at all, can he?"

When Erin shook her head silently, he continued. "You shouldn't be lifting him," he said abruptly.

Who was Blake Tanner to criticize her for doing what

she had to do? "I'm not injuring myself or this baby," she snapped before managing to curb her temper.

"I don't agree. When you signed the contract with us to have the baby, you promised to take proper care of yourself while you're pregnant. It looks to me like you're running yourself to death taking care of Timmy. And I can't believe living in this place is conducive to anyone's good health."

"It's the best I can afford and pay for Timmy's therapy."

"Are you even eating right? I haven't seen the first bite of food since I've been here."

Erin stood up and stared down at Blake. "We'd just had supper before you came. Would you like to sample the leftovers?" she asked sarcastically.

"I don't think so. But I would like to offer you a proposition." As if to accentuate his power, he stood so she would have to look up to him.

"That baby inside you is mine. I can't ignore my responsibility to it. Or to Glenna. This is what I have in mind," he told Erin. "Move out of here, bring Timmy to my house, and let me take care of both of you. At least until after the baby's born. I'll pay for whatever you need."

"You want to keep the baby now?" Erin asked, confused.

"I guess I do. I—I don't want it being raised by strangers. But what in hell am I going to do with it? My God! A baby needs its mother. . . ." Blake's hand tightened into a fist, and Erin wondered when his control would break and he would shatter her flimsy end table.

"It needs its father, too," she said softly, reaching up to touch the taut skin of his cheek and give him what comfort she could. Again, as in the kitchen, she watched his eyes glaze over and felt him mentally withdraw from her.

After a while, he sat back down, taking her hand to pull her onto the sofa beside him. "We're a hell of a pair, aren't we?" he asked rhetorically before going on.

"You agreed to do this so you could get your boy the

help he needs. I did it to make Glenna happy. Now, like it or not, we're in this together. You still need money to take care of Timmy, and I'm going to need a woman to mother that baby you're carrying. I think we might as well make the best of a bad situation and take care of each other's needs. You move in with me, and we'll muddle through this mess together.''

Shocked, Erin turned around and met his gaze. *He's serious. No, he can't be.* ''Why would you want to do that?'' she asked, hardly recognizing the sound of her own voice— and wondering why she was actually thinking of accepting Blake Tanner's strange offer.

Chapter 6

"Greg!"

"Yeah?" At the sound of Sandy's voice, Greg looked up immediately from the accountant's report he had been trying to decipher. He had been thinking of her anyhow, as he did every time he had to face the fact that unless one or both of his expensive ex-wives decided to find themselves another victim, he'd never be able to give Sandy the kind of life he knew she deserved.

God, he wished he'd met Sandy long before there had been one, let alone two former Mrs. Halperns bleeding him dry of damn near every cent he could manage to earn.

"You want to tell me what's going on with my sister and Blake Tanner?" she demanded, her voice rising with every word.

Surprised to hear Sandy screeching like his most recent ex so frequently did, Greg got up and reached out to stroke an errant strand of tawny hair away from eyes that flashed with anger. "Calm down, sweetheart," he said gently.

"Calm down? When my sister calls and tells me she's moving into Blake Tanner's house next week? What's going on? Greg, I don't want Erin hurt. I'm the one who got her mixed up in this. Erin's been through enough hell for three lifetimes as it is."

"Sandy. Don't yell at me. This is the first I've heard about your sister moving in with Blake. I haven't talked to either of them since I went to Blake's office last week and asked him to go and meet Erin. I've known Blake Tanner a lot of years, though, and I know he'd never hurt a woman.''

''But, Greg . . .''

''But nothing. Your sister needs some help now. I imagine that taking care of Timmy is quite a job for any woman, let alone one in Erin's condition. Even if Glenna were alive and well, I'd have suggested that Blake provide Erin with more help now that her pregnancy is advancing.''

''But putting her up in his house?''

''Why not? It's certainly big enough. Look, Sandy, I've got to go over to the hospital and check on Mrs. Slater. Come with me. We can eat out somewhere if she's holding on okay, and talk about this some more,'' he suggested, stashing the financial statements in his desk drawer and shrugging out of the wrinkled lab coat he wore during office hours.

''Do you really live in this great big house all by yourself?'' Timmy asked sleepily, his slight body shifting awkwardly against Blake's chest.

Suddenly pain washed through Blake at the little boy's reminder that now he *was* all alone. ''Not anymore, sport,'' he said gruffly.

''Timmy, don't bother Mr. Tanner,'' Erin cautioned in that calm, sweet voice Blake knew must be hiding her uncertainty at putting hers and Timmy's lives into his, a stranger's, hands.

He had his own doubts, that was for sure. Still, Erin was carrying his and Glenna's child, and that made her well-being his responsibility.

Blake forced a smile. ''He's not bothering me,'' he said, looking over the child in his arms to meet Erin's gaze. ''As a matter of fact, I think he's just drifted off to sleep. Shall I put him to bed now?'' He strode purposefully through the courtyard and pool area toward one of several sliding glass doors.

"I can do it," Erin replied, her voice quietly assertive despite her obvious fatigue.

Dark circles under her eyes and fine lines around her sensual mouth bore witness to the fact that Erin had been doing far more than a woman in her condition should, Blake thought as he ignored her protest and laid Timmy onto the bed. Reluctantly he moved aside so Erin could get the boy ready for a good night's rest, making a mental note to talk to Mary and make sure the housekeeper would take over most of the physical part of Timmy's care.

"It's been a long day for you," Blake said after watching Erin arrange a light blanket over her son's slight shoulders and bend awkwardly to brush soft lips over his pale cheek. "Mary put your things away in there," he added, gesturing with one hand in the general direction of a connecting door.

Should I walk her in and show her around? Where did that idea come from?

Suddenly Blake felt his gaze settle on Erin—specifically on the rounded mound that held Glenna's baby. No, not Glenna's baby now. Glenna was gone. His baby. His and this soft-spoken stranger's with a sweet, tired smile, and a look in eyes as dark as the sky at midnight that spoke of pain and suffering he knew must rival his own.

"I never realized before how exhausting moving could be. I must be almost as tired as Timmy," Erin said, tilting her head backward to meet Blake's gaze. "If you'll excuse me, I believe I'll skip dinner and make it an early night."

"Of course. There's a phone by the bed," Blake told her. "Just press the button marked 'Intercom' if you need anything, and Mary will get it for you."

Much later, as he mentally crossed off the last of the details he had taken care of to ensure Erin and Timmy's comfort and well-being, it struck Blake that he had gone several hours without being overwhelmed by the senseless,

heartrending realization of his beloved Glenna's death—
and his own emptiness.

Soft, fuzzy apricots. *That's what the floor looks like,* Erin
thought as she tried to focus her sleepy eyes. Vaguely she
remembered coming in here last night after tucking Timmy
into bed in his own room, undressing and collapsing between these cool, silky sheets. She stretched, luxuriating in
the feel of warmth that came as much from dappled sunlight
filtered through the leaves of a willow tree outside as from
the quilted satin comforter she had burrowed into like a
cocoon.

Slowly Erin awakened. Last night she'd been too tired
to notice much other than that the room Blake had given
her was close to being as big as the whole apartment she
and Timmy had just vacated. Now Erin felt Glenna Tanner's airy touch in white art deco furniture and pristine
walls warmed by the deep apricot carpet and accessories in
aqua and apricot. The last time they had met, Erin recalled,
Glenna had mentioned how she was going to use her favorite colors—apricot and aqua—to decorate the baby's
nursery.

"*I'm glad you're here.*"

"Who's there? Mary, is that you?"

Erin sat up quickly and glanced around the room.
"Where are you?" she asked.

No one answered, but Erin thought she saw the slightest
rustling of a sheer, pale apricot drapery that framed closed
French doors. *I must be losing my mind,* she told herself.

Then the door opened, and Erin watched a beaming, mid-
dle-aged woman push a tea cart ahead of her as she came
into the room. "Mr. Tanner said you'd probably sleep late,
but that I wasn't to let you miss lunch," the woman said.

"Lunch?"

"Well, brunch, you might say. I'm Mary Malone, ma'am,
and I've been running this house for just about as long as

Mr. Tanner's been alive. Will you be wanting to eat in bed or here by the window?''

''I'll get up.'' Erin couldn't imagine herself being served in bed like an indolent lady she recalled seeing in a movie once. Apparently Blake had failed to tell Mrs. Malone that he had rescued the surrogate mother of his child from a life that had never included breakfast in bed or hired help. He certainly had neglected to let *her* know just how opulently he lived, Erin thought as she slid off the bed and waddled to the small table where the housekeeper was setting up a place setting for one, complete with linen place mat, napkins, and a single rose in a cut-crystal bud vase.

''What time is it, Mrs. Malone?'' she asked as she sank—as graciously as a six-months' pregnant lady in an oversize T-shirt nightie could manage—onto the edge of the chair in front of the place where her food had been set out.

''A bit past eleven, ma'am. After you've eaten, Mr. Tanner thought you might like to take a tour around the house and grounds.'' Mrs. Malone hustled around the room, making the bed Erin had just vacated and picking up the few garments she had been too tired to put away last night.

''Eleven?'' Erin pushed back her chair and began to get up. ''Oh, no. I've got to get Timmy ready to go to the hospital for his therapy,'' she explained, washing down the last bite of a cheese and ham omelet with a swallow of tangy tomato juice cocktail that must have been made from fresh tomatoes and herbs.

''You don't worry about that, ma'am. Mr. Tanner's got your little boy's therapist coming out here, so you won't have to drive all the way downtown.'' Mrs. Malone flipped back the napkin covering a small silver basket, tempting Erin with a flaky Danish pastry.

''But how? The equipment . . . ?''

''Why, Mr. Tanner's got a gym that's got more contraptions than a body could possibly need to exercise. He already had most of what that Ms. Michelle said she'd need,

and what he didn't have, they sent out day before yesterday
from the hospital.''

Erin felt the way Alice must have felt as she was ca-
reening down that dark hole into Wonderland. Everything
was moving too fast, out of control. Yesterday she had been
struggling to find energy to take care of Timmy and herself
as well as the baby inside her. Today, it seemed, Blake
Tanner controlled every aspect of their lives. Needing to
restore some direction to her own existence, Erin headed
for the closed mirrored door she assumed hid a closet. She
would dress, find Timmy, and see to his needs in this scary
new environment.

She started to grab soft jeans and a cotton knit top; then,
picturing the softly elegant decor of the room where Blake
had put her, and Mrs. Malone in her starched, black uniform, she put them back and chose a maternity jumper of
pale gray wool that she had found a few weeks ago at a
thrift shop in the old neighborhood. Dressed in the jumper,
with a burgundy turtleneck shirt, black tights, and black
flats that looked like ballet slippers, Erin felt comfortable,
presentable, and ready to face her son and whatever new
surprises Blake had in store for her.

At least that was what she told herself as she brushed
the tangles from her hair and pulled it back in a low po-
nytail. She wasn't so sure as she followed Mrs. Malone
through the house whose casual elegance had escaped her
notice last night when Blake had brought them here.

''This is the breakfast room,'' Mrs. Malone told Erin as
they entered a bright, airy enclosure with glass walls on
three sides. As if denying the unseasonal bleakness of the
cold, rainy April day, leafy plants abounded. Some grew
tall and lush in glazed ceramic pots on the spotless floor of
Mexican tile, while others hung suspended from the vaulted
ceiling in baskets of wood, wire, and clay. Several orchids
were in rampant bloom, spilling cascades of delicate blossoms in all directions. ''Mr. Tanner usually eats here unless
he is having guests,'' the housekeeper added.

"It's beautiful." Erin's gaze took in a large round table surrounded with six matching captain's chairs, as well as a conversational grouping of sofa, chairs, and tables that faced the plant-filled glass walls. She noticed the table was already set for three, and wondered if Blake would be joining them for lunch. "Is Mr. Tanner here?" she asked with only a moment's hesitation.

"Why, certainly, Mrs. Winters. He stayed home today, wanting to make sure everything was right for you and that precious little boy. Right now, I think he's talking with Timmy's therapist out by the pool."

The housekeeper motioned toward the wide expanse of glass, and when Erin followed, she saw Blake standing by a crystal-clear pool, accompanied not by Michelle the therapist but by Timmy, whose grin warmed Erin's heart as he waved to her.

I like Timmy.

As he watched the little boy bravely endure what must be excruciatingly painful manipulation of his scarred, stiff legs, Blake could barely restrain himself from ordering Michelle to stop, to cease her torture and soothe Timmy's pain with a deep heat massage—or ultrasound—or a healing soak in the Jacuzzi over in the corner of his weight room. He felt an insane urge to grab Timmy away from the therapist, cradle him in his arms, and carry him away where no one could hurt him, not even in the name of healing.

One morning in Timmy's company had made Blake realize that Erin had suffered pain at least as great as he was feeling with his loss of Glenna. As he stood by helplessly and watched Erin's son endure hellish pain at the hands of his physical therapist, Blake recalled patches of the little boy's candid conversation as they explored the house and grounds earlier this morning.

"My mommy's going to have your baby," the boy had said when Blake asked him if he would mind letting Erin sleep a little longer. ''Will he be my brother?'' he had asked in the next breath.

''Half brother or sister.'' At the time, Blake had given the reply as technically accurate but meaningless.

''Mommy liked Ms. Glenna,'' Timmy had said then. ''Mommy said she died, just like my daddy. You must miss her a lot.''

Blake had forced a neutral reply, but Timmy came back with wisdom far beyond his tender years. ''It's okay to cry when you hurt. Mommy says so. Sometimes I cry when Michelle moves my legs around. Sometimes Mommy does, too. She says it hurts her when Michelle has to hurt me.''

''Hurt you?'' The thought of anyone deliberately hurting Timmy—any child—had incensed Blake.

''Yeah. Sometimes it hurts a lot. But Mommy says I'm lucky. They were able to fix my legs so they didn't have to cut them off, and if I work really hard, someday they ought to work almost good as new. I want them to work again.''

From Timmy's childish words, and a serious conversation with Michelle when she arrived, Blake had learned some of what Erin had gone through since the accident three years earlier that had made her a widow and nearly taken away her only child. The knowledge strengthened his resolve to care for Erin and Timmy, while it blessedly allowed him to bury the bitterest portions of his own grief.

He felt Erin's presence in the weight room before he actually saw her. Michelle had said she came every day, and that Erin never left the room while Timmy had his therapy. Today, at least, Mary had kept Erin occupied while Michelle put Timmy through hell; and for that Blake was grateful. Slowly he pushed himself away from the wall he had been leaning against and joined her next to the Jacuzzi where Timmy was soaking while Michelle massaged his legs.

''This is too much, Blake,'' Erin said, and he could see her taking in the Nautilus equipment as well as the new therapy table and ultrasound unit he had added to the gym for Timmy's use.

"Most of it was already here. I don't want you having to drag Timmy all the way downtown to the hospital every day. Michelle assures me that she has all he needs here, and in the pool." Blake walked Erin over to the door and indicated the outdoor swimming pool where wisps of steam already were forming over its crystalline surface. "It's too cold today, but you can see that the heater's working now."

"You're heating that big pool?"

"Sure. I used to keep it heated all the time. It should be plenty warm in a day or so, even if this cold front doesn't break," he observed, wondering why Erin's presence unnerved him so while he fully enjoyed her little son's company.

Hell, he knew exactly why. His baby was growing inside her, and the disdain he had felt for one who would sell her body for his money had faded into admiration for the way she had managed to provide for herself and Timmy under circumstances so dire he had trouble imagining them.

Blake swore silently. Being around Timmy had made him think of his own unborn son or daughter. And he had no trouble picturing the baby, either. It would look like Erin. And him. His gaze raked the tall, dark-haired woman with eyes nearly the same color as his, and he knew his child would have none of Glenna's blondness, no chance at all to look at him from eyes like golden honey. Intentionally or not, Glenna had chosen a surrogate mother whose features mirrored his, not hers, robbing him of the possibility of a son or daughter he could think of as hers.

"Are you feeling more rested now?" he asked, forcing the sudden anguish from his mind.

"Yes. Still, I'm not used to sleeping the morning away," Erin replied, sounding a bit annoyed.

"I thought you needed the rest. By the way, I talked to Greg Halpern this morning. He and Sandy are coming over for dinner tonight, and he said he could do your checkup here so you wouldn't have to go to his office on Friday."

"Are you planning to keep me prisoner here?" Erin asked pointedly.

"No. You're welcome to go and come as you please, just as long as you rest and take care of yourself. Greg said you probably shouldn't be making the long drive to the city, so if you want to go somewhere, let me know and I'll get Miguel to take you, if I'm not available to go myself."

Blake watched Erin's expression soften. "Thank you. I hadn't thought about the distance, not to mention the fact that I don't have the vaguest idea about bus service out here. I'll let you know if there's anywhere I need to go."

As if I would let you ride a public bus in your condition!

"Be sure you do. Let me get Timmy from Michelle and we'll take him inside for lunch. I had Mary fix us burgers and fries—I hope you don't mind. Timmy said that would be the best meal he could think of."

"He would. Wouldn't you, buddy?" Erin ran her fingers through Timmy's chestnut-brown curls, and Blake couldn't help remembering how gentle those long, slender fingers had felt on his face the night they met, when she had reached out to soothe his pain.

It felt weird to be standing next to Blake as if they were a couple, greeting her sister and her obstetrician for a friendly evening meal. Erin had napped for a couple of hours and indulged in a leisurely bath after Blake installed Super-Nintendo on a small TV set he had found and placed in her son's room. The last she had seen before retiring to her room was the two of them, controls in hand, engrossed in some fast-paced game that Timmy appeared to be winning, hands down.

Refreshed, she had put on the dressiest of the maternity clothes in her limited wardrobe and brushed her hair into a cascade of waves around her face. Blake seemed pleased with her appearance, although the dark blue rayon dress that hugged her breasts and fell in soft pleats to a hemline just below the knee could hardly hold a candle to his own obviously custom-tailored tan slacks and navy blazer.

Thankfully, no one mentioned her at-home checkup or hers and Blake's strange new living arrangements while they ate French onion soup followed by some delightfully rich concoction of shrimp and crab meat flanked with tiny, tender-crisp carrots and green beans. Erin listened to Blake's and Greg's desultory conversation, adding as little as Sandy, who looked as if she couldn't tear her gaze away from Greg for more than a few seconds at a time.

"Ready for me to check you now, Erin?" Greg asked after they had finished tiny dishes of rich chocolate custard and buttery cookies.

"I guess so." For some reason, Erin felt strange, reminded that she was in the presence of one man who had made her pregnant without ever having seen her, and another who had examined her repeatedly and minutely in his role as her OB-GYN. "Shall we do it in my room?" Surely, Blake had not gone so far as to set up an examining room somewhere in his huge, imposing house!

"That'll be fine. Blake, where did you stash my bag?"

"In the coat closet. I'll get it."

Erin stood up. Would Blake want to join Greg while he checked her blood pressure and listened to the baby's heartbeat? Would she let him if he did?

It seemed that Blake had every intention of being a part of this, Erin thought as she let him guide her to her room while Greg and Sandy followed. She shouldn't mind; less than a month ago she had gladly let Glenna join her in Dr. Halpern's examining room to listen to her baby. Still, she felt her cheeks heat with embarrassment when Blake led her to her bed and stepped back, out of the way but definitely *there*.

Sandy helped her lift her dress and lower her panty hose to bare her tummy. Erin was grateful that her sister's body blocked the view from Blake's clinically interested gaze. Greg quickly checked her blood pressure before lowering the sheet she had pulled over herself and gently probing at her abdomen.

"Want to hear your baby, Blake?" Greg asked, and Erin saw him stand and move closer to the bed.

"Do you mind?" Blake asked, his gaze studiously remaining on Erin's face.

It's his baby. He's got a right to listen to it, realize it's alive.

"No. Go ahead." Erin tried not to notice the rapt expression on Blake's face as he listened to his baby through Greg's stethoscope, but she couldn't help reacting when he drew back from the tiny hand or foot that poked out against her taut skin.

"Does it hurt? Is that normal?"

Erin didn't know if Blake was directing his questions to her or to Greg. She was about to reply when Greg did.

"No and yes. It wouldn't be normal if the baby didn't move. Here. You can feel it," Greg said, grabbing Blake's hand and pressing it gently against the spot that was rippling with the healthy movement of his child.

Erin's first thought was to protest, until she saw Blake's expression change from controlled pain to disbelieving awe—and finally to a genuine grin that lit his handsome face and brightened his eyes to the color of a clear, midnight sky.

"Does it move like this all the time?" he asked, his free hand joining the one already on Erin to cup both sides of her abdomen just above where her hipbones used to be.

"Not always," Erin replied. "Sometimes he sleeps."

Suddenly Blake must have realized that it wasn't only his unborn child that he was touching, because he jerked his hands away as if he'd been burned. "If you're done, Greg, come on and let Sandy visit with Erin while we have a drink. Erin, have a good night's rest," he added over his shoulder as he practically dragged his friend out of her room.

*   *   *

"Go on with them if you want to," Erin told Sandy when she kicked off her high-heeled sandals and sat down Indian-style at the foot of the king-sized bed.

"And miss telling you I've fallen head over heels in love?" Sandy asked, her eyes sparkling with happiness.

"You mean you've given up your crush on the much-divorced, alimony-ridden obstetrician you work for?" Erin teased.

"Don't even think that! Last night, I finally got Greg past his noble protests that he can't afford to fall in love again. And, Erin, you wouldn't believe what a wonderful lover he is!"

"I wouldn't?" Erin couldn't resist poking fun at her usually levelheaded sister.

"Never in a million years! How either one of those women he married could have even *thought* of leaving him, I'll never know. Greg is the gentlest, kindest, most caring man on earth, and I intend to have him."

Erin hoped Sandy wouldn't be too disappointed if her plans didn't work out. "What about the alimony and the teenage daughter? Didn't you tell me not a month ago that Greg was on the verge of bankruptcy, just from paying off his former wives?"

Sandy sighed. "I don't care if we have to live in a furnished room. Besides, his apartment is nice, even if it isn't big and grand like this. He took me there last night, after one of his patients lost a premature baby. Erin, Greg *cried*. He actually cried for that couple. It started out by my just holding him, trying to give him comfort. Then something happened. He started hugging me back, and then we kissed . . . and well, you know . . ."

"Yes, I know." It had been years, but Erin recalled that kind of passion—the kind that overruled reason and culminated in lovemaking that obliterated every obstacle to "happily ever after." She had felt it with Bill, enjoyed it to the fullest before it burned itself out and left her with a marriage that had lasted until his death only because of their little boy.

"Erin, I want to have Greg's baby. He's so good with little ones, so kind and caring. . . ." Sandy took in a deep breath and let it out slowly, and Erin saw the dreamy look in her bright, blue eyes.

"Greg Halpern already has a daughter. Twelve years old, spoiled rotten, and singularly obnoxious, if I recall your description of her after having taken her back to her mother," Erin reminded her sister, in a futile attempt to bring her back down to earth. "And, Sandy, he's at least ten years older than you."

"And of a different faith. And he's got a profession that will always come before his relationship with a woman. Oh, Erin, Greg has told me all that. I'm sure everybody else will tell me, too. Believe me, it doesn't make a bit of difference in the way I feel about him."

Erin smiled sadly. She had always hoped her little sister would find love, but the love she had envisioned was simpler, without the complications she imagined Sandy would find in a relationship with Greg. Suddenly Erin felt very tired. She pulled herself awkwardly out of bed and walked with Sandy out to the family room where Blake and Greg were talking and watching a fire that smoldered in the wide, brass-grated fireplace.

"Good luck, little sister," she said quietly, and then she headed back to her room.

What a day!

Sandy's suddenly changed relationship with her multi-divorced boss took a backseat to Erin's resentment of the high-handed way Blake had insisted on managing every aspect of her life.

More exhausted from Blake's treating her like a fragile depository for his precious seed than she had been yesterday from packing and moving, Erin struggled out of her clothes and collapsed in bed. Her fury built as she waged mental warfare on Blake and his implacable attitude.

"I can't stand this . . . this silk and velvet prison," she muttered aloud. "There won't be anything left of *me* if he has his way."

The room was comfortably warm, its windows and French doors securely closed against the late winter storm that raged outside. Still, Erin saw the curtains flutter and thought she felt a slight draft pass across the room. At first she tried to deny the eerie feeling that there was some intruding presence there with her.

"I'm glad you're here for Blake now. He means well, Erin, and he needs you more now than you and Timmy need the material help he can give to you."

The voice was clear . . . soft . . . hypnotic in its tone. It was strange and otherworldly but yet somehow familiar. Erin sat up suddenly, ignoring the baby's protest against her sudden movement, and strained her eyes to see in the pitch-black darkness of the room.

"Where are you?" she whispered, searching her memory for a name for that elusive voice.

"Here. By the window."

Erin looked in that direction but saw only the sheer, fluttering drapes. "I can't see you." She felt her panic rise with every second that passed. "Am I losing my mind?" she asked, whether of herself or of the disembodied voice she did not know. "Tell me who you are."

"Glenna."

"No! You're playing an awful trick on me! Glenna's dead."

"Dead, yes. At peace, no. I've gone and left Blake, and you, and the baby I wanted to the point of obsession, and there will be no peace for me until I've made amends."

"What? I can't believe this! Come on now, leave me alone. This whole situation may have me half insane, but I'm not far enough gone to believe I'm talking with a ghost!" Erin forced her swollen body to move enough so she could flip on the bedside lamp. "Show yourself, or I'll

scream for Blake,'' she threatened with more bravado than
real confidence.

Suddenly a burst of light drew Erin's attention to the
other side of the room, where what looked like particles of
shimmering dust gathered and materialized into a surrealistic female figure. Its features sharpened and solidified before her eyes, slowly but surely forming the substance of a
woman. *Glenna*—or anyhow, a dead ringer for her.

''Why are you doing this?'' Erin cried. ''Is this some
kind of macabre joke?'' Erin knew this had to be a high-
tech trick, but she couldn't imagine who would want, or
dare, to pull it in the house Blake controlled with the velvet-
clad iron fist he had so graphically demonstrated to her
today.

''Blake,'' Erin called, but the yell she had intended came
out as a muffled whisper as she felt an invisible hand clamp
snugly over her gaping mouth. Terrified, she closed her
eyes, as if doing so could erase her eerie tormentor's presence.

''Listen to me, Erin. I'm here to help, not hurt you.''

When Erin found the courage to open her eyes, she saw
Glenna perched on the edge of the bed. Her features were
clearer now than before, clear enough that Erin could no
longer deny her presence. ''What do you want?'' Erin
asked hoarsely.

''Listen carefully. I'm new at this, and I may float away
at any minute. I want Blake to laugh again. I want his baby
to have a loving mother as well as a daddy. I want you
and Timmy to have a happy, secure home and plenty of
love to share. I want you to make Blake love you as much
as he used to love me.''

Erin nearly laughed out loud. ''You must have heard me
swearing at your precious husband's macho way of con-
trolling everything. How on earth do you think I would ever
want him—and if I did, what's to say he might ever be
attracted to me in the least?''

''That's just Blake's way. When you get to know him,

you'll see he's really a big, lovable pussycat. Don't you worry about the other, either. He'll be wanting you, sooner than you think.''

"I don't believe you. I don't believe *this*." Erin watched as Glenna's image began to fade and disintegrate into the bright cloud of dust from which it came.

"Believe. Give our Blake a chance. I've got to go now, but I'll be back to help.''

The memory of her late-night visitor haunted Erin during the next few weeks. Sometimes she felt as if the whole scene had been a macabre dream; at other times, she could feel Glenna's presence just beyond her consciousness and she knew somehow that Glenna had come to her—and that she would return as she had promised.

When Blake was especially withdrawn or demanding, Erin could almost hear Glenna's voice, cautioning her sometimes to give him time and space, and other times to offer comfort and companionship. Tonight Erin felt compelled to keep Blake company, to try to ease the loneliness that surrounded him like a shroud.

"Thank you for spending time with Timmy this afternoon," she said, knowing that if Blake felt like talking about anything, he would join in a conversation about the little boy she knew he had come to care for deeply.

"He's a great kid. I enjoy his company," he replied politely, shifting his position on the sofa a bit to meet her gaze. "Are you feeling all right?" he asked, his attention focusing on the bulging stomach Erin didn't think could grow much larger in the next four weeks.

"He's worried about you. Say something funny."

"As fine as a watermelon can feel," Erin quipped with a smile, wondering why she was heeding that disembodied

voice that had started popping into her head more often
these last few days.

*"That's the way, Erin, make him smile. He really isn't
the stuffed shirt he tries so hard to be. Say something else
to make him laugh."*

It *was* Glenna, urging her to lighten up Blake's brooding
mood. It had to be. Erin didn't quite know whether to laugh
or scream. It seemed as if she were the only one who felt
this friendly ghost's continual presence.

Wondering for about the hundredth time if she was going
quietly crazy, Erin looked at Blake to see if he, too, had
heard that soft, smiling voice. Obviously he hadn't, she
decided when she noted his faintly amused grin and
watched him slide in her direction to place a gentle hand
on her tummy.

"He's being quiet tonight?"

It was more a question than a statement. She thought
Blake sounded disappointed that the baby hadn't chosen
this moment to practice kick-boxing against his father's
hand.

Heeding Glenna's eerie advice, Erin searched her mind
for another quip that might reward her with one of Blake's
disarming smiles. "For the moment. But that could change,
faster than the weather in a hurricane," she finally said.
Just then, the baby kicked, and Blake followed its motion
with his hand.

"I think I feel a foot here," he said excitedly, pressing
a little harder at the right side of Erin's abdomen. "Or
maybe it's a hand. How big is the baby now?"

"Big enough to come out, I think."

Blake smiled again. Erin wished he could always be cajoled so easily from the depression that so frequently surrounded him like a dark cloud obscures the sun before a
storm.

Blake was a paradox, she decided—unsure about his
feelings for the baby Glenna had wanted so much, yet unable to squelch the awe and pride in the development of

that baby in Erin's body. There was something sensual in the way he felt the baby move within her, yet his touch on her body felt impersonal—detached from sexuality, affection, or any emotion at all.

"Keep trying, my friend. You know, I can't say it doesn't make me feel good that he loved me so much. But he has to get over the grief, get on with his life."

This time when Erin looked up, Glenna had materialized in the corner of the room. Erin glanced away and checked to see if Blake had seen her, too. His expression hadn't changed, she noted, so she guessed the ghost's unnerving visits had to be for her alone.

Quickly she looked back toward the spot where she had seen Glenna seconds earlier. But she saw only sunlight reflecting on that now familiar haze of golden dust. Then the aura dissipated, and there was nothing at all.

"I think Blake is going to make it after all," Greg told Sandy as they finished eating take-out Chinese dinners in his apartment. He hoped so. He'd never seen anyone as devastated as Blake had been when Glenna died.

"I think so, too. Right now, though, I'd rather be thinking about us," Sandy told him, reaching out and stroking his forearm with a silky hand.

Greg reached out and grabbed her arm, giving her finger a playful nip before taking it gently into his mouth and laving it with his tongue. "You taste better than the food," he murmured, getting up and drawing Sandy into his arms.

"I love you," she said, and he believed her as he'd never thought he would believe a woman again. He loved Sandy, too, and he wished to hell he had the right to tell her so. Maybe soon he would.

It had very nearly been worth his spending his free afternoon without Sandy, letting his spoiled daughter cajole him for more money just like her mother always had, to hear Shana's latest gripe—that her mother Kay, his first wife, was about to sink her perfectly manicured talons into another, bigger fish. Greg would keep his fingers crossed that this time Kay wouldn't let her victim slip away—and that he would be freed of a big chunk of alimony that was due to end the day that ex-wife finally remarried.

"Soon, sweetheart," he murmured, putting pleasant possibilities out of his mind as he set about seducing the only woman who had ever made him feel ten feet tall and invincible.

He had a colleague taking emergency calls, no mothers threatening to have problems at the moment, a box of condoms in the drawer of his bedside table, and a burning need to see how many of them he and Sandy could use in the long, silent hours before morning would come again. Tomorrow would be soon enough to see if just maybe he might have a future to offer Sandy along with his deep, abiding love.

"Where's Sandy? This is the first time I've seen you without her in weeks," Blake commented the next morning when Greg walked into his office.

"At the office. This is just between you and me—at least for now." Greg looked a bit chagrined, Blake thought, recalling that his friend had always been a bit reticent about sharing his problems.

Blake regarded Greg with mock seriousness. "When are you going to make an honest woman of my baby's aunt?" he asked, half kidding, but half serious, too, since Erin had expressed her concern about Sandy's future and Greg's intentions toward her younger sister.

"I'm going to ask her to marry me so fast it will make your head spin—that is, if you can get either of the vultures I was dumb enough to marry to accept a hefty reduction in their blood money. You might try Kay first—Shana told me she's thinking about remarrying."

Blake leaned back in his chair and ran a hand through his hair. Greg had certainly managed to find two of the most grasping females Blake had ever had the misfortune of meeting—and he wasn't looking forward to making another futile attempt to extricate his friend from the alimony nightmare both Kay and her successor had inflicted upon him.

"If Kay remarries, the alimony stops," he said, repeating a fact he was sure Greg already knew. Blake hated working with divorces, alimony, and property settlements. The only reason he had taken Greg's cases in hand was because of their close friendship, and the way he pitied his friend for the way his original attorneys had botched their jobs.

"I'll look over the files again and see if there's any flaw I can use to justify asking for a review of the judges' respective orders. Does your accountant have current financial information put together?"

"Yeah. There's not all that much for him to record," Greg told Blake with a self-deprecating grin. "I'm serious. I'm barely surviving."

"Did you ever think of raising your fees?"

"I have. Regularly. I'm the most expensive damn OB-GYN in Dallas, unless Sam Harrell has jacked up his prices again in the last month. Seriously, there's a limit to how much most people will pay to have a healthy baby—and insurance companies are squeezing us greedy doctors more with every passing day."

Blake got up and poured himself another cup of coffee. "You want some more?"

"No, thanks. I have to get back to my office. What do you think my chances are?"

"I'll let you know after I've taken a fine-tooth comb to those papers," Blake told Greg as he walked him to the elevator.

In the last week, Blake had read the four-inch-thick file that documented Greg's two divorces in stilted legalese—several times. Now, though, he devoured each page in minute detail, looking for any irregularity he might have overlooked on more cursory examination.

The yellow pad he had used to note possible loopholes was pathetically close to blank when he finished his review and set the fat folder on the corner of his desk. Blake believed his friend's best hope for relief from court-ordered poverty was that Kay Halpern would hook the fish Greg had told him she currently had on the line. In spite of his pessimism about gaining Greg relief in the courts, Blake picked up his microcassette recorder and began dictating petitions to reopen alimony and support hearings.

He had just finished dictating the first petition when his secretary, Sharon Raston, apologetically interrupted.

"Your housekeeper is on line two," she told him. "I wouldn't have disturbed you, but she sounds upset."

"I'll talk to her. Thanks, Sharon," he said, flipping off the recorder and punching the blinking button on his speakerphone. "What is it, Mary?"

"It's Mrs. Winters. She twisted her ankle and fell, out by the pool."

"Is she hurt?"

"She says she's all right. I helped her up and into her room. She's lying down now."

Blake thought of Erin's stubborn streak of independence that seemed to keep her from accepting a lot of the help he wanted to give her. Was she truly all right? "How is she really, Mary?"

"I think her doctor ought to check her out. It's awfully close to her time to have the baby."

"Then have Miguel drive her to Dr. Halpern's office. I'll meet her there," Blake directed.

Mary sounded distressed. "Miguel isn't here. This is his day off. Do you want me to call an ambulance?"

"No. I doubt if she would appreciate that, not when she's insisting she isn't hurt. Just make Erin stay in bed until I can get home. I'm leaving now."

"Shall I call Dr. Halpern?" Mary asked.

"I'll call him from the car." He snatched up his suit coat and bolted for the elevator.

"Will you be back?" Sharon asked as he strode past her desk.

"I don't know. You'd better cancel appointments for me this afternoon. I'll be in touch." Not waiting for Sharon to reply, Blake sprinted toward the parking garage.

It usually took Blake half an hour to drive home from the office. Today he decided after making some quick mental calculations that he could make it in twenty minutes. Pulling his powerful Mercedes onto the interstate, he watched the speedometer needle climb to eighty before setting the cruise control. He thanked fate for the light midday traffic and tried not to agonize over the worst he could imagine happening to his baby—and Erin.

He wasn't having much luck turning off his worries, he decided as he pulled off the expressway and onto the narrow, winding road that would take him home. Forced to slow down now, he couldn't distract himself, and full-blown panic set in.

She could lose my baby. Glenna's baby . . . no, the baby belongs to me and the woman who holds it in her body.

Had it been just a few months ago that he wanted—no, demanded, he corrected himself with scrupulous honesty—that Erin destroy the life that had come to mean so much to him?

His lips moved, silently mouthing the words to prayers he hadn't invoked since childhood. He prayed for the baby, for Erin, and selfishly for himself, because as he thought of losing his child he realized what an important part of his life that baby had become.

More than anything except to have Glenna back, Blake wanted to see and hold the tiny child whose movement in its mother's womb enthralled him every time he felt and saw it. As he turned into the drive that led to his house, he made a silent pact with himself.

If his son or daughter was unhurt, nothing could keep him from giving that child the most secure, caring family that any child could want. He would let nothing stand in his way.

As he carried Erin to his car, and while he drove her sanely to Greg's office, plans formed in his mind to secure the life he wanted for his—and Erin's—child.

"I don't have to stay in bed, Blake," Erin protested later as he settled her in the center of her bed and straightened the covers around her tummy. "Greg said to rest, not to confine myself to bed like an invalid. I need to spend some time with my son."

"Timmy is polishing off the burgers we brought home for him, and practicing his writing for Mary. I told him that if he behaved, I'd join him later and we'd play some Nintendo before he goes to sleep."

"Thanks for stopping by McDonald's. I'm sure it wasn't your first choice for having lunch, but Timmy loves their burgers and fries. To tell you the truth, so do I."

Blake shrugged. He had felt downright foolish going into the McDonald's near Greg's office, dressed in a suit and tie, and eating a Big Mac. "It was your choice. I thought we had something to celebrate after Greg said your fall hadn't done you or the baby any harm."

"All I hurt was my pride and the skin on my hands and knees. And I don't need to be put to bed like a half-witted child. You don't have the right to dictate every move I make."

Even if I don't have the right, I'll keep on doing it anyway. "Give it up. Indulge me. Anyhow, I've been doing some serious thinking. We need to talk, and we may as well do it right here while you relax."

"All right." As if resigned to hearing him out, Erin adjusted the pillows behind her back and shifted to her side. "This is about the only comfortable position I've found for lying down lately," she explained.

"I can imagine." Blake smiled. In the last week or so,

he thought he had literally seen the baby growing every day.

"You wanted to talk?"

"Yes. I think we should marry."

Erin's eyes widened with disbelief—or was it horror? Blake assumed he would have to present the arguments he had mentally prepared for the merger he was proposing. He didn't doubt that the lady would put up a spirited defense.

"Both of us care for the baby we're going to have in less than a month. I believe we both want *our* child to have a loving, stable home life. Who can give that to him better than his two natural parents, together?"

She lay quietly for a moment, as if considering what he had said. "How does Timmy fit into this picture of domestic tranquility, Blake?"

"I'd like to adopt him. Whether I do or not, I'd expect to treat him the same as if he were mine. It should go without saying that whatever treatment Timmy should need, I will see that he gets. I really like your son."

Erin nodded. "And now you believe you will love this baby, too?"

"Yes. I hope you can forgive me for what I asked you to do after Glenna died." Blake couldn't form the words to express the travesty he had demanded. Knowing he had asked Erin to destroy his child, even when he was half-crazed with grief, made him feel like a monster.

"I forgave you the night we met."

He had no doubt as to the sincerity of her softly spoken statement; he wished he could forgive himself as easily as she apparently had pardoned him. "Thank you," he said, mentally preparing to argue his position that they must commit their lives to the goal of giving their baby a stable home.

"What made you decide so suddenly that you—and I— owe it to this baby to tie ourselves to a marriage without love?" Erin asked.

"Your accident. Knowing I might lose my child before

it had a chance at life. Actually, I've been fighting what I've known since I realized I owed this baby two loving parents. I reached that conclusion the night I came to you, intending to deny all but financial responsibility for my part in creating our child.''

Blake paused as he slid a chair close to Erin's bed, sat down, and took her hand. ''There are so many reasons we should marry, and so few that we should not. Please, don't debate them with me now; just let me throw them out for you to think about. When I'm done, I'll leave you to consider what I have said.''

''And when will you expect an answer?''

''Tomorrow morning. I'd say that time is of the essence, since our baby is due in less than three weeks.'' Immediately, before Erin could form any objection, Blake began to argue his case for their marriage.

Long after Blake finished enumerating his reasons for them to marry, Erin lay wide-awake in the darkened room, her mind in turmoil. With skill she supposed he had developed in courtrooms, he had presented his position in ways she found difficult, if not impossible, to refute.

It takes two loving parents together to give a child a stable home.

Blake had made that premise the basis of every other argument he had given, weaving in the probable ambiguity their baby would someday feel if faced with the fact that its biological mother had borne it for money and rejected the opportunity to claim and raise it.

He had reminded Erin of the joys of parenting, promised his own full participation as the baby's father—and Timmy's. He pledged his financial support without qualification and his emotional sustenance insofar as he was capable of giving it. With a smile Erin had thought was close to real, Blake had told her he would try to share control of home and family with her.

Clearly, when he had finished, Blake thought he had

made her an offer she couldn't refuse. Perhaps he had, she thought now as she turned to her other side to ease the strain on her back, trying to unscramble conflicting thoughts that filled her mind.

"Yes, I want to be a real mother to you," she told her baby when it shifted in her womb. "And your father can't wait for you to be born so he can hold and love you, too. You ought to see him with your brother Timmy. I know you'd like to have your daddy and me living together, bringing you up together. But, little one, could we really make a happy home for you when all we have to hold it all together is you?"

Before Erin was done, she had asked her unborn child all the questions for which she had no answers—answers she would have to find tonight so that she could form a decision to give to Blake in the morning.

She hated to think she might marry Blake largely to provide for Timmy's future medical care. In her mind, doing that would make her a vulture just like Greg's grasping former wives, if Sandy's frequent descriptions were accurate. On the other hand, could she *not* consider her little boy and his special needs? Did her primary responsibility not belong with Timmy? And hadn't Blake specifically said he wanted to take care of him, adopt him if she would agree?

Blake seemed to think the arrangement would be fair. Erin would get a daddy for Timmy as well as their baby, all the financial support she might need, and some measure of control over her own life. What would Blake be getting, she wondered, besides a mother instead of a nanny for their baby?

She had asked him timidly if the marriage he proposed would be real. "Oh, it will be real enough in the sense that it will be signed, sealed, and delivered. If you're asking me if we will be sharing a bed, the answer is no—at least not in the foreseeable future. I haven't wanted a woman since

Glenna died. As of this moment, I have no desire for sex with you or anyone else.''

Living without sex wouldn't be a major problem for her, Erin thought, remembering the few times she had truly enjoyed making love with Bill. Those times had been early in their marriage, when the bloom of love was still bright and full.

But she and Bill had been in love. That love had withered within the first six months after their wedding, replaced most of the time by indifference, but sometimes by downright dislike.

What chance for contentment would she have with Blake, starting out as they would be, with feelings she would describe at best as wary respect for one another? On the other hand, she thought, couldn't a couple that married with no pretense of loving one another possibly succeed better than a pair whose commitment was based on romantic love that was almost sure to fade?

Grasping for a logical decision, Erin mentally listed the reasons to and not to accept Blake's unemotional proposal. Exhausted and frustrated, she gave up when she found herself often listing the same reason as justification for saying yes and no.

Finally, no closer to an answer than she had been when she began, she closed her eyes and made a determined effort to sleep.

Chapter 8

Glenna

You, marry Erin? Blake, how could you?

For a ghost, Glenna thought wryly, she felt a mighty human burst of jealousy! But Blake was *hers*, had been hers since the beginning of time, would be hers as long as they lived.

It broke her heart to think of him alone and unhappy; yet the thought of him pledging to love, honor, and cherish another woman hurt so much more than she had thought it might when she vowed to make up for leaving him by bringing him together with the biological mother of their child. She felt tears coming and reached up to brush them from her cheek.

Idiot, you're not alive anymore. Ghosts don't cry, and even if they do, they don't have hands to brush away imaginary tears.

Glenna tried hard to force down the evil monster of envy she couldn't help but feel for Erin, who was alive and well and carrying the baby that should have been her own—and Blake's.

You want Blake to be happy, don't you?

Happy? Glenna let out a tight, ironic chuckle. What Blake had proposed was a sterile merger, not a partnership between two caring and loving people. Glenna wished she could reach down and shake some sense into that stubborn man she loved, the one who most of the time, infuriatingly, thought only in terms of black and white!

He's proposing a marriage of convenience. He doesn't want to sleep with her.

That made Glenna feel good in a purely human, feminine way; but it also made her sad. She had believed until her dying day that Blake had been faithful to her all the time they were married, even though her illnesses and pregnancies had forced long periods of celibacy on them both.

At least in the foreseeable future.

Right! Glenna thought, again resenting the fact that she was dead and the woman she was setting up to be her successor was very much alive. Blake was a healthy man, with strong physical needs. Someday soon, she knew, the sharp edges of grief would wear away, and he would need the comfort of a woman's body.

That woman has to be Erin.

I set this all in motion when I insisted that we have this baby by hiring Erin Winters as a surrogate. No matter how I wish I were still down there, loving Blake, I'm not. Erin is his baby's mother now, so she will have to heal his heart and satisfy his passion that I know won't stay dormant for long.

"I want Blake to love Erin as much as he used to love me."

Keep telling yourself that, Glenna. Maybe in time you will really mean it.

Glenna marshaled her strength to speak and be heard, to see and be seen, and materialized for the second time in Erin's bedroom.

Chapter 9

"*E*rin. Wake up."

"Oh. What time is it?" Erin asked, lifting a hand to cover her eyes in the room that had suddenly become as bright as day.

"*About three o'clock. But we need to talk.*"

Erin forced her tired eyes to focus. "Glenna," she whispered.

"*You're going to marry Blake, aren't you?*"

"I don't know. God, I don't know. Why did I ever agree to be a surrogate mother?"

"*Fate. We must all bow to fate, Erin. Look at me. I wanted to bear Blake's children, but fate decreed otherwise. But we still had each other. It was fate, too, that I persuaded Blake to accept a surrogate arrangement so we could have the baby who meant everything to me, and that I was shot before I got to hold and love that child. Now your destiny is to marry Blake so both of you can give your child a loving home.*" Glenna paused, as if going on were more than she could bear.

"*He's a good man. Underneath that cool, clear logic and the grief I've brought him by dying and leaving you to live with the results of what he gave for me with love, is a man who can love deeply and well.*"

Hearing Glenna—or rather, Glenna's ghost—talk so eloquently about Blake's sterling qualities, embarrassed Erin.

"Why do you want this?" she asked, wishing she could deny the surrealistic presence and escape into healing sleep.

"I told you before. I want to see good come from the situation I so unwittingly caused. I want Blake to be happy; I need to know the baby I wanted so much has a good, loving home; and I have to know you and your little boy will not be hurt because I needed Blake's baby to make my life complete."

The aura surrounding Glenna brightened more, making Erin turn her gaze toward fluttering curtains at French doors she was sure she had closed. "None of this was your fault," she said, feeling Glenna's pain.

"I was responsible."

"No."

"Yes. Erin, marry Blake. Give him time. He'll be a wonderful father, not only to his baby but to your little boy."

Erin trembled. That argument had been the one Blake had hammered into her, and the one that she couldn't discount as she lay and tried to decide whether she should become the second Mrs. James Blake Tanner IV. "Is that reason enough for two people who don't love each other to marry?" she asked the ghost, as she had earlier asked herself.

"Oh, no. But Blake will love again. His grief was talking when he said he was proposing a marriage of convenience. That won't last long. Our Blake is virile and sensual, as well as faithful to any promise he makes. He will want you—sooner than you think. Erin, he's a wonderful lover," Glenna's ghost added wistfully.

Erin blushed. "You're making me uncomfortable," she murmured, wishing for solitude that would enable her to make what would be the hardest decision of her life.

"Promise me you'll marry him," Glenna whispered as her image began to fade.

"I will."

Did I really say that? Erin watched her late night visitor disappear into a cloud of golden dust as she had that first night, when she had welcomed Erin to what used to be her home.

She almost felt as though Glenna's ghost was a real live, flesh-and-blood friend. There was something eerie, though, about having a friend who seemed to know everything you said and did. Was the ghost always around? Did she eavesdrop on every conversation in this big, extravagant house that used to be her home? Had she been there earlier this evening, when Blake had done his best to persuade Erin they should marry?

Erin laughed, more from nerves than from any sort of mirth. For a minute there, she had worried about Blake's unknowingly hurting the ghost of his dead wife. *That* certainly wasn't likely, she told herself as she recalled the flat, sober expression on his face when he had told her he didn't foresee wanting anyone but Glenna—that his heart belonged to her and always would. That her death hadn't altered his commitment to her.

Her friendly ghost didn't seem to mind her husband's decision to acquire a mother for his unborn baby. As a matter of fact, Glenna had been even more persuasive than Blake in telling Erin that marriage would be the best solution for them all.

"I promised Glenna I'd marry him," Erin murmured aloud, and suddenly the prospect of being Mrs. Blake Tanner, if only in name, seemed the only option that made much sense out of the muddled mess she, Blake, and Glenna had so unwittingly created. "And I'm going to do it," she told herself in a stronger tone before wriggling into a comfortable position on the bed and switching off the night-light.

Feeling surprisingly peaceful now that she—or Glenna—had made her decision, Erin closed her eyes and went to sleep.

"Have you made up your mind?" Blake asked Erin as she slowly made her way to the breakfast table in the garden room. Each day, it seemed, her abdomen grew bigger; he thought she might have the baby any day.

"Yes, I have."

"Well?" Blake stood and held a chair for Erin, using his free hand at her elbow to steady her.

"I'll marry you. I've thought it over, and I can't see any better alternative. Still, I have reservations—lots of them. And I have a few conditions, too."

"Conditions?" Blake didn't particularly want to hear Erin's reservations; he had plenty of his own.

"Timmy. I want him to believe this marriage is real."

"I agree. I'll do my part, if you'll do yours." What would making a seven-year-old think a marriage was real entail? Blake wondered. "What do you propose we do to accomplish this?" he asked in what he hoped was a calm, reasonable tone.

Erin looked confused. Maybe, Blake thought, she hadn't given the mechanics of making this farce of an arrangement look real much more thought than he had. "Do?" she asked.

"Exactly. Do we hold hands and kiss? Call each other pet names when the children are around? Sleep together?"

"I—I hadn't thought of *how*," Erin admitted. "But I don't want Timmy to think I'm marrying you because of him *or* this baby. Maybe we should just forget it."

Blake met her concerned gaze. "No. You're absolutely right that we should keep the reasons for this marriage to ourselves—for both children's sakes. We can work out the details later," he added, wondering how in hell they would manage deceiving not only a little boy and a baby, but half of Dallas as well.

And half of Dallas it would be, Blake thought grimly. When he paused to consider the situation, he realized that to keep Timmy—and eventually his baby, too—thinking his and Erin's marriage was a true love match, they would have to persuade family, friends, and even casual acquaintances of their mutual affection if not downright love.

His gaze shifted from the view of lush green grass and colorful flowers blooming this bright, early June morning to the ever-increasing girth of Erin's midsection.

Erin's question was small, reluctant. "When do you want to . . ."

"As soon as possible, wouldn't you say?" He met her gaze.

"I guess so."

"I'll make the arrangements. Saturday afternoon, if I can find a judge available at that time. Do you have family you'll want here?" As far as Blake was concerned, the simpler the better. Still, one needed family to make this farce seem real.

"Just Sandy. Our parents died when she was still a teenager. And Timmy, of course. How about you?"

Blake lifted his left hand to brush a strand of hair off his forehead. "My mother is out of the country," he replied. "Dad died a few years back." He watched Erin's gaze settle on his hand as it came back to rest on the tabletop.

"Do you intend to take that off?" she asked quietly.

Blake's gaze followed Erin's to the gold band that reflected the bright rays from the morning sun. He felt as if he were tearing out his heart as he slowly brought his right hand up to grasp the ring that had rarely left his finger since Glenna put it there, nearly fifteen years ago.

"Yes. I'll take it off. I've worn Glenna's ring since the day we married, but I obviously can't wear it when I'm about to marry you." He knew his voice sounded unnecessarily curt as he worked the wide, gold band off his finger and put it in his pocket, but he couldn't help it. "I won't wear another wedding band, Erin."

"I didn't expect you would. I don't need one, either," Erin replied, her voice tight.

"You'll get one anyway."

This might be a loveless marriage he was entering into, but Blake would provide the bride's ring that society would expect. He made a mental note to have his secretary shop for it today, after she finished making other necessary arrangements for his wedding.

"Will you be home this evening?" Erin asked as he got up and shrugged into the jacket of a tropical-weight gray pin-striped suit.

"Yes. I'll let you know what arrangements I've made, at dinner." With that, Blake hurried out of the house to arrange the ceremony that would formalize the agreement he and Erin had just made.

"You've heard from the judge already?" Greg asked as Sandy stood back to give Blake room to stride through his office door. Blake must be damn good, Greg thought, remembering that it had taken months for the last attorney he had hired to get petitions for alimony reduction written, much less before the courts.

Blake shook his head. "Hardly. I just filed the petitions this morning. We should get hearing dates assigned within a couple of weeks. These things take time."

"Then what brings you here, for the second time in so many days?" Greg asked, curious. "I told you, Erin is just fine. It takes more than a simple fall like she had to hurt a healthy baby, Blake."

"I need you to do a blood test."

"On whom?"

"Me. Erin, too, but I assume you've got her tests on record here."

"Go see your own doctor. My practice is limited to women. Wait a minute, my friend. What kind of blood tests? You certainly don't think you need proof that the baby's really yours?"

"No. Damn it, I'm going to marry Erin. I just need whatever test the state requires to get a marriage license."

Greg stood up and paced around the room while he wondered whether he should offer congratulations or commiseration. "You're going to marry her?" he finally asked to ease the silence.

Blake shrugged. ''I'm about to become a father, as you know better than anyone, including the baby's mother. Don't you think it's reasonable that I provide my child with both its parents?''

Silently but fervently Greg promised himself that he would avoid any future encounters with surrogate parenthood, as judiciously as Sandy kept him from accepting too many time-consuming charity cases.

Sandy. Greg bet she was going to be a handful when she got *this* news. His little angel was damn protective of her older sister, especially since she had been the one to suggest that Erin become a surrogate mother for Blake—and Glenna.

''What about Glenna?'' Greg asked suddenly. ''I mean, isn't it awfully soon?''

Blake's expression suddenly became fierce. ''What do I do? Wait the usual time for mourning and let my child be born without me being married to the woman who will be its mother? This baby was Glenna's fondest desire come true. Since Glenna is gone, marrying Erin is the right thing to do. I'd rather let people think I'm an ass for marrying again too soon than have them call my son or daughter a bastard.''

''When did you decide all this?''

''I guess I've known it from the minute I realized I couldn't turn my back on this baby. God knows I've fought doing it; but when I knew Erin was hurt and that the baby might be at risk, it hit me just how much I want this child— and how it will need its mother.''

Greg silently wished his friend the best of luck in this marriage, because he figured Blake and Erin were going to need all the good wishes they could get. ''Am I invited to the happy event?'' he asked, forcing a tone that was lighter than he felt.

''You're invited to be best man—again,'' Blake replied, and Greg could see the anguish in his friend's expression. Briefly he let himself remember that other union—the one that had lasted through two of his own marriages and divorces. Glenna and Blake's deep, loving commitment to each other had given Greg hope that someday he might have a relationship as enduring and peaceful.

Then he forced a grin. The last thing Blake needed was another glum face to intensify the deep sorrow Greg knew would surround him for a long time, if not forever.

"I'd be honored. When is this festive occasion to be?"

"Saturday. Seven o'clock, at the house. We'll have dinner afterward. It will be informal: just you, Sandy, the judge, Erin, and me—and Timmy, her little boy, of course."

"Good timing. Any later, and I might be attending for quite another reason," Greg quipped.

Blake's laugh sounded forced. Still, when he left Greg's office, Greg thought Blake seemed at peace with himself and his decision. He hoped Sandy would take the news of this upcoming wedding with the same equanimity as it seemed that at least one of the two main participants was accepting it.

"Your last appointment cancelled," Sandy said when Greg called to tell her he was ready to see the new referral from a colleague. "Are you ready to go eat my version of a home-cooked meal?"

He thought her voice sounded strained, but she kept their conversation focused on the day's events at the office until after they finished their salad and gazpacho and settled on the swing in the corner of her tiny patio with root beer floats. Greg grinned as he recalled their discovery at the beginning of summer that they shared a passion for the frosty fountain drinks. Since then, Sandy often fixed them instead of dessert when he came over.

"You know they're getting married, don't you?" Sandy asked, her manner quiet but serious.

"Blake told me."

"What do you think about it?"

Greg shrugged. "That they're both certifiable. But I see

Blake's reasoning. That baby does need two parents.''

"You think they're marrying just for the baby's sake? Erin gave me the impression there's some attraction between them, too.''

I don't just think it, I know damn well they're marrying because of the baby—at least Blake is.

"I got that impression; but then, Blake is the soul of logic—he wouldn't let anybody, even a close friend, in on his deeper feelings.'' Greg felt guilty, holding back on what he believed was the whole truth about Blake and Erin's coming marriage, but he couldn't very well make Erin out to be a liar to her sister.

Sandy smiled. "I'm glad you're not shy about making your deeper feelings known,'' she said, moving closer to him on the old-fashioned swing where they were slowly rocking back and forth.

Greg put an arm around her, letting his fingers rove over the silky soft skin of her bare shoulder. He loved the feel of her, the way she cuddled against his chest like a friendly kitten. He craved her when they were together, and even more when they were apart. In a few short months, she had become an addiction, one he had to have more and more of in order to survive.

"Want to know how I feel right now?'' he asked, letting his hand wander downward to cradle and caress a soft, shapely breast.

"Uh-huh.'' Her nipple beaded up at his touch, burning into his hand through the soft, flimsy material of the T-shirt she'd put on when they got to her apartment.

"Horny.'' In the past three months, he'd been that way more than he remembered having been even when he was a studious teenager whose fantasies ran to the hot and heavy—but whose limited success with the girls of his dreams had done little to alleviate the wanting.

"Want to go to bed?'' Sandy invited, standing and taking his hand to pretend to drag him inside.

"I thought you'd never ask,'' he replied with a grin,

lifting her into his arms and carrying her into the apartment.

Their loving was sweet and gentle, then hot and fast; it left Greg drained but supremely content. With Sandy he enjoyed the aftermath just as much as the actual sex act, he realized, amazed. It was wonderful, having a lover who was a friend, he decided as they lay together and let the night breeze from the open window cool their sated bodies.

The love he felt for Sandy could so easily be the kind that could endure forever. It wasn't just hot, wild passion like the fever that had made him marry Rhea, a woman he could barely stand except in bed.

And it was totally different from what he'd felt at first for Kay, whom he had married right out of college because she had been his mother's ideal of the perfect doctor's wife. Greg looked at Sandy, so young yet more mature than either of the women he had married, and he knew he would never let her go.

"I hope Erin and Blake find half the happiness that we've found together," Sandy murmured, and Greg silently seconded the wish he doubted could come true.

That day Erin had told Timmy she was marrying Mr. Tanner, called Sandy, and confirmed the news to Mrs. Malone. Blake, she had learned, had already told his household staff. Whatever else the man was, he was efficient—efficient enough to drive Erin almost crazy.

She laughed aloud. It was better to laugh than to cry, she supposed. Here she was, planning to marry the grieving widower of a ghost—the same ghost who kept visiting her and nudging her toward Blake.

Glenna's ghost doesn't nudge; she pushes and shoves. She expects me not only to marry the man, but to fall in love with him. And make him fall in love with me! What a joke!

No wonder they had gotten along so well, Erin thought, not without a bit of malice—both Glenna and Blake seemed to go after what they wanted with a singularity of purpose.

No one had seemed to be particularly shocked or surprised when she told them about the wedding. Timmy took the news in stride. He liked Blake and thought he'd make a great daddy. And he loved living here and enjoying the little luxuries that meant little to a rich man but a lot to the little boy whose life had been pretty much devoid of treats.

Erin had expected shrieks and dire warnings from Sandy. But while her sister's feelings were obviously mixed, Sandy had agreed to witness this fiasco of a wedding and refrained from showing downright disapproval. She even offered to drive Erin to the stores tomorrow so she could find something to wear Saturday for the wedding.

A maternity wedding dress!

That was how Sandy had put it. Erin laughed. How ironic it was that the first brand-new dress she had bought in more than three years would, of necessity, be one that she could only wear for three more weeks!

Oh, well, she thought, there would be plenty of money for dresses now. Blake had made it very clear last night that he would provide her with all the material things she could reasonably want. In practically the same breath, though, he had assured her that there was nothing left in him emotionally to give her. That last thought made her feel more like crying than smiling.

"Cheer up. It's going to take some time, but he's got to stop grieving soon."

Erin knew Glenna was there—somewhere. She had a feeling the ghost never slept, that she bore silent witness to Erin's every thought. "Where are you?" she asked after looking around in vain for the source of that bright, cheerful voice.

"I'm here. Look, it takes a lot of energy to pop in where you can see me. There are times, like this, I won't try. I've got a feeling you're going to need me more later than you do now. You looked like you were going to cry, though, so I thought you might need someone."

"Are you always watching, listening?"

"Most of the time. I made a hell of a mess of your and Blake's lives. I can't rest until the damages are fixed."

Erin glanced around the room, still searching for the source of Glenna's voice.

"I'm over here."

"Where?" Erin whispered.

"By the garden room door. But you won't be able to see me. I'm saving my energy. By the way, I hope you're planning to buy something special for your wedding," the cheerfully disembodied voice continued while Erin tried in vain to see Glenna.

"Are you?"

Apparently she doesn't *listen* all *the time,* Erin thought. If she did, she would have heard the plans she had just made with Sandy to go shopping. At first relieved at this bit of knowledge, she quickly realized that, even if Glenna weren't lurking all the time, there was no way she would be able to tell *when* her ghostly buddy was around!

"You met my sister, Sandy. She works for Dr. Halpern. We're going to shop for dresses later this week," Erin told Glenna quietly, after looking around the room to be sure there was no one around to decide she was nuts for talking to herself.

The weird feeling that she was never really alone didn't leave her as she went about her simple daily routine of playing with Timmy and getting more rest than she would have ever thought she needed.

It had been a busy but productive day. Blake mentally reviewed the plans he had made as he pulled into the garage half an hour earlier than usual. He smiled when he saw Timmy waiting in his wheelchair, out beside the pool.

"Mr. Tanner!"

"Timmy. How are you, sport?" Blake asked as he set his briefcase down and sank onto a patio chair next to the little boy.

"I took six steps today. And Mommy says we're gonna

marry you and live here with you and your new baby. Are we really?'' Timmy asked excitedly.

"Yes, we are." Blake paused, considering that the chance to be a father figure for this bright, brave boy was one big plus to his arrangement with the boy's mother. "Tell me about your walking," he said with a smile.

Timmy returned the grin. "Well, it's not *really* walking, I guess. But I held myself up between the bars and moved my legs all by myself. Michelle said I did good."

"I'm proud of you. Keep it up, and pretty soon you'll be good as new."

"Mr. Tanner, are you gonna be my daddy?" Blake noticed Timmy's expression had turned suddenly serious.

We have to make this marriage seem real—for Timmy's sake.

He and Erin had agreed to that condition, but Erin hadn't addressed his offer to adopt her son. Blake didn't like loose ends, and he resolved to tie this one up soon, but for now he'd have to wing his response to his future stepson's questions.

"I'll be your stepfather, sport."

Timmy looked worried. "You mean like the wicked step*mother* in *Cinderella*?" he asked in a tiny voice.

Blake reached over and ruffled Timmy's hair. "Of course not. At least I hope you won't ever think of me that way," he replied, making a conscious effort to maintain the mild tone of his voice and the smile on his lips.

"I'd like to pretend you're my real daddy."

"I'd like that, too. Only you don't need to pretend. Your real daddy can't be here for you now, so I'll do my best to stand in for him." Blake placed the issue of adopting Timmy at the top of his mental list of things to do.

"Are you and Mommy gonna sleep together? I remember when she and my . . . my first daddy . . . used to let me crawl in between them in their bed on Sunday mornings." Timmy paused, and Blake wondered what was going through the boy's agile mind. "I guess I'm too big for that now," he said wistfully.

"Yes. You certainly are getting big," Blake agreed, avoiding answering Timmy's question. He hadn't thought the boy would worry about his and Erin's sleeping arrangements; but then, he would never have dared to intrude on either or both of his parents' private space when he was a boy, so he supposed his lack of foresight was understandable.

Timmy grinned. "You think our baby's gonna be another boy? I sure hope so, don't you?"

Safer ground.

"We'll have to wait and see, sport. A boy would be nice, but so would a little girl," Blake said mildly, relieved at having been able to defer Timmy's other line of questioning.

"A girl. Yuck. I don't like girls."

"Sure you do. What about your mom? And Michelle, and Mary, and your aunt Sandy?"

"They're not girls. They're all grown up." Timmy paused, obviously in deep thought. "Do you like girls?"

"Yes, I do. Little ones as well as grown-up girls."

"You must like my mommy a lot, since you want us to marry you and stay with you and our baby," Timmy stated, but the inflection in his voice made it sound more like a question.

Blake could handle that one. "Sure. I like both of you a lot," he said, getting up and motioning toward the house. "I promised your mom we'd talk when I got home, so I'd better head on inside now. Would you like a push?"

"No, thank you, sir. I can do it myself. Michelle taught me how. What am I supposed to call you after you and Mommy get married?" Timmy asked as he rolled along beside Blake on the sidewalk that led to the back door.

"I'd like it if you wanted to call me 'Daddy,' but if you'd rather, you can just use my name."

"Blake? Like Mommy calls you?"

"Yes."

Timmy rolled along quietly for a few seconds, before announcing that he thought he'd like to think this over for a few days. Blake murmured his approval as he made another mental note to add the move of Erin's things into the master suite to his list of chores that needed doing before they married.

Blake didn't talk with Erin right away. Instead, he had Mary serve their dinner on trays after suggesting that they and Timmy watch a movie on the giant-screen TV in the family room. After helping Erin tuck the sleepy little boy into bed at nine o'clock, Blake walked her into her bedroom.

"Get ready for bed," he ordered, not unkindly, and Erin complied because she really was exhausted after having spent most of the previous night awake, agonizing over Blake's proposal.

He was still in the room when she emerged from the bathroom wearing an oversize T-shirt that stretched taut over her tummy and fell almost to her knees. Apparently he meant to see that she followed his orders, so she lowered herself awkwardly to the bed and stretched out along its length.

With what seemed almost like tender concern, he pulled the sheet and light blanket over her. "I'll be right back. We need to go over some things," he told her before striding purposefully out of the room.

Erin didn't have time to consider what was coming before Blake returned, black leather briefcase in hand. She watched as he sat down in the chair next to her bed and opened the case, pulling out several neatly typed sheets and what looked like some kind of a legal document bound in stiff, blue paper.

"I think I have everything covered," he said as he set the briefcase on the floor beside him.

Why don't I doubt that? Erin believed firmly that if Blake thought he had arranged every detail, he most likely had. "What do I need to do?"

Blake gave her two papers, stapled together. "These are the arrangements for the ceremony. Everything is taken care of except for getting the license and picking out something for you to wear. The license we can get late tomorrow afternoon. I thought Miguel might take you shopping first, then drive you to the courthouse at four o'clock."

"Sandy said she'd take me to find a dress. It would save her driving me back here if she dropped me off at the courthouse to meet you. I guess you would drive me back?" Erin knew she had agreed that Blake's house would become her home, but she couldn't think of it as such—at least not yet.

"I planned to."

Blake looked as if he were weighing the consequences of what he was about to say, Erin thought as she watched the subtle changes in his expression.

"Erin," he finally said in a somber tone, "you told me you wanted your son to think this marriage was going to be real. And I agreed. Don't you think that if we're going to succeed in this little deception, we're going to have to become a bit more comfortable with each other?"

"What do you mean?"

"He means, you're going to have to get close if you're going to pull this off without folks asking a lot of embarrassing questions," interjected a familiar voice Erin knew by now that only she could hear.

Blake shrugged, as if annoyed at Erin's lack of immediate perception. "I mean, you're going to have to be with me occasionally without Timmy there as a buffer. More than occasionally after the baby is born, because we'll have to make appearances together as a couple of people will think there's something strange about our marriage. We need to be friends, even if we're not lovers like married people usually are."

"But we hardly know each other at all," Erin protested.

And you've certainly shown no interest in becoming pals before.

She heard that voice again. *"You'd best be getting acquainted, Mommy. You two are going to spend a lifetime raising that baby, you know."*

Blake smiled, and in spite of her discomfort at knowing Glenna was there somewhere, Erin noticed how his relaxed expression brightened the deep indigo of his eyes. "You're right. My point is, we need to get to know each other. After all, we're going to be married *and* we're going to be parents in less than a month. We're going to be sharing one big master suite if not one bed. I won't bite."

"All right. By the way, I appreciated your taking the time to do something with Timmy tonight." Would Glenna approve? Erin wondered.

"I enjoyed it. You know, I don't think my parents ever spent a whole evening with me, just relaxing at home."

"He's right, Erin. His parents were something else again."

"I kn—I mean, really?"

Blake raised an eyebrow at her inadvertent slip, but he apparently chose to ignore it and give her another bit of his life history. "Really. My father lived and breathed the law, and Mother still thinks the world revolves around whatever her jet-setting friends are doing at any given time. I'm going to need a lot of guidance, but I intend to be the best parent I can be to my own children."

Blake's tone was matter-of-fact, but Erin imagined that a lot of emotion lurked behind that simple declaration. Of all the doubts she had, and there were many, one was not that Blake would be anything other than a caring father for his child. "I know you do," she murmured.

"Are you going to relax around me?" Blake asked, as if he could order immediate compliance with all his requests. "Look at you, you're as strung out as an embezzler caught with his fingers in the till."

You'd be strung out, too, if you had a ghost popping in

and nudging you nearly every time you turned around. Erin realized her hands were clenched into fists, and she imagined the strain of being here alone with Blake except for the all-knowing but unseen ghost of his dead wife showed plainly on her face.

"I'm sorry. I can't help feeling vulnerable, lying here undressed with you there, fully clothed, handing down ultimatums."

"Would it help if I took off my shirt?" Blake asked, setting the blue-bound papers on the bed and attacking the second button of his pale yellow dress shirt. His grin told her he was joking now.

"Stop it!" Frantically Erin searched the room, looking for that golden aura that usually surrounded Glenna's ghost.

"Uh, I think it's time for me to go. I'll be back," Glenna whispered as Erin watched a trail of golden dust float through the closed patio doors. She looked back quickly, but not soon enough that Blake hadn't developed a puzzled expression.

"What's wrong?" he asked.

Erin hesitated. Part of her wanted to tell him about the ghost. The saner portion of her brain intervened. If she hadn't seen Glenna, she wouldn't have believed. And there wasn't a chance in the world that she could find the words that would make Blake believe, not when he obviously had not encountered Glenna since she died. Finally she found her voice.

"Nothing. What is this?" Erin asked, picking up an official-looking document Blake had laid on the bed and leafing through it.

"It's a form we both need to sign, rescinding the surrogate arrangement." Blake stopped unbuttoning buttons and met Erin's gaze. "I don't want this baby ever to know you agreed to have it and give it up for money," he said.

He still thinks what I did was wrong.

Blake must have known that what he said had hurt, because he reached out and touched her—not her hand or face, but the round, hard mound that defined their child. "Erin, I know and understand why you did this; I respect you for doing it to ensure that Timmy got the care he needs. But you're going to be this baby's real mother now. Do you want the baby to know someday that you originally intended to have him for someone else?"

No, she didn't. But signing another paper? It had been hard enough to sign the first one. "Why can't we just rip up the original papers we signed?" she asked quietly.

"Because copies have been filed with the family court. These papers rescind the permission you gave for me to adopt our child at birth. I'll get the original papers back when I present these to the judge. Then we can tear them up. We can even burn them if you'd like," he offered lightly.

"All right." Glenna had told Erin last night that Blake was a good man who could love deeply and well. Erin could tell he was good; she could easily love *him*, and she could believe that he would love his child. But she doubted Glenna's assessment that he would someday be ready to love a woman again.

"Then get some rest. I'll meet you at four tomorrow afternoon at the courthouse, and we'll get the license. Other than that, I don't think you will need to do anything except be in the garden room at seven o'clock Saturday evening. Here, I almost forgot. You'll need these if you're going shopping tomorrow. I don't want you worrying about the costs." He pulled some credit cards out of his pocket and set them on the bedside table.

It ruffled Erin's fierce sense of independence that Blake should insist on paying for the dress she'd be wearing to marry him. She didn't protest, though. Her depleted checking account currently boasted forty-eight dollars and some-odd cents, and she doubted that would go far toward decking her out as a blushing if very pregnant bride. Besides, she had a feeling that she should save arguing with Blake for something that mattered more than a bit of tattered pride.

Chapter 10

"Keep away from that sale rack," Sandy cautioned as Erin gravitated toward a group of maternity clothes whose sign said she could take another fifty percent off the already reduced prices.

"Yes, do. And put that dreary navy blue thing back. Where do you think you're going? To a funeral?"

Erin looked around. Glenna couldn't be here, in this little out-of-the-way maternity boutique where the clothes all wore discreet designer labels and even more discreet but obscenely expensive price tags. But there she was, perched on the corner of the antique desk that served as a cash register, so dainty and pretty she made Erin feel like a circus elephant being fitted for a new tent.

"Do you like this?" Sandy asked.

Erin turned to her sister, who was holding up a pale pink organdy dress with a white linen collar.

"Only if it comes with a matching one for one's little girl."

Erin laughed at Glenna's observation. The dress, with its short puffed sleeves, Peter Pan collar, and the gathered skirt that billowed from a yoke complete with lace insertions, did remind her of much smaller ones she had seen advertised for little girls for those oh-so-special occasions.

"What's so funny?" Sandy demanded.

"Oh, nothing." Glenna grinned, Sandy looked perturbed, and Erin felt like, between the two of them, she was going to go stark raving crazy before she got out of this place. "I don't think that will do," she said, motioning toward the offending garment and pulling another one off the rack.

It was pretty and sort of festive-looking, Erin thought, holding up her selection for Sandy's—and Glenna's—approval.

"Too somber," Sandy said, apparently not impressed by the tiny white flowers on a background of black cotton. "And not dressy enough."

"She's right. If I know Blake, he'll be wearing one of those gray pin-striped suits and a somber tie. You don't want your wedding pictures to look like color film hasn't been invented yet. Here. Try this one."

Erin reached out quickly to grab the garment that almost leaped off the rack at her. It was pale blue, gauzy silk, with a low scooped neckline and a skirt that fell in soft, wrinkly pleats from the empire bodice. For a maternity dress, it was gorgeous! Then she looked at the price tag and gasped, putting it back on the rack with a sigh of regret.

"I like that one," Sandy said. "Go try it on."

"No. Sandy, you wouldn't believe the price of that dress!" Determined to find something that would please both her sister and her ghostly friend, Erin flipped through the size eight selections on the sales rack. "Here, this should do," she said, holding up a silvery gray jumper whose black silk blouse she thought would lend a slimming effect to the ensemble.

"This is not a funeral. Lord knows we've had enough of them."

Erin whirled around and looked at Glenna, shocked.

"What? I can't say that? We can't ignore it. It happened. Now put away that outfit and go try on the one I found for you. So what if it's expensive? Didn't Blake tell you not to worry about the cost?"

The dress practically fell into Erin's hands again. "I

guess I will try this one on,'' she told Sandy, figuring that she'd look like Dumbo the Elephant in it, and that would take away the initial excitement she had felt when she first saw the garment.

"You look gorgeous," Sandy said with wonder when Erin stepped out of the dressing room.

"I look pregnant. Very, very pregnant." Erin felt huge but pretty in the soft, blue dress.

"But it's his baby. He'll think you're beautiful."

"Sandy, this dress costs over five hundred dollars." *But it feels so good,* Erin thought, letting her fingers run lovingly over the crispy, crinkled silk that formed a calf-length skirt.

"Every one of Blake's suits cost more than that. And when I died, he donated clothes of mine that cost at least fifty times the price of that dress to charity, just to get them out of his sight. Erin, you've got to put things into perspective. Get the dress. It's gorgeous, and so are you."

Glenna slid off the corner of the desk and moved to a display of costume jewelry. *"I want to pick out something, just to you from me. Here. See this necklace and earrings? They will look beautiful with your dress."*

"Are you going to get it?" Sandy paced around Erin, looking at her from all angles. "The cut must be what makes it so expensive. It makes you look radiant, not blimpy. Come on, Erin, buy it. You can lend it to me someday when I'm expecting Greg's baby," she added, a dreamy look on her face.

Erin felt pulled toward the locked display case that held the pieces Glenna had mentioned. "I guess so. But it seems insane to spend this much. Even if Blake *can* afford it." Then she saw the jewelry she knew Glenna had selected.

They were roses, miniature roses crafted of gold with shiny blue dewdrops that looked like sapphires. The smaller ones were earrings, and the larger one a pendant suspended on a golden chain. The workmanship took Erin's breath away. They were beautiful, but as she summoned the quietly attentive clerk, she realized that their cost must match or exceed that of the dress she had already decided to buy.

"You like them, don't you? I knew you would. Go ahead. Take them. Our Blake isn't much of a jewelry man—I had to buy most of my own trinkets when we were married."

Erin recalled the simple string of creamy cultured pearls Bill had given her the day before their wedding, and momentarily regretted having sold them to raise money for Timmy's first long hospital stay. Blake had indicated he would be giving her a ring, but she knew that would be the only token she would be receiving with which to remember this very practical, unemotional union.

"I'll take these, and this dress," she told the saleswoman decisively. "Sandy, do you think we'll have time for me to find a pair of shoes?"

"Sure. There's a store two doors down."

As Erin gathered her packages and prepared to leave the boutique, she saw Glenna surrounded by that golden haze that always seemed to herald her arrivals and departures. She knew her mind was playing tricks on her; still, she could almost swear Glenna gave her the thumbs-up sign along with an exaggerated wink.

The next afternoon, Erin thought of Glenna's farewell gesture and felt she could use some cheering up, even if it did come from a ghost. Timmy had gone with Blake to get a haircut. Mrs. Malone was running around in circles, seeing to some details that Blake had managed to reduce to terse comments on a sheet of paper, but which required considerably more effort to execute.

Erin herself had been ordered to nap after watching Miguel and Mary move her few possessions into the gigantic bedroom that was part of the master suite, lest the coming ceremony stress her and the baby—but sleep wouldn't come. For a little while, she tried to conjure up Glenna in her mind without success; then her mind wandered to another day, another wedding.

Was I ever that young and that naive?

Erin pictured herself at twenty-one, starry-eyed as she walked slowly down the aisle. Her dress had been traditional—white on white, lace on satin, with a chapel train and a veil of silk illusion that she remembered had obscured her view of Bill's handsome, smiling face. And she had been the traditional bride, ready to love, honor, and cherish the young man who became her husband for as long as they both might live.

Erin tried to picture Bill, to recall how he looked and what he said when they cut the three-tiered wedding cake at her parents' home after the ceremony. She thought hard, trying to re-create the wedding night that had followed in a small hotel on a Galveston beach. Those memories had faded to a sepia glow, she thought sadly, letting her mind wander to scenes that came to her more clearly of the years that followed.

There had been good times for them, in spite of time and circumstances that dulled the joy of first, young love. She had stayed home while Bill worked as a successful salesman for a small electronics company. He had been the original party animal; and their life together, even after a teenage Sandy had come to live with them after their parents' deaths, was a constant round of frenzied good times that ended only after Timmy's birth.

Erin couldn't help comparing Bill's initial distaste at the idea of becoming a father with Blake's wholehearted enthusiasm for his coming child. But neither could she fault Bill as a father. He had adored Timmy from the day he was born until that rainy Saturday nearly four years earlier when he'd run his financed-to-the-hilt silver Porsche into a tree—ending his life along with their marriage, and crippling his little boy.

Now, as she began to get ready for her second wedding, Erin tried to tell herself that this rational, logical union would work out better than her first marriage that had begun with two kids in love and ended in a mass of twisted metal on a highway outside Dallas.

By the time Sandy came into her room to help her dress, Erin had a mask of calm, cool assurance firmly in place. It was only inside that she was shaking, praying silently that she was doing the right thing for Timmy, this new baby, Blake—and herself.

Blake was having similar feelings after he left Timmy with Mary and made a final inspection of the room where Erin would be sleeping after they married. In another two hours, she would be his wife, and that thought brought on sharp, agonizing pain as he saw the room not as it was today, but the way he remembered how it used to fairly shout Glenna's presence in every whimsical detail she had added through their years together.

Every item had commemorated a special time they shared. The woven Navajo rug Glenna bought while they camped in Arizona because its colors reminded her of the desert sunrise . . . that glistening rough-cut blue topaz they found in the wilds of Panama . . . even the massive four-poster bed he commissioned from a famous Appalachian craftsman while they vacationed in Gatlinburg . . .

All the tangible evidence of memories he had ordered Mary to get rid of after Glenna died were as vivid in Blake's mind as if they were still here, waiting for her to come back and restore them in fact as well as in his unruly mind.

How she had teased him about that bed! Once she decked it out like a harem couch, in crimson silk instead of the creamy crocheted lace that usually cascaded from the heavy square posts that had nearly reached the twelve-foot ceilings. And she'd seduced him handily, he recalled with more agony than the ecstasy the moment had brought.

This magic space he had shared with Glenna now existed only in his tortured memories. Reality, within the same walls of the same house he had lived in all his life, was a bland, correctly furnished suite of rooms that he could just as easily have found in any of a hundred luxury hotels.

And reality was the woman downstairs who soon would be the mother of his child—and even sooner would be his wife. Forcing bittersweet memories to the farthest reaches of his mind, Blake went into the odd-shaped office he had outfitted as his own sleeping room. After laying out his clothes, he set about methodically to shower, shave, and dress.

Adjusting a tie he had randomly selected from a rack in his dressing room, Blake went downstairs. He felt strangely detached, as if it were someone else's wedding he would be hosting within the hour.

"Blake."

He strode into the morning room and joined Greg. "Where's Sandy?" he asked, not seeing Erin's sister anywhere in his line of vision.

"She's helping Erin dress—or so she said. Want a drink?"

About a dozen. "Sure. Whatever you're having will be fine."

Blake watched Greg pour two fingers of Jack Daniels into a highball glass over a few cubes of ice. "Here's to liquid courage," Greg said as he handed over the glass.

"To courage."

"Want to talk about it?" Greg asked, sitting back down and sipping his drink.

"What is there to discuss?"

"Whatever's on your mind that you'd like to share. I've had more experience at this than you. I'll be happy to offer advice, if the price is right, of course," Greg offered, grinning.

Blake couldn't help smiling. "Advice? Remember, I'm the guy who is trying to dig you out of the alimony poorhouse with both of the women you were so sage as to marry. By the way, Si Abrams called me yesterday. Apparently Kay is amenable now to giving up her monthly checks in return for a lump-sum settlement. I told Si to forget it.''

''For God's sake, Blake! Why?''

''For one thing, you can't afford what she and Si have in mind. For another, you say she's about to marry again; and if she does, the monthly payments will stop without your shelling out any more than you already have. Trust me. Negotiating settlements is what I do for a living.''

Greg shook his head, but he was still smiling. ''I know. Damn it, though, I wish something would happen fast. I feel like hell not being able to offer Sandy anything except a mountain of debt along with the dubious honor of marrying a two-time reject fifteen years older than she is.''

''You've asked her to marry you?''

''Not yet. But I want to.''

Not knowing Sandy well, but having had the questionable pleasure of close acquaintance with both of Greg's ex-wives, Blake had his doubts that his friend had finally found a woman who could and would share a harried lifestyle that revolved around his work. ''You're sure?'' he asked, voicing his concern.

''I'm sure. For Sandy I'll fight the devils in hell. I'll even fight my exes, and talk my mother into moving in with her sister out in Phoenix, if that's what it will take to make Sandy happy.''

''Sandy doesn't meet with Mom's approval?'' Blake imagined Sadie's dislike would be a formidable obstacle—although he himself got along with Greg's mother just fine, had even called her ''Mom'' at her insistence since Greg used to take him home for holidays when they were in school.

''Too young, too independent, but she's a sweet, sweet girl, for a nice boy her own age,'' Greg said with a grin, mimicking his mother's distinctive speech pattern. ''I don't care. Mom will come around. Anyhow, she liked both Kay and Rhea, and look how things turned out with *them*.''

The doorbell rang, and Blake got up to answer it, knowing Mary was busy getting Timmy dressed up in the new, gray suit they had bought for him this afternoon. It was Judge Adkins, who joined them for a drink while they waited for the other members of the bridal party.

"Are you having one ring or two?" the judge asked, apparently planning the ceremony mentally while they talked.

"One." Blake reached into his pocket and withdrew a small, flat box.

Maybe I should look at this, he thought, recalling that he hadn't opened the box since his secretary had set it on his desk two days ago. "Not bad," he murmured as he glanced at the wide gold band that was plain except for engraved swirls that added a textured effect.

"I'll hold it," Greg offered.

"Blake!" Timmy rolled into the room in his wheelchair, with Mary hurrying to keep up with the excited child. "Look. It's fun dressing up. Dr. Halpern, how do you like my new suit?"

Greg smiled. "Looks just like one of Blake's. You sure you didn't borrow it from him?" he teased.

Timmy laughed. "Blake's too big. So he took me to the store and got me this. And a bunch of other clothes, too. Who are you?" he asked when he noticed the judge.

"Judge Adkins. And you must be Blake's new stepson, young man."

"How'd you know? My name's Timmy. I'm supposed to tell you Mommy and Aunt Sandy will be ready in just a few minutes. Mommy looks real pretty, Blake."

Greg wandered over to the stereo in the corner and picked up a stack of compact discs. "Background music, anyone?" he asked.

"Pick out something appropriate and turn it on," Blake offered.

"Certainly not *this*?" Greg asked, barely restraining his laughter as he held up a disc.

"Why not?" To Blake, one classical piece was pretty much the same as the next.

"I think we'd all find a soprano screeching in Italian a little distracting, don't you? This is an opera, some heart-rending tragedy if I recall correctly," Greg explained, holding up the cover that featured an Oriental geisha girl and identified the disc as a soundtrack of *Madame Butterfly*.

"Cut out the comments and just find some music that will do," Blake retorted, irritated. "That's all the classical music I've got."

Greg set the offending selection down and dug through the discs, finally settling on one that he inserted in the CD player. Suddenly the room filled with soft, unobtrusive harmonies.

"Where is the wedding going to be?" Timmy asked, maneuvering his wheelchair closer to the sofa where Blake was sitting.

Blake smiled. "Over there, by the windows, in that little alcove Miguel made with the plants and flowers."

"Are you going to give Mommy a ring?"

"Yes."

"And flowers?"

Flowers? Blake had forgotten that, among other things, he was supposed to have sent Erin some kind of bouquet or corsage. *Too late now.*

"No, sport, just the ones we've got in here."

Timmy looked around. "But, Blake, these are the same ones that are always in here. They're just all scrunched up in that whatever you called it over there."

"Alcove."

"Yeah. Oh, boy, here comes Mommy and Aunt Sandy. And Mrs. Malone."

Blake's gaze went to the doorway, where Erin's tightly controlled smile reminded him that this was going to be as hard for her as it was for him. She had done well with her shopping, though, he decided as he clinically appraised her from the dark, simply arranged hair that curled around her shoulders to slender feet shod in low-heeled sandals. A pretty, light blue dress veiled but did not hide his unborn child.

He made himself smile as he rose to meet her.

"Here, Mommy, you need a flower," Timmy said, plucking a fat yellow rosebud out of an arrangement on a low table beside a chair and handing it up to Erin.

Embarrassed that he had overlooked the necessary detail of flowers for his bride, Blake picked another rose from the vase. "For the maid of honor," he said lightly as he handed over the flower to Sandy.

He glanced at his Rolex and stifled the sense of longing that seeing Glenna's gift always evoked. "It's time," he said, taking Erin's hand and walking slowly across the room to the alcove where they would formalize their new arrangement.

For the second time, Sandy watched Erin repeat marriage vows. This time she knew what it should mean to say those hopeful, solemn promises. She was twenty-three, not twelve, and the man she loved was standing across from her, looking handsome and relaxed as he, too, paid close attention to Erin and Blake's mutual pledge.

"Do you, Blake, take this woman to be your lawfully wedded wife? Do you promise to love her, honor her, and cherish her as long as you both shall live?"

Blake answered; but it was Greg that Sandy imagined, making those solemn promises to her. Then it was Erin's turn to make the same vows; but in her heart, Sandy was repeating the pledge of lasting fidelity to Greg. Her gaze settled on his solemn face, and her heartbeat accelerated.

"Do you have the ring?" Judge Adkins asked Greg, who dug into his pants pocket and pulled out the band Blake would be putting on her sister's finger. Smiling, he handed it to Blake before looking back intently at Sandy.

"Repeat after me, 'With this ring, I thee wed.' "

Sandy watched Greg, and Greg watched Blake as he repeated the judge's words in a hushed, halting voice and slipped a wide gold band onto the ring finger of her sister's left hand.

"With the power vested in me by the state of Texas, I pronounce you man and wife."

Blake hesitated, just for a second, but Sandy caught the pause. Then he lifted a hand to cup Erin's chin and brushed his lips briefly over hers. It wasn't a kiss of passion. It wasn't even one that bestowed warmth and caring, Sandy thought, her heart going out to Erin—whom she was certain now had entered into this marriage for reasons having little to do with emotion and even less to do with love.

That thought stayed with Sandy as they went into the dining room to eat. The table was immaculate, covered with snowy linen edged in hand-crocheted lace. Dark blue candles flickered in silver candlesticks, casting soft light on an arrangement of multicolored roses and some lacy white flowers Sandy couldn't name.

The food was delicious, from a tangy fruit soup appetizer to the perfectly prepared chateaubriand and crisp, buttered vegetables. Sandy couldn't fault the salad of hearts of artichoke, either.

It was a lovely dinner. What bothered Sandy was that, except for crystal flutes to hold the imported champagne in a silver bucket and a small white-iced cake trimmed with fresh flowers, this could have been any company dinner at Blake Tanner's big, fancy house.

She found Blake's hospitality more subdued than ever. Erin, she knew, must be faking the gaiety that made her laugh nervously at everything any of them said. Sandy sighed. Even Greg seemed to be on edge. Only Timmy and the judge seemed honestly to be enjoying the festivities of what should be a very important day.

"I'd like to propose a toast," Greg said then, after Mrs. Malone and her helper had cleared the table, served the cake, and poured champagne for everyone. Sandy watched as he stood and grinned, first at her and then at her sister.

"To Erin. May your future be as beautiful as you are to-day," he said, his usual exuberance restrained.

Blake got up next. "To your happiness," he said simply, lifting his glass in Erin's direction before taking a sip and sitting back down.

"May I?"

Sandy noticed how Blake's expression warmed when he turned to Timmy. "Sure," he said, smiling.

"Can I make a wish for all of us?"

"Go ahead, sport."

Timmy looked first at Erin and then at Blake, who sat at opposite ends of the big dining table. "To our whole family," he said gravely, lifting his glass of sparkling grape juice and taking a big sip.

Judge Adkins cleared his throat and gave his own good wishes. "To a bright future for this wonderful family. Blake, your grandpa Jimmy would have been proud of all of you today," he added before excusing himself.

Sandy felt Greg's gaze before she realized that she, too, would be expected to propose a toast to the newlyweds. "Be happy, you two," she managed to say with a bright smile, but she wondered if that wish could ever come true.

For Erin, or for me? Maybe for both of us.

Why couldn't relationships be simple? Why was Erin starting a marriage to a man who lost his much-loved wife just months ago, one she had only met because she had agreed to be the surrogate mother of his child?

Sandy didn't know, any more than she knew why she had gone and fallen in love with Greg. No woman in her right mind would want a guy who had ruinous alimony to pay to two ex-wives, a spoiled rotten daughter who kept Daddy wrapped around her twelve-year-old finger, and a mother who gently but firmly tried to run his life.

But she loved Greg. She couldn't help loving him.

"Sandy?" Greg said, interrupting her pensive reflection.

Everyone had gotten up from the table. Timmy had gone with Mary to get ready for bed, and Judge Adkins was preparing to leave. Sandy stood and followed Greg to the door.

"I think we'll call it a night, too. Thanks for letting us be a part of your wedding. And best wishes to you both," Greg told Blake and Erin.

On the way home, Greg stopped at a small park and turned to Sandy. "They'll be all right, honey," he told her, taking her hand as they strolled down a well-lit path among fragrant summer jasmines and honeysuckle.

"It almost seemed like they were signing a contract instead of getting married," she said sadly.

"Marriage is a contract," he observed.

"It is? I thought people got married because they love each other."

She could almost feel Greg smiling. "That, too. But think, sweetheart, about the way, years ago, matchmakers wrote out detailed agreements for marriages between couples who had never even met. Most of those marriages worked out fine. Erin and Blake's will, too."

"Didn't you marry because you were in love?"

Greg stopped and turned to face her. "No. Not like I love you. I cared deeply for Kay, but I don't think I was ever really in love with her."

He loves me. Sandy's heart beat faster, and she felt like dancing with happiness. "I love you, too. But what about Rhea?"

"I was hot for her body at the time, and flattered that she seemed to want me just as much. Unfortunately those feelings didn't last much longer than it took for the ink to dry on the marriage license. I want to talk about us, Sandy," he said seriously as he toyed with a strand of her hair that had blown over her shoulder.

"Okay."

"All I could think about tonight when Blake and Erin were saying their vows was that I wished it were you and I standing there committing ourselves to each other. But I won't even ask you until I've worked out something so that

I can support you. I'll tell you this, though. I want to marry you. I want to wake up with you every morning and go to sleep with you in my arms. I want us to have a couple of kids while I'm still in good enough shape to teach them to swim and play tennis and so on. Most of all, sweetheart, I want to know you're going to keep loving me like I'll be loving you, as long as we live.''

"I'd marry you tomorrow," Sandy vowed, touched by his declaration.

Greg put an arm around her, and they walked back toward his car. "Not tomorrow, love. But soon, I hope."

Sandy thought Greg was unusually quiet as they resumed the drive back to his apartment. She didn't mind; the lack of conversation gave her time to luxuriate in the knowledge that he really loved her and wanted her to be his wife.

"We could start planning our wedding now," she said suddenly, visions of white lace and silk illusion drifting through her head. "I'd like something more traditional than Erin and Blake had."

"As long as it's legal, whatever you want will suit me just fine," Greg said. Then he paused. "We can't have a religious ceremony, but we can do as big and fancy a civil wedding as you want," he amended, sounding worried.

"Oh." Sandy hadn't thought of that. "I don't think that would bother Erin, and we don't have any other relatives. But won't your mother and sisters be upset?" she asked.

Greg shrugged. "Probably. But I wouldn't ask you to marry outside your faith, any more than I'd expect you to want me to say the most important vows of my life outside of mine."

"Greg, do you really believe circumstances are going to change with . . . with your alimony situations? I don't want to wait forever."

He nodded, but didn't say anything as he walked her to the door of his apartment.

She tried again to get Greg to confide in her. "I don't want to wait much longer. I wouldn't mind living here, and keeping on working like I do now. You wouldn't have to pay me if we were married,'' Sandy said as she kicked off her shoes and padded to the kitchen for a glass of water.

She listened to Greg protest again that she deserved better than the life he could give her now, and she damned the complications that were keeping them apart—at least in his mind and heart. Then her spirits brightened. At least he had admitted he loved her, that he was ready to commit himself to her as soon as he could give her the lifestyle his pride demanded.

Later, as she lay in his arms, she thought again about the wedding they had witnessed earlier. Try as she might, she couldn't help but think she and Greg would go through some trying times before they would stand together and say their own vows of love in front of God and everyone.

As Sandy snuggled closer to Greg's warm, hard body, her mind wandered back to Erin. Was she sleeping peacefully beside her gorgeous new husband, or lying alone in her room, married in name only?

Blake had seemed so detached. And Erin's gaiety had obviously been forced. Sandy imagined that Greg's first impression of Blake and Erin's reasons for marrying had been correct. They must have married only for the baby's sake. Any emotional attachment, any other motive they might have had for that union, certainly hadn't been evident this evening, if indeed it was ever there between her sister and Blake.

Standing, shoulders slumped, under a bright moon that reflected off the pool, Blake was anything but detached. Tremors that had threatened all during the wedding and simple reception were coming with a vengeance now. Unable to stand any longer, he sank onto a patio chair, not caring that the night dew was soaking through his pants. Elbows braced on his thighs, he supported his head between shaking hands.

Why in hell do I feel guilty?

There had been a part of him that wanted to genuinely embrace the quiet, pretty woman who carried his child beneath her heart, to thank her for the gift she was giving him and offer her far more than the sterile vows he made.

But no. He couldn't set aside the love he felt for Glenna and offer more than cold material security to Erin and her little boy, in return for their loving his soon-to-be baby. And he hated himself for doing that to them.

Blake was very much afraid that by making this marriage of convenience, he and Erin had set Timmy up for more hurt. The boy had already seen such loss and pain in his short lifetime that he certainly deserved joy—not more distress and loss. And Erin had done nothing, either, to deserve the loveless life she had just committed herself to.

She was a good woman, worthy of emotions Blake could no longer give. He had touched her, kissed her, because it had been expected of him. He imagined he would have to make such public displays from time to time, to reinforce the facade that the marriage they had entered into was real. Hell, he felt guilty about that, too.

God. I had to touch her, look at her. Damn it, Glenna, Judge Adkins would have thought it was mighty fishy if I'd treated Erin like a leper. I had to marry her—no decent man would have done otherwise.

Then why do I feel so guilty?

Because, he told himself, Glenna was everywhere, in every nook and cranny of this house where she lived with him for fourteen years.

It's as if she has just taken a trip and will soon be home. But she won't. She's gone, and she left me here with a life that's as sterile and empty as the walls of that master bedroom I can't stand being in.

He spoke aloud, barely able to recognize the hoarse, strained voice as his own. "Damn you, Glenna! You wanted this baby. I didn't. But now it's almost here and very much alive, and I've found that I do want it after all. You're gone, I have to carry on, and who could be better to mother my child than the woman who is giving it life?

"Do you remember the night we sat in the garden room and watched the snow come down last winter while we listened to those old pop songs you used to like so well? How you laughed and teased me about how I was loving you while another lover like the one in that song was carrying my child? And how I teased you back, singing along with the line that said the other lover could never have the part of me I gave to you or something to that effect?

"Well, Glenna, now I've got a hell of a problem. I gave all of me to you. There's nothing left for me to give the woman I just promised to love, honor, and cherish. I stood there and perjured myself in front of our closest friend and a judge who has known and respected my family since long before I was born. And it's all your damn fault!"

He stopped, thinking he heard someone come out of the house; then he continued his tirade, cursing Glenna for her obsession to have a baby, the idiocy of getting in front of a bullet meant for someone else, and the tyranny of leaving him alone, without his heart.

Finally wracking sobs came from deep in Blake's chest, making it impossible for him to go on railing at the woman he loved. She was gone and beyond his fury; yet her presence was very much with him in every breath he took.

He heard the intruding sound of a door closing, but placed no importance on it as he let forth the tears that had refused to come when Glenna died, or even that rainy February day when the workers lowered her casket into the icy ground.

And in the silence of the newly furnished master bedroom Blake had insisted she occupy to make the world believe she was *really* Mrs. James Blake Tanner IV, Erin curled up in an overstuffed lounge chair covered in navy blue silk damask and stared at the lonely-looking king-sized bed. She wrapped her arms around the massive bulk of her abdomen. And she, too, cried.

Chapter 11

Glenna

"You hurt her, Blake, not me," Glenna whispered, feeling more inclined to admonish him for causing Erin's tears than to refute the angry accusations he had hurled at her.

She felt compelled to go to him, ease his anguish, and tell him she had never meant to cause all this. But she knew she couldn't. She had let him go. He had to fight his own demons to tell her good-bye; and if he came to hate her, maybe that would make his personal war less painful.

Suddenly weary, for she had struggled to observe them unseen through the afternoon and evening of their wedding, Glenna wondered if perhaps Blake could be right. Counting back the time to that day when her life had been taken, she realized it had been over four months—and still Blake showed no signs of recovery from the shock of losing her. Would he ever?

Yes. He has to.

Glenna couldn't bear the thought of floating in limbo forever, watching Blake suffer endlessly because she had gone before him. She needed peace, the eternal peace of angels that could not come until she knew she had righted the pain she had so unwittingly caused to Blake—and Erin.

Their wedding had been so small, so sad, with Erin's

little Timmy looking hopefully on while Erin held the rose the child had given her when Blake had forgotten that small but telling detail.

Greg had looked as if he'd like to have been saying those vows to Erin's young sister instead of witnessing his best friend's antiseptic recitation. And Sandy seemed to be silently making her pledge to Greg. Blake had been detached, saying and doing the right things at the right time, like a robot programmed to act the happy bridegroom.

It had been Erin's sometimes hopeful, sometimes desolate expressions that affected Glenna most. She had played her part in persuading Erin to take Blake's wounded soul and try to heal it with her baby's love. Had she doomed them all to a life of living hell, and herself to eternal death without contentment?

In Glenna's troubled mind, Erin's tears mingled with Blake's anguished cries in a cacophony of sounds. His tears, she hoped, were cathartic, beginning to heal the terrible grief she had brought upon him. Erin's quiet, solitary sobs were worse. Hearing them continue for what seemed like hours in the darkness of the night moved Glenna to gather the last of her strength, to try to ease the hurt she knew Blake's anguished words had evoked.

Chapter 12

Erin tried without success to think logically and calm herself. What had she done tonight? What had she been thinking when she married a man whose grief was so intense it filled his life so nothing and no one else could have a place there?

She shifted in the chair, not willing to lie down and let the whole night pass while she shed bitter, silent tears. Then, at the door she had gone through to find out it was Blake making those muted, anguished sounds outside by the pool, she saw a brilliant golden haze—and Glenna.

"How could you?" she asked, tasting the salt of her tears as she spoke harshly to the woman who had caused her new husband—in name only—such anguish. "Why couldn't you just conjure yourself up to him and do your own comforting, instead of selling me on stepping in and trying to be the wife he doesn't want?"

Glenna's image was not as clear as it had been when she appeared on those other occasions. She seemed nearly transparent. Her features were recognizable, but through them Erin could see the flickering golden aura that before had only surrounded her.

"Can't you answer?" she asked harshly.

Glenna's image flickered, then strengthened. *"Do you think I wanted to die?"* she asked, her expression tortured as Erin had never seen it before. *"Or that I want now to*

*wander formless on this earth, seeing the trouble I've
caused my love, yet not able to make things right?''*

"Then why not go to Blake? He's out there, suffering in
a way no one should ever have to suffer. Only you can ease
him. You know that, don't you, Glenna?" Erin taunted.

She thought she saw sparkling golden tears falling down
Glenna's pale, translucent cheeks. But Erin tried hard to
squelch the pangs of sympathy she couldn't quite help feeling for the ghost. She recalled when, earlier today, she had
tried to make Glenna appear to ease her own well-placed
misgivings about the marriage she now was sure had been
conceived in hell.

*"I can't. Don't you think that if I could I would have
Blake with me now, in whatever plane of existence we might
have to live? Yes, I could go and try to comfort him. But
that's your place now."*

"He loves you. He has nothing to give to me or anyone
else. I'm sure you heard him say he had given all of himself
to you, if you've been hovering like you said, watching the
misery you've brought on us all." Erin wished she could
take back some of her accusations when she saw how
Glenna trembled, how her image began to fade and then
brightened as if by some supernatural act of will.

When Glenna spoke, her words were barely audible.
*"Blake is going to heal. And he will love again. What he's
going through tonight is a good sign, Erin. Do you realize
this is the first time he has cried? The first time he has truly
opened himself to suffer? For months he has been blocking
the truth from his heart, trying to tell himself our love had
never been and therefore could not be lost to him."*

"How do you figure that?" Erin asked, shifting in the
chair to ease the strain on her back and twisting the engraved gold band Blake had managed to get on her swollen
finger hours earlier.

"Look around this room. What do you see?" Glenna
asked.

What was she getting at? Erin wondered. "Just a room.

A huge, luxurious room with lots of angles and glass, and a curved wall behind the bed. Nice, comfortable furniture that looks brand-new. There's nothing personal here, no touches to make the room feel lived in.''

"Precisely. Would you believe it if I told you that just four months ago this whole suite looked completely different? That every piece of furniture, every accessory, had special, loving memories for Blake—and me? Would you believe Blake emptied it out of everything, and that he ordered new furniture, carpeting, and drapes without even going in person to pick them out?"

Erin looked again around the luxurious but sterile-looking room. "Yes, I guess I would. I wondered why the rooms in this wing seem so cold and impersonal, when the rest of the house has all the caring touches that make it seem like a home."

Glenna's image faded again, then brightened. *"Think, Erin,"* she said, her voice clear but weakening. *"For four months now, Blake has done nothing except deny his sense of loss, try with every trick he could think of to put my dying out of his mind. Tonight he faced it for the first time. What you heard was the guilt and anger finally coming to the surface of his mind. I've got to go now, Erin, but believe me, Blake will heal."*

"Will you be back?"

"Yes . . ."

With that last, faint promise Glenna's image disappeared, leaving Erin looking at rapidly disseminating golden dust while she pondered what the ghost of her husband's first wife had revealed.

For the first two weeks after their wedding, their lives went along pretty much as they had before. Blake got up and went to his office, seemingly unaffected by his tortured self-revelations that first night. Timmy had his daily therapy with Michelle, Mary ran the household, and Erin divided her time between her son and resting while she waited for the baby to be born.

Glenna's ghost was being quiet, but Erin couldn't help believing she was around, observing and replenishing her strength. Sometimes Erin even found herself looking for signs, searching through the house for a glimmer of Glenna's golden aura; other times she was able to put the ghost and her futile hopes at matchmaking out of her mind.

While Blake had told her she could make whatever changes she wished to her new sleeping quarters and sitting room, Erin hadn't found the energy or the self-confidence to add accessories that would have made the sterile rooms seem more like home. She had, however, taken him up on his suggestion that she furnish the empty, oddly angled room next to her bedroom as a nursery.

She ignored the small voice inside her that told her to fix the baby's room the way Glenna had described it to her, that day before she died when they met and shared lunch and talk. With deliberate intent, she set about making the nursery a small statement of her own taste.

A trip with Mary to an attic storeroom yielded an old oak crib and changing table that Miguel cleaned and polished to a high gloss before placing them in the empty room. Calls to the infant department at Saks provided linens and a layette. When Greg and Sandy brought an antique cradle where Erin could rock her newborn baby to sleep, the nursery seemed complete.

"Don't you need some toys or something in here to brighten the place up? I heard somewhere that babies respond to primary colors almost as soon as they're born." On Thursday morning of the third week they had been married, Erin turned to find Blake standing in the doorway in brief navy racing trunks, a big striped towel draped around his broad, muscular shoulders.

She surveyed the nursery. "I've read that, too. I guess I could call and order some pictures and toys. I'd thought I would wait until I could go myself." Blake had been adamant that she was not to endanger herself by going out so late in her pregnancy. She had accepted the constraint on her activity, understanding his fear that would have seemed unreasonable had she not known its cause.

"Would you mind if I picked up a few things?" he asked.

His almost hesitant attitude surprised her. "Not at all. But do you have time?"

"I've arranged my case load so I won't have to go to the office for a few weeks," he said, eyeing her at what used to be waist level as if trying to guess how much longer it would be until she exploded—or gave birth.

"You mean you'll be here most of the time?"

Blake smiled. "Yes. I'll be working on some legal matters I've taken on for Greg. Will my being underfoot disturb you?"

Erin didn't know if it would or not. It certainly bothered her to see him there, looking like he could model for a Chippendale's calendar, making her wish fleetingly that he cared half as much for her as he did for their unborn child. "No," she said, realizing she'd been standing there staring at him like a half-wit.

"I thought I'd try to keep Timmy occupied so you can rest. Maybe he'd like to go with me to find some stuff to brighten up the baby's room."

"Yes, I'm sure he'd like that. He's still talking about how much fun he had when you took him out to get his suit. Thank you, Blake," she said, realizing she hadn't expressed her appreciation for all he was doing for her little boy.

"I enjoyed Timmy as much as he enjoyed his outing." He glanced down at himself, as if he were suddenly realizing how very nearly naked he was. "I'd better go change, before I drip all over the carpet," he said as he turned to go into what had been his office/hobby room in the master suite, before he had turned it into a combination bedroom and study.

Later that day, Erin rubbed at the aching spot at the small of her back, then wandered out by the pool. She longed to jump in and cool herself in the crystal-clear water, but contented herself with watching Michelle put Timmy through his exercises. Her recent conversation with Blake ran through her mind, and she wondered what kind of work Blake was doing for Greg—and why Sandy hadn't mentioned it to her before.

"Doesn't Sandy know?" Blake asked Greg while he was confirming an appointment for them to meet with Kay's attorney later the next day.

"No. Why?"

"Because Erin seemed surprised when I told her I'd be taking care of some legal matters for you while I'm sticking close to home. I assumed she would know, from Sandy, what we're trying to accomplish."

"I haven't said anything to Sandy yet, because I damn sure don't want to get her hopes up if all your efforts don't bring results. I guess I will tell her now, before Erin does." Greg sounded stressed, Blake thought, although the reason for it could have been the difficult delivery he said he had just finished up with before returning Blake's call.

"I didn't mention what kind of work I was doing for you," Blake assured Greg. "Anyhow, I doubt that she'll say anything to her sister. Since I've been home, she's spent most of her time resting. How long is it going to be, anyhow?"

"Before you're a father? Any day now. Blake, do you want to see your baby being born?"

Blake hesitated. "I'd like to. But it's going to feel damn strange, considering the circumstances. I doubt Erin would want me there."

"Erin told me she wouldn't object if you wanted to go in the delivery room."

That surprised Blake. Erin gave every impression of being uncomfortable whenever she saw him around home dressed in tennis shorts or swim attire. He would have thought the idea of him seeing her as intimately as he assumed he would when she gave birth would really distress her. "I want to be there," he repeated to his friend.

"Then I'll bring a couple of tapes for you to watch, so you'll know what to expect. You said Si and Kay would be at your house at six?"

"That's right. You're welcome to stay and have dinner after we're done with the meeting."

Greg chuckled. "Will I feel like eating after the meeting?"

"I have no idea. But I'll see you in another couple of hours." Blake hoped that Greg would come alone; he wanted nothing to interfere with what he hoped would be the reasonable discussion of reducing Greg's troublesome alimony burden.

When Greg arrived at the house, Blake noted Sandy's conspicuous absence; and so did Erin, who had been sitting with him beside the pool, watching Timmy, when Greg arrived alone, still wearing wrinkled scrubs with an equally disheveled-looking lab coat hastily pulled over them.

"How's my favorite patient?" Greg asked Erin as he pulled up a patio chair and joined them.

"Getting anxious," Erin admitted with a smile. "Where's Sandy?"

"At the office, working. It's only four o'clock, and I'm an evil taskmaster," Greg said with a grin.

Blake stood up abruptly. "Since this isn't a social call, we'd better go inside. The other parties will be here shortly."

He had hardly had time to brief Greg before Mary came into the study and announced that Mr. Abrams and his client had arrived. "Send them in," he said, silently willing Greg to keep his sometimes acid tongue in check.

"Si. Kay. Thank you for coming here instead of downtown," Blake said in greeting, knowing that he hadn't in-

convenienced them at all, since Si's office was less than
two miles away.

Kay laughed, a brittle, tinkling sound Blake thought
matched the brilliant red of her linen suit and pale, bright
tone of her short, curly hair. "I wouldn't think of having
you leave your brand-new bride so close to her delivery
date," she replied, setting down her alligator handbag and
settling herself daintily onto a chair.

"You always were considerate, Kay," Greg offered silk-
ily from his seat on the sofa in the corner before Blake
could verbalize a defense of himself, Erin, and their baby.

Kay turned and faced her former husband. "I see you're
dressed for work, as usual. Are you planning to deliver
Blake's baby here and now?" she asked sweetly.

Blake could feel the tension building. Someone needed
to diffuse it, and it seemed that Si Abrams was content to
sit back and watch the show. "Greg came straight here
from the hospital when I told him you were willing to ne-
gotiate the alimony, Kay," he said firmly. "He can't afford
to pay me to referee a verbal war between you two—besides, that's not what we're here for. Let's cut out this
childish sniping and get down to business."

"Right," Si said with hearty enthusiasm. "Kay realizes
you're paying more than you can afford in alimony, Dr.
Halpern. Are you aware that three weeks ago I conveyed
her offer to give up future payments in return for a lump-
sum settlement?"

"He is aware, Si. As I told you, Kay's offer was unac-
ceptable. Kay, is it true that you plan to remarry shortly?"
Blake asked.

Kay nodded, letting her bright blue gaze drop noticeably
to the headlight of a diamond on her left hand. "That's
why I've asked for this meeting. I won't be getting alimony
from you after this month, anyhow, Greg, but I thought I'd
offer you a small present in celebration of my remarriage."

"Let me," Si said as Blake sat back, wondering what
would be coming next and trying to plan his line of attack.

"Kay is marrying a proud and wealthy man. He dislikes the idea of his wife receiving what he considers an excessive amount in child support. We've all talked this over and feel that a thousand dollars a month should be adequate to take care of Shana's needs until she is of age."

Blake mentally reviewed the numbers Greg's accountant had provided him with. Without the $7,500 he was paying Kay, Greg could easily afford the court-ordered monthly child support of $2,500. "Greg hasn't contested the child support, Si. Just the alimony. He wants to support his daughter."

"Of course he does, Blake. But if he isn't having to pay so much in support, he will have more to give her the little extras every girl wants." Kay sounded so sweet that Blake knew there had to be a catch to her offer.

Greg spoke up. "And who do I have to kill to make this happen, Kay?"

Kay faced Greg, her features serene. "Why, no one, darling. All you have to do is take temporary custody of our daughter for six months or so while Abe and I take an extended honeymoon. That's a trip, like the ones we never took while you buried yourself in the hospital caring for every woman in the world except me, and I got stuck vegetating in a tiny, cramped apartment I hated."

"That's all?" Greg sounded incredulous.

"That's all, and I'll even waive child support for the time Shana will be spending with you. Of course, you will have to buy a house and hire a housekeeper. I won't have my child living in that tenement you call an apartment building."

Blake studied the papers Si had handed him that spelled out Kay's proposed agreement. "It seems to say exactly what Kay has told you," he said to Greg as he worked his way to the last page.

"Then I'd be a fool to turn it down."

Si cleared his throat as Blake came to a clause that gave

him second thoughts. He seemed to expect Blake's next comment.

"Could I speak to my client alone before he makes a decision?"

"You think Greg won't like the clause that says he can't carry on with women while Shana's with him? Blake, my friend, you don't know my former husband at all. He'd rather deliver babies than make them," Kay said scathingly. "Obviously unlike you."

"Kay, let's keep this businesslike," Si implored.

"Yeah, Kay, try to hold in those talons before they draw blood," Greg drawled. "Go ahead, Blake, explain my lovely ex-wife's terms right here. I'm sure she can withstand the embarrassment."

It was Blake's turn to be embarrassed. What, he wondered, had gone on between these people who had appeared to be in love when they decided to marry fifteen years ago?

He reread the clause and handed the unsigned agreement to Greg. "What it says is you are not to expose Shana to any of your relationships with women."

"What the hell? Kay has obviously exposed Shana to this guy she's about to marry. Shana told me about him, long before today. I don't have indiscriminate flings with women, and Kay damn well knows it. I am seeing one woman, and Shana already knows her." Greg had stood during his diatribe and now was pacing across the room.

"All I want is to be assured you won't be 'seeing' your little nymphet right under our daughter's impressionable nose, Greg. Certainly you have adequate time to dally with her while you both are at your office every day."

Blake could see Greg was getting ready to explode with fury. "Sit down and calm down," he ordered quietly but firmly. "Si, we need to revise this clause. Like Kay, we want to ensure Shana's safety, both physical and emotional; but we feel that contractually prohibiting Greg from seeing a woman friend while in his daughter's company is absurd."

Si leaned over and studied the offending words. He checked with Kay and made a counteroffer; Blake studied the new wording and consulted with Greg. Blake thought they would never reach agreement—but finally they did. Greg was to be free of one albatross. Now all they had to worry about was Rhea—not that Rhea could be considered anything but a formidable opponent.

Blake got up and walked his colleague to the door while Kay and Greg indulged in one last shouting match. He was damn glad he didn't deal in this kind of law every day— or even every year.

When Kay stormed past him toward the door, Blake felt like throttling her himself for the snide comment she had directed toward him for marrying and fathering a baby so soon after Glenna's death. He wondered how much there would be of such cruelty, and if there was any way other than broadcasting the aborted surrogate arrangement to prevent the baby and Erin from being hurt by mean-spirited shrews like Greg's ex-wife.

There wasn't to be a whole lot of time to form a line of defense against what friends and acquaintances were going to think as they learned of Blake's marriage and impending fatherhood. When he walked with Greg into the garden room, Timmy was rolling toward them in his wheelchair, wide-eyed and obviously scared to death.

"My mommy's sick," the little boy said. "Dr. Halpern, please help her."

Blake stayed and tried to calm his stepson while Greg went to Erin's room to examine her. It didn't help much that he was as frightened as the boy, if not more so. Still, he forced his hands not to shake as he explained that a little discomfort was normal when a mommy was getting ready to have a baby.

"Erin's in early labor. Mrs. Malone is helping her get dressed. You bring her in as soon as she's ready, and I'll meet you at the hospital,'' Greg told Blake when he came back, heading toward the door.

"Wait. Shouldn't I call an ambulance?"

"No. She's barely dilated at all. And the baby's big. We're going to be having a long night of it, I'm afraid. I need to call Sandy before I leave," he said as he pulled a cellular phone from his pocket and punched in some numbers.

Blake turned back to Timmy. "I'm taking your mom to the hospital to get our baby. She's going to be just fine, sport."

"But she's sick," the boy repeated stubbornly.

"Dr. Halpern said she's just ready for the baby to be born. Trust me, nothing bad is happening to your mom. Go on, get Mary to fix you a hot fudge sundae, and tell her I said it's okay for you to stay up and watch a movie on the big TV. I'm going to take your mommy to the hospital now, but I'll be back and take you to the hospital so you can see your new brother or sister."

By the time Erin came out, Blake was damn near petrified with fear. Greg had said she wasn't dilated and that the baby was big. Greg had also assured Blake before he did the first artificial insemination that Erin was healthy and able to have this child without complications; but now Blake wasn't placing a lot of credence in those months-old predictions.

He was shaking when he helped her into the car, and her soft moans did nothing to reassure him. "Go ahead, scream," he told her between clenched teeth as he gunned the Mercedes into the center lane of the interstate and sped toward the hospital where he hoped to hell Greg was waiting.

Erin let out not a scream, but certainly at least a yelp, as she clutched both hands to her heaving abdomen.

"Jesus, I'm sorry," Blake muttered, sweating now. How much farther was the damn exit?

Erin's voice was strained when she said softly, "It's not your fault."

Yes, by God it is, and I didn't even give you a lover's

pleasure to make it happen. Aloud, Blake just uttered a cryptic oath.

"I'll be fine," Erin managed between groaning and writhing pitifully on the front seat.

Sure. Blake wished he felt a tenth as certain as Erin sounded even through her pain.

"Stay with me."

"I will." Blake swerved into the exit lane and moments later was pulling into the hospital's emergency entrance. Tossing the keys to a security guard and ordering the man to take the car and park it, he scooped Erin into his arms and bolted through the doors.

A nurse accosted them. "You'll have to go to Admitting," she told Blake as she tried to get him to set Erin into a wheelchair. All Blake could think of was that he had promised not to leave her.

"No. Send a clerk upstairs. We're supposed to meet Dr. Halpern in the labor room."

"I'll take your wife to him. You have to stay down here and take care of admitting her. Then you can go upstairs." The nurse assumed what she apparently thought was an uncompromising pose.

"I promised not to leave her. So you can damn well send an admitting clerk upstairs or do without the formalities. Where is the labor room?"

"Third floor," the nurse said sullenly as Blake headed with Erin for the elevators.

Blake did have to leave Erin, but only for as long as it took him to take off his slacks and shirt and don a set of shapeless blue scrubs. Then he joined her in a labor room painted in cheerful tones of blue and yellow.

She was writhing on the narrow bed, turning from side to side as pains wracked her body. "Is there anything I can do?" he asked her helplessly.

"You can sit down over there and hold her hand while Jessica starts an epidural," Greg said as he came into the small room with a plain but pleasant-looking woman Blake assumed must be an anesthesiologist. "Here now, Erin, you'll be feeling better soon."

"You're going to put her to sleep?" Blake asked Greg, surprised when Erin clenched his hand with amazing strength.

The anesthesiologist smiled. "No, this will keep your wife comfortable during labor. I will place this tiny catheter into the epidural space so that medication can be administered as needed. Is that all right?"

"Yes." The last thing Blake wanted was for Erin to suffer any more than necessary to give him this child.

For what seemed like days even though he knew it was only a few tension-filled hours, Blake sat with Erin, rubbing her back and shoulders, wiping the sweat from her forehead with a cool, damp cloth, and simply being there in case he might be needed. He felt he should be saying something, but words wouldn't come.

"It's time for the big event," Greg said jovially as he straightened up and adjusted the sheet over Erin's lower body for what Blake thought must have been at least the tenth time since they'd been here.

"Come on, Blake. Erin, sweetheart, let these pretty ladies get you ready, and we'll meet you in the delivery room." Like a zombie, Blake followed Greg out of the labor room as two nurses prepared to move Erin to this other room where their baby was to be born.

"Do you need the neonatologist to stand by?" the nurse at the desk asked Greg.

Greg grinned. "Not tonight, unless Bernie's got nothing better to do. Do you have some caps, masks, and shoe covers for us?" he asked, taking the requested items when she handed them to him.

"Delivery room three is ready for Mrs. Tanner," another nurse called out.

The head nurse scowled. "Dr. Halpern needs room four or one," she reminded the woman tersely.

"A regular delivery room will be fine tonight, Daisy. This mama and baby are as healthy as they come," Greg told the woman as he led the way to the scrub room.

Another doctor came in and began to scrub up while Greg and Blake were soaping their hands and forearms. "Want a consult, Greg?" the older man asked jovially.

"Sure, after I finish here. Sam, this is Blake Tanner, who's about to become a daddy for the first time. Blake, Sam Reed."

Reed greeted Blake with a sympathetic smile. "If anyone can get a problem baby here safely, this young man can. Good luck, son."

Blake panicked, and he looked to Greg for reassurance.

"Sam, Blake was my roommate in college. For a change, I'm getting the pleasure of delivering a healthy baby from a healthy mom. What's the consult about?"

"A thirty-eight-year-old brittle diabetic. Her seven-month fetus died in utero. I'm going in now to take it."

Greg let out a low whistle. "Doesn't sound good. Any other kids?"

"A daughter, sixteen." Reed shook his head sadly. "She married again a couple of years ago, and she's damn near obsessed to have his baby."

"You want me to see her today?"

"Not her. Her records. See if you can offer any hope for them. If you can't, maybe you can help me persuade her husband they mustn't try again."

A feminine voice broke Blake's morbid fascination. "Mrs. Tanner's ready for you in Three, Dr. Halpern," a woman said from the entry to the scrub room.

"Blake." He was touched that Erin called his name even though she was obviously exhausted.

"I'm here." He stood beside her, grasping her cold hand and trying not to shiver in the room that was damn near freezing cold despite the hot, blinding lights that seemed to be focused on them from all directions.

He watched a nurse adjust a large, round mirror above Erin's head. "Here, now you can see," she said before gliding quietly to a small stainless steel table to arrange some evil-looking instruments on a towel-draped tray.

Greg sat down on a stool positioned at the foot of the table and murmured his approval. "You're doing great, sweetheart," he said, his voice radiating confidence Blake hoped to hell was not misplaced. "Come on now, give this baby a little push. Look, can you see? The kid's got lots of dark hair."

Blake listened to his friend coax and cajole. "Hey, little one, you've got a mommy and daddy just waiting to spoil you rotten. I bet you've already got more toys than lots of kids see in a lifetime. Again now, Erin, push!"

Blake was listening to Greg when he heard an indignant howl. His baby was born! He took two long steps to stand beside Greg and watch firsthand while the wet, wriggling mass of humanity emerged from its mother's body.

"What is it?" Erin asked excitedly.

"A baby. A furious, squalling little baby," Blake exclaimed, enthralled as he watched Greg gently turn the baby's shoulder so he could work its body free.

"It's a boy. Congratulations, Blake, Erin." Greg spoke as he held the baby Blake thought was the tiniest and most indignant human he'd ever seen, gently suctioning mucus from his nose and mouth. Then he turned to Blake. "Here, take him over and get him weighed, and show him to his mom while I finish up down here." He handed Blake his naked, screaming son and turned his attention back to Erin.

Blake had never felt such pure, heady adoration as came over him when he held his baby. He hated relinquishing his precious burden long enough for a nurse to weigh and measure him, and when she handed the baby back, wrapped snugly in a blue receiving blanket, he examined the infant's features with wonder and love. Then he went to Erin's side.

"Thank you for my son," he said and, feeling rather than thinking, he bent and kissed her gently on lips parched from her ordeal.

Blake was awed. Seeing this woman he had never lain with giving birth to his child was the most intimate yet innocent experience of his life. It was sweet, yet erotic beyond anything he could recall.

As if it were his perfect right to do so, he brushed aside the loose, worn cotton of her hospital gown to bare one full, firm breast. Then he carefully laid his newborn son down and guided her rose-tipped nipple to his avid little mouth. As he watched, his long-dormant sexuality emerged, and he felt his body quicken beneath the concealing cloth of the baggy scrub pants.

He could have been there for seconds, or it could have been hours when Greg stood and told the nurses they could take Erin into the recovery room. Blake watched as they rolled her and their baby separately away, and then he followed Greg out another door that led back to the sinks where they had scrubbed.

"Thanks, Greg," he said when they finally sat down in the lounge with some of the strongest coffee he had ever tasted.

"My pleasure. What's his name?"

Blake shrugged. "You mean you can't guess?"

Greg chuckled. "The Fifth? What I meant is, what are you and Erin going to call him?"

"Erin can decide if he's going to be James, Jimmy, JB, Blake, or some other nickname. After all, she went through hell getting him here."

"Not really. Compared to most, it was a fairly easy labor and delivery," Greg said as he refilled his cup from the urn on a small, crowded counter. "I guess you didn't have the chance to look at those videos I brought by."

"Hardly. What happens next, with Erin and baby?"

"Erin will be in recovery until the epidural wears off. She's probably taking a well-deserved nap. I'll check her in a few minutes. Meanwhile, John Kaplan will be coming sometime within the next few hours to give the Fifth a thorough exam—that is, unless you have another pediatrician you'd rather use. I called John because Erin said he's Timmy's regular doctor."

"He knows what he's doing, doesn't he?" Blake asked.

Greg shrugged. "Clinically he's one of the best. I've always thought his bedside manner with parents and colleagues left a good deal to be desired, but from all I hear, his little patients love him."

"Then he's fine with me. The baby's all right, isn't he?" Blake asked, concerned.

"The little slugger looks healthy as a horse to me. He's damn near as big, too. Nine pounds, three ounces—biggest baby I've delivered for a long time!"

Blake grinned; then he thought of the ordeal Erin had just gone through to deliver his lusty, bouncing baby boy. "How is Erin, really?" he asked.

"Fine. She'll be tired and sore for a few days. I could probably send her home tomorrow, but I'd rather keep her here for two or three days. Hell, you can afford the extra assurance that she and the Fifth are okay."

Blake grinned, now fully reassured that there were no problems lurking in the background for Erin or their baby. Suddenly he remembered the meeting he and Greg had had earlier, before Erin had gone into labor.

"I seem to recall you're in the market for a house," he said, voicing a thought that had been lurking in the back of his harried mind. "There's a place down the road from me that's just gone on the market."

Greg laughed out loud. "Really? What bank do you suggest I rob to pay for an estate in the most expensive damn area of Dallas?"

"It's not an estate—just a small house and pool on less than an acre. From what I hear, the Campbells' heirs are anxious to unload it."

"How small?" Greg asked.

"Four or five thousand square feet, I guess. It used to be a guest house for the Trayne estate that's next door to me; but during a recession back when I was a kid, they got in a bind and sold off this place and several other small parcels of land."

"Hmmm. Suitable for my little princess and cozy enough that I just might be able to swing buying it, you think?" Greg asked thoughtfully.

"It's a possibility, anyhow."

"Maybe I'll make an appointment and take Sandy over to see it tomorrow. Oh, my God. Sandy. I promised I'd call her just as soon as we got out of the delivery room." As if he'd been shot from a cannon, Greg bolted out of the easy chair where he'd been slouching and grabbed the phone on the counter.

Blake grinned at his friend. "I'm going to stop by the nursery and look at my son again. Then I've got to get home and let Timmy know he has a baby brother. Will I see you tomorrow?"

Greg nodded and waved as Blake hurried out of the lounge.

Blake had seemed to be glued to her side while she and baby Jamie were at the hospital, and Erin thought he was just trying to make the world think theirs was a normal marriage. But when he brought her home, he showed no inclination to reestablish their relationship as polite strangers. In fact, Erin decided, Blake was even more attentive when he was not being hindered by the presence of nurses and doctors who dictated the amount of time he could spend with the little boy.

He hadn't stinted on the time he spent with Timmy, either. Instead, Blake had gone out of his way today to make her son feel he was just as important as the new baby in the house. Maybe Glenna had been right when she told her that with time Blake would set aside his mourning and want to build a real family with the boys, and her.

Off and on during the day, Erin found herself searching for signs of Glenna, from the moment Blake brought her to her room and laid her gently on the bed. *I know she's here.* But wherever the ghost was, she apparently wasn't ready to show herself, Erin decided after the first few hours of having her newborn son at home.

That night, Erin was tired but happy when Blake strode into her room, his squalling son cradled securely against his chest.

"I think he's hungry," he told her, a sappy smile on his face as he watched her prop herself up with several pillows and adjust her nightgown.

"Here, I'll take him now." The feel of his callused fingers brushing against her bare breast as he laid Jamie in her arms made her tingle clear down to her toes. Chastising herself for fantasizing about how it would feel to have him put those big, strong hands on her body in passion, she forced her attention to her nursing baby.

With determination, Erin attributed her sudden burst of purely feminine fancy to hormones that must have kicked into high gear after Jamie's birth. She certainly hoped Glenna's ghost hadn't picked this particular time to pop into this dimension and read her mind—almost as much as she hoped Blake didn't share his dead wife's penchant for reading minds.

"May I stay?"

Blake's question forced Erin to meet his intense, indigo gaze. "Of course," she replied, surprised because while she was in the hospital, he'd shown no reticence at watching her nurse his son. Here in the home he had shared with Glenna, she supposed he might feel more deeply the boundaries he had defined for their marriage.

One thing Erin knew: Blake adored Jamie as much as she did. His love showed in awed expressions and in the endearing way he wanted to take part in every aspect of the baby's care. When he lifted the sleeping baby out of her arms and gently admonished her to get a good night's rest, she lay back, content to let him have time alone with the baby they had made together—yet separately.

Chapter 13

Glenna

I knew you'd love him.

For the longest time Glenna hovered out of sight, watching Blake stand there by the crib just looking with adoration at his sleeping baby. It was all she could do to keep from joining him there, sharing in the moment she had waited for, for so many years.

Finally he bent over and gave Jamie one last tender pat on his upthrust little backside before walking out and leaving the baby alone. Instantly Glenna materialized in the spot where Blake had been standing, and she, too, stared down into the antique crib with wonder and awe.

My God, how long have I been standing here, staring at this child?

Yearning, yet feeling almost shy, Glenna reached out and stroked the baby's velvety-soft, dark head as he slumbered undisturbed.

"My baby. My sweet, precious angel Jamie. I'm glad they decided to call you that now, but I bet you'll be JB by the time you get to school." Glenna's fingers drifted down to trace Jamie's plump, ruddy cheek, choking back an almost human urge to weep.

"You would have been mine. And I would have called you JB right from the start."

Her gaze took in every detail of him, from the fine, dark hair and long eyelashes that reminded her of his daddy to the determined way he clenched his tiny fists. Gently she eased back the yellow and dark blue blanket that didn't quite go with the things she had planned to use in Jamie's room.

It pleased Glenna that Jamie was robust, nicely filled out, and already stretching the blue footed sleeper he was wearing. He'd grow to be a big man, like Blake, she thought with satisfaction. Perversely, though, she kept looking, searching for some feature that would mark the baby as hers.

"You're your daddy's baby. And hers. There's nothing of me in you, my angel."

Glenna felt like screaming with the unfairness of it all. This baby, the one she had wanted and waited for years to get, wasn't hers at all. He was Blake's—and Erin's. She would never hold him, never dry his baby tears, never beam with pride as he hit his first home run or won a prize at school. She was gone. Dead.

It's not fair. Erin has Timmy. Now she has you, too. And soon she'll have your daddy.

This baby was not and never would be hers. Even the nursery that she had planned in her mind, down to an aqua padded rocker and the whimsical porcelain clowns she'd picked out but never had the chance to buy before she died, bore nothing of her.

Dispassionately she took in pale yellow walls, antique oak furniture, and accents of indigo and royal blue. Erin must have fixed up the room with Blake's favorite colors in mind, Glenna thought as a new wave of jealousy swept over her. Viciously she struck down that uncharitable but human reaction as she focused her attention again on Blake's newborn son.

You're Blake's all right. You're the son I couldn't give him.

Memories of the babies she had lost flooded her mind as

she watched Jamie's eyelids flutter and his little fists un-
clench and tighten again around a section of the loosened
blanket.

*The last one would have been sitting up by now, explor-
ing her small world with eager enthusiasm. Would she have
been big and dark-haired like you, or little and blond like
me? Oh, Jamie, I wanted her and the others so, so much.
I wanted you, too. Would you have filled the empty spaces
they left in my heart?*

Jamie stirred again, as if he had heard her thoughts. As
he uncurled his fingers, Glenna wished she were alive so
she could feel him curl a trusting, curious hand around her
own finger.

Being a ghost had its downside, she thought wryly as
she wished, just once, she could become flesh and blood
again, so she could feel the joy of loving and being loved
by a part of herself and a part of the man she loved.

Then she smiled. She couldn't come back. She couldn't
have the joy of raising Blake's baby as her own. But, being
a ghost, she could do her best to see that Jamie had two
parents who loved each other as well as him. Allowing
herself one last, loving look, Glenna willed herself to fade
away so she could observe the family she could no longer
be part of and guide them, through Erin, back into the light.

Chapter 14

*B*lake kicked off his tennis shoes and sat on the bed to strip down. He'd have to get the hang of positioning a towel or something over his shoulder while he held his son, he guessed, not really minding that Jamie had burped up some of his dinner all over the collar of his shirt.

It was a heady feeling, this being a father. Fleetingly Blake let himself reflect on the babies Glenna and he had wanted so deeply, yet who had never seemed as real to him as the living, breathing little guy across the hall.

Those babies he'd lost before they had really existed didn't even seem as real, or as much a part of him, as Timmy. This afternoon Erin's son had called him Daddy for the first time. And damned if he didn't feel like a father, not only to Jamie but to the little boy whose life had begun with the passion of another man.

Blake also felt horny. For the past three days he had stayed half hard most of the time, and the constant state of sexual tension was driving him nuts. He couldn't will away the unwanted condition as he had been able to do so many times in years gone by, and that annoyed the hell out of him, too. Determined to work off his frustration, he wrapped a towel around his waist and headed out to the pool.

Not once in the nearly five months Glenna had been gone had Blake felt the slightest twinge of desire—not until three nights ago, when he had first watched his newborn son begin to suckle tentatively at his mother's breast. It had happened then, and every time since then when he'd punished himself by watching Erin nurse their baby. Hell, he'd even gotten hard just thinking about how creamy smooth her firm, full breasts would feel and taste and . . .

"Come off it, Blake. You've never been a breast man, anyhow," he grumbled to himself as he stripped off the towel. "Not to mention most folks would tell you you're some certifiable sex maniac to be lusting after a woman who has just had your baby."

Unfortunately his body didn't listen half as well as his mind did. Shedding the towel, he dove cleanly into the tepid water of the pool, determined to force those stray, annoying hormones into submission.

Twenty laps later, he hauled himself out of the water and replaced the towel, cursing the heat of the night and the fever inside him that wouldn't subside as he strode back into the house.

In the sterile confines of the study he had turned into a monklike cell, Blake lay in the dark and took the irritating problem in hand. With determination, he kept the image of the woman he had loved and lost at the forefront of his mind. He had to; otherwise he could never keep at bay those inappropriate yearnings for the woman who had brought him to this state.

When the dam burst and the musky, heated essence of him spurted onto his own naked flesh, though, the woman Blake saw was Erin. And moments later, when he stepped under the warm, pulsing jets of water in the shower, he tried hard to wash away the persistent wanting along with the guilt that had come with it.

Blake had always taken pride in his ability to analyze and evaluate the feelings of others accurately and incisively. Why, he wondered, was he now suddenly unsure about his own agenda? And why was he acting so out of character?

He had vowed never to open this drawer, yet here he was, rifling through it and cradling the photo he'd swept off his office desk the day after the funeral. *Glenna*. This had been her favorite picture, taken six years ago when she had just learned she was expecting the second baby they'd lost.

Blake's heart beat faster, then slowed. Glenna was dead, lost to him forever. He had wanted to die with her, to bury the love and desire she had created in him when they were kids.

"You *had* to have a child, even if it killed you," he said to the sweet, unmoving face that haunted his every memory. "And by God, it did! It wasn't enough that you had me, was it? My loving you wasn't enough to fill that need—that obsession—inside you."

He felt the tremor in his voice, but for once he couldn't control it. "You left me alone, Glenna. Damn you, you should have stayed home. You didn't need to buy out Neiman's for a baby that wasn't even close to being born."

But Jamie is here now. And I love him.

"I wanted a child as much as any man would. But I wanted you more." Even as he spoke the words, Blake wondered if they were true. Had he somehow conveyed to Glenna with words he never spoke that having a child would make him feel the elation and pure, prideful joy he had felt when he first held his newborn son?

He searched the still, smiling face in the picture before replacing it in the drawer and turning the key in the lock. Glenna had been his safe anchor, his emotional harbor. Now she was gone, and his mind warred with conflicting feelings. He loved Glenna. He always would grieve for her.

Yet he exulted in the knowledge that he had a healthy, beautiful son across the hall. And he wanted his son's mother, and that made him feel guilty as hell.

"How does Greg do it?" Blake asked aloud as he lay in bed and pictured his friend's uncomplicated, joyful relationship with Sandy—a relationship seemingly unaffected by the love Greg once must have felt for not one but two other women who had shared his name and life.

"I think we'll like living here," Greg said, stretching his bare legs out and enjoying the view of Sandy's scantily clad body against a backdrop of flowing water and natural stone that dominated his smallish backyard. "I hope Shana will like her room."

"I'm sure she will." Greg knew his daughter's choice of a pricey, avant-garde-style bedroom set that mirrored her mother's taste had irritated frugal Sandy. But he didn't quite know what to do about it. "Honey, Shana will settle down once Kay gets married and she comes here to live with us."

"Here? With us?"

Sandy sounded stressed, a state of mind Greg had seldom before observed in his competent young fiancée. Maybe he should have told her about his arrangement with Kay earlier, before they decided together to buy this pleasant, roomy house less than a mile from her sister—and Blake.

"Just for a few months, sweetheart. While Kay and her fish take a prolonged honeymoon. Don't tell me you're afraid of a twelve-year-old," he teased.

Sandy sank onto a patio chair, one of the set that was the first furniture purchase they had made together for their new home. "Shana doesn't like me, Greg. I'd hoped we could get to know each other . . . well, more gradually."

Greg was beginning to *feel* stressed. As well as anyone, he knew his daughter could try the patience of a saint. Still, he loved the little girl Shana had been and had hope that this time with him—and Sandy—could bring him close to Shana again. He tried for levity when he replied.

"Shana doesn't much like anyone who tries to tell her what to do; but then, from what I've heard, most kids her age are like that. I'll bet you gave Erin and her husband some rough times when you first went to live with them."

Sandy smiled, a nervous little motion of her lips that

didn't reach her eyes. "I guess," she said softly, her gaze focused on the spa and pool that, set in native stone, looked like a natural feature of the backyard landscape. "Greg, I don't know how to be a stepmother."

"You'll learn, love. And I'll be here to help smooth over any rough spots," he told her, sounding a hell of a lot surer of himself than he felt.

"But you're away so much at night, and I'll be here with her all by myself. Greg, what if I can't make her like me? I already loved Erin when I moved in with her and Bill."

"Hush. I've hired an associate, and he'll be taking call every other night. Besides, you took my office in hand and made it run like a top. I have no doubt that you'll be able to handle just one girl less than half your age."

"All right." As if determined to put the prospect of becoming a full-time stepmom out of her mind, Sandy got up and came to Greg, sighing happily when he pulled her onto his lap and tweaked her nipples through the flimsy material of her red string bikini top.

Her fingers tangled in the hair on his chest as she searched out and teased at his nipples just as he was doing to hers. He groaned when she shifted around to face him fully, wrapping her legs around his waist and cradling his suddenly burning erection to her warm, moist center.

"Interested, are you?" she asked, leaning back and looking pointedly at the eager flesh that was swelling out from the confines of his tight, black swim trunks. He shuddered and felt himself grow even harder when Sandy slowly stroked the exposed tip of his throbbing penis with a teasing finger.

She had a way of making him feel as if he was the only man in the world, Greg thought through a haze of need totally devoid of civilized restraint. Vaguely his mind registered the fact that she had freed him completely from his swimsuit to continue exploring him with nearly clinical precision.

Desperate to bury himself in her willing warmth, he

clasped the warm, naked skin of her buttocks, slid aside the tiny T-back scrap of cloth that she might as well have left off for all it covered, and raised her to meet his needy thrust.

He forced his eyelids not to close. Looking at Sandy when they were making love was worth the effort of holding back, teasing her with long, lazy strokes that made her writhe against him and tighten around him like a loving vise. The way her mouth slackened and she cried out his name made Greg feel ten feet tall. Not until he felt her jerk and constrict around him did he close his eyes and let go, thrusting one more time and giving himself up to a shattering climax.

"I love you, baby," he said, holding onto her silky thighs, not wanting to give up the pleasure of being deep inside her even after the fire inside him had been doused.

"Baby?"

"Yeah. You're my sweet, loving baby."

Sandy nuzzled at his neck like a friendly kitten. "I'm your woman, not your baby. Shana's your baby."

"Shana, and the ones we're going to have together. Still, I'll call you my baby if I want to." Greg felt himself hardening again inside Sandy. It had never felt so good, so natural, before. He had felt her hot, welcoming wetness ease his way, their body fluids mingling when he spilled his seed deep into her womb. He hadn't protected her!

"We may have one of those babies sooner than we planned, honey," he murmured as he lifted her off him and adjusted their bodies to fit side by side on the generously wide chair. "I forgot to use a condom."

"I know."

"And you didn't say anything?"

Sandy reached out and caressed his cheek. "I think I said 'Please.' " Greg met her gaze and felt the love he had been searching for since he was a boy. "I wouldn't mind getting pregnant now. I want your baby. Several of them. By the way, it's the twelfth day of my cycle," she told him with a twinkle in her eye.

"It's my professional opinion that you should start planning your wedding, then, Ms. Daniels," Greg told her, half in jest.

He wouldn't worry about how the two women he loved would get along, living for a time in the same house. Life was too short for agonizing—he would let each day take care of itself, and this time he had a feeling that while he, Shana, and Sandy would all have some adjustments to make, everything would work out just fine in the end.

Finally Greg had found a woman he could love without reservation. He hoped his good friend and new neighbor would soon be able to set aside his sadness and learn to live again.

Every day, Blake gave Erin conflicting signals. One moment he would be warm, friendly, and teasing; then he would turn cool and distant, but only with her. In the month since Jamie was born, Blake had shown nothing but constant admiration for their little boy—and Timmy, whose finalized adoption papers Blake had just brought home to her yesterday afternoon.

Blake was full of surprises, too. First, he had admitted a love for horses that he hadn't indulged for years. Tomorrow they were all going to fly out to his great-uncle's ranch southeast of Lubbock so he could pick out two or three well-behaved riding horses to have shipped home for them to ride. Excited at the prospect of renewing a childhood passion of her own, Erin stepped into the stable at the back of Blake's property, anxious to see the results of renovation work that had been going on since last week.

"I'm glad you ride. It always made me feel bad for Blake that I was scared to death of horses. You know, I think this is the first time I've ever been inside this stable."

Erin recognized Glenna's voice at once, although it took a few minutes for her to find the ghost who hovered behind the shield of a half-closed storeroom door, as if afraid of nonexistent equines in newly refurbished stalls.

"I always liked to ride. It's been years, though, since I've been on a horse."

"Blake, too. He got rid of his horses when he realized how much they frightened me. His dog, too."

Erin smiled. "I wondered if Blake would mind Timmy having a puppy. After his next surgery, that is."

"He won't mind. He would go as nuts over a dog as he has over the boys. Well, maybe not quite that nuts, but close," she admitted with an impish grin.

"Glenna, I don't know what to make of Blake. Sometimes I think you're right, that he's giving *us* a chance for a marriage that's real. But he changes with the speed of light, closes up, and won't let me in to help him heal."

Erin watched as Glenna glided closer. She could almost feel the ghostly aura. *"Those times when he shuts you out are going to get shorter and farther apart, Erin. Hang in there. Much as I hate to admit it, you're going to be a better match for our husband than I ever was. What you need to do now is get back to the house and set a scene. It's Jamie's one-month birthday, in case you forgot. Celebrate with Jamie. Then start seducing Jamie's daddy."*

Erin felt her mouth drop open. "But it's too soon for that."

"Not for candlelight dinner and a preview of what can't be for another couple of weeks, it isn't. Mark my words, Erin. Blake already wants you. Make him so hot for you that when Greg gives you the go-ahead, he won't be able to resist. I would, if I were still alive."

Erin watched as Glenna's image brightened then faded away. Then, as if compelled by some force outside herself, she strolled back to the house and made the preparations a ghost had suggested for their mutual husband's eventual seduction.

Strange as it seemed, Erin thought she heard Glenna's murmur of approval when she asked Mary to fix broiled steak, rare, with baked potatoes and a simple salad for the evening meal. After telling Mary she would see to setting the table, Erin went into the impressive dining room and stared indecisively at the table that would seat at least a dozen diners with ease.

"Not here. You want intimate, not elegant."

Erin looked around but saw nothing. Still, she was sure it was her friendly ghost when she whispered her reply. "Where, then?" she asked, certain that a reply would be forthcoming from wherever the voice had come.

"The patio. No. Too many memories for him there. I know! Your room."

"My room? No!" What would Blake think if she lured him into her bedroom for an intimate dinner, Erin thought, aghast at the ghost's audacity.

"Why not? Oh, I know! Your sitting room. It's perfect. I hated that strange-shaped little alcove—never used it. Blake won't have any old memories in there. Is there a table?"

"Yes. It's triangular. And there are two chairs. They're covered with blue paisley print that would go with those dishes," Erin offered, more comfortable knowing she wouldn't be eating a meal with Blake while a king-sized bed dominated their view. She pointed toward a stack of dark blue pottery plates. "But there's nothing romantic . . ."

"Not now. But there will be. Get two of those awful plates. They used to belong to Blake's grandmother. He likes them because they'll hold a huge hunk of steak. And find his mother's gold-plated silverware. I hated it, so he hasn't seen it for years."

Erin felt as railroaded as she imagined Blake was going to feel when she tricked him into an intimate meal for two, for God's sake, to celebrate their baby's one-month birthday. "Will these glasses do?" she asked, barely whispering for fear Mary would hear her and think she had gone over the deep end.

The two crystal flutes levitated out of Erin's hand as if by magic and returned to their places in the china cabinet. As she stood aghast, two pale carnival glass saucer champagne glasses levitated gracefully out of the cabinet and nestled in her hands. *"Use these,"* the voice commanded sweetly.

When the table setting met her exacting standards, Glenna's ghost nudged Erin up into the attic where she found a pleasant landscape scene and several accent pieces to lend some of her own personality to the coldly elegant bedroom and sitting room.

"He'll like it—and you," were Glenna's parting words as Erin surveyed the scene.

While she nursed Jamie, Erin looked forward to the two hours she would have to ready herself for what the ghost was sure would be a momentous evening at home with Blake. Impulsively she called Mary on the intercom and asked her to feed Timmy early so he could have a good rest before the next day's planned excursion. Then she handed her well-fed, sleeping baby to Miguel's daughter Theresa and closed herself into her dressing room with a sigh of relief.

She rifled through her limited wardrobe, finally choosing a body-skimming caftan woven of dark blue cotton shot with metallic threads of gold. It had to have appealed to Blake in the store, she assumed, since he had bought it for her the day after Jamie was born. Erin hoped that tonight it would appeal to him even more when it skimmed curves finally pared almost down to size after a month's careful eating and exercise.

She opened a drawer and pulled out a set of the plain white nursing bra and panties that had become her lingerie "uniform" since her baby's birth. Then she put them back and got out a scandalously brief navy satin bra and panty set Sandy had laughingly given her before she married Blake.

Holding the scrap of a bra up against her swollen breasts,

Erin grinned. She could wear the set and look far sexier than its maker had probably intended—and she would, even if Blake never knew that beneath his tasteful, luxurious gift was underwear that Sandy had assured her would raise the interest of a dead man.

Luxuriating in the ritual of beautifying her body, Erin methodically waxed her legs. She had always hated the feel of razor stubble, so much that she hardly felt the sting anymore when she jerked off each strip of hardened wax.

Next, she dumped fragrant oil into the tub while it filled with water, letting the hot dampness permeate her naked body as she shampooed her hair and applied a light cleansing mask to her face. Now, she thought self-indulgently, she was ready for her bath.

"You're going to knock him clear off his feet." Glenna laughed when Erin reflexively crossed her hands across her breasts. *"What's that fragrance?"*

"Something Sandy got some free samples of at *Le Parfumerie*. The bath oil came out of that tube over on the makeup table."

She watched Glenna glide over and pick up the tiny sample container. *"I don't believe this! Erin, this is an omen."*

"What do you mean?"

"Do you know what this is?"

What was Glenna getting at? "It's *La Mer l'Été*. It means 'Summer Sea.' Just like it says on the package."

"Blake bought me a huge bottle of the perfume once, after he smelled it on a woman in the shop. He loved it. On her. Unfortunately, when I put it on, I smelled almost like a scared skunk. He was awfully disappointed."

Glenna's grin told Erin her memory was happy, not sad. "You don't think I should wear it?"

"Oh, yes, you definitely should wear it. You should run out and buy the biggest bottles you can find—perfume, bath oil—the works! It smells the way it's supposed to on you. Blake won't be able to keep his hands to himself, not that he would be for long, in any case."

"You really think so?"

"Yeah. I do. Relax and enjoy your bath. I'm going to make myself scarce." With that, Glenna faded away, leaving Erin to her bath and her reading.

Half an hour later, the timer's shrill buzz brought Erin from the fantasy world she had found in her book, a historical romance that featured a feisty noblewoman helplessly in love with the scoundrel who had abducted and seduced her. She set the book down and climbed reluctantly from her bath to subject herself to icy needles of water pulsing from four jets in the separate shower.

Rough-soft terry cloth soaked up the water from her skin, leaving a faint, sweet smell of lemon, flowers, and herbs. Beginning with her toes and working all the way up to her neck, Erin massaged cool lotion into her skin, strengthening the fragrance just a bit. Finally she took up the tiny, precious vial that held pure essence of *La Mer l'Été* and dotted drops of it between her breasts, at each elbow, and on the back side of each knee.

For the first time in more years than she could count, Erin felt pretty and sexy as she stepped into tiny bikini panties and looked critically at her image in the mirror. Her tummy still looked a little convex, and her legs could use a bit more firming exercise—but all in all, she was pleased. If tonight was to be the night for Blake to see her body for the first time, she imagined that he wouldn't be too disappointed.

After all, he saw her breasts almost every day when he watched her nurse their baby. And he'd seen *down there*, too, Erin recalled, blushing at the memory of his stepping down to get a good look at Jamie emerging from her straining body. Not a sight to set a man's blood boiling, she told herself as she lifted her breasts into the underwired half-cups of the navy bra and snapped the front fastener closed.

Erin glanced at the clock. Blake would be home soon, and she wanted to be ready. Hurriedly she dried her hair, applied light makeup, and slipped into the caftan, noting with satisfaction how it lightly skimmed her body, emphasizing her new slimness with a subtlety that totally belied the frankly sexy way she felt inside. As she stepped out of the dressing room, she heard Blake's voice from Jamie's room.

"Would you like to bring Jamie in the sitting room?" Erin asked as she joined Blake in the nursery. "He could join us while we enjoy his birthday dinner."

Blake regarded his sleeping baby. "Maybe we should let him sleep. I brought him a pony," he said, reaching into the crib and showing Erin the black-and-white stuffed animal. "It's got a music box inside." Before setting it down, he wound it up and grinned as a tinkly version of "Home on the Range" began to play.

"You're spoiling him." Erin's words were mildly scolding, but her smile conveyed approval. "We have dinner waiting," she told him.

"Where?"

"In the sitting room."

At least it wasn't in her bedroom, where Blake knew damn well he wouldn't be able to keep his thoughts off that wide, inviting bed! "I'll wash up and join you in a minute," he told her as they left the nursery together, trying to remember where he had smelled that perfume of hers before.

I should have brought Jamie in here with us. Timmy, too. But Blake doubted that much of anything could take his mind off that clean but strangely seductive smell of Erin's perfume. He tried to put it out of his mind, but he couldn't. It evoked some memory, as well as getting him so hard he could barely stand it.

The food was great, but for all the enjoyment Blake got from it, the prime New York strip steak might just as well have been old shoe leather. Try as he might, he couldn't take his eyes off Erin. She had always been attractive. Tonight, though, with her shoulder-length hair loosely curled around a face that glowed with good health, Erin was striking.

Her blue eyes sparkled, complemented by the dark blue of the caftan he had impulsively bought for her while she was in the hospital. From what he could tell, for the graceful garment loosely skimmed the body he was dying to explore, her ripe womanly curves were honed to firm perfection.

God, how she and that elusive, airy scent she was wearing turned him on! Blake wanted her badly, and from the looks she gave him, he knew she wanted him, too.

What else could they talk about? he wondered. Before they had finished their steaks, they had exhausted the subject of their planned trip to his great-uncle's. They had proudly praised Jamie and Timmy's accomplishments over salad. Blake was desperate to keep the conversation going, if for no other reason than to keep his mind off what he knew he could not have—at least not now.

"Greg bought Sandy a ring today," he confided as he sank a fork into a piece of apple pie. "What would you think about our giving them an engagement party three weeks from this Friday?"

Erin's smile nearly took his breath away. "Sandy would love it! She told me yesterday that she wished she could afford to give a small party so she could show Greg off to her friends from school. It won't be too expensive if I have her keep her guest list small. I can handwrite the invitations, and we can serve cake and maybe some simple sandwiches."

Blake held up a hand to stave off Erin's enthusiastic planning. "I'm not worried about the cost, Erin. Greg is one of my closest friends, and after all, Sandy is my sister-in-law. Besides, the party will be a good setting to introduce you as my wife," he added as he recalled Kay Halpern's snide remarks the day Jamie was born.

"Oh. How many people are we talking about?" Erin asked warily.

"A hundred or so, plus your and Sandy's friends—give or take. A cocktail dance would probably work best for that many guests, don't you think?"

Erin raised her eyebrows expressively. "I think that's an awfully big party to put together in three weeks' time. I suppose I can do it, though." The long, slender fingers of her left hand tapped out a nervous rhythm on the smoked glass tabletop.

"You'll have plenty of help," he said, wanting to allay her obvious discomfort at the thought of hosting such a large gathering.

He felt her smile all the way down to his stomach, and beyond. It made him want to leap across the table and gather her in his arms. "Sharon will do the invitations and make most of the arrangements," he said, trying to focus on anything except Erin's soft, infinitely kissable mouth.

"Sharon?"

"What? Oh, Sharon's my secretary. Remember, she came to visit while you were in the hospital."

"Oh. She won't mind? I don't imagine that planning parties is part of her job description." Erin's blue eyes twinkled when she teased Blake, and that only made him want her more.

"Actually, it is. Sharon has always taken care of planning personal as well as business entertaining. I think she gets a kick out of it. How long will it take you to get together a list of people you want to invite?" he asked.

"I can meet with Sandy after we get back tomorrow, and give you names and addresses in a day or two. Blake, we're going to need every bit of space we can find to accommodate such a big crowd. Do you think the weather will still be nice enough to use the patio as well as inside?"

Blake forced a smile. He and Glenna had hosted many a glittering party here, and the house was plenty big to entertain two hundred or more people in comfort. But there were too many memories. "I want to have the party at the country club," he told Erin decisively.

"Why?"

Because I'm not ready. I don't know if I'll ever be ready to laugh and be happy in the home I shared with Glenna.

"Because it will be easier for you," he replied without his usual candor. He didn't want that soft, pleased expression to vanish from Erin's lovely face. He couldn't bear the thought of hurting her. He wanted . . .

Abruptly Blake stood and went to Erin with two quick steps. Grasping her shoulders, he pulled her to her feet and held her at arm's length.

"Oh, hell," he muttered, drawing her close enough that he could feel her warm, moist breath against his chest, "this is what I want, and you've been telling me all evening with those sweet, soft looks that you want it, too."

When he heard no protest and felt her pulse quicken against his fingers, he bent and kissed those soft, inviting lips. Gentle at first, feeling his way into uncharted territory, Blake soon unleashed the fierce desire that had been riding him for weeks. His tongue sought and found entrance, and he drank in her sweetness like a man long starved.

It was heaven, holding her—and hell, knowing he couldn't invade her body the way his tongue was ravishing her mouth. Still, he sought more torture as he tugged down the zipper of her caftan and stroked the satiny fullness of breasts barely contained by some silky scrap of a bra.

She smelled like flowers and musk and woman, he thought as he laid a path of openmouthed kisses down her neck. When he reached her bra, he nuzzled it out of the way and closed his lips around a tight bud of a nipple that he had been dreaming of for days. With his tongue he teased at the pebbly nub until it rewarded him with a sweet, hot taste of the milk that sustained his son.

He was so hard he thought he just might die. And she wasn't helping the matter, either, the way she pressed her hips to his and rocked languidly back and forth against the swollen evidence of his need. Following the oldest instincts in the world, Blake scooped Erin into his arms and headed for the nearest bed.

"We can't," she protested as he laid her down and stood back to get rid of his clothes. "It's too soon. The baby . . ."

"I know."

What had he been thinking of? Hell, he knew exactly what he'd been thinking with, and it certainly wasn't his brain! "I'm sorry." He sat down on the edge of the bed and reached for Erin's hand.

"It's all right." Her face was flushed, her eyes dreamy. She had obviously wanted him as much as he wanted her— if that were possible.

He held her gaze and rubbed his thumbs across the palms of both her hands until he found his voice to speak. "Erin, I know I told you before we married that I didn't want a sexual relationship—in the foreseeable future, was the way I think I expressed it. Well, in case you haven't already guessed, I'd better tell you I foresee wanting one damn soon now."

He felt her hands curl and tighten around his. "All right," she said, her voice low and husky, and sexy as the devil.

Suddenly he pictured Glenna's face, and he drew his hands away from Erin's. "I hope that doesn't bother you half as much as it's tearing me up inside with guilt," he whispered, barely loud enough for himself to hear, as he stood and mentally prepared himself to face another hard, lonely night alone.

"Blake was the one who thought of our having this party for you and Greg," Erin replied when her sister began thanking her effusively for all she and Blake were doing to celebrate her engagement. "Don't ask me what made him think about it in the first place, but he brought up the subject last week while we were having dinner to celebrate Jamie's one-month birthday."

Sandy grinned. "I wouldn't have believed your husband

had a romantic bone in his gorgeous body,'' she remarked casually.

''I don't know that he does.'' But Erin hoped the new, friendly way Blake had been treating her lately might mean he was thinking about her with more than just the physical attraction he had reluctantly confessed that night. Needing someone to talk with, she told Sandy about the dinner and what had followed.

''I worried about Blake all that night, after he stormed out of my room, but by the next morning he seemed to have shaken off whatever remorse he'd been feeling,'' Erin concluded. ''For the most part, he has acted like a different man from the one I'd gotten to know.'' Erin lifted a deceptively plain black silk dress that looked almost like a floor-length slip from a Neiman-Marcus dress box and put it onto a padded hanger in her closet as she chatted with her sister.

''Different how?'' Sandy asked, her eyes bright with excitement as she reviewed the list of guests who had accepted invitations to her engagement party.

Erin smiled. ''More open. I don't know. It just seems that once he took the boys and me to his great-uncle's last week, Blake has been easy to be with. Fun. Would you believe he looks even better in tight jeans and cowboy boots than he does in his suits?''

''I'd believe that.''

''You would. I never would have thought Blake loved being outdoors the way he does. Until we went to get the horses, the only exercise I'd seen him doing was pumping iron in his gym—and swimming. But he rides like a rodeo champ, and I can almost *feel* his excitement when he's around the horses. I believe Blake would be as happy being a rancher as he is practicing law.''

''How many horses do you have? And how long have they been here?''

''Three. A black colt, a dappled gray pony, and the chestnut mare he picked out for me. They arrived Monday, in an air-conditioned horse trailer, no less."

"You must be thrilled. I remember how much you used to love to ride." Sandy set aside the guest list and curled up on the love seat in Erin's bedroom.

"I am. I was shocked when I found out Blake loves horses as much as I do. I probably never would have found out if I hadn't gotten curious and asked why he kept that big field behind the house fenced in, with nothing except grass growing in it. After he showed me the stable and told me about the horses he'd always had when he was a boy, I admitted that riding used to be one of my favorite pastimes."

"So he just decided, like that, to go get some four-legged transportation?" Sandy shook her head.

Erin smiled. "Well, he did arrange to have the stable fixed up first. That took two weeks. Then, last weekend, Blake loaded Timmy, Jamie, and me into the plane he keeps over at the executive airstrip and flew us to his great-uncle's ranch outside Lubbock. He picked out the horses there."

Sandy sighed. "I don't suppose he'd let my future stepdaughter ride one of them. On top of everything else I've got to do, Shana has decided she *has* to ride every day after she comes to stay with Greg and me. Guess who gets to take the princess to her riding club? It's twenty miles one way, so I'll be stuck there for two hours every evening while she has her lessons."

"You can ask him." Erin still didn't know Blake well enough to guess his feelings about sharing—especially something he cared about as much as he did those horses. What few comments she had heard him make about Greg's daughter hadn't given her the impression that Shana was one of his favorite people.

"I will."

Erin smiled. No one could accuse her little sister of lacking nerve. She hoped that spunk would keep Sandy going when dealing with her husband's daughter became a fact of her daily life.

Looking at Sandy greeting friends and strangers with equal aplomb, Erin couldn't help feeling an almost motherly pride. Her baby sister was all grown up, poised and sophisticated in a forest-green halter gown of silk charmeuse. Sandy had chosen well. The deceptively simple gown and upswept chestnut curls accentuated her beauty and made an elegant backdrop for Greg's engagement gifts—a beautifully cut diamond solitaire and the modest diamond studs she wore in her ears.

As Sandy stood there between Greg and his mother Sadie, greeting their guests and acting as if she had been doing this society thing all her life, she radiated confidence Erin was trying hard to emulate. No one would guess, Erin knew, that Sadie's approval had come grudgingly, or that the absence of Greg's daughter from the receiving line had been a subject of much dissention.

They presented a picture of unity that belied underlying ripples of one-upmanship in the game of jockeying for first place in poor Greg's life. Erin shuddered inside. She would hate having to tiptoe around Sadie Halpern. Never mind that the woman was currently beaming and chattering her approval of her son's coming marriage to everyone she greeted. Beneath Sadie's disarming smile and glittering gown of royal blue sequins, Erin knew, was a mother whose major function in life was trying to manipulate her only son.

"Where's Shana?" Blake whispered during a lull in the stream of arriving guests.

Erin tilted her head to meet his gaze. "Over there. She decided to skip the receiving line."

He looked away from her toward the sullen preteen whose expression of studied boredom would have done justice to a jaded thirty-year-old. Erin thought of Sandy at that age, when she had come to live with her and Bill, sweet

and eager to please despite having just lost her parents—
and the comparison made her furious. Shana was doing her
level best to make Sandy's—and her father's—lives hell
on earth, for no reason Erin could see except perhaps that
doing it amused the kid.

"I don't envy Sandy or Greg, either, having to deal with
the little monster Kay has created," Blake offered under
his breath, sliding the hand at Erin's back up a little and
massaging at skin left bare above her waist with a circular
motion of his thumb. "Judge Adkins. You've already met
Erin," he said heartily to the man who had performed their
wedding. "Erin, this is the judge's granddaughter, Julie."

*"She's a lawyer with the state attorney's office. Tried
that mass murderer last year."* The voice of the ghost came
out of nowhere, into Erin's ear.

"I'm glad to meet you, Julie. I followed the Harvey case
on TV. It must have been exciting, working to convict
him."

Julie smiled and murmured thanks for Erin's praise.
More guests came in, and Erin turned to greet them, too.

Blake suddenly bent his head and whispered into Erin's
ear. "Oh, God! I didn't realize we'd invited *her*!"

*"For God's sake, Erin, don't compliment this one on
her dress. You'll never get rid of her. She'll tell you who
designed it and why she wore it tonight. If you let her, she'll
even tell you who designed and why she didn't wear everything else in her closet."*

Glenna's ghost was driving Erin nuts; but as the evening
went on, she noticed Blake's admiring glances. He seemed
to like the tactful way she was able to greet his guests.
Finally they disbanded the receiving line and adjourned to
a big, round table at a corner of the dance floor.

The volume of the music from a small, skilled band increased almost imperceptibly. Erin watched waiters scur-
rying around to keep the buffet tables filled and drink
orders flowing from three bars.

This is a cocktail buffet? Erin stood at the serving table, a plate poised in one hand as she tried to choose from an array that included the cold roast beef, turkey, and cheeses, and trays of vegetables and dip that she had suggested, along with a selection of hot dishes that came as a complete surprise to her.

There were meatballs, croquettes, and several savory-smelling casseroles. Erin counted at least five different shapes and varieties in the silver basket filled with delectable-looking rolls and muffins. She selected some food and went back to the table.

"My mom has a diamond three times as big as this," Shana was saying after lifting Sandy's hand to inspect her ring. "The ring Dad gave Mom was even bigger and better than yours. She had it made into a pendant, you know."

Greg had gone to fill Sadie's plate, and Shana was on the loose. Glancing at Sandy with sympathy, Erin suppressed an urge to shake Greg's daughter until her bright, silvery braces popped out of her head.

"Shana. That's enough," Sadie said sharply before turning to Sandy, whose mouth was trembling almost imperceptibly. "Sandy, dear, don't mind her. Every little girl is just the least bit jealous of any woman who attracts her dad's attention."

"Here you go, Mother." Greg set a plate down in front of Sadie and took his seat between her and Sandy. "What's the matter, princess?" he asked Shana, whose pout let everyone know she wasn't happy with the situation.

"None of my friends are here," she groused.

Erin could have reached over and kissed Blake when he spoke up. "Whose fault is that, young lady? Sandy and Erin both asked you who you would like to have here. And my secretary spoke to you again before the invitations went out. Come on, relax and be happy for your dad."

The conversation warmed, and Erin could see Sandy relaxing again, basking in Greg's obvious adoration. She was watching Sandy float gracefully around the dance floor in Greg's close embrace when her ghostly friend appeared in a haze of pale gold dust on the other side of the room.

"Ask him to dance," she mouthed, inclining her head toward Blake as her image faded away.

Blake looked surprised when Erin tapped his shoulder and gestured toward the dance floor, but he politely rose and held her chair. Taking her hand, he led her onto the highly polished raised surface and took her in his arms.

"You look beautiful tonight," he murmured politely as they swayed in time to a sweet, romantic tune.

"You, too." Blake looked good enough to eat in stark black formal attire, Erin had decided the moment he came into her room, ready to take her to this party. The brilliant white of the crisp, tucked shirt made his healthy, tanned skin seem vibrant with life. She hadn't wanted to stop looking at him, as if he were a tempting sweet placed just outside her greedy reach.

"Sandy and Greg make a good couple."

Erin sighed. "I hope they can survive adjusting to Shana," she said, her body relaxing against Blake when she felt his arm tighten around her.

"And Mom Sadie. At least she won't put up with Shana's being outright rude."

"I noticed."

"Do all kids get obnoxious like that when they get to be her age?" Blake asked, his tone conveying a tiny bit of alarm at what might lie ahead for them with their boys.

Erin tilted her head back and looked into his eyes. "I hope not," she replied, smiling.

"Me, too. Come on," he said when the music stopped and he headed them toward the bandstand.

Blake's arm felt good around her as they stood there and he made the formal announcement of Sandy's engagement to Greg. She felt herself flush with pleasure when he adlibbed, "And for those of you who haven't met her yet, this is Sandy's sister—my beautiful bride, Erin."

The next time they danced, Blake was the one doing the asking. And Erin thought he held her a little closer . . . felt the rush of his warm breath against her hair . . . allowed a hopeful anticipation to grow in her that he was starting to feel more for her than just the tentative friendship they had begun to form.

"Do you know what you do to me?" he growled as they danced the night's last dance together. Now he molded her body to his own and held her there with both arms wrapped like tender tentacles around her waist. His fingers played havoc with her senses when he rubbed them softly over her bare back.

"I think so." Erin knew exactly what she was doing to him, because he was doing the same thing to her. She felt warm and languid, her whole body sensitized to his. Deep inside her, she melted and readied herself for the hard, hot length of him that burned through the layers of their clothes.

She wondered if tonight he would act on the desire he could not hide, and her heart beat faster.

Chapter 15

"I'll see you in the morning," Blake told Erin brusquely after they had checked on Jamie. He practically ran from the nursery into the room where he slept, because he knew that if he didn't, nothing in the world would keep him from betraying his wife and making love to the woman who had him so hard and aching he could hardly stand up.

Erin had wanted him to stay. He knew from the look in those dark, entrancing eyes that his abrupt departure had hurt her. God, he didn't want that, any more than he wanted to indulge his body while he subjected his mind to the worst kind of guilt trip he could imagine.

For a long time, Blake sat there staring into the darkened hallway. He tried to picture Glenna, but only Erin came to mind.

"Damn it to hell!" he muttered as he got up and started to undress. He could take care of the throbbing ache in his groin the way he'd done several times this last month and a half. Why didn't that appeal to him one tenth as much as tossing away his misgivings and crawling into bed with the enticing woman across the hall?

My wife. The mother of my son. No, sons. But she's not really my wife. Glenna is, and she's gone.

He heard the nursery door close softly and turned to glance into the hall. The pale, yellowish light from Erin's room cast shadows on the walls. He looked toward the light.

Her hair was loose, wild, and windblown now, when at the party it had rippled against her shoulders in soft, ordered curls. He watched her raise her arms to lift off that clinging, satin gown that had left the supple skin of her back bare to his touch.

She had on black panty hose, so sheer they hinted at the ivory skin beneath them. No, by God, they were thigh-high stockings held up by skinny, black, lace straps. Then she tossed aside her dress and bra. She just stood there in plain view, her body backlit by that soft, diffused light, wearing nothing but those stockings and the flimsy black garter belt that held them on her. Blake felt ready to explode.

Don't look, he told himself, but there was no way his senses were going to obey. He had denied them for months; now they were going to have their way. Almost as if under a tantalizing witch's spell, Blake took that first step toward Erin.

By the time he reached her door, he had his cummerbund off and cuff links loosened. When he stopped three feet away from her and met her gaze, he'd worked loose all but two of the onyx studs that secured his shirt. In the time it took for him to walk into her outstretched arms, Blake managed to toss his suspenders and shirt carelessly onto the floor.

"Witch," he muttered as his lips clamped down on hers and drank ravenously of her sweetness. He let his hands roam freely, from the tender small of her back that had tantalized him all evening long to the firm, shapely cheeks of her backside that filled his hands with velvety, naked skin and the textured feel of lace garters that pressed against his palm and reminded him how damn hot and hard he had gotten, just watching her strip off that slinky black satin gown.

Her hands were exploring him, too, first hesitantly and then with a fervor that hinted at her need. When he felt her working at the buttons of his tux pants, he damn nearly came on the spot.

"Some other time, honey," he rasped out as he captured her questing hands and brought them to his lips. "Your little striptease has me so ready, I don't trust myself to let you touch me." With more haste than finesse, he undid his pants and lowered them along with his briefs.

"Oh, my."

"Oh, what?" Blake was in a hurry, and his socks didn't seem to want to cooperate.

"You're . . ."

"Do you like what you see?" The second sock finally came off, and Blake threw it into the corner of the room before dragging Erin down onto the bed and covering her body with his own. "I asked you, honey, if you approve," he prompted as he cupped a silky breast with one hand and nuzzled at the nipple with his mouth.

"Uh-huh. You've got a great body."

"So do you." He splayed his hand across her newly flattened belly and felt a few faintly raised spidery lines that only heightened his desire. "Is this okay for you?" he asked, reminded that only seven weeks ago she had borne his son.

"It's fine."

She stroked him, from the back of his head where her fingers gently tugged at strands of his hair, down his back and lower, where she tickled at the indentations at the base of his spine. She was driving him to the brink of insanity.

"Tell me what you like, honey. I'm not going to last very long tonight," he murmured against the velvety softness of her breasts.

As if in answer, she opened to him, inviting a more intimate touch. As carefully as he could, he stroked the heat of her womanhood, testing her readiness before venturing inside her wet, waiting warmth with a gentle finger.

"There's a condom in the drawer," she told him breathlessly as he withdrew his finger and started to pull her hips into position beneath his.

For a moment he just stared at her. Why would she worry about *that*? They were married, weren't they? Then, unwilling to spoil the moment with conversation or wait longer to fulfill his body's aching need, he reached over and fumbled for a small, foil packet.

"May I?" she asked, propping her head up with one hand as she visually inspected him.

His hands shook. He wanted her so badly, he'd never get the thing on by himself. On the other hand, if she touched him, it just might be all over. Gathering the last shreds of control he could find in himself, he handed her the packet and muttered between clenched teeth, "Be my guest. Just hurry."

By the time she sheathed him, he'd lost his sanity. Without finesse, he rolled her over and entered her in one long, hard stroke. He felt her shudder, and wondered through a fog of mindless passion if he had hurt her. Then, when she wrapped her smooth legs possessively around his waist, he knew it was desire, not pain, that drove her now.

He wanted to bring her pleasure. But it had been so long, and she felt so damn good! He gritted his teeth and tried to hold back, but when she tightened around him and milked him when he partially withdrew, it was too much. He couldn't stop himself. He pounded into her with short, hard thrusts until just seconds later he buried himself to the hilt and came.

He seemed completely drained, Erin thought as she held him against her breasts and stroked his silky hair off his forehead. Drained, not satisfied. For the first time since their sad, separate wedding night when he had sobbed alone, she had seen Blake lose control.

He was a magnificent specimen, she decided as she watched him in the dim, seductive light that neither of them had bothered to douse. He didn't have a lot of body hair, but the light dusting of silky, dark curls that shadowed his muscled arms and chest just emphasized his masculinity.

She knew he had shaved before the party; still, just hours later, she could make out the stubbly beginnings of a heavy beard. Her breasts tingled, as if they liked the prickly feel of his cheek as much as she had relished it while they were making love.

Remembering the sterile terms of their marriage agreement, Erin tried to tell herself that what had just happened was just pure and simple sex—a man and a woman put in close proximity with one another, giving in to the universal need to satisfy an urge to mate. But she was afraid that, for her, there was much more to it than that.

Just then, Blake stirred, his lips making contact with her nipple and teasing it to attention. "Again?" she murmured as her hands moved to stroke his hard, flat belly.

"I always try to give as good as I get, honey," he told her sleepily as he moved lower, grazing her belly with a rough, pebbly tongue . . . nuzzling at the damp curls between her legs before placing gentle nips on the inside of her thighs. Then he took her in his mouth and loved her that way until she begged for mercy.

"You want more?" His pupils were dilated, the muscles of his neck constricted. Erin lowered her gaze and found he was more than ready to take her again. "Yeah, I want you, too," he growled. "Reach over and get another one of those damn things if you really want me to use it this time."

She reached down instead and cupped him gently in both hands. "Greg didn't want me to take the pill while I'm nursing Jamie," she told him regretfully, because there was nothing at the moment that she wanted more than to take his naked body into hers and feel as if they were one. He was big and hard and beautiful, and for just this moment, he was hers. "You don't want to take a chance on another baby so soon, do you?"

Blake scowled, but the softness of his voice belied his

expression. "I just don't like it. The guy who said it felt like taking a shower in a raincoat had a point," he teased as she smoothed soft, pliable latex over him with what she knew was excessive attention to detail.

This time, their loving was slower—and more tender, Erin thought as she came down from an explosive climax. They had come together, something that had never happened to her before; and she felt sleepily content.

"G'night," Blake muttered, his head half covered by a pillow. Then he sat up as if stunned. "Oh, my God!" he said, and Erin didn't know if he was praying or swearing.

"What's wrong?" She reached out to touch him, but he moved out of her reach as if she were poison.

He picked up one of the gossamer sheer black stockings he had skimmed down her leg an hour earlier and crumpled it in a trembling fist. It seemed to Erin that he was groping for words to express whatever it was he was feeling.

Finally he spoke, his voice hardly more than a whisper. "Glenna's dead. She's hardly been gone six months, and here I am making love with you. What's more, I enjoyed every minute of it. I could do it again right now, and several times more before the sun comes up."

Blake paused, his fingers loosening around the stocking he had worked into a tight, wrinkled mass. He met her gaze before going on. "Erin, I'm not over Glenna. I don't know if I ever will be. Every time I touch you—hell, every time I look at you, and want you, I feel this awful guilt. I'm not being fair to you when I feel like this. Damn it to hell, I feel as if I'm being unfaithful to her!"

Erin felt silent tears rush down her cheeks as she watched Blake storm out of the room. She had thought she could make him care for her; the ghost of his dead wife had believed she could. But they were wrong. Glenna's hold on Blake, even in death, was so strong Erin knew now it would never let him go.

And Erin realized that she had fallen in love with Blake—deep down, head-over-heels in love. She curled up where they had made love moments earlier and pictured a long, miserable life ahead, tied by her love for her children to a man to whom she would never be more than a friend— and maybe a lover on those occasions when his libido over-ruled his heart.

Blake didn't want to be alone, yet he couldn't stay with Erin and not want to touch and taste and devour every square inch of the body that turned him inside out and made him forget he would always belong to Glenna. Still naked, he went into the nursery and scooped his sleeping baby gently out of the crib.

For a long time, he just held Jamie, rocking back and forth in the old oak chair he vaguely remembered from long ago, when any one of several faceless nannies had soothed his childish dreams and given him the affection neither of his parents had had time for.

That affection had been paid for by the hour. Blake hadn't known honest caring until he was five, when a tiny blond angel befriended him, he reminded himself as he absently stroked the baby's back through the soft terry cloth of his sleeper. He choked back a cry.

As if he felt his father's anguish, Jamie began to stir against Blake's chest, his little mouth open and searching. "That's one thing I can't do for you," he said, his melancholy lessening as he deftly changed a soggy diaper and stuffed the baby into a clean, dry sleeper.

In the weeks since Jamie's birth, Blake had taken him to Erin countless times. Tonight, though, he hesitated at the door he himself had closed behind him when he left her bed. At the sound of the baby's impatient howl, he pushed aside his reluctance and strode into Erin's room.

"He's hungry," Blake said unnecessarily, for their son was making that fact abundantly clear.

Erin's head emerged from under the embroidered navy blue sheet. Had she been sleeping, or hiding from the hurt he knew he must have inflicted on her earlier with his

abrupt attack of conscience? Blake thought he saw the re-
mains of tears on her smooth, soft cheeks, but he couldn't
be sure because she turned away when he laid the baby in
her arms.

"Do you want a gown or something?" he asked, noticing that she wore nothing except the precariously draped
sheet.

"Don't you?"

"What? Oh, yeah." Blake scooped up his briefs from
where they had fallen and jerked them on. *Funny,* he
thought, *I can't get my pants on fast enough now, and just
a few hours ago I nearly killed myself getting them off in
record time.* Self-conscious, he practically ran into Erin's
dressing room and rifled through drawers to find something,
anything to shield her from his gaze.

"Here," he said, thrusting the first garment he had found
at her, "put this on. I'll hold Jamie," he added, taking the
baby and turning to stare out the window at the pool.

He knew Erin was putting on whatever he brought her,
because he could hear the soft rustle of material as she
shook it out and slipped it over her head. But he wasn't
going to watch. He couldn't. With softly murmured words,
he tried to soothe an indignant baby who suddenly wanted
nothing except his mother.

"I'll feed him now."

Blake didn't want to turn around and face her, but he
walked to the bed and deposited Jamie in her arms. "I'm
sorry about tonight," he said, reading the sadness in her
solemn gaze. When he felt she was going to open up his
wounds again by rehashing his parting words, he added,
"Can we talk about it later?"

"All right."

"I'm not very good company, I'm afraid. I'll see you in
the morning." And with that, he left her to nurse their baby.
But he couldn't make himself close the doors between their
rooms.

Chapter 16

Glenna

*B*lake!

It was all Glenna could do to stay in the shadows, to restrain herself from materializing and giving him a piece of her mind.

Glenna sighed as she settled back in a dark corner of the expansive hall that connected the rooms of the suite she once shared with Blake. She had expected to feel jealousy tonight, for all the brave words she'd spouted to Erin about wanting her and Blake to have a real, loving marriage together.

There was a twinge of envy, I'll admit. But mostly I felt relief. Relief that Blake was finally coming out of the darkness I inflicted on him and getting ready to live again.

And anger! Now I'm just damn mad.

She had felt a sort of smug self-satisfaction when she'd watched Blake stalk across the hall, disrobing as he went. Seeing them together earlier at the party they gave for Greg and Sandy, she had known Blake's resistance to his new wife's charm was hanging by a thread.

Glenna had deliberately left them alone as they sank onto the big, new bed in a tangle of long arms and legs. Staying would have been too hard. Her love for Blake didn't allow her that kind of detachment, even if she could have with-stood feeling like a voyeuristic intruder.

She hoped Blake had, at least, given Erin pleasure before he broke her heart with some infernally honest admission of ... of what? All she *knew* was that after Blake slammed out of the big master bedroom, Erin had lain there, covers clutched tensely between long, slender fingers while her shoulders trembled and tears poured down her cheeks.

And she had seen Blake take refuge in the nursery, holding on to baby Jamie like the lifeline Glenna suspected he had suddenly become, emerging and giving Erin a half-hearted apology only when the baby demanded succor at his mother's breast.

"*What am I going to do with you?*" Glenna asked her husband in a tone so hushed that only she could hear. Suddenly she could hear Blake's parting words from some place far, far away.

"*Erin, I'm not over Glenna. I don't know if I ever will be. Every time I touch you—hell, every time I look at you, and want you, I feel this awful guilt. I'm not being fair to you when I feel like this. Damn it to hell, I feel as if I'm being unfaithful to her!*"

Glenna stomped her foot silently against the granite slabs that paved the hallway. "*How could you?*" she asked.

I know what I'd have done if you'd ever pulled a stunt like that on me! You'd better be glad you never brought another woman into our marriage bed, Blake Tanner!

I wouldn't have lain there with tears in my eyes and let you get by with telling me you loved someone else and walking out. It wouldn't have made a damn bit of difference to me whether the woman were dead or alive! I'd have ...

I'd have snatched up that big amethyst crystal I used to keep on the nightstand by the bed and cracked it over your dumb, unfeeling skull. Then ...

Glenna grinned at the mental picture of hard, brittle crystal fracturing over Blake's unsuspecting head. It felt exhilarating—almost as if she were alive again, she decided—

to give a human emotion like jealousy and anger free rein, if only for a moment.

Could I go to Blake? Make him realize I'm gone and that he needs to let go of what's in the past and live for now and tomorrow?

Glenna shook her head. Never could she reveal herself to him, no matter how much she wanted to. She had decided that months ago, and nothing had happened to make her change her mind. Willing herself into Erin's presence, she materialized at the foot of the king-sized bed.

What can I say to make her hurt less?

At a loss for words, Glenna stood and looked down on Erin, who had finally fallen asleep with tiny Jamie curled contentedly in her arms. She wouldn't wake Erin now, she decided.

Maybe she would leave the task of smoothing Erin's battered feelings to her husband—he had always been good at giving comfort, at least to her. After all, Glenna couldn't help feeling that since Blake had been the one dishing out the pain, he was the only one who could truly ease it.

"I hope Blake's hurting as much as he hurt her tonight with his thoughtless honesty," Glenna whispered to the wind as she slowly faded into the limbo she couldn't escape until she righted the wrongs her well-meant actions had brought to the ones she loved.

Chapter 17

Blake pounded a fist into his pillow. He might as well get up, because tonight sleep was out of the question.

Visions of a dark, sensual lover mingled in his head with those of a sweet madonna nursing her baby. And a disturbingly fuzzy picture of Glenna tortured Blake throughout the night.

He might as well never have gone to bed at all, he told himself as he watched the sun rise through a long, narrow window that overlooked the stable.

Cursing Glenna and Erin and the whole damn situation he was in, Blake stumbled out of bed and called Greg. He figured a long, hard ride would either wake him up or get him so damn exhausted he might be able to get some rest. Then he threw on jeans and a shirt before tugging on his boots and hurrying out to saddle the horses.

"You look like hell," Greg observed when they met outside the grassy paddock.

Blake managed a tired grin. "You're a great one to talk. Did one of your patients keep you up all night after you left the party?" he asked as he checked the cinch on his saddle.

"No. Sandy did." Greg's expression darkened. "Is this horse tame?"

"Gentle as a kitten. I picked her out for Erin. Her name's Blaze."

"What brought on the invitation for an impromptu early morning ride?" Greg asked as he swung easily onto the mare's back and stroked her neck.

"Impulse. And the realization that I wasn't going to get any sleep no matter how long I lay in bed today." Not ready yet for serious discussion, Blake snapped the reins and took off on Renegade toward a wooded bridle path that wound around the back of his property.

The soft thud of hooves against the moist clay of the trail and intermittent squawks of birds frightened at the equine invasion of territory long left to them reminded Blake of times long ago when he had made this trek every morning before school. Times before Erin . . . even before Glenna.

"Simpler times."

"What?" Greg asked.

Blake glanced over at Greg, realizing he had spoken out loud. "I was just thinking how much simpler life was when we were kids."

"As in?"

"Feelings. At the time, I never realized how easy I had it, when my biggest worry was whether to spend the day riding, or studying, or lounging by the pool."

Greg let out a sigh. "Those were the days, all right."

"Dealing with one woman is hard enough. How do you manage, juggling not one but three and sometimes four or five?" Blake asked, recalling the degree of tension he had felt while Greg's daughter, mother, and fiancée took civilized potshots at each other last night—and he wasn't the one directly involved with them.

"I don't—at least not well enough." Greg shifted slightly in the saddle before going on. "Sandy lets Shana snipe at her, and then lets me have it over my kid's nasty behavior. Shana whines to me about everything under the sun. And Mom gives me hell over them, Kay, Rhea, and everything else she can think of. I guess I just give a good shot at letting everything any of them says go in one ear and out the other."

Blake cleared his throat. "Well, if you can come up with ten thousand dollars cash, your worries with Rhea will be over. Her lawyer called me yesterday."

"Why didn't you say so earlier? Ten grand's just five months' worth of alimony."

Blake shrugged. "The party, remember. Somehow it didn't seem the proper place or time to bring up your ex-wife."

"Why didn't someone drill that idea into my daughter's head?" Greg asked with a self-deprecating grin.

"Sadie tried."

Greg looked surprised. "She did?"

"Yes. While you were at the buffet getting your mother some food, Shana took it on herself to tell Sandy how her mom's engagement rings—current and past—were so much bigger and better than Sandy's. Sadie shut her up before she could reduce your fiancée to a state of total fury."

"So that's what really set Sandy off," Greg commented thoughtfully. "I wondered. Couldn't see much reason for the way she was screaming and ranting over the way I let my kid get away with murder."

"How did you settle it?"

"The usual way. Soft words and hot sex. The thing that worries me is that I didn't really settle it at all. The only difference between this morning and last night is that for the moment Sandy at least believes I love her to pieces and can't keep my hands off her."

"But that's not enough for her?"

"It was, at the time. But Shana isn't going to turn into Little Miss Muffet, and Sandy's not about to give an inch to her. Kay won't be back soon enough to keep the fur from flying, and Mom's getting too old to be the referee for their fights."

Blake felt for Greg, who might as well have been on a medieval rack, the way his emotions were being tugged in all directions by the three strong-minded women he loved.

"How do you take it?" he asked as they reined in their horses in front of the stable and dismounted.

"One hour at a time. When I'm working, I just put it all out of my mind and concentrate on the patient at hand. Hell, I know I should have picked some quiet, biddable woman without an independent thought in her head—but then she wouldn't give me the fire and lightning I've gotten with the ones I've chosen," Greg admitted with a grin.

Greg had himself pegged. Blake figured his friend must like having unrealistic demands placed on him. If he didn't, he wouldn't have taken up medicine at all, much less the sometimes heartbreaking subspecialty of high-risk OB. He had to thrive on demanding women as well, Blake decided as he mentally compared young Sandy with her predecessors in Greg's life.

"Unlike you, my friend, I like living in peace. I'll take my well-behaved boys and my lovely, tranquil wife—and leave the constant fireworks for you to handle." As Blake made his casual observation, he realized that it was Erin and not Glenna he had been thinking of when he spoke.

Erin had brought Blake a degree of peace when he most needed it, he admitted to himself while he silently rubbed down Renegade and put away the tack. Her calm and tranquil manner, the soft and soothing timbre of her distinctive west Texas drawl, the gentle sway of slender hips when she moved, all joined to create a restful aura in his home.

That aura is helping me to heal.

"Blake?"

"Yeah, Greg?"

"Are you going to rub all the skin off that big black beast of yours?"

Blake looked at the currycomb in his hand, realizing suddenly that he had been going over the same spot on Renegade's muscled shoulder for a long time now. Sheepishly he hung the grooming tool on a peg and joined Greg. "I was just thinking," he said by way of explaining his strange behavior.

"Let's have some breakfast. Then I'll go tackle taming Shana while you sit back and enjoy. . . ."

"If you and Sandy aren't doing anything tonight, come on over. Bring Shana, too. We can barbecue some steaks and play around in the pool," Blake suggested.

Greg accepted his invitation quickly, almost too quickly, as if he were grasping at ways to keep a buffer between himself, Sandy, and his daughter. As Blake walked back toward his house, he wondered if he, too, might be looking for excuses to delay facing up to how he had hurt Erin by venting his own grief and guilt.

"Did you enjoy your swim?" Erin asked Shana when she joined her and Timmy at a table beside the pool that afternoon.

"It was okay. Your pool is bigger than Dad's." She glanced over at the grill, where Blake and Greg were busy preparing the coals for steaks Erin had just brought from the kitchen. "You're a lot older than Sandy, aren't you?" Shana asked, her appraising gaze returning to Erin.

"Ten years. Sandy came to live with me after our parents died. She was just a few years older than you are now."

"You must have been awful to her. I bet that's why she's such a witch to me." Shana's nose wrinkled with disgust.

Erin restrained the urge to snap off a rude reply. "How do you figure my sister's being a witch?" she asked mildly, privately deciding Shana had it mixed up as to who was the witch in her father's life.

"*You* wouldn't understand."

A car horn blared, and Shana practically leaped out of the chair where she'd been sitting. "That's Marisa and her mom. We're going riding."

As she watched Shana grab her designer gym bag and sprint toward her friend's car, Erin noted that Greg's daughter was gorgeous when she really smiled. Pity, neither Greg nor Sandy seemed to have the ability to inspire the least bit of joy in the spoiled young girl.

"She's gone?" Sandy sounded relieved when she came outside, a carafe of wine in hand.

"Yes." Erin didn't know what to say to relieve the tension that hung heavily in the air. She almost wished Blake hadn't cooked up this impromptu get-together, even though she had welcomed the idea of it this morning as a diversion for her own tattered emotions.

"Well, sweetheart, you can breathe easy now," Greg told Sandy with false heartiness when he came over and joined them. "Hey, Tim, how's it going?" he asked, playfully ruffling Timmy's hair. "Want to swim?"

Timmy had already been in the water twice, first with her, then with Blake and Shana just a few minutes earlier. Erin wasn't surprised when her son shook his head and told them he thought he'd go inside and practice Nintendo.

"Sandy?"

"What? No, Greg, I think I'll just sit with Erin and watch the sun go down."

Was there trouble in Sandy's newly found paradise? Erin wondered. Sensitized by her own raw feelings, she felt a subtle undercurrent of dissention between affable, easygoing Greg and her strong-minded young sister.

She had no time to find out what was going on, though. Before she could ask Sandy, Blake was there, not asking but insisting that she help him check out the steaks.

"Something's going on between Sandy and Greg," she murmured just loudly enough for Blake to hear.

She watched him nod. "One word. Shana," he whispered as he held up a big T-bone steak at the end of a long-handled fork and pretended to examine it in minute detail.

"What do you mean?"

"That Greg's having one hell of a time trying to keep his little girl and Sandy from tearing him in two."

"I can't believe Sandy would deliberately try to turn Greg against his own child," Erin said, looking over at the telling scene of Greg doing determined laps in the pool while Sandy sat at a table, looking more than vaguely annoyed as she swirled her wine rhythmically around in a stemmed glass.

"It's not deliberate, at least not on Sandy's part, or at least that's the impression I get. Still, Greg is smarting over the knock-down-drag-out argument they had last night over the way Sandy thinks he lets Shana get away with anything short of murder."

"I don't blame her! It was all I could do last night to keep from grabbing that spiteful little girl and shaking her silly." Erin frowned. Blake had been the one to step in and tell Shana to knock off her complaining. She didn't need to protect her sister from him! "You noticed how rude Shana was acting, too," she pointed out quietly.

"I noticed. So did Greg. But underneath that laid-back attitude he shows the world, Greg's burying a soul that's just about brimming over with intensity. He never says much, but I believe he's burying a bunch of guilt for not having done more to give his daughter a stable, two-parent family to grow up in." Blake set the steak back onto the iced platter where it had been and replaced a domed, thermal lid to keep the meat chilled until they got ready to cook.

Erin nodded, briefly allowing herself to muse that Blake himself seemed to be carrying around more than his own share of misplaced torment. "I know it's been hard on Sandy, too. She loves Greg so much, she wants to love Shana, too—but Shana wants no part of her."

Blake reached out and caressed her open hand, as if to reassure her. Despite the way he left her last night, and the fact that he had avoided the talk he admitted they must have, Erin felt a jolt of heat at the casual contact. Reflexively she jerked her hand away.

"You want no part of me now, either, do you?" His mellow voice sounded strained.

"You said we needed to talk, Blake. Last night wasn't the time or place for you; now's not right, either. We need to entertain our guests," she reminded him with forced cheer as she lifted the lid from the steak platter and speared a piece of meat. "It's just about time for dinner."

As the evening wore on, Erin tried to make Sandy laugh. Blake teased Greg until he instigated a game of pool tag that forced both couples to touch and communicate—at least on a superficial level.

"Here, catch," Sandy cried, tossing the bright yellow beach ball at Erin. Blake leaped high, captured the prize, and passed it neatly in Greg's direction before Erin managed to grab him from behind and pull him underwater.

"Oh, no, you don't!" Sputtering and laughing, Blake took off after Erin. Pretending terror, she squealed before taking a deep breath in preparation for her own dunking.

"You can do better than that, Blake," Greg called from the other end of the pool, and Blake took up the challenge by lifting Erin high in the air.

She braced herself to hit the water, but it didn't happen. Instead, he lowered her slowly, stopping when their gazes met and locking their mouths together in a voracious kiss. When they came up for air, Erin burrowed her face into his chest to conceal the way she knew she had to be blushing like a besotted teenager.

"Hey, you guys, that looks like fun," Greg yelled, breaking Erin's concentration and forcing her to look his way in time to see him scoop Sandy up and nuzzle suggestively at her neck.

If Blake hadn't made her burn with his every teasing touch, Erin could have laughed herself to death at his and Greg's childish game of one-upmanship where she and Sandy were their helpless pawns. They must have kept at it for half an hour or more, Erin thought by the time Blake picked her up and carried her out of the pool.

It seemed to Erin as if Blake was determined to keep up the game while they sipped on after-dinner cocktails. Greg went along, too, giving her a glimpse of the fun-loving kids they must once have been before failed relationships molded Greg and tragedy touched her husband. Sandy had opened up, too, laughing and taking part in the men's sensual banter.

Erin knew she was dangerously close to falling in love with Blake, the dark, tortured man she had come to know. Tonight she decided she genuinely liked this new Blake who could go out of his way to make friends forget their woes.

By the time Sandy and Greg left, Erin noted with approval that the obvious, physical bond between them was alive and well. Her hot, aching body told her there was nothing wrong with the chemistry between her and Blake, either—or at least that *her* hormones were alive and well.

Wanting to savor her feelings for this new carefree Blake, Erin bade him a friendly, warm good night and went inside to tuck in Timmy and nurse baby Jamie. She hoped her smile would beckon Blake to join her—to put out the fires he'd stoked rather than to rehash guilty feelings she knew lurked not far below the surface of his mind.

"May I come in?"

Last night Blake hadn't asked—but then Erin had invited him with blatant actions instead of words. Tonight he felt the intruder in this space he had designated as hers.

"Of course. Jamie's just about done nursing," Erin said, smiling down at the dark-haired baby who was nodding off to sleep at her breast.

Self-conscious, Blake took a seat on the edge of the bed. The thinly veiled sexual foreplay and suggestive conversation he had initiated for the benefit of Greg and Sandy had certainly backfired on him, because he wanted nothing more right now than to haul Jamie off to bed and hurry back to take his fill of Erin.

"I promised you we'd talk," he said, when all he wanted to do was bury himself in her and forget all the reasons that desire made him a total jerk. "I didn't mean to hurt you."

"I know. Here, you put Jamie to bed, and I'll slip into

something more comfortable.'' She smiled when he cuddled his baby snugly against his chest.

If Blake didn't know better, he'd have thought Erin was out to seduce him again. He doubted if that was going to happen, though, after the way he left her last night. Tucking a blanket around Jamie's plump, warm body, he checked the baby one more time before going back to Erin's room. This time he settled himself on a chair, out of temptation's way, before meeting her solemn gaze.

But was she solemn? Blake would swear he saw fire in those deep blue eyes, strung out need in the way she clasped her fingers against the quilted satin coverlet. He couldn't help noticing pale, narrow straps across her slender shoulders, or the top of a lacy nightgown that barely veiled her beautiful breasts.

Every day he was learning there was more to Erin than the calm, rational mother . . . big sister . . . friend . . . that she displayed. Last night, she had shown him an earthy sensuality the likes of which would have caused wet dreams when he was a boy. And her fierce defense of Sandy proved she could fight tough and dirty if need be, for someone she loved.

If it wasn't for the damn, strangulating guilt that he couldn't set aside, Blake knew he could come to love this woman who was his wife. And he couldn't let that happen. It wouldn't be fair to Glenna.

''I shouldn't have said what I did last night,'' he ventured gruffly. ''I wanted you just as much as—probably more than—you wanted me.''

''I doubt that.'' Erin smiled, a slow, seductive grin that hit him hard, below the belt.

''Let me apologize, Erin.''

''Don't. I understand.''

Blake shifted in the chair. ''I'm glad you do, because I'm having a hard time understanding it myself.''

''Look. We may be married, but we don't know each

other all that well. Maybe the chemistry between us has something to do with . . .''

"Damn it, don't tell me I can barely keep my hands off you just because you had my baby! I've tried persuading myself that, and it won't wash. I want you because you're gorgeous and sexy and *mine*, and wanting you is eating me alive.

"If I stay away from you, I hurt. And I feel just as guilty if I don't touch you as if I do—because I want you so damn much."

Blake watched Erin slip gracefully out of bed and cross the room to kneel at his feet. "Glenna wouldn't want you to go through life alone," she said, taking one of his hands and sandwiching it between her own in a gesture more comforting than arousing.

"How would you know what she would want? You didn't even know her! And even if you did, can you possibly be honest and say it wouldn't hurt her to know I was enjoying some other woman's bed hardly six months since she's been gone?" He let his head droop onto his chest, and he tried hard not to feel the gentle touch of Erin's fingers as she massaged his scalp.

"I know."

How could she sound so certain? She had met Glenna just once, the day before she died. He, on the other hand, had known and loved Glenna for the better part of his life . . . had been secure in her love for him, too. And Blake still couldn't reach into Glenna's mind and soul and get the vaguest idea of what she would expect of him today.

He had almost found the words to express his doubt when Erin's voice commanded his attention. "Let's forget last night," she suggested quietly. "We're hardly more than strangers in a lot of ways. Why don't we ignore the chemistry, get to know each other, and try to be friends?"

Blake felt her hands go still, then withdraw before she stood up and moved to the chair at the other side of what seemed at the moment to be an insurmountable expanse of sliding glass wall. While he murmured his approval of her suggestion, he wondered how in hell he was supposed to forget the way she turned him hard as stone and single-minded as a teenager hot on the heels of his first real sexual encounter.

"Blake, is there anything we can do to help them cope with Shana?" Erin asked, and Blake silently blessed her for distracting him from what he'd like to be doing.

"How about buying a one-way ticket for Miss Shana to use to join up with her mom and stepdad over in Athens or wherever they are?" he asked, only half kidding.

He liked the way Erin smiled, and the sassy look she gave him when she said, "Be serious."

"A muzzle?"

"Blake!"

He thought for a minute. "I could talk to Greg about the way he buys that child everything under the sun."

Now Erin laughed out loud. "This from the man who hardly ever comes home without some new present for Jamie and Tim?"

"Yeah. Do I buy them too much stuff?"

He could almost feel her mulling his question over in her mind. "No," she finally said. "It would be too much if you didn't give them just as much of your time and attention, though."

"As far as I know, Greg has spent all the time the courts allow him with his daughter," Blake said, meeting Erin's gaze and regretting their decision to turn down the heat on their relationship. "Hasn't he?"

"I guess so. Sandy's never said otherwise."

"Then maybe Shana's just reacting to the prospect of having a stepmother who's closer to her age than Greg's," Blake suggested, grasping at straws. Hell, what did he know about the care and feeding of a twelve-year-old girl?

"You may be right. I don't know, though. Sandy came to live with Bill and me when she was just sixteen, and she never gave me the kind of grief Sandy's putting up with now.''

Blake shrugged. ''The girl may be just antsy about having any stepmother at all. Or Kay may have poisoned her mind about Greg, or Sandy, or both of them. I wouldn't put it past her,'' he muttered, recalling the woman's penchant for damning people with innuendo only slightly veiled with the cloak of civility.

''Would Greg's ex-wife actually do something that mean?''

Erin obviously had never met Kay Halpern, Blake thought as he assured her that there was almost nothing Kay wouldn't do if she were provoked enough—that on occasion the woman would go for someone's jugular just for the fun of it.

''Oh. Maybe I should let Sandy know what kind of influence Shana's been living with for all these years. It might make her go easier, be more understanding. . . .''

''I'm sure she knows. There are damn few people close to Greg that he hasn't discussed Kay's antics with. When the two of them actually get together in the same room, I try to be sure there's a fire extinguisher on hand.''

''They get together?''

Blake laughed. ''Only to fight over alimony and child support, so far as I know. I'm surprised you didn't hear the fireworks when we had that meeting here, the afternoon before Jamie was born.''

''I was otherwise occupied, I'm afraid,'' Erin replied with a smile. ''I didn't know you did divorces.''

''Just for Greg. And I didn't 'do' the divorces for Greg. Kay and Rhea, his second wife, both took him to the cleaners. He asked me to attempt some damage control so he could afford to marry Sandy.''

''I guess you were successful.''

''Moderately. Kay's remarriage had more to do with my success than any skills I may have.''

''I doubt that,'' Erin said with conviction, and Blake felt

a surprising wave of contentment at her vote of confidence. "But we're not going to solve the world's problems—or Sandy's and Greg's, either—tonight. Don't you think it's time we got some sleep?"

Blake could think of several things he would rather be doing than sleeping. Nonetheless, he got up and walked Erin to the king-sized bed, tucked her in, and brushed his lips briefly across hers before going across the hall to his own lonely room. He wondered as he tried to sleep why he hadn't crawled in with Erin and let her sweet, hot warmth envelop him and give him peace.

Chapter 18

$\mathscr{P}$eace was not in the cards for him tonight, Greg knew. The minute they arrived at her apartment, Sandy laid into him again, this time over his giving in and lifting Shana's latest restriction to let her spend the night with her friend.

"She's just a little girl," he said in his most conciliatory tone.

Sandy stood up and put her hands firmly at her luscious hips. "Shana is a miserable spoiled brat. I know you're not entirely responsible for that, but you certainly do your share. Why did you say she could go riding and then spend the night tonight with Marisa?"

Greg shrugged his shoulders. "Would you believe so we could have some time alone?"

"Normally I would, if you hadn't told your daughter just this morning that she'd be grounded for the rest of the weekend because she was so darn rude at our engagement party! Greg, you can't give in to her every little demand. Don't you know anything about being a parent?"

"You don't like Shana. That's what all this boils down to, doesn't it?" Greg asked, smarting from Sandy's assessment of his parenting skills.

Sandy whirled around to face windows that looked out onto nothing but an empty street. "I'm trying really hard to like her because she's your daughter. But she's tearing us apart. Can't you see what Shana's doing to us?''

''She's my little girl, sweetheart.''

''And she's determined to make my life miserable!''

Greg moved closer and tentatively touched Sandy's tensed shoulders with both his hands. ''You two got along all right before Shana came to stay with me,'' he pointed out with what he thought was perfectly reasonable logic.

He could feel her stubborn refusal to turn and face him. ''That was because all I did with her *then* was haul her wherever you told me to, which meant she considered me nothing but just another one of the hired help.''

''Be reasonable. Shana's having to adjust to her mom being gone, and living with me for a while—us, after we get married next month. Try to see things as she does.''

Sandy turned on him, her eyes flashing blue-green fire. ''You mean, see you as a never-ending supplier of designer furniture and designer clothes that are never quite good enough for her royal little self? And myself as the combination maid, cook, chauffeur, laundress whose sole purpose on this earth is to cater to her every whim?''

''Sandy, sweetheart, cut the kid some slack. It's not easy to grow up in a broken home. Besides, you don't know Shana's mother.''

''What does your ex-wife have to do with your daughter's being a brat?''

Greg had to laugh. ''Shana is her mother's daughter. Practically a carbon copy, personality-wise. It's as much my fault as Kay's, I suppose, since I never fought to be a bigger part of Shana's life after we divorced.''

''Why?''

''Because at first I was too busy, trying to finish my residency and establish a practice. I let Kay get the divorce and worked like a dog to make enough money to pay her the alimony and support she demanded. I couldn't afford to take Kay back to court. But I've always seen Shana as often as the judge's decree allowed me to.''

Sandy scowled. ''And you've catered to her as if she

were a precious little princess. You've never insisted that she behave or followed through with punishing her when she decides to be unbearably rude. You've helped her mother create a monster, and damn it, Greg, you're still at it!''

"Please, sweetheart, getting mad isn't helping us solve anything," he replied, deliberately reaching out and drawing her trembling body close to his heart.

"M-making love isn't going to solve anything, either," Sandy stammered, her voice muffled by the cloth of his shirt as she burrowed tighter against his chest.

"It won't?" He, for one, thought they needed to ease the tension—or rather convert its direction from anger to passion.

"No."

She sounded so sad, yet so certain, Greg thought as he sank onto a little sofa and pulled her onto his lap. "What do you want me to do?" he asked as he wiped away a tear that was making its way down her flushed cheek.

"I don't know. Greg, I need some time to think. I'll see you at work on Monday," Sandy said as she got up and slowly walked toward the door.

He was losing Sandy. He could feel her withdrawing bit by bit, and he didn't know what the hell he could do about it. On the way home, and later in a bed that felt cold and empty without her sharing it, Greg tried to hold on to his anger, if only to hold the fear in his gut at bay.

He didn't doubt her love for him. Not at all. But it was becoming painfully clear that love wasn't going to be strong enough to weather the storms that hit every time Sandy had to endure one of Shana's snide attacks.

He could, and would, reach his daughter somehow. He would let her know he loved her but that he expected—no, demanded, he mentally amended—that she treat Sandy with the respect that was due her as his fiancée. How he would accomplish this, he admitted to himself ruefully, he would have to decide as he went along. That determined, Greg fell into a restless sleep.

And in the morning, after he visited his hospitalized patients, he picked up Shana from the sleepover that had set Sandy off.

"Shana, we need to reach an understanding," he said sternly as they pulled into the driveway of the house he had just bought and furnished in order to bring his daughter home.

"Shana's just a child," Erin pointed out reasonably to Sandy as she turned Jamie around to nurse at her other breast.

Sandy shook her head with disgust. "She's a monster. And Greg won't do a damn thing about it."

"Why don't you tell this to him?" Erin asked, hating that she had no ready answers for her sister as to how to handle a recalcitrant preteen.

"I have. He just makes excuses for her, says she's the way she is because she comes from a broken home and all that psychobabble. Darn it all, our folks died when I wasn't a whole lot older than Shana, and I came to live with you and Bill. I had just lost my mom and dad, and on top of that, I had to leave all my friends back home. I was hurting a whole lot more than a kid whose biggest gripe is that her daddy won't buy her more than fifty pairs of jeans! But I didn't act that way. Did I?"

Erin smiled. Sandy hadn't been exactly a model teen, but then she had never had a mean bone in her body, either. "No. Not exactly. But it took a bit of adjustment for us, too, before you really accepted me as any kind of authority figure."

"Really?"

"Yes, really. And as I recall, you never really took much Bill told you as law, until I backed up his orders. Trying to be parents to a girl who was just a few years younger than he was taxed his patience just about to the limit—

many times,'' Erin said, remembering the stress that having responsibility for her sister had often placed on an already shaky new marriage.

Sandy stood, her stance indignant. "I was never rude or mean or . . ."

"Yes, you were. Not often, but sometimes when you'd get really homesick, you got to be a real pain."

"Bill used to say I was jealous of Timmy," Sandy said quietly, as if she were trying to remember those times when she was more typical teenager than angel.

"Even before Timmy was born," Erin said, her memory taking her back to those months when she had felt so helpless—helpless to divide her loyalties adequately among her husband, her young sister, and her then-unborn son. "Not all of that tension had to do with you," she added, unwilling to let Sandy shoulder the blame for a situation long ago where Bill—and she—were more at fault than the sixteen-year-old whose life had been forever changed by their parents' untimely deaths.

Jamie had stopped nursing and gone to sleep, Erin noticed when she glanced down and watched the baby's dark eyelashes flutter closed against his soft, pink cheek. "Let me put him in his crib," she murmured, carefully lifting herself out of the padded rocker and moving to the crib.

"What should I do?" Sandy asked bluntly as they moved out onto the patio to continue their visit in the warmth of a late September afternoon.

"What do you want to do?"

"I'm going to give Greg his ring back. I can't cope with his daughter."

Erin couldn't help it. She had to smile. "That's what Bill told me he would have done if we hadn't already been married when you came to live with us," she confided.

Sandy's eyes widened. "That jerk!"

"And you're any less of one?"

"W-what do you mean?" Erin couldn't tell if she were hurt or just plain angry.

"Do you love Greg?"

Sandy's reply was instant and indignant. "Of course I do. I love Greg with all my heart. But I can't cope with Shana!"

Six months, even three months ago, Erin thought to herself, she would have questioned the wisdom of a match between her sister and a man who, in addition to being fifteen years older and saddled with the emotional baggage of two failed relationships, was very obviously married to his work.

Since then, though, she had come to know and respect Greg; and she had seen how he was changing his lifestyle to make Sandy, not medicine, the focal point of his life. Most of all, Greg had shown not just Erin, but everyone he came in contact with, that he loved her sister with the kind of fervency Erin herself had always hoped for.

Bill didn't love me that way, and Blake doesn't, either. Fool, she told herself, *Blake doesn't love you at all.* Then Erin shook off that sudden wave of self-pity and met Sandy's questioning gaze.

"What were you thinking?" Sandy asked quietly.

"About you and Greg, and how sad it is that you love each other so much."

"What do you mean, it's sad?"

"That you're going to break up because you're such a coward you can't handle one kid who isn't even a teenager yet," Erin said soberly, intentionally baiting Sandy now.

"What do you mean, I'm a coward? I've tried everything I know how to do to make Shana like me."

Erin met her sister's accusing gaze. "Maybe you've been trying to make her like you, when you should be working at earning her respect."

"I don't think she respects anyone," Sandy said, her tone of voice flat, defeated.

"Sadie."

"What about Greg's mother?"

Erin smiled. "Shana respects her. Remember night before last, when just a word from Sadie shut her up like a clam?''

''Well, that's different. No kid would be out-and-out rude to her own grandmother.''

''The way we grew up, Sandy, we wouldn't have dared be rude to *anyone* older than we were. But it's obvious that Shana hasn't learned that fine point of courtesy as yet. What do you think makes her toe the line for Sadie?'' Erin asked calmly.

''Is that a trick question?''

''Is it?''

Erin watched Sandy's expression change from one of despair to one of tentative hope. ''I think Shana won't buck her grandmother's orders because she knows Sadie would chew her up and spit her out again,'' she finally replied.

''But you're so weak you can't put the pressure on one child? Is that what you're saying when you're threatening to walk out on the man you love to distraction?'' Erin watched Sandy closely, taking heart when her sister's face took on a fiercely determined expression.

''No. I'll bring her around if I have to kill her to do it,'' Sandy declared through clenched teeth. ''No twelve-year-old is going to get me down. She's not going to make me give up her daddy, either. By the time I'm done, that little wildcat will be as tame as that big, fat Persian cat that used to live across the road from us when we were kids.''

Greg had stalled as long as he could, he knew as he headed out to his patio, carrying a chilled bottle of raspberry seltzer for his daughter and an icy can of beer for himself. *I should have grabbed the whole damn six-pack,* he thought as he approached Shana. God, how he hated that bored, pouty look she affected whenever he tried to get her into anything bordering on a real conversation.

''Thank you,'' Shana muttered, stretching coltish legs out on the chaise as if she were some movie star or something, and he were the lackey charged with seeing to her needs.

Holding on to his temper by reminding himself that whatever Shana was, he was just as much at fault as Kay, Greg pulled up a chair and sat down, close enough to touch the child he loved but did not understand. Before he spoke, he chose his words as carefully as if he were trying to cushion the blow of devastating news to one of his patients.

"What's wrong?" he finally asked.

"I hate you and that simple *child* you're going to marry. I hate this house and having to stay here when I could be having lots more fun at home. And I can't stand the way all of you treat me like I'm a baby, too!" Shana concluded, her dramatic announcement accompanied by the tears that came close to breaking Greg's heart.

"Maybe we treat you like a child because you act like one. Actually, you *are* still a child, honey."

"Whatever," Shana said, fixing her petulant gaze on some point on the other side of the pool.

Greg had to remind himself this child was the daughter he had walked away from when he left her mother. "We need to discuss your manners, young lady," he managed to tell her in the tone of voice that got nurses and interns cracking to follow his orders.

"My manners are just fine. Mother's made sure I know which fork to pick up and what to wear. Has little Sandy been whining again?"

Greg felt like dragging her off that lounge chair and shaking her until she begged for mercy. Damn it to hell, he decided, if Shana could get down and dirty, so could he! "We're not talking about my fiancée, we're talking about you. And from what I've seen in the week you've been with me, I'd say your mother has sadly neglected your education in basic human relations. She may let you get away with being rude and snide, Shana, but I've got news for you. I won't."

"Whatever."

"Remove that disgusting expression from your vocabulary," Greg snapped. Sandy was right; this girl could be impossible.

Shana sat up straight and stared him down. "Whatever," she repeated, and Greg practically leaped to his feet.

"You're grounded for a month," he shouted as he felt his blood pressure begin to soar. "Forget your riding lessons. Forget seeing your friends outside of school. And don't even think about going shopping. If you're lucky, maybe I'll let you out of your room long enough to apologize to Sandy for the way you've been treating her."

"And what makes you think I will? I don't like her. All my friends think you must be a dirty old man, marrying an outsider who's young enough to be your kid. You're both *disgusting*." She drew out that last word, emphasizing every syllable.

"That sounds like your mother talking, Shana. And it's a damn stupid statement to boot. I'd have had to be pretty precocious to have fathered a baby when I was fourteen," Greg retorted before he realized it was childish to take his own child's bait. "Besides, it's not your business."

"Whatever. Nothing's my business. But it screws up my life just the same. Mother didn't ask me before she decided to marry Pop Abe, who's got grandchildren older than me. You don't care that I can't stand Sandy. Do you have any idea how *humiliating* it is to admit I'm going to have a stepfather as old as Grandma Sadie, and a stepmother who's not much older than me?"

That hurt, because at least the first of Shana's impassioned statements was true. He *hadn't* considered his daughter's feelings about his engagement to Sandy, any more than he had consulted her several years ago before he married Rhea. And he knew damn well Kay's only thoughts when she decided to become Mrs. Abe Goldman were of herself. Kay was that way.

Humiliating? Now that was a bit extreme, Greg thought in his own defense. "There's nothing for you to be upset about, Shana. It's natural for men and women to want to share their lives with someone else. You know, honey, differences in age get less important when we get older. I love Sandy, and I'm sure your mother feels the same about Pop Abe," he told his daughter quietly. "But we both love you."

Shana turned on him like a riled-up wildcat. He grabbed her wrists to keep her from pummeling his chest with furious fists. "Sure you do," she snarled. "Mother cares so much, she left to cruise around the world with *him*; and the only reason I'm here instead of stuck in some geeky boarding school is because she *bribed* you to take me!"

"What?"

"Don't try and say she didn't. Mother told me she let you out of supporting us to make you take care of me while she and Abe play kissy-face on some stupid tour."

Greg wished Kay were around so he could strangle her. "I wanted you with me," he said, watching tears that threatened to erupt from his little girl's dark eyes that were so much like his, and wishing he could take away the pain he knew had to be buried under her brittle, sullen exterior. "Sandy wants you, too," he added, telling himself that at least at first that had been the truth.

"You wanted to quit giving *us* money so you could afford to marry *her*. Mother said so."

Greg reached out and stroked Shana's damp, flushed cheek. What could he do or say that would sweep away the bitterness Kay had instilled in his only child? "There's a lot of animosity between your mom and me, honey," he said when she didn't immediately pull away from his touch. "That doesn't mean we don't both love you."

Shana shook her head and backed away. "You mean you didn't want the money?"

"The only thing I wanted was to be able to make a home for myself—and you," he said. Reading the disbelief in Shana's gaze, he went on. "To do that, I had to ask your mother to accept less alimony. She made that possible when she decided to get married again.''

Tossing her dark hair over her shoulder, Shana sat back down, looking up at Greg with those dark, mistrustful eyes. ''Why did you and Mother ever have me? Why couldn't I have parents like Marisa's? They're divorced, too, but they live just around the corner from each other. Her mom and stepfather even play cards once a week with her dad and stepmom. They're cool.''

The swinging pathologists? He just bet they were playing cards when they got together! Greg closed his mouth before he could burst his daughter's bubble. It wouldn't make Shana feel better to know Tom and Elaine and Mark and Cecelia had swapped off for years before they had made what hospital gossips insisted was a purely fanciful legal change of partners. Instead, he felt compelled to apologize for the way he and Kay had hurt their child while attempting to injure each other.

''I'm sorry we're not cool, as you say. Your mom and I both tried, but I guess neither of us tried hard enough to keep on loving each other. Before I left, we'd said and done too many mean, bitter things. There was no way we'd ever be friends. But Shana, honey, we're both entitled to a little slice of happiness for ourselves. My loving Sandy doesn't take away any of the love I feel for you, and I'm sure your mom doesn't love you less because she loves Mr. Goldman, too.''

Greg could tell Shana wasn't buying into what he was saying. He watched the way her fingers tapped impatiently against the wicker arm of her chair. ''*He* treated me just fine until he married Mother and they dumped me here with you,'' she finally said, sharing at least a piece of her thoughts.

''They deserve a little time to themselves, don't you think?''

''Six months?''

Privately Greg thought Kay and her aging millionaire

had gone overboard on their honeymoon plans, but it wouldn't do for him to say so. "It isn't really that long, when you think about it," he said neutrally.

"Whatever. Do I get to stay here with prune-faced old Mrs. Watson while you take a trip around the world or something?" Shana asked, her voice dripping sarcasm.

"No. I can't take that much time away from work. We'll just be taking a long weekend out at Possum Kingdom. You will be staying with Nana Sadie. Look, Shana. We've gotten off track here. I'm sorry you feel so put-upon, but we were discussing your behavior."

"Daddy, what do you want me to do? Lie and pretend I'm all happy because you're going to get married again? I'll never get to see you at all."

Greg offered up silent thanks to God that he had decided against a specialty in child psychiatry. He would never understand kids, if his own daughter were any indication! "What makes you say that?"

"Sandy doesn't like me any more than I like her. Once you're married, she'll make sure you don't have any time at all for me. Rhea did, and she was sweet as sugar to me when you were just dating."

Greg thought he saw Shana's lower lip tremble, but he wasn't sure. "Rhea fooled me, too," he said lightly. "You're here now, and you're staying until your mother gets home. We're going to be seeing a lot of each other, especially since you're acting like such a brat that I have to keep you on a tight leash."

"Oh, Daddy, you won't do that, will you?"

Now he had a feeling he was being conned. "I will, and there will be no wheedling your way out of your punishment, either."

"A whole *month*?" Shana's expression reflected horror along with a goodly dose of skepticism.

"Look, Shana. I'll make you a deal. We'll do this a week at a time. You apologize to Sandy and mean it. And you remember to treat her, and everybody else you come in contact with, with respect and kindness. We'll talk about parole next Sunday.''

Shana's mouth dropped open. ''You're really going to marry her, aren't you?''

''Come hell or high water, honey. Give her a chance. Sandy isn't your mom, but she would like to be your friend.''

They talked for a few more minutes before going inside. That night as he tried to get some sleep, he hoped to hell he had gotten through to the little girl who looked like him, but inside seemed to be almost a carbon copy of Kay. At least, he assured himself, his daughter wouldn't dare keep needling at the woman he loved.

''How do you do it?'' he asked Blake when they met the next morning to exercise the horses.

Blake hadn't the vaguest idea what Greg was talking about. ''What?'' he asked, half asleep.

''Make your stepson crazy about you.''

''My son. I've adopted Timmy. I guess he likes me because I like him and show it. He's a fantastic little kid. I wish I had half his courage.'' The cool, dry morning air was doing its job; Blake was beginning to shake the cobwebs off his sluggish brain.

Greg sighed. ''He is a brave little guy. How's his therapy coming?''

''Erin and I have to meet with his doctors next Monday. From what Michelle tells me, she's done about all she can do with physical therapy, until he goes through another operation.''

''Who's his surgeon?''

Blake pulled up his mount and met Greg's gaze. ''A guy named Dan Newman. Do you know him?''

''Yeah. He's good. Who's he working with?''

''What do you mean?''

Greg shifted in his saddle. ''Newman's specialty is microsurgery on the nervous system. He'd get an orthopedic guy and maybe someone who does plastic and reconstructive surgery, too, to make up a surgery team for Timmy. I think. Sandy described what happened to him. Damn rotten shame!''

Erin hadn't told *him* much, Blake thought, perturbed. Not that he didn't know, in his head, most of what his little boy had gone through before he and his mother became Blake's responsibility. He had talked with Michelle, and Timmy himself. ''Greg, is he going to be all right eventually?'' he asked, suddenly afraid for Tim.

''I'm a women's doctor, my friend,'' Greg reminded Blake with a grin. ''What's more, I've never looked at Timmy's legs from a medical standpoint, or studied his records. Your therapist would know more than I do about what your boy's future holds.''

''I'm scared.'' And that was the truth. Most things Blake could control. But not that. All he would be able to do was stand by and offer comfort while Timmy did all the suffering. ''I don't want him to hurt anymore,'' he declared, wishing for the power to make his child whole and strong.

Greg met his sober gaze. ''No one does, my friend. You know, they say that kids make the best patients, because they quickly forget the pain and get on with their lives. Maybe that's true in the sense that they can cope better with physical discomfort than adults. But it damn sure is a pile of cow dung when it comes to psychological hurting.''

''Erin's done nothing but love Timmy.''

''I wasn't thinking about your boy then, Blake. My mind was on the emotional wreck Kay and I have managed to make out of Shana.''

''Shana? She's got more confidence in herself than most grown women I know.''

Greg shook his head. ''She puts on a good show. But deep down, she's just a frightened little kid who doesn't think she means much to either Kay or me.''

Blake doubted that ''frightened'' fit Shana Halpern nearly as well as ''spiteful'' and ''spoiled rotten,'' terms he remembered hearing Greg's fiancée use with every other breath last night to describe the behavior of her soon-to-be stepdaughter. But he hesitated saying that to the girl's father, no matter how good friends they were. "You and Sandy are going to have a time with her," he said.

"If Sandy doesn't decide I've got too much baggage to take along with me, and call the whole thing off."

"From what she told Erin, Sandy has no intention of letting you slither away. If I were you, though, I'd warn Miss Shana to be on her best behavior. Your fiancée has decided that your daughter's no match for her, my friend." Blake noted the relieved expression on Greg's face as they walked the horses back to the stable.

After Greg left, Blake quickly showered and headed to his office. Before he surrendered his little boy to more suffering that he couldn't prevent, he wanted to do something really special, something Timmy would remember for years to come.

Between appointments that morning, Blake considered and discarded a dozen or more attractions he had heard friends say their children loved. Disney World . . . Six Flags . . . the Grand Canyon. Timmy wouldn't be able to run and ride and do all the things that made those places fun, Blake thought dismally.

And then it came to him. He would take them to Possum Kingdom, to his cabin on the lake where he hadn't been for years. They could do as much or as little as they felt like, and he and Erin could get to know each other while spending uninterrupted, quiet time with their boys.

"Erin?" he asked when he recognized her soft voice on the phone. "We're going on a little trip. Can you and the boys be ready to leave early Thursday morning?"

Chapter 19

$\mathcal{P}$ortable crib . . . stroller . . . two huge boxes of disposable diapers . . . changes of clothes for three days and nights . . . vitamins and lotion and baby powder, and plenty of clean linens for Jamie's bed. Erin looked at the neatly stacked supplies by the door that led to the garage and wondered if it all would fit in the trunk of Blake's car. Then she grinned. She had nearly forgotten what a production it could be to prepare for a trip with children.

Blake loaded it all, even Timmy's folded wheelchair, into the car. And then they were on their way. Both Timmy and Jamie went to sleep in the backseat almost as soon as the car started moving, while Erin sat back with a steaming mug of coffee and admired the confident, competent way Blake maneuvered in the morning traffic.

She wanted to reach over and stroke his hard, muscled thigh that beckoned through faded jeans. Blake should wear jeans more often, she thought, as her gaze shifted to take in broad shoulders encased in a soft, old Longhorns sweatshirt, and his rugged, handsome profile.

"What kind of car do you want?" he asked suddenly, surprising Erin.

"Car? You have three of them already." In addition to the Mercedes sedan Blake was driving, a late-model pickup truck and an older station wagon were in the garage behind the house. Miguel used the wagon to take her shopping and to the pediatrician's office, and she guessed Blake kept the truck for hauling feed and lawn supplies.

Blake shot a quick glance Erin's way. "See that minivan in the far left lane?" he asked. "Wouldn't you like to have one to haul the kids around in?"

Erin smiled. "I appreciate the thought, but I haven't driven for a long time."

"It's not something one forgets, I don't think."

"I'm sure you're right."

"Are you afraid to drive?" Blake asked.

For a moment Erin thought about his question. "I don't think I am anymore. For a while after the accident, the idea of even getting into a car put me into a cold sweat. But I got over that pretty quickly. If there had been any way, I would have bought a car about the time I had to start taking Timmy to therapy almost every day."

Blake didn't reply for a few minutes as he concentrated on pulling off the Interstate onto a state highway that would take them to Possum Kingdom. "You'll need some wheels to get back and forth from the hospital," he pointed out after he brought the car back up to highway speed, reminding her of Timmy's impending surgery that she would just as soon forget for now.

"Can't I use the station wagon? It seems wasteful to buy another car when there's a perfectly good one right in your garage."

"The wagon's ten years old. Besides, Mary needs something to go grocery shopping in. And the truck won't do for you—it's a stick shift, and none too easy to drive. Come on, Erin, most women would be thrilled to death at the prospect of getting a new car." Blake's words were serious, but his teasing tone took the edge off and made Erin smile.

"All right. Never let it be said that I wasn't like most women," she said, figuring it was better to give in than to spoil the day with a meaningless argument.

As they drew farther from Dallas, Erin watched the scenery, mentally comparing fall in the north-central Texas hill country with the west Texas ranch where she and Sandy had grown up. Trees had been scarce there, an occasional scrub oak, mesquite, or cactus punctuating an otherwise bare, dusty horizon.

Here she reveled in a riot of color. Dark evergreens and deciduous trees whose leaves were turning shades of scarlet, gold, and orange, nestled in valleys that often featured some red-toned river or stream. The colors repeated themselves in patches on the hillsides, contrasting with pale, golden beige sandstone and red, Texas earth. She could hardly wait to get to Possum Kingdom to enjoy the beauty of the countryside up close.

"Pretty scenery, isn't it?" Blake asked as he turned onto a secondary road and slowed down to maneuver around a poorly banked curve.

Erin nodded. "I've never been out here in the fall before," she told him, recalling her summer camping trip here with Bill the year before Timmy's birth and wondering if Blake had brought Glenna to Possum Kingdom during the lazy days of Indian summer.

"Mommy?" Timmy sounded sleepy. "I think Jamie's waking up."

Twisting sideways in the bucket seat, Erin turned around to check on the boys. Jamie's eyelids were twitching, an almost sure sign that his nap time was nearly over; and Timmy looked as uncomfortable as Erin knew he must be after an hour and a half of sleeping sitting up. "Blake, we'll need to stop soon so I can feed the baby," she said as she straightened in her seat.

"Hang in there, boys," he said, grinning. "The turnoff's right up here."

"You're taking a shortcut?"

Blake shook his head. "The cabin is just a mile or so down this road. It's on the southern end of the lake."

"Oh." Erin had assumed they would be staying at the lodge in the state park, some miles farther down the two-lane highway. When she saw the big, rustic-looking old house with its porches all around, her heart nearly stopped. "This is beautiful, Blake," she murmured, her gaze darting from the house to a sturdy rock and wooden dock nestled among trees and shrubs decked out in breathtaking fall colors.

"I thought you might like it here," he said, chuckling as he pulled the car to a stop at the side of the house. "My great-grandfather built it back in the twenties, as sort of a semiretirement cottage. Come on, let's get the kids and gear inside so we can enjoy just doing nothing."

Blake looked happier and more relaxed than she had ever seen him, Erin thought as she watched him carry Timmy up the four wide steps and deposit him on a weathered oak rocking chair. Had he brought Glenna here? she wondered, and then she chided herself.

Certainly he brought her here, idiot. They were married for what? Fourteen or fifteen years?

"Fourteen. We came here a few times, but not too often. You know, I wasn't much of an outdoor girl. Forget me and enjoy yourself."

Forget Glenna? How could she, when she never knew whether the ghost was lurking about? *Like now*, Erin thought as she looked around. It was Glenna's voice she heard as clear as day, but she couldn't see her ghostly rival.

"I'm going to float away for now, Erin. Enjoy!"

Erin laughed at herself. She had thought of Glenna, and abracadabra! There she was, out of sight but answering questions Erin had asked only in her mind. Today the antics of Glenna's ghost struck her as funny—maybe that was because she was here in this magical place and wasn't willing to let anything stand in the way of having a perfect family weekend with the man who was both Glenna's husband and her own.

"What's so funny?" Blake asked as he made another trip to the car for the last of their gear.

Erin visually searched the area one more time for Glenna. "Nothing. I'm just so happy to be out here in this gorgeous place with nothing to do except take care of you and the boys for three whole days.''

''Here, if you can grab these, we can start having fun,'' Blake said, handing her Jamie's diaper bags before wrestling the porta-crib from the trunk and setting it on the ground. Dazed, Erin watched the play of muscles in his neck when he lifted the nursery equipment and headed for the house.

''Mommy, Daddy! Aren't you gonna bring Jamie in?'' Timmy called from his vantage point on the porch.

Erin looked at Blake, and he stared back. She saw his grin turn into a full-fledged belly laugh just about the time tears came rolling down her own cheeks. They had relaxed, she guessed. Even if just a few short minutes had passed, she and Blake had gone without thinking of the tiny boy whose existence was the only reason they were a family now.

''I think we've got both of them plain tired out,'' Erin said later, after they had backpacked Tim and Jamie on a long but leisurely trek through the woods that ringed the lake.

Blake murmured his agreement as he set Timmy gently on his bed and began to remove the little boy's clothes. ''Can you hand me his pajamas?'' he asked Erin, hoping their walk hadn't been too much for her.

''Here. Timmy, do you want something to eat?'' she asked, leaning over to smooth a stray lock of hair from the boy's forehead.

''No. I'm stuffed. Night-night, Mommy. Daddy.''

Blake had sort of figured the two peanut butter and jelly sandwiches and assorted candy bars that Timmy had scarfed down during their hike would take the edge off his appetite tonight—but what the hell. This weekend was for his son; it would be a long time before Timmy would be recovered from this surgery that was coming up, too long for them to be able to promise the boy a return trip out here before the weather turned too cold to enjoy what nature had to offer.

Digging back into memories of long, long ago, Blake wove a story for Tim about when Possum Kingdom was a wild and wooly no-man's-land where outlaws hid from the Texas Rangers. He had no idea if the yarn was true, but he had loved it when his grandpa used to tell the tale to him when he lay here in this same bed, tired from swimming and running in a wilderness that had by that time been made safe for little boys.

"Tell me another story, Daddy," Timmy begged, but Blake could see he was fighting sleep.

He leaned down and kissed the little boy's windburned cheek. "Tomorrow, sport. You need your sleep now."

Quietly he got up and doused the light. Why was it, he wondered, that he felt a sense of peace here that eluded him when he was home? He banished the question from his mind, not willing to risk spoiling the good, simple feeling of contentment by pondering reasons for it.

He found Erin putting Jamie into the little crib they had brought and felt a twinge of jealousy for the simple and unconditional love she gave to both her boys. She fairly glowed when she gazed down at their sleeping baby.

"Join me by the fire?" he asked, surprised at the huskiness in his own voice.

Erin looked up and met his gaze. "I'd like that," she said in a tone that reminded Blake of milk and honey and soft, naked woman. He pushed that thought from his mind. This time was for the kids, especially Tim—and for getting to know this woman who was his wife, but who had accurately pointed out just days ago that they were strangers.

She seemed tense, curled up at one corner of the U-shaped gray leather sofa in front of a fireplace where he had laid a modest fire. Her brow was creased, as if with worry, and he detected a tightness in her shoulders beneath that soft, dark red robe that covered her from neck to toes.

"Are you worried about Timmy?" he asked, echoing his

own fear that had triggered this impromptu vacation.

Erin looked up and met his gaze. "Yes," she said, bringing her bare feet up close to her hips and hugging her knees with both slender arms. "I'm glad you thought of bringing us here. Timmy hasn't had many chances to enjoy the out-of-doors the way he did today, with you being his 'horsie.' "

"I enjoyed it, too. I thought I'd take him fishing tomorrow. Would you like a drink before I sit down?" Blake asked, thinking that might be just the ticket to help Erin relax and set her worries aside for a while.

She smiled. "What are you offering?"

"Beer, wine, hard liquor. Water and cola to mix with. Probably seltzer, too. I'll look and see what other mixers might be lurking behind the bar."

"A beer would be good," Erin said, and Blake brought two frosty cans from the bar refrigerator. "Thanks."

"You're welcome." Intentionally Blake settled in the other rounded corner of the sofa. He wanted to talk, not make love—but he knew that if he got close to Erin, his unruly libido would overrule his brain. "What was Tim like before he got hurt?" he asked.

"Like any bright, curious four-year-old, I guess. He's always been a basically happy child." She paused, as if she were sorting out the thoughts inside her head. "He's quieter. I think it's more than just his age and not being able to get around the way he did before."

"How did you stand it? Having Timmy hurt so badly and losing your husband at the same time?" Erin hadn't ever said much about her marriage, and Blake wondered if a part of her were still grieving over her loss.

"I didn't have a whole lot of choice, Blake. Bill was dead. Nothing was going to bring him back. And all I could do for Timmy was be there for him. . . ." Erin's voice trailed off, and she looked away, out the windows toward a starry sky.

"Tell me about it. I'd gladly go through what's in store

for Tim next week if I could. All I've done since we talked with the surgeons is wonder if there's anything, no matter how insignificant it may be, that I can do to make it easier for him.''

Erin turned back to Blake. She felt as if she was looking all the way to his soul. ''All we can do is love him. He'll have the surgery, and he'll be able to walk again or he won't. Timmy knows we'll be there for him either way.''

Through her simple words, Blake saw a strength in Erin that he hadn't realized before. She had gone through hell, might very well go through a lot more of it before Timmy's rehabilitation was complete. At best, she would suffer each and every one of her son's pains and disappointments as he moved slowly toward recovery. At worst, she could find that all his suffering had been for naught—that Timmy would never again be whole and strong.

He slid closer to her and took her hand. ''I'll be there for him, too,'' he told her quietly, and he meant it as he hadn't meant the vows he had made when they married.

''I know.'' She brought his hand up and brushed it against her lips. ''Timmy's lucky to have you, Blake,'' she said quietly as she burrowed her head against his shoulder.

This feels so right, Blake thought, letting his fingers sift through her hair that looked and felt like dark, shimmering silk. ''Tell me about Tim's mom,'' he prompted as he leaned back against the couch pillows, bringing Erin with him.

''There's nothing special to tell. I grew up on a little ranch about halfway between Midland and San Angelo. Until I was nine, there was just Mom and Dad and me. Then Sandy was born. In high school, I edited the school paper for me and went out for cheerleader to please my mom. I graduated and got a scholarship to SMU. Four years later I had a degree in journalism and a brand-new husband.''

''Did you ever work?''

Erin chuckled. ''Outside the house? No. It had been my dream to write all kinds of compelling feature articles and sell them to magazines and newspapers—and I wrote a few pieces, but they didn't sell. Bill wanted me at home. He was a sales representative, and he had to entertain customers a lot. After he died, I tried writing some more, hoping I could make a little money to help out with Timmy's medical bills. Again, no luck—or maybe just no talent.''

This was a new facet to Erin, one Blake hadn't gleaned from bare facts Greg had passed along before they made the surrogate arrangement over a year ago—or sharing a house with her for months. She liked to write but had given it up to be the kind of wife Bill had wanted. He liked the tenacity he saw in her that had let her try again and not become bitter at rejection. Did she still have dreams of a home-based career?

"You could write now," he murmured, his hand going still at the curve of her neck.

Erin tipped her head back and met his gaze. "I've thought about it. Now I have time, even with both boys. Have I thanked you for hiring Theresa? It really wasn't necessary, but I appreciate her help.''

"She needed a job. And Mary's not as young as she used to be. I don't want you tied to the house and kids twenty-four hours a day. I didn't marry you to be a nanny," he replied, knowing when he said it that it was a lie—at least, it had been, the day they said their vows.

"Anyway, thanks. Would you like some coffee before we go to bed?''

Bed?

"Not unless you do. Isn't it about time for Jamie to have his midnight snack?" he asked, telling himself her innocent question hadn't been an invitation and damning the desire that slammed into him like a sledgehammer.

How could he ever have thought this woman plain? Blake pictured her as she had been that first day they met, tired and worn and pregnant with his son. And he told himself that then he'd felt nothing but anger at the situation that had brought them together. It didn't do any good.

"Damn," he muttered. She drew him like a moth to a flame, and there wasn't a thing he could do to make himself stop wanting her. Pushing week-old promises and old, tearing memories from his mind, he pulled her closer and sampled the sweet temptation of her mouth.

When he knew that if he didn't stop now, he never would, Blake ended the kiss and cradled Erin's head gently against his shoulder. "You go on and get ready for bed, before this fire inside me builds to the point that I forget all my good intentions. I'll check on Tim and change Jamie before I bring him in to you," he said.

As he watched her go, his body protested in no uncertain terms at the torture it was enduring because he and Erin had agreed to this time of being just new friends, getting to know one another as they hadn't before they had given in, just once, to a mutual chemistry like nothing he had ever experienced before.

"This place will be perfect for Sandy and Greg to have their honeymoon," Erin murmured, her gaze on their baby who was nursing contentedly at her breast.

"Uh-huh."

Blake seemed to have lost his usual articulate way of speaking, she decided. For fifteen minutes he had just sat there in an old oak rocking chair, staring at Jamie and her as if trying to memorize their features. Every time she tried to start a conversation, he gave some monosyllabic reply, as if he would really rather address some deeply private thoughts.

"Blake, what's wrong?"

"Nothing."

Not one to give up when they had been communicating so nicely earlier, Erin tried another tack. "I told you all about me. Now it's your turn," she coaxed gently.

He met her gaze, and she could see sadness as well as the desire he hadn't been quite able to mask when he held and kissed her less than a half hour ago. When he finally spoke, his voice was raspy, as if the words were being tortured from somewhere deep inside his soul.

"We're here together because fate took . . . Glenna . . . away," he said, as if he could barely stand to speak his late wife's name. "But of course you know that. You know as much as I do. One day she was here, happier than I'd ever seen her before, and the next she was dead, shot down by that psycho. . . ." He sounded as if he was choking as his last words trailed off.

Then he continued, his voice strengthening. "You've been through as much as I have, though. Maybe more. We've both been handed a lot to deal with. But in one way I don't think fate's treated us as badly as it could have."

Hope sprang into Erin's heart, but she beat it down, unwilling to risk disappointment if she was misunderstanding what Blake was trying to say. "What do you mean?" she asked when he didn't elaborate on that enigmatic statement.

He seemed to be struggling to voice what was on his mind. "We got together because of *him*," Blake said, nodding at their sleepy baby. "And because of my losing . . . *her*. But it could be worse, much worse. You love that little guy, and so do I. I've got two boys now who give me more joy in living than I ever thought I'd have again."

He paused, his dark blue gaze holding her in thrall. "Erin," he finally said, continuing, "I think we've got a whole lot more going for us than some couples do. I like you and I believe you like me, too. And neither one of us can deny the chemistry between us, honey."

She had hoped for more, but expected less. Blake still couldn't bear to hear Glenna's name. Erin doubted if he would for a long time, if ever. But he could admit liking her and wanting her. She felt the corners of her mouth turn up in an accepting smile.

"Are you saying we're luckier than we could have been because we're not stuck in a marriage of convenience where neither of us can stand to look at the other?" she asked, lightening the mood.

"Yeah. I could look at you a long time without getting tired of the view," he drawled, following her lead. "Is our son asleep?"

She nodded.

With infinite care, Blake lifted Jamie and anchored the baby firmly against his shoulder with one muscled arm and hand. "Good night, sweetie," she whispered to the sleeping infant—and the man she was coming to love far, far more than she had ever loved Bill all those years ago.

"May I come back?" Blake asked, his hooded gaze more compelling than the simple words.

She tried to find the words to say no, but her heart screamed, "Yes." Loving him could—almost certainly would, she mentally amended—hurt her. Still, denying him would hurt her, too.

Maybe he was right. Fate had scarred them both; but it could have dealt each of them a rougher hand than it had. She would play the game like seven-card stud, betting that the next card falling would bring them not a royal flush, but the love they had lost in other games of times gone by.

Erin nodded her head and smiled. What would be, would be.

Chapter 20

What would be tonight was pure, sensual pleasure, Erin knew as soon as Blake walked back into the room. Newly shaved, barefoot, and naked to the waist, he nearly took her breath away.

Unbuttoned jeans only emphasized his impressive masculinity, already aroused and straining against dark blue briefs she could see in the gaping vee of his fly. And the look in his eyes told her he was on the prowl, a predatory male animal now who bore only slight resemblance to the loving father who had walked in the woods today with her and their boys.

"I intend to spend the night in here," he said, and there was no way Erin was going to suggest otherwise. Every pore in her body ached for him, and one short coupling wasn't going to put out her fire, either.

"Come here," she whispered.

He just stood there and looked at her. She burned from the intensity of his gaze. Breathless now, she slid off the bed and took three steps, stopping when she was close enough to reach out and stroke the muscled expanse of his chest.

Slowly he pushed those soft, faded jeans down his legs and stepped out of them. He held her with a hot, needy gaze. She heard rather than felt the teeth of her robe's zipper whisper, sensed his long, nimble fingers tugging at the tab. Then the soft breeze from an open window caressed her naked skin. She moved one step closer, close enough that she could hear his heart beat, see his pulse in the muscled column of his neck.

"We've got all night, Erin," he murmured as he caught her questing hands and brought them gently to his lips. She shuddered when he sucked one finger into his mouth and laved it with his tongue.

She felt herself falling more deeply under his sensual spell. This wasn't the impetuous lover who had taken her in a frenzy of passion and then come back to satisfy her needs. It wasn't a grief-stricken man torn with guilt, either. Tonight Blake was weaving an erotic fantasy like nothing she had ever imagined before.

"Touch me," she implored while he ministered to each of her fingers in turn. Suddenly the cool air might as well have been a blazing furnace. She burned from the tips of her fingers that he was seducing with such leisurely fervor, to a spot deep inside her that ached to be filled with him.

"Patience is a virtue," he murmured, but he released her hands and slid his under her open velvet robe. The warm coarseness of hardened and callused palms sweetly abraded her skin. "Are you hot?"

She wasn't hot. Hot was too tame a word. She was smoldering from the inside out. That was how he made her feel. And she wanted more. She wanted him to love her until she fell apart in a conflagration of sensual delight. "You're making me burn," she whispered, her hands burrowing into his soft chest hair to find and tease taut masculine nipples.

"Not yet." Again he took those talented hands off her to halt her own exploration. "Let me show you slow and easy."

When she stilled her hands, he released them and returned to caressing her shoulders. This time, though, his hands moved down her arms, slipping the smooth, soft velvet before them. She felt the robe puddle at her feet, and the night breeze caress her from head to toe.

He must have seen her shiver and thought it was from cold air, because he came closer and wrapped her in the cushion of his arms. He wasn't holding her tightly, but she still felt branded by the heat of his erection that pulsed hard and strong against her stomach through the insignificant barrier of his briefs.

She couldn't help the way her hips sought his, how they moved in sinuous rhythm against heat barely contained in the last barrier to their joining. And she felt his control slip, in the fast, shallow breaths that ruffled her hair against one ear.

"Shower time," he told her, punctuating his words by lifting her as if she weighed no more than Timmy and striding in fluid, efficient movements into the adjoining bathroom. Setting her down in the pristine, white shower stall, he slid off his briefs and joined her.

He was rock-hard. She couldn't help but wonder if he was in pain. She knew she was hurting, hurting for him to fill her. But he seemed not to be in any great hurry, she thought resentfully as she watched him adjust the twin showerheads and sigh as pulsing warm water prickled his gorgeous body.

Turning, he grasped her waist and positioned her where the water pounded at her skin. She gasped at the contrast of sensation when he caressed her with soapy smooth, callused-rough hands. She felt her nipples tighten and bead up at his touch. Her stomach muscles flinched in response to the water's sting, then relaxed as he moved his hands over the sensitive skin of her mound, protecting it from the tingling spray.

Weak with all Blake was making her feel, Erin leaned back, welcoming the smooth, impersonal coolness of the tile against her back. She still felt dizzy, more so when he stopped and lathered more soap in his big, capable hands. When he knelt before her, she had to move her legs apart to keep from falling in a heap of quivering limbs and frustrated need.

Rivulets of water streamed from his thick, sable hair and down a face she thought must be part angel, part devil to enslave her this way. His hands were magic, branding her with fire as they moved up her legs, unconcerned about the yearning, throbbing core of her that was fairly screaming for his touch.

As if she were a helpless baby, he soaped her ankles— calves—the outside of her trembling thighs. He had to know what he was doing to her, she thought, resentful that he had her trapped here, where she couldn't reach out and touch him, torture him with caresses that enflamed yet did not satisfy.

She wanted to be on her knees, taking his big, throbbing penis in her mouth. Her hands itched to weigh his hot, velvety soft scrotum while her tongue teased his hard, pulsing erection. Maybe then he would know the sensual torment he was now inflicting on her!

Through a haze of half joy, half pain, she felt his hands reach between her legs and wash her. She opened further to him, willing him to ease the ache that was building to a fever pitch. He didn't touch her, not the way she wanted him to. Instead, he reached for the lower showerhead, pulled it off its stand, and directed its needlelike flow to rinse off the soap.

"Blake, please," she murmured, nearly out of her mind now.

"Soon, honey."

He replaced the showerhead. With maddening lack of haste, he turned back to her, using his hands to caress her inner thighs and spread them farther apart. She held her breath, waiting—knowing when he took both hands and opened her to his gaze that he had only begun his sensual assault.

His breath was hot, searing her like a brand when he finally leaned toward her and rested a clean-shaven cheek against her mound. She felt his tongue snake out, wrapping itself around the tiny nub that felt so hard by now she thought she might scream.

"I need you now," she croaked, opening herself even more as he sucked more strongly at that tiny bud and insinuated two, then three long fingers deeply inside her.

He muttered something, but it melded in the haze of sexual excitement that was bubbling toward a climax. She didn't want it this way! But she couldn't make her body move away. There was no will in her to close herself to Blake, make him stop and give her of himself, not just of his passion.

Her fingers tangled in wet strands of his hair as she leaned back harder against the shower tiles. Shudders of ecstasy wracked her body; then she came down again to earth, only to succumb again to the ministrations of his eager hand and tongue. The second time, she collapsed into strong arms suddenly supporting her against his rock-hard body.

He wasn't done with her yet, she knew in a tiny sane part of her mind that registered the rough-soft feel of a big bath sheet instead of the piercing needles of water that had sensitized every pore on her body. His pulsing sex beckoned, and she weighed him in her hand before he scooped her back up into his arms.

She let him carry her back to the bedroom. It was his turn now, she decided, to let her feed her fantasies on his helpless flesh. "Sit on the edge of the bed," she ordered in the most compelling tone she could manage.

If she hadn't been his helpless prisoner just moments earlier, Erin doubted she could have found the courage to sink to her knees and bury her face against the unyielding hardness of his belly. Her tongue swirled around his navel, testing the textures of firm, smooth skin and fine, silky body hair. He smelled like the soap he had used to tease her, she thought as her mouth traveled lower.

With the tip of her tongue, she circled the knob of his engorged penis, liking the way it twitched and grew under her shy caress. Could she take him in her mouth? she wondered, her fingers measuring the length and thickness and . . .

"Erin, you're killing me," he muttered, but he sounded more impassioned than tortured. Encouraged, she took the tip of him inside her mouth and suckled while her hands captured and cradled the heavy sac that held his seed. Her lips curled with pleasure at the sound of his raspy, tortured breathing.

He was so big and so hard. So strong. Taking a deep breath, she relaxed and sank further down on him, swallowing reflexively when she took him deep into her throat. His body hair tickled her lips and made her draw back, but she felt a thrill of power when he flexed his hips and made her take all of him again.

"Stop!" he cried as she was just about to climax from feeling him stretch and caress her throat while she lightly squeezed his scrotum between her questing fingers. She didn't want to stop. She wanted to feel him come the way he'd made her explode with his mouth.

Vaguely she felt him lie back and lift her onto the bed, twisting her body until she straddled him. Yet she held on to her prize.

She felt him take her nipples between his thumb and forefinger. He tugged and squeezed in a rhythm that matched what her mouth was doing to his hot, hard sex. Then he moved his head between her widespread legs and plunged his tongue deep into her wet, ready body.

He had the control of an iron man, she thought as she worked up and down his erection with eager lips and tongue. What he was doing to her turned her bones to jelly. Certainly he couldn't take much more!

She felt him lift her shoulders, and she cried out at the loss of her sexual toy. With total efficiency of motion, he positioned her facedown on the bed, raising her hips and seating himself deep inside her in a single powerful thrust.

For long moments he didn't move inside her, choosing

instead to tug her nipples gently and roll them to tight, moist buds while he let her milk him with internal muscles that seemed to have a mind of their own. She felt him suckle at the tender skin of her neck.

Then he nearly withdrew before plunging deep, so deep she thought he touched her womb. The pressure inside her built, with every thrust of his hips that took him ever deeper, ever harder inside her, with each feathery touch of his fingers on her nipples and each love bite from his lips. She felt a part of him, more than she had ever felt before, and she wanted more.

Bracing herself, she met his next wild plunge with one of her own, and she felt the pressure inside her build. Her breasts cried for their loss when he moved his hands, lifting her buttocks higher off the bed; but her body soared when he began to stroke and tease the slick, tight bud of her desire with nimble fingers while his huge, hot penis sank harder and deeper into her eager warmth with every stroke.

She felt a gush of new moisture and ground her hips backward into his. Before she succumbed completely to the carnal feast, she heard him shout and felt him give himself to her in an explosion of the mutual passion neither of them could deny.

He didn't leave her as he'd done before, Erin thought with satisfaction some time later as she lay on her side, still joined intimately with Blake. He filled her yet, even sated as he was, she learned as her own overworked muscles gripped him as if they would never let him go.

Blake awakened to the sound of his baby's plaintive wail. For a minute he was disoriented. Then he felt Erin's warm, pliant body next to him and realized he wasn't alone.

They had spent the night together. And what a night it had been! Reflexively Blake reached out and touched her face, so relaxed and peaceful in sleep. Then he slipped out of bed and stretched tired muscles he had severely taxed after long inactivity.

There's nothing wrong with you, he thought, as he pulled up briefs over part of him that should have been wrung out and hung up to dry. He grinned. He might be thirty-eight and aching, but he could still wake up with a hard-on like a randy fifteen-year-old.

Humming a sprightly tune, he looked in on a sleeping Timmy before answering Jamie's escalating demands. "You're a real screamer, aren't you?" he asked the baby while he cleaned him up. "You've got to take it easy on your mom this morning, son. I'm afraid I kept her from her sleep last night."

When he brought Jamie to Erin, he shed his jeans and joined them in the bed. The old demon, guilt, washed over him, but he fought it down. Glenna was dead, he was alive.

Blake reminded himself it had been Glenna who had insisted before she died that someone bear his child for her. He had agreed. When she died, she had left his son short one mother, so he had supplied one.

Erin deserved if not his love, then his respect and his passion. And he deserved the pleasure he had found with the mother of his children, he told himself as he adjusted the pillows behind his head.

Feeling more than the sexual satisfaction he could readily understand, Blake extended his arm and pulled Erin against his chest. "Does that feel good?" he asked as he watched his baby suckle greedily at her full, pale breast.

"Not as good as it does when you do it," she replied with a soft smile. "But it makes me feel useful to know Jamie needs me as much as I need him."

"Lucky baby," Blake murmured, his index finger stroking her breast lightly, close to his son's busy little mouth. He grinned when Jamie grasped his finger in a tiny fist and tugged at it with surprising strength. "Did you nurse Timmy?"

"Only for a month or so. It bothered Bill—he thought enlightened mothers bought formula in disposable bottles."

"It turns me on to know you're nourishing my child,"

Blake murmured, a trifle embarrassed to feel himself hardening again beneath the concealing sheet and blanket. "You know, I never saw a baby nursing before. Never expected to. But I like it."

Erin shifted Jamie to her other breast. She seemed as unconcerned by her nudity as he usually was with his own—until that day not long ago when she had brought his dormant sexuality to a resounding state of wakefulness.

"You're the sexiest woman I've ever met." Gently he reached down and stroked the velvety soft folds of skin that concealed her sex.

"You're good at making me feel sexy," she replied, reaching under the covers to tangle her fingers in the thick hair at his groin before tracing the length of him gently with her palm.

Blake wasn't used to such honest, easy sexuality, his woman telling him straight out without the slightest guile that she liked his body and what it could do for her. But damn! She made him want not only to give and get sexual relief, but to experience every form of human sensuality, every nuance of erotic pleasure he had ever experienced or heard about.

"I'll give you about an hour to stop that," he growled as he bent and suckled at the breast his son had almost—but not quite, emptied.

She squirmed, opening her legs further as he fondled her. God, how hot and smooth she felt! That little rose-red nub of flesh that peeked impudently at him from silky, pouting lips was hard as stone. He felt her finger stroke the very tip of his erection, coaxing out a pearl of moisture to slicken and ease the gentle friction that was driving him insane.

"Jamie's gone to sleep," she told him, her voice languid as she kept up the circular motion that was threatening to make him come.

"Good." He raised his lips from her breast and licked away the drops of milk that lingered there.

She acted as if she never wanted to let him go. "Just a

minute," he told her, tossing back the covers and dragging a soft quilt off the bed. Quickly he folded it into fourths and set it on the floor. "Give me the baby," he said, and when she did, he settled Jamie on his makeshift bed.

"We should have about an hour before Timmy wakes up," Erin said as she looked from the digital clock to his straining sex. "You're magnificent, you know."

"So are you." He feasted on her with his gaze, from the top of her tousled head to narrow feet with neatly painted toenails. But it was her velvety woman's place that beckoned like the sirens of old. She lay there naked, without props like see-through nighties or erotic toys, raw desire in those expressive eyes that reminded him of a calm, still sea. Desire for him.

He bent and swirled his tongue down her body, savoring the tremor he felt when he laved her mound. Playfully he flicked at that impudent little nub of flesh that demanded his attention before nipping at firm, slender thighs and the soft lips that veiled her sex.

"Blake." Her hands tugged and pulled at his leg until he gave in and straddled her. At first she teased him with gentle puffs of breath that tickled his balls while he attended to readying her with nimble fingers. Then she took him fully into her mouth, and it was his turn to shudder.

Her tongue teased and tormented, her fingers tangled in his hair and drew him deeper down her throat. His nostrils full of the smell of her and him and sex, he buried his face between her legs and devoured the hot sweet essence of her. He sent his tongue deep inside her again and again, then drove three fingers into her and rode her hard while his teeth caught her clitoris for his tongue to flail.

When her mouth went slack on him and she gasped for breath, he reversed positions and draped her legs over his shoulders. Mindful that the night's activities might have left her sore, he entered her slowly, an inch at a time, until his balls rested tightly against her wet, satin skin. Deliberately he ignored her begging and withdrew, taking time to sheath himself before joining their bodies again.

He watched her writhe, wanting more, wanting all he had to give her. But he wanted more, too. Rhythmically he slid in and out, delving deeper each time until he could feel the tip of her womb. His gaze fastened on her face, damp with sweat and slack with passion, took in eyes half shut, focused unashamed on the part of him that was part of her.

He looked down, torturing himself by going slowly, savoring the eroticism of visualizing what before he had only known by touch and feel. God, he was going to come, and there wasn't a thing he could do to delay it, he thought as he desperately worked his fingers on her nipples to bring her with him.

"Blake! God, Blake, don't stop. Please don't stop."

"I won't. I can't." His breath came in short, shallow spurts as her body bucked and convulsed against him. He let go and let her storm carry him over. A long time later, he got up to take care of his sons.

Erin hummed happily as she slipped into jeans and a bright plaid Western-style shirt for the day. She felt like pinching herself to see if she were dreaming. Before last night, she would have laughed if anyone had told her it was possible to make love three times in one night.

But Blake had been insatiable, waking her twice in the night. And again this morning! She still felt aftershocks of pleasure from their last wild lovemaking.

He was a moaner, not a talker, she had quickly determined. Still, it heartened her when he said, "I think we should make this a real marriage." Those had been his parting words as he left to get the boys ready for a boat trip around Possum Kingdom Lake.

Erin couldn't help thinking, as she brushed her hair, that he had never mentioned love. But he wanted her. And she had no doubt that he loved Jamie—and Tim. Maybe in time she could love away the emptiness that still so often darkened his heart.

"Do I smell coffee?" she asked brightly as she joined Blake and Timmy in the big, old-fashioned kitchen.

Blake grinned. "It's instant. I hope you don't mind."

"Not at all." She dumped a spoonful of crystals into a mug and filled it with the water Blake had boiling in a kettle on the stove. "Don't tell me you made breakfast, too!"

"Daddy made pancakes in the microwave," Timmy offered excitedly when Erin joined him at the table.

"Better eat up, sport. We've got a big day ahead of us." Blake pulled another package of pancakes out of the freezer. "Want some, Mommy?" he asked.

"Sure. Where's Jamie?"

"Taking another nap. I just cleaned him up again, so all we have to do when we finish up here is collect him and hurry on down to the dock."

Later, as they had a picnic lunch in a secluded cove surrounded by trees and bushes in all their autumn glory, Erin watched Blake teach Timmy how to bait a hook and cast his line. Neither of them caught a fish, but then they didn't have to. Just being together, all of them, this way seemed enough to put them, and Erin herself, into a wonderful, relaxed mood.

On the way back to Dallas, Erin could feel that sense of well-being slipping away. Despite herself, she worried about Timmy's upcoming surgery; and she knew that subject was on Blake's mind, too. If that weren't enough, she had taken on much of the planning for Sandy's wedding— a wedding that just might not be happening if those two couldn't reconcile their differences over the care and handling of Greg's willful daughter.

At least, she reminded herself, she and Blake were of like minds about the problems that loomed immediately in their future.

*   *   *

I hate hospitals, Blake thought vehemently as he waited for Dr. Newman in a small anteroom off the main operating suite at Children's Medical Center late the following Friday afternoon. He found this place where helpless children suffered and died even worse than the ones where most of the patients were adults.

"Sorry to keep you waiting, Mr. Tanner," Dr. Newman said briskly as he hurried into the room through sliding doors. "Come on into my office."

Blake glanced around a sparsely furnished cubicle that did nothing to inspire confidence in its occupant's stature, before taking a seat in the single, scarred oak armchair. "I appreciate your making time to see me," he said politely, his gaze coming to rest on a wall full of diplomas displayed in mismatched frames.

"You said you had more questions about your son's coming operation," Newman said, his tone expectant.

"Yes. What are you going to do exactly, and what results do you expect?"

The surgeon rifled through an untidy stack of papers on his desk and came up with the folder he apparently was looking for. "This will be Timmy's fourth operation," he said. "I've gone over all this before."

"I'd appreciate your running through the details again with me. For my own peace of mind, you understand." Blake reminded himself that Greg had given this guy a vote of confidence.

Newman started at the beginning, when Timmy had nearly lost both legs, and continued to chronicle in graphic detail each operation and therapy regimen Timmy had endured over the past three and a half years. Blake shuddered.

"Basically, I'm going to go in and do more nerve grafts in his left leg. The orthopedic team will graft more bone and replace some of the hardware in his right ankle, if they find the leg is viable," the surgeon explained. "If not, they'll amputate it just above the site where we reattached the severed right ankle and foot. We'll do the procedures on both legs simultaneously, to reduce the total time your son will be under anesthesia. The operations, while long, aren't particularly risky in terms of life and death.''

The doctor's matter-of-fact explanation made Blake shudder, deep inside. "How many more operations is my boy going to have to endure before he's as good as he's going to get?''

Blake watched the expression in Newman's deep brown eyes. The doubt he saw there increased his apprehension. "I asked you a question," he said when the doctor hesitated.

"I'm hopeful that this surgery will be the last on Tim's left leg.''

"How about the other one?" Blake asked, forcibly maintaining a facade of calmness.

"That depends on what the orthopods decide. If they believe the leg can be saved, long-term, they'll have to go in periodically until Tim is grown—or until they change their minds. He'll need nerve grafts as well. On the other hand, if they amputate, that should be the last surgery the boy will need.''

What a choice! Blake thought bleakly. "I—I didn't know his leg was damaged that much," he ground out, knowing he sounded like a blithering idiot.

Newman shrugged his narrow shoulders. "Mr. Tanner, Timmy's legs were both nearly severed in the accident. But the right foot and ankle were crushed as well. From just below the knee to the toes, that leg is a hodgepodge of hardware. No nerves or muscle to speak of. In my opinion, Tim will never be able to use it fully.''

"You recommend . . . amputation?" The word stuck on Blake's tongue.

"Yes. If they go that route, Tim could be mobile in just a few months with an intelligent prosthesis. If not, he will be wheelchair bound at least most of the time, with a non-functional natural leg that will need frequent surgical lengthening. The decision, though, is not mine. It belongs to the orthopedic team. They are deferring judgment until they open up the ankle and take another look.''

Feeling poleaxed, Blake bid Newman a somber farewell and drove silently home. As he drove, he wondered how in hell Erin had lived with Timmy's uncertain future and constant pain for all this time, how she managed the brave face she showed her son.

Hell, he thought as he pounded the steering wheel with a tightly fisted hand, he didn't even know what he should be hoping for. He wondered whether, if he were consulted, Timmy would opt for losing part of himself to gain faster and surer mobility and freedom from pain. As he pulled into the curving driveway, Blake let out his frustration in the form of several virulent Anglo-Saxon curses he hadn't used since the day Glenna died.

With determination, he put on a smile and went to find Erin. If anyone needed distraction, she must. And he intended to let her know he was and would be right beside her, no matter what.

''What's that?'' he asked when he found her sitting at the table where they had shared Jamie's birthday dinner several weeks earlier, an assortment of boxes and papers strewn over the tabletop. Apparently she had found her own way of keeping her mind off Timmy's surgery.

Erin looked up and returned his smile. ''This is a bunch of old family pictures. Sandy's going to wear our mother's wedding gown, so Greg asked if I could find a picture for him to give the florist. He's a thoughtful man, wanting to surprise Sandy with a bouquet that looks like Mom's.''

''Uh-huh.'' Blake pulled out a chair and sat down. ''May I help?'' he asked, needing to put his mind on something, anything except the worries his private visit with Dr. Newman had fed more than alleviated.

''Here, you can look through this box.'' She used a rag to dust off a tattered shoebox before dumping its contents onto the glass-topped table. Blake sorted through snapshots of Erin and Sandy at various stages while they were growing up, and of the pleasant-looking couple who must have been their parents.

Realization of this other loss that Erin had suffered hit him hard as he stared at the smiling bride and groom in a formal photo he found. He knew her parents had died less than a year before Timmy was born; yet she seldom spoke of them—at least to him. "You must miss them," he murmured. "Here, take a look."

He looked along with her at the faded image that revealed a dark, rugged-looking groom who looked proud but out of place in an ill-fitting black tux, and a delicate-looking bride in a simple white gown that emphasized her tiny waist and hugged trim hips.

"Did you wear her dress, too?" Blake asked, wondering why the thought of Erin marrying another man sent a jolt of jealousy through him like a knife.

She laughed. "I'd never have fit into it. I'm at least five or six inches taller than Mom was. Besides, the dress is velvet, and I got married in the summer."

Both times. Or didn't our wedding count?

That sad little ceremony hadn't meant a marriage to him at the time. But each day he was feeling more like a husband. He was wanting more of Erin than he trusted she was willing to give.

He watched her root through her parents' wedding pictures. "Look, Blake," she said, her voice ringing with excitement, "I found a shot of Mom's bouquet. Now I remember, she always liked to tell us how she'd picked poinsettias instead of orchids!"

She certainly had, Blake agreed as he looked at the photo, apparently taken at a reception. The bouquet formed a centerpiece on a table draped in white lace. Sprigs of holly decorated a tiered cake and candlesticks that held skinny, red candles.

"They must have had a Christmas wedding," he commented warily.

"Yes. Christmas Eve. Daddy used to call Mom his little

Christmas rose. Someday I'll get it all arranged in albums. Here, help me put this stuff back in the boxes. But leave that picture out. I'll take it to Greg.''

Blake sat there, staring at the picture. "Erin, this is really pretty, but . . ."

"You don't like it." She sounded hurt.

He chose his words carefully. "I like it. It's beautiful. Except, what color dresses are Sandy's attendants going to be wearing?"

"Royal blue."

Blake breathed a sigh of relief. "Then if I were you, I'd tell Greg to have the florist use white poinsettias. Otherwise the color scheme will be sort of reminiscent of the Stars and Stripes."

Erin laughed, and Blake relaxed. "You're right. Unless there's some kind of big flower that's blue?"

"None I can think of. Why couldn't they reverse the colors?"

"You mean, use white poinsettias—or orchids? And tiny blue flowers around them?"

"Yeah. That would work. Be sure and tell Greg, though, or he's likely to have the florist make up a bouquet exactly like the one your mother had." Blake knew Greg would, if he thought it would please Sandy. And he could just imagine what Greg's mother would have to say. "Are they coming over tonight?"

"No. Sandy called. She and Greg want us to come to his place and have dinner. Do you mind?"

"Should I?"

Erin tossed a saucy grin his way. "Sandy's making dinner, she said, and I'm afraid cooking isn't among her finer talents."

"Well, we survived my efforts in the kitchen out at Possum Kingdom. I'm sure your sister's masterpiece won't kill us," he replied, standing up and bending to brush his lips across her cheek. "Should I change?"

Erin's gaze shifted downward from his face to his lap,

and he wished for a minute that they could forget about eating and spend the evening in bed. "You can if you want to," she said. "Sandy doesn't do fancy. I'm going to wear what I have on."

He noted with approval that Erin had chosen a soft, chic jumpsuit they had found at Saks, on the shopping trip he had insisted on to distract them both after their joint meeting with Timmy's doctors. He loved the way the soft, off-white wool skimmed her slender frame and made her look sexy as hell—but still elegant and ladylike. "Are you wearing that teddy I picked out, too?" he asked, fighting down the flow of blood he suddenly felt pooling in his groin.

She nodded, and he got a whiff of the perfume that turned him six ways from Sunday. "I'll show you later. If you're going to change, you'd better hurry. We're supposed to be there at eight. I'll just go in and check on Jamie," she said as she walked away.

"Erin looked happy tonight," Sandy told Greg as they watched Blake help Erin into his car.

"Yes, she did. So do you." He pulled her back against him and bent to nip gently at her ear.

"I think it was a good idea to let her plan our wedding. If she weren't so busy, all she would do would be worry about Timmy. Greg, stop it," Sandy said, pulling away. "Shana's upstairs."

He turned her to face him. "And it's Mrs. Watson's night off, so I can't even go home with you tonight. I'm learning that full-time fatherhood has its drawbacks. Honey, I wish to hell I didn't have to wait four more weeks until I can take you upstairs to bed in front of God and everyone."

She met his gaze, and the longing in her expression mirrored his own need. "Behave, darling," she murmured, patting his shoulder the way she might pet a friendly but troublesome mutt. "At least one of us has to act like an adult instead of a horny teenager. Besides, we still have some addresses to copy down for the calligrapher."

Greg let out an exaggerated moan. "Okay." He stuffed a hand into his pants pocket and felt the picture Erin had slipped to him earlier. He made a mental note to drop it by the florist's tomorrow, between making hospital rounds and going to his office.

"Why don't we just write out the damn invitations ourselves?" he asked as he finished copying what seemed like the thousandth name from his dog-eared address book onto a white index card.

"Just because."

"Because, why?"

"Because you write like a doctor," Sandy said, a saucy grin on her face.

Greg shook his head. "You're making me print on these cards. If the calligrapher or whatever you call this person who addresses wedding invitations can read the cards, certainly the mailman could read addresses if I printed them on envelopes."

Sandy tossed her head back and laughed out loud. "Quit griping and let's get this done. Don't you want our invitations to be pretty? And uniform-looking?"

Greg couldn't see the point of fussing over putting names on envelopes that everyone would toss in the trash as soon as the things were open, but he felt good. Sandy wasn't making noises about cancelling their plans. And the past week, since he grounded Shana, had been peaceful.

Sandy and his daughter must have come to some kind of truce this afternoon, he guessed. He wasn't sure he wanted to know exactly what went on, but he had noticed with satisfaction that the two managed to tolerate each other's company at dinner without major bloodshed.

"Get busy! I've filled out twice as many cards as you have." Sandy picked up her cards and set them on top of his much smaller stack.

"Okay." He had to know, but he hated to risk opening up barely closed wounds. "Did you ask Shana if she'd like to be a bridesmaid?'' he asked, reaching out and taking Sandy's hand.

Sandy met his gaze. ''I asked. She said no. But she did agree to come to the wedding.''

Why couldn't his kid be a little angel like Timmy? Greg asked himself. ''Her not coming was never an option. I'll talk to her again,'' he promised, frustrated with his daughter's stubborn refusal to wish him and Sandy well.

''Greg, don't. You'll just back her into a corner, and she'll have to rebel. Let it go. I promised I'd take her shopping for a really special dress, one she can wear to the wedding and maybe later to a dance at school.''

''Are you okay with that?''

''Yes. I think Shana and I are starting to come to an understanding . . . but we're nowhere close to being friends, not now and probably not for a long time yet. It's too much to expect her to set aside all her fear and hostility at once.''

He took Sandy's hand and toyed with the sparkling diamond he had thought she would be tossing back in his face. ''I'm sorry, sweetheart,'' he said, wishing he wasn't coming to her with the baggage of two broken marriages and a troubled child he wasn't at all sure he could control.

''You haven't done anything to be sorry for.'' Setting the cards she had filled out into a neat stack, she got up and moved behind him, her talented fingers kneading the tense muscles of his neck and shoulders. ''I love you and you love me, and don't you ever forget it,'' Sandy said, her tone determined.

''I won't. Don't you ever forget it either.'' Greg leaned back and let her magic fingers lull away his doubts and tension. ''By the way, your dinner was great,'' he murmured, knowing how hard she had worked to fix that practically inedible meal.

''You don't have to lie, Greg,'' Sandy replied, stopping her sensual massaging and facing him, hands on hips. ''I know I can't cook worth beans. But I'll learn. Maybe your mother . . .''

"Honey, I don't care if you burn water trying to make us coffee. We'll just get Mrs. Watson to fix some stuff and leave it for us to warm up on her days off—or maybe I'll just have to make a standing date to take you out two days a week. Would you like that?"

Sandy pouted, but Greg could see the sparkle come back into her eyes. "I want to be a good wife. A good mother."

"You will be. Just wait and see. You're already the best thing that ever happened to me. You're the best office manager I've ever had. And in four weeks, you're going to be the best little wife in Texas!"

"Really?"

Greg stood and took her in his arms. "Really. Now you'd better get your gorgeous little tush out of here before I decide to hell with protecting my kid from the facts of life and drag you upstairs to our bedroom," he told her, nuzzling playfully at her neck.

Chapter 21

"Who was that?" Blake pulled his head out from under a pillow and stared at the digital clock on the nightstand in Erin's room.

"Sandy."

"What did she want? To be sure we'd survived without getting our stomachs pumped?" he grumbled.

"Blake! For all you know, I can't cook either!" Erin shared his thoughts about the charred casserole they had choked down earlier, but still she felt the need to defend her sister.

Blake grinned, a sleepy sort of look that nearly took her breath away. "At least you don't *try* to, honey."

Erin laughed. "Actually, I'm a pretty good cook. Mom taught me. I guess I neglected Sandy's education after she came to live with us." Last night's sampling of her sister's cooking hadn't dampened her enjoyment of being out with Blake, temporarily distracted from worrying over Timmy.

"What are you going to do today?" Blake asked as he rolled to the edge of her bed and dragged his body into a sitting position.

Erin stretched, trying to shake the cobwebs from a brain still fuzzy with sleep. "I thought I'd spend the morning with Timmy and Jamie. The caterer's coming over at noon so Sandy and I can go over the menu with her. How about you?"

"I'll be in court this morning. If you'd like, I can rearrange some appointments and spend the afternoon with you and the kids."

"You don't need to. Blake, I appreciate the extra time you've been making for us lately, but there's no reason for you to disrupt your routine at work."

Since the doctors had scheduled Timmy's surgery, Blake had made extra time for Erin as well as her son. Whether they rode the horses, talked with the caterers or florist, or just sat inside when the weather turned rainy and cool, Erin felt him lend her his strength each day. And at night she loved the way he held her for hours after they made slow, hot love.

She knew Blake hardly slept when he shared this bed in the room he had lived in with Glenna for so long. She felt his reluctance, knew the room brought memories he hadn't been able to sweep away when he had ordered the room stripped down to bare walls. Still, he lay there each night, holding her long after she had gone to sleep. Knowing that being there for her taxed Blake's endurance, Erin appreciated his kindness all the more.

Chapter 22

Glenna

It's been a long time since I've been in Blake's office. Since she popped in on Erin when they first arrived at Possum Kingdom, Glenna had pretty much sat back and watched Erin and Blake's relationship develop. Even though she drew the line at checking out how they were progressing in a physical way, she surmised from the way Erin glowed that they were getting on just fine in her bedroom, where Blake had been spending most of his nights.

She had no doubts, either, that Erin was deeply in love with Blake. How could she not be? Glenna thought smugly. *Her* Blake was nothing if not lovable!

Her worry was Blake. It hurt her to see his beautiful eyes still cloud with grief sometimes when he was deep in thought. And it bothered her that he could want Erin as much as he obviously did, and still withhold his heart.

I'm going to give it back to him.

And that was why she was here, to jar him into realizing what he had now was so much more than what he had lost—so much more than *her*. Clutching a paper bag in her hand, she crossed the room and stopped in front of Blake's cluttered desk.

Glenna felt a pang of sadness when she noticed the

empty spot on the credenza. Every time she had come in here when she was alive, she'd begged him to let her swap that picture of her in her wedding gown for a newer, less formal shot. But he had been adamant about that particular portrait, so it had stayed.

Maybe, she thought, he had finally started to get on with his life and put it away. Then she remembered. When she had been here just days after her funeral, seeing him suffering and wanting baby Jamie's life destroyed, the picture had been gone, along with everything in the suite of rooms at home that had apparently reminded him too much of her.

"Just as well," Glenna murmured as she set down a brand-new, brushed silver frame in the place where Blake used to keep her wedding portrait. *"These go better in here, anyway."*

She took a moment to stare at this, her favorite of some photos Blake had captured of his new family at Possum Kingdom. Erin, Timmy, and Jamie lay stretched out on a blanket under a tree, looking happy but tired out from a long day's play. This was the kind of family Blake deserved—the kind she hadn't been able to give him.

It had been quite a task to lift the negatives she had found in Blake's study at home, materialize in a photo shop she'd never frequented as a living being, and get this shot blown up and framed. But it was worth it, she thought as she perched on the windowsill next to a couch in the corner of the office and settled down to catch his reaction.

Chapter 23

*B*lake hadn't slept worth a damn, but he shrugged off his own fatigue and put on a determinedly cheerful face for Timmy and Erin as he drove them to the hospital. He felt bad about leaving them there alone, but the case he was defending was at a crucial point, and he could hardly delegate the final arguments to one of his young associates. He had to be in court at eleven, and in his office for a while before that, to review some new notes his clerk had made.

Thoughts of Timmy and the ordeal he would face tomorrow distracted him as he drove to his office. With determination, he shelved those worries in a corner of his mind, so that his client might get the benefit of his full attention.

"What the hell?"

"Is something wrong?"

It took a minute for Blake to realize he'd yelled out loud, and that Sharon was standing beside him, looking at him as if he had lost his mind. Still, he couldn't tear his gaze from the picture.

"Did you put that there?" he asked.

Sharon shook her head. "I never saw it before."

"I have. At least, I think I have. I took a picture like that last weekend out at Possum Kingdom. But I didn't have it enlarged or framed, and I didn't bring it here."

"Maybe Mrs. Tanner . . ."

"She hasn't been here."

"Do you want me to put it away?" Sharon asked, her tone relaying a bit of exasperation as well as a lot of confusion.

"No." As the shock of seeing Erin and the children smiling back at him from the very spot where he had kept a picture of Glenna as a bride wore off, Blake realized that he liked having an image of his new, odd family here where he could see them. "It's all right, Sharon. Maybe Erin had it framed and delivered. Would you ask Jared to bring in the research he did last night?"

"Right away." Sharon turned and hurried out, as if anxious to get away from what she must have decided was her newly insane employer.

Blake turned back to the photo, picking up the frame and looking closely when he had a strange feeling that the thing was nothing but a figment of his imagination. It was real, all right, as real as the one he had taken down the day after Glenna died and locked into his credenza's bottom drawer.

He didn't know what compelled him to waste time like this on a day when he had to appear in court, but before he began reviewing the additional precedents Jared had found in some old, obscure cases, Blake fumbled in his top desk drawer for the key to the credenza, opened it, and took one longing look at the image of his first, lost bride.

Despite the late start and the nagging question about where that picture had come from, Blake wrapped up his summation at three and heard the judge's ruling before four o'clock. Usually a victory as big as this one gave him an adrenaline rush; today he only felt relieved that the case was finished and he would be able to stand by his son—and ask Erin about that blasted picture.

Blake strode into Timmy's hospital room minutes before five, loosening his tie as he went. "How's Tim doing?" he asked, forcing a casual demeanor he hoped Tim and Erin wouldn't see straight through.

"He's fine. But you look tired," Erin replied as she

looked up from the novel she had been reading. How was your day?"

"Good. The judge ruled in our favor. XCon offered a compromise settlement, and my client agreed. Where's our boy?" he asked, noticing that Timmy's bed was empty. Trying hard to relax, he shed his suit coat and settled into the other lounge chair.

"He's having an MRI. It shouldn't take much longer."

Just then an orderly opened the door and wheeled Timmy in on a child-size gurney. "Daddy!" he said, his eyes bright as they settled on Blake.

"Hey, sport."

Blake stood up and helped the orderly transfer Timmy into bed. For an hour or so, he asked his son about what he had done and people he had seen. It had felt right, he decided as he walked with Erin to the car, to promise Timmy they would both be back early the next day, before he had to go to surgery.

But Blake could feel Erin's fear, and it fueled his own apprehension. In the car as they drove home, and later when he held her, he tried to shake off the sense of foreboding that had begun last week and escalated today, when he kept trying to project confidence about what lay ahead—confidence he did not really feel.

He wanted to share his fear with Erin, and he wanted to ask her about that picture that had appeared as if by magic in his office, but he couldn't find the words. All he could do was hold her, be there for Timmy, and hope for . . . he wasn't sure just what he prayed tomorrow would bring.

"He's going to be all right."

Erin wished she felt as confident as Blake sounded. "Blake, I'm sorry. I've never been such a basket case before, not even the first time they operated on Timmy. I don't know what's gotten into me," she told him as she choked back tears.

Timmy had been in the operating room for hours. Here

in this VIP lounge with its cherry-smocked attendant who offered freshly brewed coffee and a selection of fragrant home-baked sweet rolls with annoying regularity, Erin felt just as distraught as she ever had when she waited in the big, spartan main surgery waiting room whose only refreshments came from quirky vending machines, with as many as fifty strangers who were waiting for news of their own loved ones.

Nervous, she paced across the room and looked out from a wide expanse of windows onto neatly manicured grounds. The glass reflected her image, so different now when she was wearing a fine light wool coat dress and matching burgundy heels than it had been the last time she waited in that other place in her tired old jeans and a faded sweater.

Her gaze shifted and took in Blake—then he had been only the source of funds for Timmy's surgery. Now, Timmy called him Daddy; and she looked to him for strength and comfort.

She was glad Blake had come. Nothing seemed to faze him, she thought as she watched him pull back a lever and settle into a recliner, coffee and rolls at his fingertips on a nearby table. Then he met her gaze, and she saw plain, stark fear reflected in his expression.

He's afraid, too.

Suddenly Erin needed to give as well as receive reassurance. "Timmy will come through this just fine," she murmured, echoing his earlier words as she knelt beside the recliner and sandwiched his hand between her trembling palms.

He nodded. "Sit down, Erin. Try to relax," he said softly.

She sank onto the sofa and tried to smile. "It's been nearly four hours," she said as she glanced at the stylized clock on the opposite wall.

"Dr. Newman warned us this would take time."

"What will happen to Tim if this doesn't work?" Erin pictured her little boy as he was last night, excited and certain that soon he would be able to run and play like other kids.

Blake sighed. "We'll just have to help him cope, I guess. Show him there's more he can do than there is he can't."

"Of course." What he said made sense; still, Erin didn't think she would be able to bear seeing Timmy watch his baby brother grow and develop, learning to walk and run while he was confined to a wheelchair.

"Everybody has disabilities, honey. They just don't all show. There are plenty of things Tim will be able to excel at, even if he can't use his legs."

"Blake, do you know something I don't?" Had Timmy's doctors talked to him alone, told him something they hadn't said when they had spoken to them together?

He met her questioning gaze. "I know Timmy's not likely ever to be an Olympic runner. I believe that's what Dan Newman said when I tried to pin him down. Erin, my work demands knowing when I'm hearing the unvarnished truth and when I'm being snowed. We were getting a snow job when we met with Timmy's treatment team. I went to Newman later and made him give it to me straight."

"Straight? And all he said was that Timmy would never be in the Olympics?"

"That's all he would predict outright. Erin, they don't know whether all this surgery is going to work. They don't know if Tim's legs are going to grow properly. Hell, they don't even know that they aren't going to have to take his right leg off."

Though she had heard the same warnings repeatedly since Timmy's accident, Erin felt terror tear through her. But then she looked at Blake and saw that he was hurting, too. "And you've known this for . . ."

"Four days." His tone was bleak as he got up from his chair and joined her on the sofa, putting his arm around her.

He'd known for four days what she had lived with for years—four days he had spent trying to keep her spirits up, she realized, and she leaned against the muscled strength of his chest. At that moment, as they shared their fears for Timmy, she loved him even more than before. And she felt that maybe his love for her son was spilling over and encompassing her.

They sat there for a long time, sharing what strength they could in silence while they waited helplessly for news.

"Mr. Tanner? Mrs. Tanner?"

Erin jumped at the sound of a woman's voice.

"Yes?" Blake said, that one word reflecting all the tension she had felt in his warm, hard body.

"I took the liberty of ordering you some lunch," the woman said, making a motion toward a small table draped with white linen and centered with an incongruously cheery bouquet of orange and gold chrysanthemums.

Erin made herself smile as she stood on legs that were trembling so much, she wondered if they would hold her. She welcomed Blake's steadying presence when he put his arm firmly around her waist and led her to the table.

"Eat, honey. You need to keep up your strength," he said when she sat there, just looking at a plate that held a club sandwich garnished with a variety of sliced, raw vegetables that came with a tiny cup of some creamy-looking dip.

He was right. She had to keep going, not only for Timmy but for baby Jamie—and Blake. When she met his gaze, she saw the toll that waiting was taking on him. Gamely she picked up a triangle of the large sandwich and took a healthy bite out of it.

"That's my girl."

Only when he saw that she was eating did he dig into the food on his own plate. Erin remembered those other times, when she had sat alone in that other waiting room even though she had been surrounded by so many other worried parents, and her heart filled with gratitude and love for Blake.

And those feelings carried her through until, as the sun

was setting in a blustery late autumn sky, a haggard-looking Dr. Newman came to tell them Timmy's surgery was done.

"His left leg should be nearly good as new," Newman told them as he sank down onto a chair that faced the sofa where Blake and Erin had settled down to wait.

"And?" Blake prompted.

Erin's muscles tensed. They had warned her when Tim had his first surgery that, even if the leg survived, it might never work again. Every time Tim had gone to surgery, the operative permits she had signed had included . . .

"We did all we could. We took the leg off just above where we had reattached it."

We took the leg off. That was all Erin heard before blackness overcame her.

Blake felt as if he had been slammed into a brick wall. He gasped for breath. It took moments for him to realize he was cradling Erin's unconscious body tightly against his chest, and that Dr. Newman appeared to be waiting for something.

"Do you want me to call someone?"

Blake looked down at his unconscious wife. "Greg Halpern."

Newman picked up a phone from the table beside him and punched out four numbers. Blake listened as he told someone to get Dr. Halpern; then he felt Erin begin to stir against his chest.

Newman set the phone down and met Blake's gaze. "I know it's a shock, but the news I brought was good, no matter how it sounded. Your son will be able to walk, even run. Soon. He will be minimally disabled."

Blake shot the surgeon a disbelieving look. He couldn't get the words out, but apparently his expression mirrored his horror.

"Better to get around almost normally with a prosthesis than to sit in a chair all your life with a leg that won't grow and won't work for you," Newman said with a tired-sounding sigh.

"How would you know?"

Newman kicked the table leg hard with his left foot. Blake's mind registered a hollow, metallic sound immediately, but it took a moment for the significance to set in. "You?"

The surgeon nodded. "Bone cancer. I was nine years old and damn lucky they got it before it spread," he explained before Blake could voice a question. "I was up on a prosthesis in three months, and out of therapy in six months. Kids bounce back a lot faster than adults do."

Blake tried to remember if there was anything about the way this man moved that should have tipped him off. He couldn't. Maybe he was losing the keen power of observation that made him a good attorney. "I couldn't tell," he admitted, more to himself than to the doctor.

"Most people can't."

Erin stirred again, and Blake watched her dark lashes flicker against pale, smooth skin. "Blake?" she said, her voice just the barest whisper of sound in the still, quiet room.

"I'm here, honey," he said, watching as her eyes slowly opened.

"I—I'm sorry. Dr. Newman, is Timmy . . ."

"He's in recovery. Because the operations took so long, it's going to take him a while to wake up. But he came through the surgery just fine."

Blake met Erin's newly determined gaze and knew she was going to demand all the details Newman had just provided him. He wished she wouldn't. He would rather tell her himself, in the familiar surroundings of home, where he could emphasize the positive and offer her the comfort of his body.

Greg strode in, Sandy right behind him. Blake had never been so glad to see his friend, he decided when Erin let her sister hug her and share her tears while Greg digested Newman's detailed medical explanation that Blake himself was in no state of mind to grasp.

"You all can stay here as long as you want," Newman said, drawing Blake's attention from Erin and Sandy who were quietly weeping in a corner of the pleasant room. "I'm going to check on Timmy before I go home."

"How can he be so damn matter-of-fact?" Blake asked Greg when Newman had left. "And so technical? The man's a walking, talking robot." He knew he wasn't being fair. Newman had a human streak, the one he had shown when he revealed his own disability to ease Blake's mind.

Greg shook his head. "He knows shit happens, but that life goes on. I guess he found that out young. If he didn't, a few years working in his particular surgical specialty probably taught him pretty fast. Timmy's going to get along okay, even if it won't be quite as easy for him to accept as Newman thinks it will."

"I knew the guy was a quack."

"Blake, he's not. He and his team are as good as you'll find anywhere in the world. Trust me."

Blake looked over at Erin. "How . . . how . . ."

"How can you make Erin not hurt anymore?"

"Yeah." Blake noticed her heartrending sobs had stopped, and that she was determinedly wiping at her tear-streaked cheeks with a tissue Sandy had dug out of her voluminous purse.

"Just love her."

Blake met his friend's solemn gaze. "Love?"

"Don't you?"

Did he? Of course he didn't. He loved Glenna and Glenna alone, since before he could remember and until eternity. Before he could blurt out the negative reply, he checked himself. "I love Timmy," he replied. "I like and respect Erin."

"Well, I hope that's enough. Come on, Sandy and I are going to take you two home. There's nothing any of us can do here, not tonight."

*   *   *

"Are you okay?"

Blake's question, voiced with obvious concern, startled Erin and made her body involuntarily jerk. She couldn't help smiling when Jamie yelped his protest at the interruption of his late evening snack. "I will be. How about you?"

"I think I'll make it, too. Did our little guy miss his mommy today?"

"Some. I think I missed him more. It's not too bad to skip nursing him once, but three times . . ."

"I should have had Theresa bring him to the hospital," Blake muttered apologetically.

Erin smiled. "A hospital's no place for a baby. I'll be fine when he finishes nursing." Deftly she turned Jamie and offered him her other aching breast.

Seeming almost afraid to voice his feelings, Blake skirted around the subject of Timmy until he finally blurted out, "What in hell can I say to him?" in a tortured voice.

"Tell him how he'll now be able to get out of that chair and walk. Let him know how great you think it is that he'll be able to go to school like other kids." Erin paused, realizing that while she had been prepared for this for years, Blake had been given only four days to digest the reality that Timmy's physical abilities would never be free of compromise.

"I'm going to be there for his therapy, while he's in the hospital at least. It will be too hard on you," he said suddenly.

Erin's heartbeat accelerated, for she read genuine care for her in his generous offer. "Thank you," she said simply, and she held those other words, words of love and sharing, deeply in her heart.

Blake glanced at Jamie. "Is he done?"

"Yes. He's sleeping now."

"I'll put him to bed." He got up and took the baby from Erin.

"Come back?" She needed him to hold and comfort her,

but she thought from his haggard expression that he might even need her more.

"Sure."

Through the night she lent him her warmth, waking when harsh dreams wracked his mind and body and holding him as she often held Timmy. With every gentle touch, each soothing motion of her hands across muscles tense with churning emotions, Erin silently gave him the love she hoped someday he might consciously accept.

She told herself that she, Blake, and all the family and friends who cared for Timmy would help him accept what fate had decreed for him today.

Chapter 24

Glenna

You're so little, so helpless. What you need is a guardian angel, but I guess you'll just have to make do with a ghost.

A ghost who loves you as much as she loves those sweet babies she wasn't able to nurture in her body until they were ready to nurture in her arms.

Glenna leaned against the icy windowpane and watched over Timmy as he slept, seeing but not seen. She fought back an urge to stroke his face, smooth back an errant strand of hair that curled damply against his pale forehead.

Her gaze wandered to Timmy's legs, one heavily bandaged from thigh to toe, the other wrapped like a mummy to its blunted end a few inches below his knee. Then, as the sun was coming up, she noticed his little body twitch, and focused on his dark eyelashes as they fluttered against baby-soft cheeks. It was all Glenna could do to stay back and let Dr. Newman get up from the bedside chair where he had spent the night, and perch on the edge of the narrow mattress.

He's going to tell him what they did.

Glenna wanted to scream out, *"No!"* Timmy would need his mom and dad to help him face this, she thought furiously, but she was powerless to still the doctor's voice.

"We had to take your right leg off, Tim," she heard him say in a tone that was so matter-of-fact, she wished she could make her presence known and slug him. But she couldn't. All she could do was will Timmy to feel a caring presence, to reach out for Blake and Erin's love that would see him through.

"Why?"

The way Tim murmured just one word expressed all the horror Glenna knew he had to be feeling now. And the look on his face told the same tale when he raised his head and stared, as if not believing, at the empty space on the bed where his lower leg and foot should have been.

I wish I could hold you, sweetheart, erase that look of terror from those innocent eyes. Where are Erin and Blake? What are they thinking? They should have been the ones to tell you your life is going to be changed forever.

Newman's explanation was simple enough that Glenna imagined Timmy could understand. "Hey, there," the doctor said gruffly when he apparently realized tears were running down Timmy's cheeks. "You'll be running and playing soon. No more wheelchairs—or crutches."

Glenna felt like balling up a fist and letting this callous jerk have it! Who was he to tell Timmy he would be grateful that he no longer had half of one of his legs? She dragged her gaze away from the little boy's anguished face and focused on the doctor.

What was he doing? She watched him swivel toward Timmy and roll up the left leg of his baggy surgical scrubs. And then she knew.

"Look, Tim," he said, unfastening a leather brace that cradled his knee and extended halfway up his thigh, "I've had this since I wasn't much older than you. I'll bet you didn't know."

Timmy shook his head, his wide-eyed gaze fixed on hands that worked the prosthesis off and set it aside, then peeled off a white sock and held up the leg so Tim could see.

"Will I look like that?"

Newman grinned. "Well, you won't quite look this neat, since you already had a fearsome bunch of scars, pal. But the length and shape's going to be pretty much like this."

"And I'll get a leg like this one?" Timmy gave the prosthesis a visual once-over.

Newman replied as he pulled the sock back over the stump of his leg. "Eventually. Until you quit growing, yours won't be exactly like this, because they'll have to make yours so they can adjust it as you grow. If you got a leg like this one now, you'd have to get a new one three or four times a year until you're grown."

"How do you put it on?"

"Like this." He showed Timmy how the stump had to fit in the socket of the prosthesis just so, and explained how it stayed on by itself. "You may not need a brace. I wear one because my knee bothers me when I have to stand up a lot, like I did yesterday."

Newman answered every question Timmy put forth, from how long it would take his legs to heal, to whether he'd be able to wear his new leg in the pool. Soon, Timmy was chuckling with the doctor over what Glenna figured had to be a private joke.

Erin and Blake came in then, windblown and looking as if neither of them had slept a wink. Glenna saw Blake look at Newman, and watched the doctor nod his head. Blake clutched Erin's hand, and they moved together to the other side of Timmy's bed.

"Mommy! Daddy! Look. Dr. Newman fixed up this leg just like he said he would. And he cut the bad one off so I can get a new leg and run and play."

Glenna could see that Tim was giving Erin and Blake what he considered fantastic news—but her heart went out to Erin, who obviously was fighting a new wave of tears. And Blake. Blake looked as ravaged as he had that day she had gone to his office and witnessed what she had done to him by dying.

Timmy didn't need her now. And there was nothing she could do that would ease Erin or Blake. Silently Glenna floated away, leaving them all to cope with life's realities while she lingered in this spaceless limbo. Each day the promise of heaven beckoned her, while those she had loved compelled her to stay and help them find their way.

Chapter 25

The following afternoon, Sandy gasped when Greg told her they were stopping by the hospital on the way to her apartment. "Go see Timmy? Greg, I can't. He's going to know the minute he sees my face."

Greg looked up from the chart he had just finished annotating and met Sandy's anxious gaze. "He's going to know, love, with or without seeing your face. Newman said they were going to tell him the minute he woke up last night. Come on, cheer up. Tim's going to be better off in the long run."

"Without his leg?"

They had been over this already, in the late hours of the night before and again this morning here in the office. Greg didn't envy Blake having to be strong for Timmy's mother, knowing his friend was damn near as upset as Sandy over what the surgeons had had little choice but to do.

For what he felt was at least the third time, Greg patiently explained the reasons for the radical surgery, finishing by telling Sandy, "Timmy's going to be able to walk again soon."

Sandy sniffed. "Still, Greg . . ."

"Yes, I know. It's not fair that Tim was hurt. It's sad that he's going to have to live with being less than a hundred percent. But, honey, he's going to be okay if we all let him know we love him. Come on, get your purse and let's go.''

For the first time since he and Sandy had become a couple, Greg realized just how young she was—not only in years, but in life experience. She was able to cope, just barely, with his difficult daughter, whose failings were invisible to the naked eye, but the shock of knowing her nephew would have to live life as an amputee seemed to be more than she could handle.

He would help her get through this. Love demanded that from him. Instead of herding her through the door and to a sad confrontation she was nowhere near ready for, Greg enfolded Sandy in his arms and led her to one of the chairs in front of his desk, where he sat down and cradled her in his arms as if she were no older than Timmy.

''Cry it all out, love,'' he whispered, his breath making spun-gold strands of her hair tickle his nose. ''I know you're hurting. So am I.''

Two hours later than he'd intended, he and Sandy finally met Blake outside the door to Timmy's private hospital room.

''Don't go in if you're going to cry,'' Blake warned.

Greg held Sandy's trembling hand. ''I'm not,'' she said, her voice almost steady. ''Is Erin with Timmy?'' Greg could feel tiny tremors still rocking her body, but he was proud of the determined set of her shoulders and the smile on her lips.

Blake nodded. ''I just brought her back a few minutes ago.''

''Don't you want to go in, too?''

Greg doubted the hospital would enforce its two-visitor's-at-a-time rule with Blake, but he figured to cut his friend some slack. ''Go on, Sandy,'' he said encouragingly. ''Blake and I will visit for a while out here.''   .

''Thanks for coming,'' Blake murmured to Sandy's back as she took a deep breath and opened the heavy door, her jaunty manner belying the tension Greg knew lurked inside her heart and mind.

Blake looked like hell, Greg thought. "Come on, there's a lounge down the hall here. You look dead on your feet."

"I feel worse. Erin and Sandy must come from tough stock. How they can go in there and smile, act like nothing's wrong, is beyond me. I lasted about five minutes before I knew I'd break down if I didn't get the hell away."

Greg made himself grin. "You're talking about your wife who fainted dead away yesterday afternoon? And Sandy? I just spent hours with her, trying like hell to persuade her that Timmy's losing a leg didn't mean he couldn't have a good, productive life."

"Maybe someone needs to persuade me." Blake's voice was flat.

"Intellectually, you know. It's just taking your emotions a while to listen to your head."

Blake smiled, just the least bit, when he met Greg's gaze. "Did they teach you that in med school?"

"No. It's just something I've picked up, observing folks reacting to the 'Good news, bad news' scenario."

Blake looked puzzled.

"Think about it. Hundreds of times, I've walked out of surgery and told someone, 'Your baby's fine, but there can't be any more.' Or, 'Your wife's alive, but I couldn't save the baby.' It takes a while for a loved one to figure out that the good news outweighs the bad. And it must be tougher when it's a little kid who can't be fixed just as good as new. But the idea's the same."

Blake nodded. "I know."

"Does Timmy realize . . ."

"Yes. Erin and I came back this morning, and we were there when Newman told him."

Greg didn't envy his colleague that job. "And?" he prompted.

"Timmy cried a little. Then he asked when he could get his new leg."

"What did Newman say?"

"That Tim would be up walking before springtime, and running by the time school starts next fall."

Greg thought Blake sounded skeptical. "That's true. I don't know a whole lot about rehab therapy, but when Sandy told me about Timmy's injury, I did a bit of reading. Below-knee amputees, especially kids, get fitted right away for artificial limbs and start using them as soon as the swelling goes down." He figured that the sooner Blake realized Tim would be up walking quickly, the sooner he would stop agonizing over the boy's tragic but not fatal loss. "So Timmy's taking it pretty well, would you say?"

Blake shrugged. "I guess so. He's drugged up with painkillers, and both legs are bandaged like a mummy's. Come on, let's go see him. I tell you, Greg, Timmy's the bravest little kid I've ever seen."

Greg figured that in the fifteen minutes he and Blake had talked, Sandy would have reached the limit of her endurance and be straining to drop her determined cheeriness—outside her nephew's view. But when she looked up from her perch at Timmy's bedside, she gave him a genuine, brilliant smile.

"Can we stay awhile?" she asked.

"Sure. Mrs. Watson's with Shana, and I'm not on call." Greg glanced at Erin and decided she was just about as strung out as Blake. "Hey, Timmy. How's it going?" he asked as he ruffled the boy's light hair.

"Okay. I feel sleepy. Did you know I'm gonna get a new foot?"

"I heard."

"Wanna see?"

"Later, okay?" Shooting a reassuring glance toward Sandy first, Greg glanced across the bed at Erin. Blake had his hands on her shoulders, and both of them looked as though they were about to drop. "Why don't you let Mommy and Daddy go home and get some rest now, Tim? Sandy and I will stay until you go to sleep."

"Okay. Mommy, give Jamie a hug for me. And bring my Game Gear tomorrow and my box of games. Daddy, you know where they are." Timmy hugged Erin first, then fiercely held on to Blake's neck when he bent to say good night.

"Can I show you now?" Tim asked, shaking Greg out from his silent concern about Blake and Erin. Greg nodded, concerned for Sandy but determined not to create distress in Timmy by opting out of what the boy obviously considered a rare opportunity for him.

Greg rested both his hands at Sandy's slender waist while Timmy lifted the top sheet up and to the left. "See? The doctors cut off my old leg 'cause they couldn't make it work. Dr. Newman says I'm gonna get a new one so I can walk again, just as soon as *that* leg gets well," Timmy told them, his voice excited even though he was hoarse and weak as he motioned toward his left leg.

"That's great, Timmy," Sandy exclaimed, bending over and giving the bandaged limbs Tim seemed so proud of a close look. Greg took his cue from her and pretended to examine the bandaged stump, before rearranging the sheet and blanket and encouraging the little boy to sleep.

And when he and Sandy walked out together, Greg had yet another reason to love her. She would be good for him, better than he had dreamed about, for instead of a strong-willed girl, she had just proven to him that she had it in her to be a strong, caring woman.

His woman, he thought with pride as he took her in his arms that night at her apartment and gave her all his love.

Blake gave Erin the smoldering of his passion, comforted her when she woke in a cold sweat, and treated her as if she were a fragile mannequin made of fine blown glass. When she thought of what he gave in those terms, she got quietly furious.

"I want more than you have in you to give," Erin whispered to the silent walls that greeted her the morning before

Timmy was to come home—three days before Sandy's wedding. She had felt Blake get up, watched him tiptoe across the hall an hour earlier, but the sleepless night had taken its toll on her composure.

Nothing he had done had soothed her. Not his sweet, thoughtful lovemaking, or the way he had held her, letting her sob for Timmy's yet unformed dreams that now could never come true. Not even his bringing their baby to her had helped.

For while Blake freely gave her his body and his kind, caring concern, he kept withholding the one thing Erin thought might see her through this sad, trying time. His love.

"You love Timmy," she said bitterly. "Why can't you love me, too?"

"He does. He just doesn't know it yet."

Erin looked around, searching for the source of Glenna's now familiar voice. Shivering when a sudden gust of cold air brushed her sleep-warmed skin, she turned toward the patio doorway. "You startled me," she said to the ghost who had perched on one of two matched chairs that flanked the door.

"Sorry. I've been lurking around these last few days, seeing how you and Blake handle worrying about your precious little boy. You've gotten along just fine on your own, but this morning it seemed as though you might need a friend."

Erin felt herself blush at Glenna's reminder that she was always there, hearing and seeing but not always being seen or heard. Had this sweet woman, the ghost of Blake's only real love, watched when he held her? Had Glenna seen them making hot, passionate love?

"Don't worry. I may be a pest, but I'm not a voyeur. He is a wonderful lover, though, isn't he?" Glenna paused, then continued. *"You don't need to answer—I can see it in your eyes. You love him, don't you? I knew you would!"*

It never ceased to amaze Erin that Glenna wanted, expected really, the marriage that came about because of her own untimely death and Jamie's imminent arrival to become a love match. "I love him," she replied softly, wondering if part of the reason why could be the fierce loyalty her husband had inspired in Glenna—a loyalty so strong, it seemed, that it kept on going for months after Glenna had died.

"Tell him. He's hurting now, more than you know, and not just for your little boy. Haven't you noticed how hard he's been trying to keep your spirits up?"

"I know. Blake's a good man. And he loves Timmy as much as if he were his birth father. That's just one of the reasons why I've gone and fallen in love with him." Erin met Glenna's ethereal gaze and smiled. "But you're wrong about one thing. He doesn't love me. He can't. He still loves you."

Glenna got up and stomped her foot. There was no noise in the gesture, which gave Erin an eerie feeling even as she had to smile.

"He will love you. He's no dummy, and he knows I'm never coming back. You tell him. Do it tonight, after you come home from seeing your boy at the hospital. By the way, something tells me Timmy's going to get along just fine.

"I'm going now. These visits take a lot out of me, and I have a feeling you two are going to put me through a lot more worry before you settle down to the kind of loving marriage I intend to see you enjoying with Blake before I can have any kind of peace."

Glenna's image was fading, but Erin still strongly felt her presence. "I'll try," she promised in a hoarse whisper before she found herself alone again, trying to persuade herself that Timmy's life would be better, not worse, now—and that she truly had a chance to have Blake's love as well as his passion and concern.

*   *   *

Timmy certainly had Blake's love, Erin thought as she watched him learn to change the bandages on her son's legs the day after Timmy came home. He had spent the day talking with Michelle and the prosthetist and encouraging Timmy to do all the painful therapy the doctors had prescribed.

Most of all, Blake had given her a chance to breathe, to finalize some of the plans for Sandy's wedding and keep her mind off Tim. More than anything he could have given her except a declaration of his love, she appreciated that. Glenna's words floated in her head as she halfway listened to Blake and Timmy's bantering, and later while she and Blake walked across the patio to their suite.

"Tell him you love him."

"I will."

"What will you do?"

Erin hadn't realized she had spoken out loud. "I don't know," she replied, afraid to come right out and do what she'd decided she would.

Blake shot her a peculiar look, but didn't pursue the subject. Grateful that she would have more time to conjure up enough courage to follow her ghostly pal's advice, she forced in a deep breath of cool, crisp air and took Blake's hand.

"Thanks for the picture," Blake said, giving her hand a squeeze.

Erin stopped and turned to meet his gaze. "What picture?" she asked, confused.

"The one of you and the boys that I took out at Possum Kingdom."

"You should be thanking yourself. You took them," she pointed out, disappointed that there had been no one there to hold the camera and get at least one shot of all of them together.

"But you or someone got that one where you were sitting on the blanket under the tree and had it enlarged and framed. It turned up in my office the day before Timmy's surgery.''

''Really? I'd like to take the credit, Blake, but it wasn't me.''

''I did it. But you can't tell him!''

Glenna! Erin heard her, plain as day. This was too much, her playing with Blake's mind, Erin decided, and she mentally began planning the scolding she was going to give the next time the ghost surfaced.

She thought Blake sounded doubtful when he said, ''Well, it certainly was strange. It wasn't there the night before. I'm sure of it. Sharon got to work about a half hour before I did, and she said no one went into my office then. I'd meant to ask you about it before, but with the surgery and all, it slipped my mind.''

''That's understandable,'' Erin replied, hardly able to contain her annoyance with Glenna's ghost. ''Did you like the picture?''

''Yeah. You're a beautiful woman, Erin, and we've got two good-looking kids. I'm damn proud of the way Tim's holding up, aren't you?'' he asked in a voice rich with feeling as he started walking again, toward the softly lit patio doors that opened into the bedroom.

''Yes, I am. You know, you're a lot of the reason he's accepting this operation so well. Thank you, Blake.''

He didn't respond except to whisper in a husky voice, ''It's been a long day, honey. Let's shower together. We can get to bed faster that way.''

Erin thought of that other shower they had shared at Possum Kingdom, and she felt her heart beat faster and her cheeks heat up. ''That sounds like a good idea,'' she murmured as her hands went to the fasteners on her jacket before they even reached the door.

She had felt his passion, experienced his skill at making love before, but tonight she sensed more as he loved her with infinite tenderness and care. A tiny voice inside her head whispered that what he was feeling might be compassion, but she pushed that warning aside and let herself believe that he was finally expressing love for *her*.

He touched her everywhere before they exploded together in a fiery climax, but most of all he touched her heart. And she finally trusted that she had reached and touched the part of him he had guarded with a vengeance for so long.

As they lay together in the darkness, half asleep, their arms and legs entwined, savoring the quiet aftermath of what had been the most profound experience of her life, Erin found the courage to gamble with her heart. "I love you, Blake," she said softly and waited for his reaction.

He stirred. She held her breath, wondering if he had heard her. Then he turned and locked her in his arms, burrowing his face into the crook of her shoulder. "Oh, Glenna. I love you, too," he murmured so softly Erin could barely hear him.

She felt him breathing softly against her neck and knew he had fallen back to sleep. Loving him the way she did, she couldn't disturb him; so she lay there in the dark and held him, tasting the salt of her own tears as the world she had let herself dream of shattered along with her broken heart.

Chapter 26

Glenna

" *I never thought I'd say it or even think it, but, my darling Blake, you're a goddamn first-class asshole!''*

Glenna had known tonight would be crucial in Blake and Erin's marriage, so she had forced aside that lingering jealousy and lurked in the shadows of their darkened room, listening and looking only enough to see that Blake was making love, not simply gaining release from pent-up sexual desire, as Erin had hinted she thought he did.

I was right. They belong together. The sparks they make could wake the dead!

Yes, she was dead but she wasn't gone yet. And she wasn't about to go until her stubborn ox of a husband put her to rest and admitted that he loved Erin as much as he had ever loved her.

No! Blake would have to admit he loved Erin more! The jerk came alive in every nerve in his gorgeous body the minute he looked at Erin, while sometimes Glenna had found it necessary to resort to elaborate seduction and erotic toys to awaken his desire for *her*.

An hour ago, Blake had been hard as stone before he and Erin had even touched—before either of them had shed a lick of clothes! And he'd worshipped every inch of Erin's long, lithe body with his hands and mouth before giving in and slaking that obvious need of his. He wouldn't have done that if all he'd been looking for was to relieve his damn male lust!

Blake had been the perfect lover to Erin, and she had risked giving him the words of love she wasn't sure he was ready to hear. And what had he done?

Glenna laughed, not a laugh that meant mirth, but one that conveyed disdain. She cut the laugh short and swore out loud. *"The stupid, unfeeling asshole had to call her by my name!"*

Glenna watched him now, sleeping on Erin's shoulder without a care in the world while Erin quietly sobbed, and she wished she had the power to conk him on the head. The guy might have graduated fourth in his class at law school, but he didn't have a lick of brains!

"What do I have to do to knock some common sense into your thick skull?" she asked, almost forgetting that he couldn't hear her, so she wouldn't get an answer. *"Damn it all!"* she added, slamming an ineffectual fist silently onto the sleek glass top of a new, sterile-looking table. *"I know you love her, Blake. What do I have to do to make you realize it?"*

Weary of this constant one-sided conflict with the man she had once loved more than life, Glenna sat down and tried to think of tricks she could pull to force Blake to see the light. She had to do it quickly, for she knew her time on earth was running out.

Events here had become chaotic, too, leaving her too little time to bring Blake to his senses before she had to go forever. First Jamie's birth, then Timmy's operation, and now Greg's wedding to Erin's sister were cutting into her time and space!

Glenna sighed. She would have to get some rest tonight, because if she wasn't sadly mistaken, she'd have to deal with an irate Erin in the morning! Maybe by then a way would come to her that would accomplish her purpose here and let her rest in peace.

Still muttering curses at Blake for his unfeeling faux pas, Glenna faded away, but the picture of Erin sobbing as if her heart were broken weighed heavily on her mind.

Chapter 27

*I*t had been all Erin could do to hold her tongue while Blake whistled his way from bed to his dressing room, and later down the hall toward the center of the house. When she was sure he was out of earshot, she leaped up out of bed and jerked on a disreputable-looking pair of sweats.

Last night, she had hurt; this morning the pain had turned to anger. No, not anger, she corrected herself, but plain, unvarnished fury!

She may have agreed to be a stand-in mother for his baby, but she damn sure never consented to be a stand-in bedmate for his meddlesome dead wife! Fuming, Erin stomped into her dressing room and started opening drawers.

If Timmy didn't love Blake so, she would take him and Jamie, leave this place, and never come back no matter what threats Blake might try to stop her! Since leaving would hurt her son, though, Erin would content herself with moving back to the other wing, where she had been before the farce of a wedding that brought her to this damnable master suite. And she didn't give a hoot who found out she and Blake had a marriage in name only!

She wished she could find Glenna's interfering ghost and give *her* a piece of her mind, too! None of this would have happened if the woman had just stayed wherever it was that ghosts should hang their hats and left Erin alone.

Grabbing an empty pillowcase, Erin emptied a drawer of her lingerie chest into it and opened the next drawer. She repeated the process until the pillowcase was bulging at its seams.

"He didn't mean it, Erin."

Erin refused to look and see whether Glenna had decided to appear in person. If she saw her, she would want to strangle her, and she wasn't sure it was possible to wreak physical havoc on a damn ghost. Then she realized the implication of the ghost's words and looked up to meet that familiar, glowing gaze.

"And you didn't mean to eavesdrop, either, did you?" Erin spat out viciously.

"Well . . ."

She had never heard Glenna hesitate before. "What's the matter? Do you actually have the decency to be embarrassed, admitting you invaded my privacy and watched us—me—in bed?"

"You're not leaving. You can't," Glenna said, her tone practically pleading now.

Erin widened her stance and set both hands on her hips. "No, I'm not leaving. You saw to it that I couldn't—not now, with my son so attached to Blake. But I damn well am moving out of this room, and there's nothing you can do to stop me!"

Whirling around, she opened another drawer and began emptying it into another pillowcase. When she filled it, she turned to set it by the first one she'd stuffed with undies, only to notice the bag was gone.

While Erin gawked, the second bag floated out of her hands as if by magic, and clothes settled once more in the drawers she had just emptied.

"What do you think you're doing?" she asked Glenna, who had settled down on top of a tall, skinny chest of drawers to grin down at her.

"Saving you from yourself. Erin, you don't want to do this."

"Why not? How would you like feeling like an overpaid nanny who earns her keep by filling in for Blake's *real* wife in bed each night?" With determination, Erin opened another drawer and began to empty it. "How would you like having the man you love call you by someone else's name?"

"The guy's a real ass, isn't he?"

While Erin gawked at Glenna, hardly believing the ghost would say a word against her husband who did no wrong, Glenna managed to get the latest sack of clothes she had filled replaced in the drawer from whence it had come.

She was getting frustrated now. "Leave me alone," Erin implored. "Haven't you done enough to me?" She watched as Glenna floated down from her perch and landed between her and the clothes she was trying to pack.

"Don't you move. If you're really that mad at Blake, make him go back to sleeping on that daybed in the den where he hid out for God knows how many months."

That was the first halfway sensible suggestion Erin had heard come out of Glenna's mouth this morning. Still, she balked. "It's not far enough away," she pointed out coldly.

"What will Timmy think?"

Erin choked back a bitter retort; she knew it would distress her boy to think she and his new wonderful "daddy" weren't getting along. Timmy already had more than enough for a seven-year-old to cope with. "You know how to deal low blows," she muttered, but she reached around the ghost and closed the only drawer that still gaped open.

"I'll do whatever it takes to see you all happy together," Glenna said, her voice strong even as her image began to fade.

"You stay here," Erin ordered, not ready to let the ghost escape without her having her say even though the worst of her anger was spent. "I've listened to you for long enough. Now it's your turn to hear what I have to say."

Glenna smiled. *"Hurry. I'll stick around as long as I can."*

"Okay. First, don't you go planting pictures or playing mind games with us anymore. Second, keep your nose out of what's going on between me and Blake. You didn't make me love him—I pulled that dumb trick all by myself. And get it through your head that you can't make him love me either."

Glenna's lower lip seemed to tremble, and Erin thought she read contrition in the ghost's benign expression. Suddenly she felt guilty. "Look, Glenna, I'm not blaming you. I'm glad you've let me get to know you, even if it had to be this way." Erin gestured toward the golden aura that gave the ghost an otherworldly look. "But you can't push me and Blake around like we're a couple of wooden puppets. Life doesn't work that way."

"I know," Glenna said softly as Erin watched her fade away.

"It's almost time for us to get ready for the rehearsal," Blake said jovially as he strode into the suite early that afternoon. He felt good—damn good, after having watched Michelle put Timmy through his paces in the gym.

"I know."

"Need help with any last-minute details for tomorrow?" He paused to drop a quick kiss on Erin's inviting lips. The chill he had heard in her voice suddenly intensified when she pulled away from his touch. "What's wrong?"

"Nothing. If you consider calling the woman you're sleeping with by someone else's name nothing, that is," Erin informed him in a tone that fairly dripped with venom.

"What?" His good mood disintegrated in the face of her anger.

"Do the words, 'I love you, too, Glenna,' ring a bell?"

Blake hesitated. Of course those words rang bells—lots of them. He *did* love Glenna. "I've never confused you with Glenna when we were in bed together." He cursed himself silently, for the way his body hardened when he thought back over times the past few weeks when he and Erin had shared erotic pleasures he guessed most couples only dreamed of.

"Maybe you didn't say it consciously. Whether you remember or not, though, you said it. And it hurt. You'd best go back to sleeping across the hall. I can't sleep with you, wondering when you might next mistake me for *her*."

He must have talked in his sleep. He certainly couldn't remember uttering those damning words! And he was sure he would never have been so boorish as to whisper words of love to one woman while he was with another—even if he'd been thinking them.

When he searched recent memory, Blake realized that when he was having sex with Erin, Glenna never crossed his mind. And that sudden cognizance produced not the tearing guilt he would have expected, but rather a gentle sense of sadness.

The last thing he wanted to do was move back into that lonely bed to toss and turn and try in vain to sleep! Now, though, was not the time to argue. He sensed that Erin's tight, controlled expression masked feminine fury best kept contained until this wedding was over and their time was once again their own.

"If that's what you want. For now. I'm sorry for whatever I said that hurt you." He laid a hand gently on her shoulder, and although she trembled, she didn't pull away.

She met his gaze with sad, dark eyes. "I know. If you'll excuse me, I'm going to spend some time with Timmy before we have to leave."

Blake watched her cross the patio to Tim's room. Women! He'd never understand them, not if he lived to be a hundred.

Erin knew he loved Glenna; he had been nothing but honest about *that* when he argued that they should marry. He had reiterated the same feelings when he told Erin he wanted her in his bed.

These past few weeks not even Timmy's surgery or the preparations for the coming wedding had interfered with Blake's enjoyment of home and family. And Erin. He liked her more each day, and wanted her with an intensity that strengthened rather than waned.

Blake shook his head. Apparently he had vowed his love for Glenna in his sleep, and that got Erin incensed. Rightly so. He would straighten out this problem as soon as things settled down, he decided as he tried to focus on Sandy and Greg's wedding and his duties as surrogate father of the bride.

Erin's heart ached with envy at the obvious love her sister shared with Greg. She felt good about the welcome Greg's flamboyant family members were giving Sandy—and her as her sister's only living relative. Still, seeing them so happy made her hurt for the lack of an honest, loving relationship of her own. She tried to banish her bittersweet feelings when Blake stood to greet the members of the wedding and their escorts.

Sandy's face mirrored excitement and joy, as it should on this, the night before her wedding. And Greg fairly beamed with pride as they made the rounds of all six tables, meeting his bride's young attendants and introducing Sandy to his family and friends.

Sandy had been right to want this dinner to be casual. To an understated, piped-in accompaniment of instrumental music that ranged from soft popular tunes to country and western, young college friends of Sandy's mingled with Greg's far-flung family members and older, more sophisticated colleagues. Somehow in denim and khaki, without trappings that broadcast personal taste or finances, the group integrated, apparently intent on celebrating their friends' commitment to one another.

The differences were there, she knew as she watched facets of light play off huge diamonds one of Greg's Houston cousins displayed when she laughingly pressed perfectly manicured fingers against a chest clad in ruby-red denim that bore the unmistakable mark of a famous designer. Self-consciously, Erin touched the collar of her own jeans dress and toyed with its trim of turquoises and silver conchos. Then her gaze settled on Katy, Sandy's childhood pal and maid of honor, who wore simple Levis and a Western shirt.

Sandy laughed at something Katy said, and gave Greg a quick, hard hug before they moved to the next table. Even without their matching shirts, no one would have trouble identifying her sister and Greg as the bride and groom. Erin watched them exchange a few words with Shana, and she was glad Greg's daughter had apparently decided to share the fun instead of causing havoc tonight.

"Erin?"

"What?" She dragged her gaze from the happy bride and groom to Blake in his blue plaid shirt, snug jeans, and hand-tooled black boots. Why did he have to look so good that he made her mouth water, when his heart belonged to someone else?

"We should mingle."

Mingling was the last thing on Erin's mind. She would prefer sitting here at the head table, vicariously sharing her sister's happiness, to playing the contented wife of this man who had married her only to give his child a mother. "In a minute," she said, taking a deep breath along with an analytic look around the room.

Sandy's attendants epitomized the joy of youth, Erin decided as she watched the play between them and their young husbands and boyfriends. She shrugged off their carefree exuberance as the province of the very young, and turned her attention to the older guests.

Greg's cousin with the apparent penchant for precious jewels had her arm draped around her blond, patrician-looking husband, who smiled at her with what looked to Erin like total devotion. Feeling like a voyeur for intruding on what she imagined was a very personal moment, she turned her attention to another couple at that table.

They, too, looked like lovers—lovers who shared a quiet, deep devotion Erin envied fiercely. Surely she wasn't the only person in this wedding party who lacked for love!

Her gaze settled on Greg's best man, the youngest of his Houston cousins. Darkly handsome like Greg, but taller, broader, and more deeply tanned, he smiled at something Sandy said, then turned to the model-slender beauty next to him. Erin saw pain in his dark, brooding expression and realized he, too, seemed to be feeling left out of all this love and goodwill that abounded tonight.

"I'm ready now," she told Blake, and she let him take her hand.

They made the rounds, but Erin's heart wasn't in the bright smile she kept firmly pasted on her face. It hurt to have Blake so close, to feel the warmth of his body against her when they stopped to greet their guests. She murmured all the right words, she guessed, but she felt a sense of kindred spirits when Blake introduced her to the brooding best man and the gorgeous woman at his side.

She could feel animosity stirring beneath a veneer of conviviality, and for a moment her own self-pity fell aside in a burst of sympathy for this tense couple. Alice, the blond, spoke just enough to keep from appearing rude, while Jake struck up a conversation with Blake about some oil rights problem. Erin assumed Blake was handling some litigation about the problem, but she thought it odd to bring up business on a festive night like this.

"I think Greg's cousin has a serious problem on his hands," Blake observed as they strolled back to their own table.

"The one you two were talking about?"

"No. The one he brought to the wedding."

Erin wouldn't have thought Blake would notice even the most blatant undertones of marital dissention—he certainly hadn't given any indication that he realized *their* marriage was in serious trouble! "Alice?" she asked, needing to make sure they were on the same wavelength.

"Alice. They're barely speaking to each other."

"How well do you know them?"

Blake paused for a moment. "I've known Jake since I've known Greg. Close to twenty years. Of course, Jake was just a kid back then."

"And you weren't?" Blake's making himself sound old struck Erin as being incongruous—and unreasonably funny.

"At the time I thought I was pretty grown-up, compared to Jake. Greg and I were freshmen at UT, and Jake couldn't have been more than eight or nine. He spent a weekend with us, and we took him along to a Longhorns football game. He and Greg have always been close—neither of them have brothers—so our paths crossed regularly while he was growing up. For the past few years, my firm has handled his oil company's legal matters."

"What makes you think there's something wrong?"

"Jake doesn't talk business when he's having fun. And he doesn't ordinarily ignore his ex-Miss Georgia wife. I'm surprised you couldn't feel the tension between them, even considering you never met them before."

"I felt it. We'd better circulate some more," Erin said, afraid to voice the question as to why her husband could so easily read others' feelings when he appeared unable to decipher hers. As they expressed their congratulations to her sister and his good friend, she wondered if perhaps she hadn't asked because she didn't want to hear that Blake's lack of insight into her thoughts and dreams meant he just didn't care.

Later, when she crawled into a bed that suddenly felt too big and empty without Blake, Erin let down her defenses and cried.

Blake sat on the daybed across the hall, wondering why and how he had said the damning words that got him tossed out of his wife's bed. All he could remember was feeling sated and totally relaxed last night as he lay on his side with Erin's soft, fragrant body curled comfortably against him.

And the lovemaking that had gone before. Blake let out a frustrated sigh. He still couldn't believe the chemistry that made him want Erin more each time than he had the last. Hell, he had trouble accepting that the part of him now throbbing against his zipper in protest of less than twenty-four hours' denial was the same one that had placidly waited out long periods of celibacy in years gone by.

The walls felt as though they were closing in on him, and his breathing became harsh and erratic. He had to get out of this room! Bolting off the daybed, he headed for Erin, then changed his mind. He had to honor the damn agreement she had insisted on this morning. Instead, he jerked around and headed outside.

He needed the burst of cold air that hit him the minute he opened the door. By the time he reached the stable, the throbbing in his groin had simmered down to a dull ache, but the turmoil in his mind raged on. Absentmindedly he went over and stroked Renegade's glossy black neck as he tried to make sense of his jumbled feelings.

He loved Glenna. Of that much he was sure. For years she had been his friend, his wife ... his lover. Leaning against the cool, smooth stall door that still smelled faintly of fresh paint, Blake let his mind wander back through the years.

He could almost see Glenna's smiling face the way it had been the day he had brought her home as his bride. She'd been so *alive*, so thrilled at the prospect of putting her mark on their home.

Renegade bumped his head against Blake's hand, as if to remind him he was still there, wanting attention. And Blake remembered how, from the day he brought Glenna home until scant weeks ago, he had given up the pleasure of riding every day. It wasn't that Glenna ever asked him to get rid of his horses, he reminded himself in the interest of fairness. But all animals *had* frightened her almost to the point of hysteria.

I'm not the kind of wife you need, he recalled Glenna having said sadly as they watched the van pulling out of the drive with his four horses and Beau. God, how he had missed that mixed-breed mutt he had rescued from the pound and turned into a fat, spoiled pet.

"She was wrong. She gave me all I needed." He felt Renegade's head tilt forward, as if the colt understood his words. Then a picture filled his mind. As crystal-clear as day, he saw Erin, laughing as she rode beside him as she had one day last week. He had wanted to reach over then, drag her off her mare, and have hot, satisfying sex with her in the shade of a venerable oak tree near the bridle path.

Who was he kidding? He always wanted sex with Erin, craved the hot, honest response his body found in hers. He tried to recall a time when he'd had trouble keeping his hands off Glenna.

They had been sixteen, friends who had suddenly discovered that touching and feeling excited them even more than openmouthed kissing. Blake smiled as he recalled the awkward, quick encounter that had ended his and Glenna's virginity simultaneously, in the backseat of a brand-new Bronco his father had bought him for his birthday.

If it hadn't been for Glenna's sense of humor, Blake knew he would have been mortified. He had barely pressed himself inside her, and it was over. He had been pretty sure he hurt her, too. But she had laughed it off, teasing and telling him they would try again and again until they got it right.

And they had. His technique had improved with practice, and Glenna had appeared to delight in learning new, titillating tricks to turn him on. They had been good in bed. But he had never burned for wanting Glenna, even during the long periods of time when they had been forced to abstain.

Blake waited for the gut-wrenching shame, the guilt for

infidelity that he expected to feel from that traitorous admission; but it flickered and then floated away on the gust of cold, crisp air that suddenly roared through the stable.

Instead, memories assailed him of his smiling playmate . . . his best friend and confidant . . . his lover and soul mate with whom he had expected to share the rest of his life. Glenna had been his promise of love and family, his anchor against his own nearly rootless beginnings.

They had clung together, the boy from new Texas money and the girl who sprang from old Dallas aristocracy, and made their place together. Glenna had been the breath of fresh, pure optimism he had so desperately needed.

Somehow remembering their time together didn't hurt so much now, so he let scenes long lost to him gently wash through his mind. Every time winter turned to spring, she had found some new horizon for them to explore, giving him joy and laughter and a bit of her zest for life. And when the leaves began to turn in autumn, she had brought him the promise of winter and a new, more brilliant spring that would follow.

He had traveled before their marriage, but it had been Glenna who had shown him lush, verdant beauty in tropical forests and stark majesty in deserts and snow-capped mountains. While he had trekked through those forests, explored the deserts and climbed the mountains, she had given him the gift of seeing and appreciating them for themselves as much as obstacles put there for him to conquer.

But Glenna had been an observer, and he had molded his life to mesh with hers, Blake realized as he stroked Renegade's velvety nose. It wasn't just about the animals, either, he realized, recalling how, when he had climbed mountains, she'd cheered him on from the valley below. And he pictured her, reading under an umbrella on the beach while he had surfed in the wild waves off Maui.

She had tamed him, domesticated him. He had known *that* for sure one day during a September week in Wyoming when she had politely put her foot down and said, ''You can't,'' after he had impulsively entered the bronc riding competition at an amateur rodeo.

Yes, Blake admitted to himself, Glenna had controlled him well, with no more tools than his love and a tiny iron fist protected with a velvet glove.

He had loved Glenna. He would always keep her memory somewhere deep within his heart. They had shared their seasons, some triumphant, others not; but now Blake realized it was time to let her go, that in his grief he had built his feelings for her from healthy love to almost obsessive worship.

As Blake left the stable and walked back to the house, he mulled over events that had mushroomed because Glenna had been obsessed to have his child.

I married Erin to give Glenna's son a mother. She married me so she could keep Jamie and get help for Tim. Fate brought us together. But I'll be damned if I don't love Erin now with an intensity I never felt for Glenna.

And it's not just the mind-boggling sex, or the way she loves to ride and fish and hike in the woods with me. I love her fierce way of caring, her strength and protectiveness over those she loves. I love the way the smallest considerate gesture can make her face light up with joy.

"Good-bye, Glenna," he whispered aloud, saying farewell to the muted warmth of spring and fall with their soft promises. Inside his room again, he began preparing to seduce the woman he knew now was his destiny.

Erin was his future, his reality. Loving Glenna had prepared him for this vivid woman who had it in her power to give him the heat of the fieriest summer day and the frost of the coldest winter night. He had felt Erin's love before, when he hadn't been ready to accept it. And, like a blind, dumb fool, he had damn near thrown it away.

As he made hurried phone calls to formalize his plans, Blake vowed he would earn Erin's love again.

Chapter 28

Glenna

Finally, Blake! You've seen the light! I just hope your talents for persuasion don't let you down—and that you don't put your big foot back in your mouth by telling Erin all about your stroll down memory lane.

Oh, don't get me wrong, darling. You had to look back, before you could look to today and tomorrow. I wish you hadn't, in a way, because you won't remember me as kindly.

But maybe you will. You loved me, faults and all, and I believe we made each other happy. Maybe someday, somewhere, we'll meet again. It will be kind of sad if we do, because what you're going to have with Erin is going to make what we had pale by comparison.

From her perch on an oak limb just outside Blake's window, she could see him flipping through an address book, making calls. She grinned. Her determined, methodical Blake would follow through and make Erin forgive—and forget—his tardy realization that their falling in love had been destined from the start.

At least, Glenna hoped she and Blake hadn't already made such a tangled mess that Erin would never open up her heart again!

No matter. If she balks, I'll be there.

And as Glenna faded slowly away into the pink of dawn's first light, she let out a huge sigh of relief that rustled the old oak tree's branches like a sudden gust of wind.

Chapter 29

A cold breeze blew pale fox fur around, tickling Erin's chin as she came back home from making a last-minute check on the decorations and flowers. Blake had assured her the caterer would follow through, but she had needed to see for herself that nothing would mar her sister's wedding.

He was home now, she noticed. When she had left an hour earlier, he had been gone—where, she had no idea, she thought with annoyance as she walked briskly to the house. While he had no obligation to keep her informed about his comings and goings, she had expected that to-day—a Sunday when he was ordinarily home, not to mention the day of this wedding—he would have had the common courtesy to stick around.

She and Blake were going to have to have a talk! Erin's moods swung like a pendulum between fury and hurt, and she had no intention of spending too much more time in this limbo of emotion! Closing the door to her rooms a bit harder than was necessary, she slid off her fur jacket and kicked off shoes in favor of the fuzzy slippers Theresa must have set out by the door.

What a gorgeous day for a wedding!

The sun had come up bright in a cold, cloudless sky this Sunday in late November, and Erin was glad. Sandy and Greg would have a beautiful wedding day. According to a

saying her mother had repeated the day Erin had married
Bill, good weather for a wedding bode well for a good
marriage.

"Erin?"

She turned and looked at Blake, who stood in the doorway to her room, looking hesitant about his welcome—as
well he should, she thought uncharitably as she tried hard
to tell herself she didn't want his strong, gentle arms around
her now.

"Where were you?" she asked, trying to maintain an
indifferent facade.

"I had to go downtown. Look, Erin, something's come
up, and I'm going to have to fly to Jackson Hole tonight
after the reception."

She hoped her expression didn't reflect the disappointment that slammed into her. "Really?"

"Yes. Something came up with a client. I hate to spring
this on you at the last minute like this, but you're coming,
too. He's bringing his wife, and she'll need someone to
keep her company while we conduct our business."

"But, Blake, what about Timmy? And Jamie?"

"Mary and Theresa can handle them—along with Michelle, who has agreed to live in while we're gone. It will
only be for a few days."

Erin didn't know what to do. She should be here for
Timmy—and the baby. But a small voice urged her to go,
to try once more, away from this house and all its memories, to gain Blake's love. "I can't," she said sadly when
responsibility won out over desire.

"Think about it, at least," Blake told her as he turned
and left the room. "I've already had Theresa pack your
bags."

Hours later, as she began to dress for the wedding, Erin
was still undecided about the impromptu trip with Blake.
Michelle had confided that Tim would be starting lessons
tomorrow in using his new prosthesis, and that those les-

sons might go more smoothly if doting parents were not around.

Still, she hesitated. She had risked her heart and gotten it battered. Why should she do it again, for the sake of pleasing a husband whose heart belonged to someone else?

"I wouldn't go if I were you!"

Erin set down a tube of concealer and looked for the ghostly source of that unwanted advice. She found Glenna, hovering near the ceiling in the corner of her dressing room.

"I thought I told you to mind your own business," she said, resigned that neither Glenna's ghost nor her grieving widower would pay a bit of attention to her requests.

"I couldn't help but hear him. He's got one awful nerve, asking you to do him a favor after what he said to you."

"Why do you care?"

"I've decided I want his love all for myself. I can wait for him to join me, out there somewhere." The ghost tossed out her challenge like a gauntlet, making Erin burning mad.

"You can't have him. You're not even alive. In fact, all I think you are is an apparition sent from hell to make me pay for planning to give away my baby."

"I gave you your chance. You failed."

"We'll see about that. I'm going to go with Blake, and there's not a thing you can do to stop me!" With that, Erin stepped out of the dressing room and waited for the damn ghost to disappear.

Chapter 30

Glenna

Glenna hovered just outside the house and chuckled, delighted with the success of her desperate ploy with Erin.

I should have tried reverse psychology before.

The look Erin had given her could have frozen ice cubes on a July day in Dallas. That was good! She had begun to wonder whether Erin had a temper.

Blake would need a strong woman as well as one who loved him, to drag him into a future that she, Glenna, had not been meant to share. Erin would fit his needs just fine, as soon as their sometimes slow-witted husband managed to convince her of *his* love for her!

I'd give anything to see him eating those words he used to get her to marry him!

But Glenna knew she had to leave Erin to Blake now. She had done what she could—she'd even tricked Erin into making this trip she would lay odds had nothing to do with any of Blake's clients, alienating her in the process!

Blake will do all right for himself. I just hope he remembers he isn't in a courtroom. Erin needs him to talk to her from his heart, not his head.

Satisfied for the moment, she floated away to haunt the beautiful Victorian mansion where in less than two hours, her friend Greg would marry Erin's pretty young sister. That she didn't intend to miss!

Chapter 31

Feeling decadently opulent in an ebony mink jacket Blake had pulled from a huge Saks box and draped across her shoulders moments earlier, Erin watched him stash their bags in the trunk with trepidation. And excitement.

He had raked her from head to toe with his gaze when he came into her room, making her feel as if her royal blue, floor-length velvet sheath covered no more of her than the sheerest of negligees. Then, his touch as gentle as the breeze, he had wrapped her in the soft, dense fur.

"You'll need this in Wyoming," he'd told her, and that had been the only comment he had made about her decision to accompany him.

"Are you ready?" he asked, placing a hand at her elbow to help her into the car.

"For the wedding? Yes." Erin doubted very much if she were ready for three nights alone with Blake in some undoubtedly romantic setting at a ski lodge in Jackson Hole— without the buffer of children, nannies, and housekeepers.

"They were lucky to get the Manse on such short notice," he commented as they drove along the silent streets where, like Blake's, homes generally sat well back away from the view of passersby.

"They'd had a cancellation for tonight."

"Change of plans?"

Erin smiled. ''The other couple's parents decided to hold the wedding at a temple instead.''

''That was good for Sandy and Greg.'' He pulled into a discreetly marked drive and brought the Mercedes to a halt at the front of the hundred-year-old mansion an enterprising young couple had bought several years ago and renovated into an upscale wedding chapel. ''Here we are,'' he said as he got out of the car and tossed the keys to a uniformed attendant who had just opened the door for Erin.

Sandy had fallen in love with the old-world charm of this place, and Erin was glad. While Blake's home could easily have accommodated the wedding, she had hesitated to suggest that after he had told her he wasn't ready for mass gaiety and laughter there. She let Blake take her jacket to hand over, with his black cashmere topcoat, to a waiting butler, before peeking into the ballroom to be sure the caterer had all the last-minute details in hand.

''I told you Caitlyn's would take care of everything.''

''And they have. Oh, Blake, look at the flowers! They found blue columbines. Sandy will be thrilled.'' She leaned down to sniff one of the small topiaries that topped each snowy-white covered round table, pleased at the effect of fragrant herbs and pert, blue wildflowers that the florist had tucked in among miniature gardenias and pastel roses.

''They look just like little replicas of *those*.'' He strode over and inspected four giant arrangements that marked off the corners of a raised, polished dance floor. ''Erin, you look beautiful tonight,'' he murmured suddenly when she joined him beside one of the eight-feet-tall floral creations.

''Thank you.''

He took her left hand and lifted it to his lips. ''I should have bought you diamonds.'' For a moment, he just stood there and traced the swirly design on her wedding band with one finger, a half smile on his lips. She wondered what thoughts were going through his mind, behind his enigmatic smile.

Sandy's attendants had her well in hand, Caitlyn's had

the food ready and all the candles lit. A photographer and video crew were waiting to capture the wedding for posterity. Erin had nothing to do but wait until the time came for one of Greg's cousins—Scott, she thought—to get her and escort her to her seat.

Did Blake think she was going to bolt and run away? He had never hovered so closely before, but tonight she couldn't move without him by her side. Restless, she circulated among the nooks and crannies off the big ballroom. Blake followed.

She could almost feel his pulse; his body heat warmed her, and the subtle cologne he wore kept reminding her of his nearness. Part of her welcomed the feeling of pride and belonging she couldn't suppress, while another, more cautious voice in her head told her not to set herself up for another fall.

"Blake. Erin?"

"Is it time?" She smiled at Greg's cousin, then turned to Blake.

"Just about. They're signing the marriage contract now," Scott told them. "May I?" He extended his arm for Erin.

"Blake?"

"I'll just wait for them out here."

The melodious sounds of an organ wafted softly through a ballroom lit by thousands of tiny white gaslights in three magnificent chandeliers. Erin let Scott seat her at a table larger than the rest.

How Mom would have loved this!

She swept that sad thought away. Today was Sandy's wedding, a day for joy, not for fretting about what should have been. Erin watched Shana float toward the table on the arm of Greg's best man.

"Take care, little Shana," Jake said in a teasing tone as he held her chair.

"Little Shana?" Erin couldn't hold back her words; the nickname was so incongruous.

"His sister's Big Shana. She didn't come," Shana said matter-of-factly. "I wouldn't let anybody but Cousin Jake call me 'little,' though."

I haven't seen Jake's wife tonight, Erin realized as she glanced around the ballroom. Then the piped-in stereo music stopped and a seven-piece combo began to play a lilting, romantic piece. The guests quieted down, and Sandy's wedding began with a formally attired Judge Adkins taking his place in the center of the raised dance floor.

Erin watched the young women who had spent many hours around the kitchen table at her house when they and Sandy were in high school. Tonight they looked like Victorian ladies in bell-skirted gowns of sapphire velvet, ivory illusion and lace filling in low scooped necklines and dripping at their wrists.

A groomsman, resplendent in white tie and tails, escorted each bridesmaid. Katy came last, wearing a gown identical to the others except for its lighter blue color, on the arm of Greg's cousin Jake. Erin smiled. Everything, from the gowns to nosegay bouquets that featured the same flowers in the table decorations, had turned out just the way Sandy planned.

Greg followed Jake and Katy, escorted by his mother and uncle. Erin sighed. He looked ecstatic, and she couldn't help envying her sister for this man who loved her so devotedly.

The music faded, then rose again with the traditional Bridal March from *Lohengrin*. Tears came to Erin's eyes as she watched Sandy glide slowly into the room, looking radiant in their mom's simple velvet gown and the pearl-encrusted tiara with its floor-length veil of gossamer silk illusion. Her flowers were perfect, blue columbines and tiny rosemary sprigs surrounding several perfect, white poinsettias.

But it was Blake who took Erin's breath away! Even as she tried to concentrate on Sandy and Greg as they prepared to say their vows, she couldn't help the tiny voice inside her that reminded her of the nights together she and Blake were about to have—business trip or no.

"We have gathered here tonight to share Sandy and Greg's joy as they celebrate their marriage."

Erin met the judge's gaze as he spoke almost the same words he had said the night not long ago when she had married Blake. *Same words. Oh, so different people and feelings!* She forced down her envy and concentrated on the ceremony.

"Who gives this woman in marriage?"

Blake turned and Erin met his gaze. "Her sister—my wife—and I do," he said quietly as he placed Sandy's hand in Greg's and stepped down to join her at the table. Erin felt him reach out and grasp her hand as she listened to the judge explain that the bride and groom would make their vows in their own words.

"Sandy, I'll love you for the rest of my life. I'll do everything I can to keep you happy and secure, and to keep harm and sadness away. I'll be there for you always, no matter what, to take care of you or let you try your wings, whatever you need. I promise to be faithful and to provide for you and any children we may have. By provide I don't just mean material things, honey; I'll provide quality time for you as well."

"I think the traditional words say it all, Greg. I promise to love, honor, and cherish you, to be faithful, in sickness and health, for richer or poorer, for better or worse, as long as we both live. I love you."

Tears rolled down Erin's cheeks, partly from joy for the bride and groom and partly from envy for the mutual adoration they so obviously shared. Dabbing a hanky at the corners of her eyes, she watched and listened as Sandy and Greg exchanged the matching wedding bands they had chosen together.

Her gaze shifted to Blake's ringless left hand, and she nearly started to cry again. Judge Adkins's words saved her, though, drawing her attention back to the bridal party.

"By the power vested in me by the great state of Texas, I pronounce you husband and wife. You may kiss the bride."

As Greg and Sandy enthusiastically embraced, Erin's eyes filled with tears. Those vows, spoken so sincerely and with so much love, made her ache for what she wanted so much to have with Blake. She met his gaze, and he gave her hand a gentle squeeze.

"You did a great job with the wedding," Blake said later as they flew in the otherwise empty first-class section of a commercial jet toward Jackson Hole.

Erin smiled. Sandy's wedding had been beautiful, down to the last detail. "Surprising Sandy with that video must have been Greg's idea," she murmured, glad he had thought of doing the picture montage that featured highlights of their lives both separately and together.

"Uh-huh. They did one for his cousin Shana's wedding a few years back, and she liked it so well, Greg decided he'd put together one for Sandy."

"Speaking of Shana, she acted like an angel tonight." The girl had sat at the table next to her uncle Jake, and she'd actually behaved as if she were happy about the marriage, Erin thought, pleased.

"Greg thought so, too. He said he figured Jake had given her a talking-to this afternoon—that they spent most of the day together. Apparently she idolizes him."

Erin frowned. "Where was Jake's wife?" Her sympathy had gone out tonight to Greg's handsome cousin, whose jovial smile had never quite reached dark, empty eyes.

"She went back to Houston this morning. Jake asked me tonight to recommend a good divorce lawyer there for him—that the marriage was over."

"I'm sorry. They were a beautiful couple." Erin paused. "Do they have children?"

"No. Jake wanted them, though."

"She couldn't . . ."

"Wouldn't. Last month she had an abortion that she told him about last night, during a whopper of an argument—or so Jake said."

Any sympathy Erin might have felt for Jake's coldly beautiful wife dissipated instantly. But she felt tears well up in her eyes for the misery *he* had masked so well tonight, except for that haunted look in his eyes.

"Erin?"

"What? Oh, sorry, I was just thinking."

Blake cleared his throat. "Were you thinking of the time I asked you to do that to Jamie?"

"No. Of course not," she said quickly, reaching out to touch his arm reassuringly. "I was thinking of how hard it must have been for Jake to act the charming, happy best man tonight."

He took her hand and rubbed a callused thumb over her palm. "Yeah. You're right. Erin, the wedding's over. Sandy and Greg are out at Possum Kingdom, and the guests have all gone home. We'll be landing in a few minutes, and there's something I've got to tell you."

Erin felt the muscles in her neck grow tense. "What?"

"There's no client. No meeting. I tricked you into coming with me so I'd have a chance to court you, somewhere where there aren't any memories to haunt us. Honey, I want us to fall in love."

He wants us to fall in love? Doesn't he know I love him already?

"Blake, I—I . . ."

"I know I've hurt you, but I'm asking for this time to convince you what we've got is worth building on. Please, give us a chance."

Erin wanted to shout, but all she could manage was a tight smile and a heartfelt sigh.

"We don't have to sleep together until you're ready. Hell, we already know we're dynamite in bed. All I'm asking is that we spend this time alone together, do some of the fun things most couples do before they say 'I do.' "

If Blake hadn't been observing her so closely, she would have pinched herself. But she reined in her elation and simply said, "All right."

And for the rest of the night and the following day, Erin let Blake pamper and cosset her. She felt like Cinderella in fur-lined boots instead of glass slippers, with her fantasy prince in his Scandinavian knit sweater and snug, sexy ski pants.

He made her feel young and carefree as she hadn't felt in years. The heady combination of this fairyland of pristine, powdery snow—and a laughing, teasing Blake—lifted years of worry from her shoulders and let her just enjoy the moment.

What moments they were! If she lived to be a hundred, Erin knew she'd never forget the exhilaration of speeding down a snowy hill on a two-man sled, secure in Blake's arms. Their impromptu snowball fight had left her panting from exertion, while Blake had scarcely been winded at all—even when he'd picked her up and tossed her into a snowdrift, following her down and pretending to wrestle her into submission. She could hardly wait for the moonlight sleigh ride Blake had promised.

That night the moon shone bright against newly fallen snow, and Blake pulled Erin tighter against his side under the cover of a woven woolen blanket. He watched her smile as sleigh bells jingled against the horses' harnesses. Not able to resist the sweet temptation of her lips, he bent and gave her the gentlest of kisses.

"Having fun?" He raised his head to meet her gaze. When she looked at him with sparkling eyes, he realized again how much he loved her.

"Oh, yes."

Seeing the brightly lit lodge up ahead, Blake reined in the matched pair of grays. "Hungry?" he asked.

"Are you?"

You know what I'm hungry for. "Uh-huh. Let's go eat."

He hardly tasted the prime rib he ate. And he saw that Erin barely touched her salmon steak. "Would you like to go dancing?" he asked, glancing across the dining room toward the muted sounds of soft, romantic music.

"I'd rather spend time just with you."

Thank you, God. "Upstairs?"

She nodded, apparently shy about voicing her own needs. That was all right. If she was prepared to listen, he was ready to voice the words he hoped she still could echo from her heart.

"Let's go, then," he said, scribbling his name and suite number on the bill. Eager now, he took her hand and led her to their room.

The staff had done well. Candles, flowers, and a blazing fire in the fireplace on an inside wall in the big bedroom created the scene exactly as Blake had envisioned. He had gauged Erin's reaction well, too, he decided as he watched her bend and sniff appreciatively at a creamy gardenia in the mixed bouquet.

"You didn't have to do all this," she said, rubbing her cheek against his shoulder.

He nudged her down onto the sofa where he'd slept last night before conscientiously sitting down a respectable distance away. "I told Glenna good-bye, Erin. I'll always remember her with love, just as I'm sure you'll remember Bill. But I've put her in the past. She's gone. I'm alive, and I want to do more than go through the motions of living."

"What are you trying to say?" Erin's eyes were bright, and her tone of voice conveyed what sounded to Blake like hope.

"That I'm ready to love again. That I'm ready to love you, if you're willing."

"Do you mean . . ." Her voice trailed off, but she stared at him with what he wanted to believe was plain and simple sexual need.

"That, too." He chuckled. "Let me make love to you, Erin."

She felt as if they were making love, not simply satisfying the compelling chemistry that had first brought them together like this. He kissed her so gently, so carefully, she might have been made of glass. Then he scooped her up in his arms and carried her to the king-sized bed.

With a total lack of haste, he undressed them both, before lifting her onto the bed and staring down at her as if she were a priceless work of art. For the first time in her life, Erin felt truly beautiful, because she was seeing herself mirrored in his soft, adoring gaze.

Then he touched her, not like an impatient lover but like a man in love. The feather-light strokes of his fingers against the wind-sensitized skin of her cheeks produced tiny sparks of arousal that enticed rather than enflamed, and brought a warm glow that spread lazily throughout her body.

"I love the way you respond to me," he murmured as he bent and traced the line of her jaw with gentle love bites.

"M-mmm." With his slightest touch, with just a wanting glance, he could make her wet and ready, she thought as she sensed a delightful tingling in her most erogenous places.

She felt the bed shift when he stretched out on his side beside her, his head supported on one hand while he used the other to stroke softly around the undercurve of one taut, aching breast.

"You're uncomfortable."

His tongue snaked out and circled a nipple, and she realized what he intended before he took it fully into his mouth and began to suckle. After a few minutes, he switched sides and relieved the tightness in her other breast.

She was sure he merely meant to ease her discomfort, but what he was doing aroused her nearly to a fever pitch. She couldn't help draping one leg across his muscular thigh and rocking her lower body rhythmically against his rock-hard sex.

Finally he stopped his delicious torture. Raising his head, he took her lips in a soft, openmouthed kiss, bathing her lips and teeth with a tongue that tasted faintly of sweet, warm milk.

She moved her hips harder against him, coaxing him to fill her; but without breaking their kiss, he stayed her with a callused hand that pushed her back against the satin sheets. Then that hand began playing havoc with her senses, too, as it drifted over her abdomen and lower.

She squirmed beneath his light, teasing touch as he dipped into her belly button with one finger, then traced across her mound. When he finally touched her intimately, she was already aching with arousal; all it took to make her shudder and beg for more was a flick of his fingers.

He plunged his tongue deep within her mouth, then withdrew and positioned his big body between her legs. She opened fully to him, expecting him to fill the void inside her. But he didn't.

Sliding down farther on the bed, he bent his head and swirled his tongue across her belly before lapping his way downward. Every pebbly swipe of his tongue against the sensitive places between her legs made her crazy. And when he kissed her there, the delicious suction coaxed out climax after climax, leaving her sweating and drained, but still wanting to feel the heat and hardness of him, filling and stretching her, taking up the void in her body and her life.

''Blake. Please,'' she implored as she tried to drag him upward by pulling at his broad, muscular shoulders.

He was letting her position him the way she wanted, she knew when it suddenly became ridiculously easy to make him stop his erotic play. But when she tried to make him enter her by pulling at his narrow hips, he balked, poised just outside her, holding himself high above her on extended arms.

"Let me say this first." His voice was raspy, breathless sounding. "Erin, I love you. I think I've loved you since long before we ever did this."

She felt the tears come—but they were tears of joy this time. "I love you, too, Blake." No one else's name intruded now, she thought before she felt him plunge inside her and drive them both quickly to oblivion.

He loved the way Erin embraced every new activity, Blake decided the last day of their short vacation as he watched her follow him down the bunny slope. Actually, he loved everything about her—and he told her, every chance he got.

He wanted to do something special, something Erin would remember always about this magical place where they had discovered their love. Should they have a romantic continental dinner in that quaint restaurant downtown? No, what he had to say was too important, much too personal to do surrounded by strangers—or even friends.

Suddenly he knew. The room where they had laughed and loved these last few days, softened with candlelight and a flickering fire, would provide a perfect setting. When they returned to the lodge for lunch, he would make the necessary arrangements.

"Come on. Let's try the snowmobiles," he urged her later when he saw she had finished her cup of mulled red wine.

For the past hour, he had enjoyed observing her sun-kissed cheeks and the deeply contented look in her eyes as they warmed themselves before a blazing fire in the lobby. Now, though, he wanted to keep Erin away from their room long enough for the staff to set his scene.

"Can we ride on one together? My legs feel like jelly already from the skiing we did this morning."

"Sure. Do you feel like cuddling?" he asked, more than willing to oblige her if that was what she had in mind.

"Always."

"Then let's get to it."

With that, Blake got up and made a show of helping Erin to her feet. Like carefree kids, they blazed a trail up the mountain on a snowmobile, stopping often to share the majestic beauty of snow-capped evergreens and the occasional winter-coated deer or elk.

To Blake, everything around him seemed bright and new. For the first time, he realized that, while he had set himself free from a painful past, it was Erin who had shown him how to live again.

When they got back to the lodge at dusk, he stopped her at the door to their room and lifted her into his arms. "I think I forgot something the day we got married," he told her with a smile.

"You'd have had a time of it, trying to do this *then*."

And not only because you were just about ready to deliver our son. But I'm a different person now.

"Come on, Erin, indulge me." Fumbling with the old-fashioned brass key, he opened the door and stepped inside.

"I wanted us to have a special evening all to ourselves," he told her as he set her down in front of the fireplace.

"Oh."

She sounded stunned and thrilled all at the same time, he thought as he watched her eyes widen at the sight of a dozen candles that lit a small buffet and the round table set for two with fine china, sparkling crystal, and sterling silver.

"Shall we get more comfortable?" He shrugged out of his insulated nylon jacket, then helped her take hers off. "Our dinner will be arriving shortly."

She met his gaze with smiling eyes. "How comfortable?"

"That's up to you, love."

"Robes?"

"Sure. Want a quick shower?"

"Together?"

That suggestion sounded good—too good, because making love was not on his agenda just yet. "Well, maybe we

should dine as we are, and save that shower for later. But
hold the thought,'' he told her huskily.

"All right. Would you like some wine?" She headed for
the silver bucket on the bar, but he reached out to stop her.

"Let's wait."

They talked for a few minutes, and Blake began to wonder if he would ever have a minute alone. He needed to get
into one of his bags without attracting Erin's attention.
When she finally excused herself to freshen up, he practically dived for his luggage, then rushed over and tucked
his gift into the wine bucket just as he heard a discreet
knock at the door. Their dinner had arrived—not a moment
too soon for Blake's purposes.

"Aren't we going to have some of that wine?" Erin
glanced toward the wine bucket on the buffet, apparently
curious because they had finished their entrée—chicken
cordon bleu—without his breaking open that bottle.

"It's champagne. I thought we'd save it for dessert."
Blake got up and removed their dinner plates, setting them
on the buffet before taking a plate filled with little cream
puffs and éclairs to their table.

"Those look fantastic—but fattening," she told him with
a grin.

Blake didn't get nervous. He *never* got flustered. But he
was all that and more tonight! "I'll just take these over and
fill them while I'm up," he muttered, snatching up the
empty saucer champagne glasses and turning back to the
buffet. Resolutely he set them down and worked the cork
out of the chilled bottle of Dom Pérignon, making sure he
stood where his body blocked Erin's view.

"Do you need help?"

"No, thanks. I've just about got it opened." A sudden
loud pop confirmed his words.

But her innocent question had nearly made him drop his
surprise noisily into one of the glasses. Catching himself,
he managed to salvage the moment and finish pouring the
bubbly wine without incident. He felt his heart racing as

he brought the glasses to the table and set one down in front of Erin.

Then he sat back down and looked deliberately into her dark, sparkling eyes. "I've been thinking the last few days. About you. Me. Us. About how we're married but we aren't, not really. Most of all, I've been realizing how much I love you now, and how happy it makes me that you love me, too.

"I want us to say our vows again, this time with feeling." Needing desperately to touch her, he took her hand and brought it to his lips.

"Erin, will you marry me? For all the right reasons this time?"

He watched her reaction, an astonished look that transformed itself within seconds into a breathtaking, lovely smile. "Yes, Blake. Oh, yes," she murmured softly as she reached out and caressed his cheek.

"Then I think it's time for us to drink a toast," he said smoothly, raising his glass. "To us."

How long was it going to take her to notice the ring? Her movement was ballet in slow motion, fueling his impatience as she lifted the glass off the table and brought it up in a graceful arc.

Seconds ticked off in his brain. Then she let out a piercing scream.

"Oh, my God! Blake, you didn't. Yes, you did!"

Grinning, he helped her fish the diamond solitaire out of her glass and slipped it on her finger, in front of the wedding band that had sealed a business deal.

"How did you get this? When?"

"Sunday, before Sandy's wedding. I persuaded a client who's a diamond wholesaler to open up his showroom and help me pick it out."

"It's beautiful. I love it. I love you. But you didn't have to do all this." Erin could keep protesting all night, but Blake could tell by her reaction that his giving her that chunk of prehistoric carbon had made her happy.

He watched as she moved her hand at different angles, observing how the three-carat brilliance glowed, reflecting light from the fire and candles. And he, too, was caught up in the magic of its sparkling message.

"Do you really want us to have another wedding?" Erin asked later, as they lay in bed, content and sated.

"Yes. I want to commit myself to you and mean it."

"Me, too." She stroked his hand, and he felt the love in her touch.

I won't wear a ring. He had meant that when he had taken off the wedding band Glenna had given him. But now the words rang harsh in his mind as he looked at the bare ring finger on his left hand. He wondered whether Erin, too, recalled that conversation, and if she did, if his grief-inspired words still caused her pain.

Shifting his gaze to capture hers, he said, "This time I'd like to wear your ring. Will you get me one?"

She did that, and much more, after they got home. How she had managed to keep from floating in a haze of pure euphoria, she didn't know; but she'd managed to keep functioning somehow, since that magic night a week earlier, when Blake had convinced her of his love.

Erin stood in their room, holding the etched gold band with three modest diamonds and reading the inscription she had written. "From Erin, with all my love," it said simply but from her heart.

The jeweler's courier had just delivered it, and she could hardly wait five more days to put it on Blake's finger!

Funny, how love could turn darkness bright, make problems seem to fade into insignificance. Erin smiled as she looked out and saw Michelle walking beside the pool with Timmy, whose mastery of crutches improved each time she observed him. Soon they would go the way of his wheelchair, as he healed and became accustomed to using Buddy, as he had whimsically named his new prosthesis.

"Would you like the baby now?"

She turned and smiled at Theresa. "Yes." She'd feed Jamie before heading for Saks with Sandy in her search for the perfect dress to wear when she and Blake renewed their vows.

Later, as she searched through designer gowns a helpful saleslady kept bringing out, Erin remembered another day, another store, where she had been looking for a dress to wear—not for a wedding but for what had almost been a cruel farce. And she thought of Glenna's ghost, who had brought a light, cheery bit of humor to what could have been a somber experience.

I wonder where Glenna has been hiding, she thought as a deceptively simple ivory sheath of soft, silk crepe caught her eye. "I'll try that one on," she said decisively, remembering how Sandy and the ghost had coaxed and cajoled to get her to buy the dress she had worn *before.*

Moments later, Erin and Sandy left the store, their mission accomplished. Often, though, as she was loving Blake and looking forward to their pledging themselves honestly to each other, she found herself feeling guilty about having run off Glenna's ghost.

Not about loving Glenna's widower. No, nothing could dull the joy Erin had found in his love. But she had *liked* Glenna—and she had a feeling that without the ghost's downright pushy interference, she and Blake would have floundered around for years before they found happiness together—if ever.

"What are you thinking about?" Blake asked the afternoon of their wedding day when he joined Erin, who had been staring out a window in the garden room.

He would think she'd lost her mind if she told the truth—or even if she mentioned ever having seen and talked with Glenna's ghost. Erin was certain of that, so she merely smiled and said, "Tonight."

He grinned. "Me, too."

She had been right that day they had met. When he was

happy, he could break hearts with that ruggedly handsome face. He certainly had captured hers!

"This is for you," he told her, setting a narrow velvet box on her lap before joining her on the sofa.

She said he wasn't much into buying baubles.

Glenna had said something like that at the store. Well, she must have been wrong, Erin thought smugly, noting the solitaire on her hand as she picked up the box that could hardly contain anything *but* a piece of jewelry.

"Aren't you going to open it?"

"Oh. Yes." She snapped open the lid and gasped. It was a sapphire as big as a marble, as dark as Blake's mesmerizing eyes. A sunburst of sparkling diamonds surrounded it, reflecting its brilliant color in their twinkling facets. Set in gold, the pendant hung suspended on a finely worked chain. "The sapphire reminds me of your eyes," she murmured when she found her voice.

"It reminded me of yours. Will you wear it tonight, for me?"

Erin nodded as she moved into his arms. For a long time, he held her, until it was time for them to dress and greet their guests.

Chapter 32

"If I keep officiating at weddings, I'm going to have the ceremony memorized," Judge Adkins commented good-naturedly as Blake ushered him into the formal living room.

"That's good." He and Erin had opted for tradition, instead of rewording the promises they would give each other. Uncharacteristically nervous, Blake straightened his bow tie and adjusted the cuffs of his pleated shirt.

Blake had greeted the fifteen or so people he and Erin had invited to share their joy. He had cuddled Jamie for a while before handing him over to Theresa, and he'd taken the time to introduce Timmy to the friends who had come. Now he was getting impatient to see his beautiful bride.

Suddenly Erin appeared in the doorway, a vision in creamy white silk that gently skimmed curves of her body that he could hardly wait to explore again in minute detail. Every time she moved, the long slit skirt swayed so he could glimpse a shapely calf and thigh. He liked the way she was wearing her hair, too, artfully tousled and loose against her bare, tanned shoulders.

She had on the pendant he had just given her, nestled just above the upper curve of her breasts. And the fragrance of *La Mer l'Été* and a scent of the roses she carried mingled to assail his senses.

Looking radiant, like a woman in love, Erin nearly took

his breath away. He reached out to her and took her hand. Slowly she moved close to him, until he could feel her warmth against his side.

In a small, sane corner of his mind, he realized that Greg and Sandy had come to stand beside them. As if he were dreaming, because this felt too good to be real, Blake met Judge Adkins's gaze and nodded his head.

The words were familiar. He—like Greg, yet for different reasons, he thought with just a twinge of regret—had repeated them not once but twice before.

Yet the vows seemed new and fresh tonight, like his love for this strong, beautiful woman who miraculously loved him, too.

"Erin, with this ring I marry you and pledge my faithful love," he said, holding her gaze as he slipped a new, wide band on her slender finger.

The judge's voice intruded on Blake's thoughts. "Erin, repeat after me. . . ." He let the instruction fade off in his mind; his thoughts were on his bride.

"Blake, with this ring I marry you and pledge my faithful love." She spoke softly, her tone low and melodious. He liked the solid feel of her wedding band on his finger, he decided as he glanced down at the ring which, like their love, was fresh and new.

Judge Adkins cleared his throat and said, "You may kiss your bride."

Gently Blake took Erin in his arms and gave her a tender kiss. Then they turned back to the judge.

"These rings you have exchanged have no beginning and no end. May your commitment to each other be the same. My friends, it is with the greatest pleasure that I introduce you to Mr. and Mrs. Blake Tanner."

His arm possessively wrapped around Erin's slender waist, Blake turned them to face their guests. Suddenly a bright, golden aura nearly blinded him.

He stared, unable to tear his gaze away, and slowly he

was able to make out the image as it crystallized from the gold dust. *Glenna.*

He felt Erin squeeze his hand. Did she see this, too? Or had the Scotch whisky he'd had just one shot of earlier gotten to him?

"Mr. and Mrs. Blake Tanner. Has a nice sound, doesn't it?"

Now this vision talks, *too.* Blake didn't believe this! He stole a glance at Erin. For some reason he didn't understand, he was sure she could see and hear this ghostly apparition, too. It surprised him that she appeared unaffected.

He wanted to interrogate this—this *ghost*—as he would ream a witness in the courtroom. But he couldn't. Judge Adkins and everyone else in the room would *know* he'd taken leave of his senses and haul him off to the funny farm if he started talking to someone—or something—that wasn't there!

"Don't mind me, darling. I just came to say good-bye. I've accomplished what I wanted for you two—a real, happy marriage filled with love. You're going to get along just fine without me now."

Blake watched the specter of his beloved wife's face turn soft and dreamy as it faded into the golden aura that shone around her. He had to strain to hear her parting words.

"Now I can go. It seems I've discovered three adorable little girls who belong to me, and it's time for me to start being a mother to them."

Nonplussed, Blake watched the surrealistic presence of his dead wife slowly fade away. Then he turned to Erin.

"Did I just see what I thought I saw?" He voiced his question in a whisper, for her ears only.

She smiled and gave him a quick hug. "Uh-huh. And you know what, my love? She's been around here the entire time."

"You've seen her before?"

"Seen her. And talked with her. I've listened to her advice. I've even argued with her."

Blake leaned closer and whispered in Erin's ear. "About what?"

"You. You've had at least two women who loved you to distraction, Mr. Tanner," she replied, pretending to nuzzle at his neck. "I've had a feeling she was gone for good—but I'm glad she came to tell us good-bye. Aren't you?"

Erin shot him an impish grin. He couldn't help returning it. Soon those grins dissolved in gales of laughter. Was it hysteria or relief? He wrapped his arms around his wife and held her for a long time.

"Is it all right—that she came?" Erin asked quietly.

He hesitated. "Yeah. It's okay now." Not getting to tell Glenna good-bye before she died had been a bitter reality for him to swallow. Now, even if Glenna's ghost had been a product of his and Erin's imagination, she had given him the gift of closure, the freedom to love Erin with all his heart.

And he did! Erin was his greatest miracle of all.

Later he would tell her. Now duty called. Wishing this party, joyous as it was, was over, Blake took Erin's hand and walked with her to greet their guests.

And now for a preview of the next
Haunting Hearts romance

Eternal Vows

Coming in January 1997 from Jove

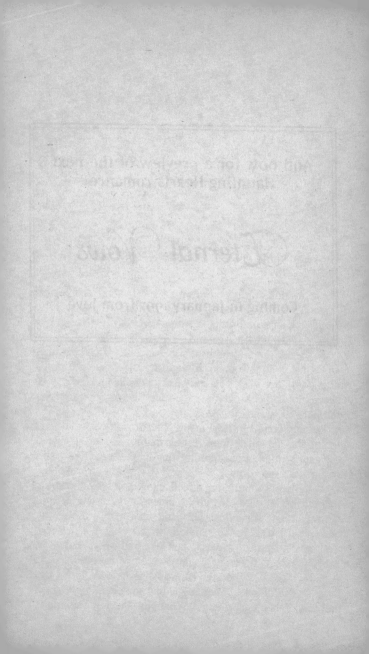

New Orleans, French Quarter
May 26, 1897

It was midnight, and the drums were beating near Congo Square. As the incessant, driving rhythms filled the sultry Louisiana air with primal yearnings, a beautiful young bride restlessly awaited her groom's return.

In the master bedroom of a newly built Victorian mansion, the young woman closeted her silk and lace gown, along with her thick veil and pearl-encrusted headpiece. As she removed her stockings, she found herself entranced by the pulsing sounds in the nearby park.

Marina wondered how many other lovers were out there this night, entwined upon feather mattresses, lured beneath the gauzy cloud of mosquito netting by the seductive primal call of the *vodu* drums.

A flash of glimmering green caught her eye, and she paused to admire the exquisite emerald-encrusted band on her finger. She slanted her left hand, charmed by the sparkle of faceted jewels in the candlelight.

''Your magnificent eyes,'' her love had whispered at the altar only a few hours ago, ''they were my inspiration. . . .''

Robert had designed the ring, just as he'd designed this large splendid house. She laughed as she began pulling off the rest of her underthings. What joy she felt this night.

Her groom, as gifted an artisan as he was a lover, had at long last become hers.

Passing by the full-length mirror on the bedroom's mahogany and rosewood amoire, Marina glimpsed her reflection and stopped. For a long moment, she observed her naked form.

Outside, the drumming continued. The primitive rhythm seeped into her body, and throbbed in her veins. Slowly, she lifted her hands to shamelessly cup her bare breasts. With a restless sigh, she closed her eyes, happy in the knowledge that her strong, handsome husband would soon be here to take whatever pleasure he desired from them.

A smile graced her wide mouth and very full lips—the only hint of her true heritage, the only sign that her blood was not all lily-white, but mixed with the inheritance of a darker lineage and the ancestry of a great spiritual people. Perhaps that is why the beating drums in the nearby park did not frighten her as they did so many others. It often amazed her how residents and new visitors to this bustling port would grow pale merely at the strangeness of another people's ways.

By the light of ten flickering candles, Marina reached up and unpinned her hair. Curling tresses cascaded past her shoulder and waist, blanketing her soft skin in a fall of deep auburn color. *Yes,* she thought, her gaze taking in the reflection of ivory skin and flaring hips, perhaps she *was* of value—something worth bartering.

Despite that rich bastard's ugly scene at her wedding celebration, despite his terrible insults and threatening words, Marina gloried in the knowledge that the "bargain" her late father had made with that vile man no longer mattered.

No one can take me from my love now. No one.

Too restless to lie down on the intricately carved fourposter bed, the bride paced the room. Pushing open the French doors, she stepped barefoot out onto the master bedroom's balcony. The night air was cloying, drenched with the thick, sweet scent of magnolia blossoms and her favorite flower—white roses. She inhaled deeply, recalling the day her love had planted them. Dozens of white rosebushes now graced the garden of the house—now *their* garden and house.

No. Their *home*, she corrected.

It would be a *home*, filled with great love, as well as great passion.

Leaning against the rail, she found herself wondering how many times in the past weeks she had stood on this very spot. How many times had she crept from her father's house on Esplanade Avenue to come here? How many times had she searched this shadowy street in the Quarter, waiting for her love to turn the corner and look up, his intense expression filled with barely contained need.

She wished her groom had not left her, even for this short half hour. But he'd insisted that she see his wedding gift to her. It was a surprise. All she knew was that he'd commissioned an artisan friend to make it for their new home.

She looked down toward the street corner, but dense fog had enveloped the port of New Orleans, and nothing but the faint, yellow halos of the city's streetlamps could burn through it.

No matter. Marina welcomed the dark, ethereal blanket. Welcomed it as a misty curtain of privacy.

Her late father may have bartered her to another man—bartered her like a horse, or a sack of grain, or a *slave*, she thought with controlled fury—but the days of slavery in this country were good and over. Now no one could deny her and her love what they had rightfully claimed.

Tonight, behind this thick curtain of mist, inside this pounding circle of drums, they would consummate their marital vows and protect the power of their love forever.

Suddenly a noise came from inside, and Marina turned to see the master bedroom's door opening. *Finally*, he was here.

Robert stood stock still, clearly taking pleasure in the

sight of his young bride. In the candlelight, her rich auburn curls seemed to shimmer like gold. Her curving, naked figure was framed by the balcony doorway, and against the backdrop of the dark fog, she appeared to be the breathing embodiment of a great painter's finest work.

But she was more than a mere artist's image. Tonight, with each step closer to the edge of that frame, this woman became more and more real to him.

Marina, in turn, surveyed the awe in Robert's expression—the reverence and love. She watched as it quickly turned to desire and need; watched as he set the large wrapped wedding gift upon a nearby silk-covered chair, flung the hat from his blond head and slipped off his black cut-away. With quick, efficient movements, he pulled off his white bow-tie and removed his waistcoat. As he unbuttoned his shirt, he began to walk toward her in measured, determined steps, the wedding gift momentarily forgotten.

With the sculpted, smooth muscles of his chest bared, he flung away his shirt and the rest of his clothing. Then he stood by the bed, magnificent and proud in his nakedness— and more aroused than she had ever seen him.

"My bride," he whispered, "let me touch you . . ."

Marina's breathing became labored as her bare toes moved forward. She felt the roughness of the balcony's planks give way to the polished cypress of the bedroom floor.

Robert watched as she moved beyond the door's wooden border, with each step confirming to him finally that *yes*, she was more than the semblance of a work of art.

She was real. She was here. And she was his.

She had stepped beyond the frame to become a warm, breathing reality in his life.

As Marina moved toward Robert, she found herself poignantly aware of the many moments that they had already shared. The many moments of their past. She was more than ready for the countless moments of their future.

Enjoying love, raising children, growing old—the future's promise stretched out before them like a long, soft carpet. All she had to do was take the first step.

With the sound of the pounding *vodu* drums echoing in the distance, Marina took it—and found herself in Robert's arms. Immediately she felt his strength and love completely envelope her, like the thick mist blanketing the city.

"You're home now . . ." Marina whispered.

"*Our* home now," Robert answered, his eyes shining with pleasure. Then his head lowered, and his mouth claimed hers in a kiss that promised a lifetime and beyond. Past, present, and future—three points of a circle that surrounded them, a circle of love that could never be broken.

This was a promise.

They knew it more than in their minds or flesh, but in their spirits. And as she returned his kiss in kind, they barely noticed the smashing, violent noises from one floor below, the voices and the heavy footsteps on the stairs.

"In here!"

They barely heard the growing sounds of disaster, the crash of the master bedroom door, the cocking of a weapon.

They barely comprehended the glare of a gas lantern flame, the long gray barrels of the shotgun, or the shards of jagged metal exploding toward them, ripping into their bodies.

It was in that instant that a shattering scream of blood and terror ascended through the night fog, a terrible testimony to the violent act that would brutally slaughter a destiny.

The cry traveled into the night and up to the heavens, and for a long, full minute—as if the beating drums had heard their heartrending wail—all sound stopped.

Across the shadows and fog of the port city, thousands of listening lovers suddenly stopped with them, chilled to the bone by the deadly silence.

Until the drums began again.

*   *   *

NEW ORLEANS, FRENCH QUARTER
ONE HUNDRED YEARS LATER

Tori Avalon slammed the door of her blue rental compact
car and started toward the old mansion. After plucking at
the peach-colored silk blouse that clung annoyingly to her
damp sticky skin, her slender, manicured fingers moved
north to push at the auburn bangs of her forehead.

Tori swore she'd sell her soul in a minute for a good
stiff breeze off the Mississippi. She had come here straight
from the airport, leaving a temperate New York May for
the heart of this sweltering hothouse. It had been a long
time since she'd been in Louisiana, and Tori had simply
forgotten how oppressive the Delta's humidity could be.

Licking her dry lips, she could almost taste a sip of that
cool, mint iced tea—the kind Aunt Hestia used to brew in
a jar on the porch of this very house. Tori smiled at the
memory of those days years ago when her aunt took a
young niece by the hand and showed her how to step with
care through the herb garden to pick the tender sprigs of
fresh mint.

It seemed to Tori that Aunt Hestia would be around forever, growing fresh herbs in her garden and conjuring up
Creole gumbo, pecan pralines, and café au lait for guests.
But Hesti hadn't resided here for ten years, and now Tori's
aunt was gone from this life, leaving Tori the fourteen-room
guest house before her—a large Victorian relic that had
once seemed like a grand palace to a shy little Northern
girl.

Tori's smile at past memories soon disappeared with the
onset of the gloomy realities that faced her now. Weeds
and tangled vines obscured the stone path as she approached the mansion. Thorns scratched at her legs, prick-
ing her silk stockings and deflating her spirits. Even the
scent of lilacs in full bloom could not soften the sight of
the unkempt and overgrown state of the house's surrounding grounds.

She stopped at the old wrought-iron fence—the very feature that had supplied this house's name. The clever pattern in the grill gave the impression of budding roses on the vine, but it was now far from the beautiful feature she recalled.

Streaked with ugly grime, the filigreed fence was in need of repair in many places, starting with the gate, which hung by a single twisted hinge. Tori stared at the gate glumly, deciding it compared with her own life—unstable and precariously dangling on a tenuous prop. The metal groaned as she pushed it out of her way and stepped gingerly over the thorns of an overgrown bush, unhappily barren of a single flower.

Finally, she could get a better look at the house itself. But it didn't help. Like a stone vanishing under the waves of the muddy Mississippi, Tori's heart sank with the realization of what sat before her. It was Blanche Dubois in the last act of *Streetcar*—a grand belle tragically reduced to an old woman, her once-prized beauty ravaged by the hardships of years passing, her haughty dignity cruelly stripped from her by careless handling.

There was no getting around it. The once-elegant Rosegate Mansion Guest House bore the scars of too many years of conscious neglect.

Aunt Hestia had hired a management company to run the guest house for the last decade. Clearly they'd done a terrible job with the upkeep, but on top of that, the house had been completely empty for over a year.

Still, like Blanche, there was some fleeting shadow of grandeur left in her, the notion of how truly majestic she once had been . . . and perhaps, still could be again.

Presenting all-new romances —
featuring ghostly heroes and heroines and the passions they inspire.

Haunting Hearts

__STARDUST OF YESTERDAY
by Lynn Kurland   0-515-11839-7/$5.99
A young woman inherits a castle—along with a ghost who tries to scare her away. Her biggest fear, however, is falling in love with him...

__SPRING ENCHANTMENT
by Christina Cordaire   0-515-11876-1/$5.99
A castle spirit must convince two mortals to believe in love—for only then will he be reunited with his own ghostly beloved...

__GHOST OF A CHANCE
by Casey Claybourne   0-515-11857-5/$5.99
Life can be a challenge for young newlyweds—especially when the family estate is haunted by a meddling mother-in-law...

__HEAVEN ABOVE
by Sara Jarrod   0-515-11954-7/$5.99
When Blake Turner's wife passes away, her ghost wants Blake to begin a family—with the surrogate mother of their child.

Payable in U.S. funds. No cash orders accepted. Postage & handling: $1.75 for one book, 75¢ for each additional. Maximum postage $5.50. Prices, postage and handling charges may change without notice. Visa, Amex, MasterCard call 1-800-788-6262, ext. 1, refer to ad # 636b°

Or, check above books Bill my: ☐ Visa ☐ MasterCard ☐ Amex _____
and send this order form to: (expires)
The Berkley Publishing Group Card#_____
390 Murray Hill Pkwy., Dept. B   ($15 minimum)
East Rutherford, NJ 07073   Signature_____
Please allow 6 weeks for delivery. Or enclosed is my: ☐ check ☐ money order

Name_____ Book Total $_____
Address_____ Postage & Handling $_____
City_____ Applicable Sales Tax $_____
               (NY, NJ, PA, CA, GST Can.)
State/ZIP_____ Total Amount Due $_____